HOW
QUICKLY
SHE
DISAPPEARS

HOW QUICKLY SHE DISAPPEARS

RAYMOND FLEISCHMANN

BERKLEY

New York

BERKLEY
An imprint of Penguin Random House LLC
penguinrandomhouse.com

Library of Congress Cataloging-in-Publication Data

Names: Fleischmann, Raymond, author.
Title: How quickly she disappears / Raymond Fleischmann.
Description: New York : Berkley, 2020.
Identifiers: LCCN 2019019798| ISBN 9781984805171 (hardback) |
ISBN 9781984805195 (ebook)
Subjects: LCSH: Twin sisters--Fiction. | Missing persons--Fiction. |
Women--Crimes against--Fiction. | Alaska--Fiction. | BISAC: FICTION / Suspense. |
FICTION / Crime. | FICTION / Literary. | GSAFD: Suspense fiction. | Mystery fiction.
Classification: LCC PS3606.L45275 H69 2020 | DDC 813/.6--dc23
LC record available at https://lccn.loc.gov/2019019798

First Edition: January 2020

Printed in the United States of America
1   3   5   7   9   10   8   6   4   2

Jacket art: mountains by Andrew Merry/Getty Images;
northern lights © plainpicture/Design Pics/Composite Image photography
Jacket design and composite by Emily Osborne
Book design by Laura K. Corless

For Madeline,
of course

Now that you have gone
and I am alone and quiet,
my contentment would be
complete, if I did not wish
you were here so I could say,
"How good it is, Tanya,
to be alone and quiet."

"Except" by Wendell Berry

HOW
QUICKLY
SHE
DISAPPEARS

PART

1

CHAPTER 1

July 1941

The rattling buzz of a bush plane awoke her that morning and, as it just so happened, Elisabeth had been dreaming of her sister.

She had been back at her childhood home in Lititz, Pennsylvania. Like all of the dreams about her sister, Elisabeth imagined Jacqueline as she was when she was eleven years old, when *they* were eleven years old, 1921, the year that Jacqueline disappeared forever.

But beyond the broadest details—her sister's sad eyes; the vast, creaking farmhouse; the clattering stalks of corn that surrounded their yard like an interminable forest—the rest of the dream was lost to Elisabeth as soon as she opened her eyes, that distant world and all its distant comfort obliterated by a postal plane grinding through the sky on its way into town.

Wait, Elisabeth thought, blinking sleep away. *Oh, yes.*

She was back in Alaska—Tanacross, Alaska, a village with a population of eighty-five people. About two hundred miles southeast of Fairbanks, Tanacross was a place so far from Pennsylvania that it sometimes felt like a different world.

Elisabeth sat up, one hand sweeping through her hair. Her husband,

John, had been away at a seminar in Juneau for almost a week, and she never slept soundly without him, purely out of habit. And then there was the light, that ceaseless summer light. In Alaska in July, the sun hardly ever went away. More often than not, Elisabeth's nights were filled with dreams: sometimes about her sister; sometimes nonsense; sometimes music, just music, an indistinct melody playing in circles. No matter the dream, she rarely slept well in the summertime. They had been living in Alaska for three years, and each passing summer had been more difficult than the last.

"Mama, are you awake?"

Margaret was standing in the frame of the bedroom's open door. She was dressed in the cotton nightgown that Elisabeth had made for her last Christmas. Glinting white light shined through the windows beside the bed, and Margaret's blond hair and pale skin made her look like a ghost. She looked, Elisabeth thought, very much like she and Jacqueline had looked when they were eleven years old, the same age that Margaret was now.

"Yes, honey, I'm awake," Elisabeth said. "I'm sitting up, aren't I?"

Margaret padded across the room. "I thought you might be a somnambulist," she said, hopping up onto the bed. Margaret leaned back against Elisabeth, collapsing into her arms like a happy cat.

"I might have thought the same about you," Elisabeth said, smiling, pulling her close. She glanced at her wristwatch on the nightstand. It was five fifteen in the morning. "What are you doing up so early? Studying your vocabulary?"

"No, I memorized everything last night. I've already . . ." Margaret paused, tugging at a loose button on her gown. "I've already learned all the requisite words."

"I can tell." Elisabeth leaned closer to the top of Margaret's head. Her daughter smelled like sleep: musty yet also vaguely sweet. "From what I hear," Elisabeth added, "I'm sure you'll do very well on your test. You always do."

That she did. Though Margaret was just eleven years old, she acted and read well beyond her age. Since moving to Alaska, Elisabeth and John had educated her themselves, at home, and Margaret took to everything they taught her with a speed and retention that was sometimes shocking. She eschewed Nancy Drew for H. G. Wells, traded toys for books of logic problems. For Christmas, in addition to the nightgown, Elisabeth and John had given her the first three letters of an encyclopedia series, a massive book that she read from one cover to the other as if it were a novel.

Tilting back her head, Margaret looked up at her. "Was that Mr. Glaser's plane?"

"Probably," Elisabeth said. "He's supposed to come by today. He's awfully early, though."

"He woke me up."

"Me, too."

"Will he have my book?"

For weeks, Margaret had eagerly awaited the arrival of a science book Elisabeth had bought through a catalogue. It contained instructions for thirty different experiments that children could conduct at home. Baking soda and vinegar became volcanic lava; paper clips defied all logic and floated on water; vegetable oil and club soda mixed to make an alien sea, its waters churning with fluorescent yellow globules. Once a week, the post office delivered mail, groceries, clothing, books, and medical supplies—anything they ordered, though certain requests took longer than others. They had sent for Margaret's book six weeks earlier.

"Maybe he'll have it," Elisabeth said. Closing her eyes, wishing for sleep again, she pulled Margaret tighter. "We'll just have to wait and see."

"If he doesn't have it, can you ask him what's taking so long?"

"I'm not going down there right now. I'm not meeting him."

"But Mr. Glaser—"

"He'll leave his deliveries on the landing strip," Elisabeth said. "He doesn't need any help."

And Elisabeth didn't want to give it. Walter Glaser was nice enough—nice, though always in a hurry—but there were few things that seemed less appealing right now than stepping out of bed, getting dressed, and meeting someone, *anyone*, on the landing strip at five fifteen in the morning. But Margaret wouldn't let it go.

"Please," she said, "please," and she wiggled out of Elisabeth's arms. Margaret knelt, bouncing lightly in front of her. "I need the book for my lessons," she said. "I have a lesson next week I need it for."

"Which lesson?"

But Margaret didn't hear the question. "Please ask him what's taking so long, Mama. Please. Mama—"

"If he doesn't have it, he doesn't have it."

"But you can ask him why."

"He's probably already left."

Margaret hopped off the bed and pulled a curtain aside from the nearest window. "He's still there," she said. "I can see the tip of his tail fin over Mr. Wallis' house."

Elisabeth was pushing the sheets away from her legs.

"Mama, please," Margaret said, bouncing on her toes. "Mama—"

"Let me think about it," she said, but they both knew that this was code for *Okay, okay. I'll do it*. If she took her time going to the bathroom and pulling on her clothes, by then Mr. Glaser really would be gone. Raising children, and Margaret in particular, was partly a question of winning battles by sleight of hand, and at times Elisabeth could be masterful in that respect. Margaret dove onto the bed.

"Thank you, Mama," she said, beaming. "I'm so obliged."

E lisabeth dressed, fed the dog, did her business in the outhouse. Then she headed for the landing strip. Tanacross shined in the morning light, the sun already high and hot in the sky. About twenty-five homes comprised the town, each of them squat and square, single story, their walls built from the hewn trunks of pine and hemlock trees. There were no paved roads in Tanacross, only roads made of dirt, and these were as hard as rock in the winter but almost liquid in the summer. Elisabeth moved quickly, her Oxfords sucking against the mud. She walked with her head down, both hands pulling her cardigan up and over her chin and nose. The summers in Tanacross were filled with swarms of mosquitoes unlike anything she had seen in Pennsylvania. Here, the insects flew in bunches as dense as floating ink. In the summertime, it was always best to move quickly and dress in layers. Today Elisabeth wore a pair of wide-leg slacks and a plain cotton blouse beneath her cardigan.

The landing strip lay on the north side of town. It seemed that everyone was still asleep, everyone except for Henry Isaac and his grandfather, who were splitting wood in front of their home. Though Henry was strong and young—twenty-nine, two years younger than Elisabeth—his grandfather was doing all the chopping. Henry just stacked the pieces of wood. Both of them nodded and smiled as Elisabeth approached, and Elisabeth did the same.

"Why aren't you the one chopping?" she said, pausing in the road a few feet away.

Henry threw up his hands. "He insisted. I couldn't stop him."

"Lies," Elisabeth said, and she smiled again. "Tell *ch'endĕddh'* he's got a lazy grandson."

Chuckling, Henry turned to Mr. Isaac and said a few words in their native Athabaskan. Mr. Isaac laughed, speaking quickly in response, too quickly for Elisabeth's meager understanding. Henry turned back to her.

"He says if it wasn't for lazy grandsons and all the extra work they make, he'd probably be dead."

Elisabeth laughed. "Fair enough," she said, and she started walking again. "*Naa su'eg'ęh*, both of you."

She knew that wasn't quite the right phrase. She had told them *Good luck*, or something to that effect, an expression as close to *Have a good morning* as she could manage. But even if she was far from the point, Henry and Mr. Isaac didn't seem to hold that against her.

"*Naa su'eg'ęh*," Mr. Isaac said, nodding and smiling. Then he raised the ax once more.

Twenty minutes had passed since Mr. Glaser arrived, and Elisabeth had every hope that he would already be on his way out of town. He wasn't airborne yet—she would have heard the plane taking off—but, as she turned the corner and approached the landing strip, she felt certain that she would hear the first catch and clunk of the plane's engine, and a minute after that Mr. Glaser would be gone.

But when she stepped onto the gravel runway, Elisabeth found that it wasn't Mr. Glaser who had landed. About two hundred feet down the landing strip stood an unfamiliar plane, its nose slightly crooked, its front left wheel resting in the grass. Equal parts white and canary yellow, the plane resembled most others that Elisabeth had seen in the Alaskan bush, except for one detail: Painted to the left of the propeller was a black-and-white German *Balkenkreuz*, which stood out like a mole on the side of someone's nose. The plane's wings stretched across the top of the fuselage like a huge rounded paddle and, directly in the center, just above the cockpit's windshield, a man sat with his knees pulled up against his chest.

For a moment, Elisabeth thought that he was fixing something— tightening a bolt, adjusting a panel, aligning this or that. No matter the season, the conditions in Alaska were tough on planes, and she had seen Mr. Glaser fix such things in the past, sometimes with the help of Teddy Granger, a local who had briefly served as a mechanic in the army.

But this man was just sitting there, motionless, his back turned toward her. He was staring at the trees that lined the landing strip, woods as dense as the cornstalks that had once encircled Elisabeth's home. He didn't notice her approaching. A haze of mosquitoes flickered around his head, but he didn't seem to notice that either.

"Good morning," Elisabeth said, and she came to a stop a few yards from the plane.

The man jolted, sitting straighter. Then he turned his head and gazed over his shoulder. His eyes were wide and dazed.

"Hello," he said. "Oh my goodness. Hello." His voice was a peculiar blend of German and British accents, quick and sharp with the consonants, slow and soft with the vowels. He pushed himself to his feet and stood staring at her from atop his plane. "I'm sorry. I didn't hear you walking up." He flashed a nervous smile. "My apologies."

For the most part, he looked normal enough. Mid-forties. Tall and rather slender. He wore a plain white button-up shirt, brown slacks, black suspenders, knee-high boots. He parted his hair to the right with his bangs swept up in a wave, a match for the neat, curving moustache that bent across his face. Elisabeth could tell that he had once been very good-looking. He certainly wasn't ugly in his middle age; it was just that his cheeks and nose were too pointed, too bony, though it was easy to imagine how he might have looked as a softer, younger man. As it was, from his angle high above her, the man owned a certain look of intensity that wasn't especially inviting. He reminded Elisabeth of a falcon or an eagle. Somehow, even as he smiled, he seemed to scowl.

"I'm sorry I startled you," Elisabeth said.

"No, no," the man told her. "That's all right. I'm fine. That's quite all right."

An awkward second passed between them. Still smiling, the man stared at Elisabeth as if waking from a trance. She wondered if he had been drinking.

"I'm Elisabeth Pfautz," she said.

Cordially, the man bowed his head and lowered his eyes. "Alfred Seidel," he said. "Very pleased to meet you, Mrs. Pfautz."

She took a single step forward. "What were you looking at?" Elisabeth turned to the woods, half expecting to see the hulking shadow of a moose or a caribou. But there were only trees—ragged, tired trees—endless as ever. Tanacross was the largest settlement for a hundred miles.

Alfred lowered his eyes again, bashfully. "I was just looking at . . ." he began, and paused for a second, "oh, just everything." He started walking down the spine of the plane.

"Everything?"

"Yes, you know," he said, gesturing with one hand, "all of it. The woods. The bush. All the beautiful world." He hopped to the ground, facing her now. His eyes were an iridescent shade of blue, and they narrowed at her as he walked a few steps forward. "Did you say your name is Pfautz?"

"I did."

Alfred set his hands on his hips. "You're a German, then?"

"Pfautz is my husband's name," Elisabeth said, "but yes, I'm German, at least by stock. My father was from Hamburg, and my mother was from Bremen."

"Munich," Alfred said, and he tapped two fingers against his chest. "I'm a German, too."

"I can see that," Elisabeth said, motioning at the German cross on his plane. Alfred briefly turned.

"Oh, that," he said. "You wouldn't believe how uncomfortable that makes some people. But I have no shame in my heritage, never mind what's going on now." He grinned, and his eyes flashed as if they had just shared a secret. "I'm sure you understand," he said. "As a countryman, I mean. By God, it is good to meet you, Mrs. Pfautz. I'll tell you: Countrymen are rare up here in the wilds." And as he said that word—*wilds*—he puckered his lips as if the word itself tasted foul.

Elisabeth shook it off. "What brings you to Tanacross?"

"The post office," Alfred said. He paced back to his plane and unlatched the cabin door.

"Where's Mr. Glaser?"

"In Lincoln, Nebraska." Alfred leaned inside the cabin and retrieved a single white box of mail, filled only halfway with envelopes and packages. He set it on the ground between them. "I fly a route west of Fairbanks, but I'm pitching in for Glaser this week. His daughter is getting married."

In a flash, it came back to her. Months ago, Mr. Glaser had mentioned his daughter's coming marriage. He had been unhappy about the location and how far he had to travel. *But your little girl getting married only happens once,* he had said, and then paused, adding, *Or it damn well better.*

"Well, it's good of you to fill in," Elisabeth said.

Alfred shrugged. "It's only my job," he said, but then a shadow seemed to pass across his face, and he rolled his head side to side like a boxer dodging punches. "I do have a favor to ask, however."

"A favor?"

He nodded. "I've been flying all day and all night. My route and Glaser's, you see. I'm exhausted. I need to rest. I need a place to stay, Mrs. Pfautz, and I've been told that you have a guest room." He lowered his chin, and his eyes steadied on hers. "So, if you'd be so kind, I'd like to stay with you."

A place to sleep. It wasn't an odd request in itself. Elisabeth and John's home was the largest in Tanacross: three bedrooms, two fireplaces, a dining room adjacent to the kitchen, and a living room not far from that. And all of this was only one half of the house; the southern half served as the local school, the reason they had come to Tanacross in the first place. Their move was John's first post with the Office of Indian Affairs. During the past three years, he had helped renovate and update the school, both the building itself and its curriculum. He taught writing, mathematics, and biology, the last of which involved monthly field trips to study the flora and fauna of Glaman Pond, a sickled body of water not far from the house. They had hosted many guests in the past: officials from the Department of the Interior, officers in the army, other teachers on their way to other posts throughout the territory. The third room was meant to be a guest room, particularly for those connected in some way to the government.

But there was something about this man that unsettled her, and there was something strange in the way he had looked at her and spoken to her. He wasn't inviting himself into her home, and he wasn't demanding an invitation. He *desired* it—*I'd like to stay with you,* he had said—and somehow a desire felt more unnerving than a demand. Elisabeth had no wish to know anything about this man's desires, and she had no wish to fulfill them.

And yet she felt trapped. The guest room was intended for exactly this type of stay. Even with John out of town, what option did she really have? It was her job—hers and John's—to put Alfred up. She felt trapped by obligation, trapped by situation, trapped by a dozen different things at once. But mostly, her eyes locked on him now, she felt trapped by Alfred Seidel.

"The room is free," she said, hoping that he would hear how this wasn't the same thing as an outright invitation, "but don't you have more deliveries to make?"

"You're my last."

Elisabeth shuffled her feet, briefly glancing down. "The room isn't much," she said. "It's not exactly the Ritz. Are you sure you'll be comfortable?"

He smiled. "I'm always comfortable with my countrymen."

"I see," Elisabeth said. "Well, you should know that my husband is away on business, so it's just me and my daughter," and again she hoped that this would dissuade him, that he would understand her awkward position and all its implicit discomfort.

He didn't. Alfred smiled merrily, holding up both hands.

"That's fine," he said. "Countrymen. Countrywomen. I'm sure I'll feel right at home." Turning back to his plane, he reached inside the cabin again, this time retrieving a large green duffel bag. He began to close the cabin door, but then he stopped himself. "Oh, I nearly forgot," he said, and he dropped his bag to the ground. He leaned inside the plane and started digging around a mass of empty boxes and padding blankets.

Elisabeth leaned to the side, trying to sneak a better look. "Do we have another box?" she said.

"Not quite," Alfred told her, "but I do have a special delivery." He turned to her and handed Elisabeth a flat package wrapped in brown paper. A note was affixed to it. *For Margaret Pfautz,* it read. "Our dear Mr. Glaser set it aside," Alfred said. He grinned, and again his eyes seemed to flash. "Margaret. Your daughter, I presume? Such a pretty name."

CHAPTER 2

To his credit, Alfred Seidel wasn't rude or unfriendly in any way. He wore a daft, cheerful smile almost constantly, and he chatted good-naturedly about the weather, Alaska, Bob Hope's performance in *Road to Zanzibar*. He thanked her effusively for everything; judging from his reactions, the guest room might as well have been the Ritz, and the coffee might as well have been champagne.

Not the least bit rude, no. But he was peculiar. During bouts of silence in a conversation, his lips would continue to move as though he were still speaking, though Elisabeth could never quite discern what he was saying to himself. In the guest room, he removed his boots and set them on his pillow—muddy soles and all—and he pushed his hands against each of the four walls as if testing their sturdiness. Before breakfast, in the midst of describing his favorite recipe for mincemeat pie, he reached inside his shirt pocket and retrieved a handful of pebbles, which he tossed into his mouth like grapes.

"Good for digestion," he said, answering Elisabeth and Margaret's puzzled stares.

Minutes later, after learning that Margaret had recently read *The*

War of the Worlds, Alfred described at length how he had sometimes seen enormous, faraway aircraft hovering above battlefields during the Great War.

"The men on the ground couldn't see them, but those of us in the air certainly could," he said, calm and matter-of-fact, undeniably serious. "They weren't zeppelins or observation balloons. These were made of metal. Shining steel. I can't guess what they were. I can only say that it seemed as if they were watching us—just watching the show."

Even Margaret, credulous and always curious, lowered her eyes and went on eating her eggs and hard roll without offering much of a reaction. Elisabeth cleared her throat.

"You were a pilot, then?" she said. "In the war, I mean?"

Alfred nodded. "Two years," he said. "I flew a Fokker *dreidecker*. Wonderful plane. I miss it every day."

"Did you ever meet the Red Baron?" Margaret asked.

"No, little one," Alfred said. "I'm afraid I never had the chance." He looked at Elisabeth. "Such a delightful child. So bright and well-informed. And your spit and image, Mrs. Pfautz. Your absolute twin."

At that, both Elisabeth and Margaret tensed, but Alfred didn't seem to notice any hint of awkwardness. He turned back to Margaret.

"I suppose you could teach me all sorts of things," he said, and then made a show of scrunching up his face in thought. "Let's see. Who was the fifth president of the United States?"

"James Monroe," Margaret said, "but that's an easy one."

"Well, then, who was the thirty-fifth?"

Margaret chewed, thinking. "We've only had thirty-one," she said. "President Roosevelt is number thirty-two."

"Ah, so I've stumped you," Alfred said. "You see, my dear, *you* will be the thirty-fifth. You, my darling," and with one finger he touched her nose and roared with laughter.

Finally, with breakfast finished, Alfred went to the guest room and slept. And almost at once, his sleep was a presence like nothing else in their home. His snoring howled through every room, his sleep so loud that it sounded greedy, as if he was sucking up all of the home's air for himself alone. And it was endless. Hour after hour passed, and the snoring went on. No more meals. No trips to the bathroom. Not a single, silent pause. By lunchtime, it was humorous. By evening, annoying.

"How long is Mr. Seidel staying?" Margaret asked as Elisabeth cooked dinner, a meal of seasoned pork chops and thyme-sprinkled radishes from the greenhouse behind their home. Margaret sat on the floor with her back against the icebox, reading her encyclopedia while idly stroking Delma, their three-year-old malamute.

"Just tonight," Elisabeth said. She flipped the pork chops in the enamel pan, and they fizzled in their pool of lard. Grease nipped at her knuckles. "Perhaps he'll leave even sooner. He's slept a lot already."

Margaret turned a page. "He said I look like your twin." She didn't look up from her book. She kept on reading, or pretending to read. "Is that true? Do I look like Jacqueline?"

Margaret knew only the basics about Jacqueline. She knew that Elisabeth had once had a twin sister, and that Jacqueline had disappeared when they were children. But apart from the simplest facts, Margaret didn't know much, though she knew that her mother rarely spoke of the matter. She knew to tread lightly, and Elisabeth was glad to do the same.

"I'd say you look like me," she told Margaret, poking the chops around the pan. "But in a sense you look like her, too, yes."

Margaret nodded, still reading. "I hope Mr. Seidel leaves soon," she said. "He smells bad," and the moment passed, to Elisabeth's relief.

After dinner, both of them were itching to leave the house. Elisabeth went to visit Mack Sanford, and Margaret went to Betty Northway's house to play Which, What, or Where?, a geography trivia game that they had inherited from their predecessor at the OIA school. Though Margaret excelled at so many things, geography had never been one of her strong suits.

It was strange; geography seemed so much easier than everything else, so much simpler, yet Margaret struggled with it more than any other subject. She could recite the definition of *acrimony* and rattle off the multiplication tables without missing a beat, but when it came to correctly labeling Alabama and Mississippi, suddenly she would find herself at a loss. Elisabeth chalked it up to a simple lack of interest.

"Why do I have to learn about places so far away?" Margaret had asked her once. She was staring down at a map of the South Pacific.

"Because those places aren't actually far away at all," Elisabeth had told her, trying to whet her interest. "Think about it. Everyone lives on the same globe. If an earthquake happens on one side of the world, it can make a wave that travels across the whole ocean. Those places may seem far away, but they're not as far as you may think."

Margaret was quiet, still staring at the map. Then she looked up. "Can I just learn about earthquakes?" she said. "Those are much more interesting than maps."

Spelling, math, and science—those were the subjects that Margaret enjoyed, and that was why Elisabeth was visiting Mack. She needed motor oil for Margaret's first experiment, and Mack was the only person in town who owned a motorized vehicle: a small bulldozer speckled with constellations of rust. There were no cars in Tanacross, no plumbing or running water. The town's only source of electricity was a small hydroelectric generator in the Tanana River, and this powered one thing only: the army radio intended strictly for emergencies. During Christmas, Father Ingraham, the priest who had run the town's Episcopalian mission for nearly thirty years, would sometimes play choral music from a crackling windup gramophone, but apart from that, as far as technology went, Mack's bulldozer was the beginning and the end.

Mack was their closest friend in Tanacross. Witty and gregarious, quick to laugh, quick to joke, he had always reminded Elisabeth of John—John in the early years of their marriage, the good years, before they had soured, before they had gotten too used to each other. Mack and John even looked alike in certain respects: broad shoulders, barrel chest, thick legs. Mack was shorter than the other Athabaskan men, most of whom were tall and lanky. Still, he was all Athabaskan, and he bore many of the traits so common among the people in Tanacross:

almond eyes, dark skin, wavy black hair, eyebrows that were thick and flat—qualities that made them look almost Asiatic, much different from the Indians outside of Alaska, or, rather, much different from the pictures and drawings Elisabeth had seen of them.

And that, it seemed, was a fair enough summation of the town as a whole: different, unexpected. Before moving to Tanacross, what Elisabeth had known about the Athabaskans was what little she had learned from books and pictures—grainy photographs of dour-faced men clad in heaps of fur, dogs pulling rickety sleds, hollow-eyed children huddled against their unsmiling mothers. The pictures always showed a place untouched by the rest of the world, and that was what Elisabeth had expected to find. The frontier. The edge of civilization. A town the world had yet to reach.

But instead, what she had found was this: The rest of the world had already gotten here. Yes, Tanacross was isolated. Yes, it was free of certain conveniences, and, yes, Tanacross existed inside a kind of bubble, but that bubble wasn't as impenetrable as she had been led to believe. Away from the cold, the men wore slacks and button-up shirts. The women wore blouses and tulip skirts and fussed about their hair. People gossiped, fought, worried about the war and the sons and brothers who might soon be fighting in it. They went to church, smoked cigarettes, played cards, read the newspaper. Of course Tanacross had its own culture—in writing letters to friends and family back home, Elisabeth still used quotation marks whenever she mentioned sweat baths or potlatches—but the town didn't feel as foreign as she had thought it would. It still felt lonely. It still didn't feel like home, and Elisabeth was certain that it never would. But foreign? Not exactly. Not entirely.

Mack lived a few hundred feet from the landing strip, on the north side of town. His house was smaller than most of the other homes in Tanacross, but Mack didn't need much space. Years ago, his wife and infant daughter had died from tuberculosis, and now he lived alone. He had scores of family in Tanacross—brothers, nieces, nephews, cousins near and distant—and he could lend an able hand for nearly any task or problem. He could fix chairs, clocks, lanterns, guns, boats, fishing reels, traps, and sleds. Two summers ago, he had helped John reinforce the roof and windows of the school. Not long after that, he and John had built the greenhouse out back.

Mack also bred dogs. Malamutes. It was Mack who had given them Delma—the runt of a litter who would have been drowned had they not taken her in. Mack kept the dogs in three large kennels beside his house: one for the males, one for the bitches, and one for the mothers and their pups. The kennels were long and narrow and lined with chicken wire.

The dogs began to stir as Elisabeth approached. Some of them paced while others jumped against the mesh, bracing their front paws on the wire and wagging their tails as if they expected Elisabeth to feed them. Despite their excitement, none of the dogs barked; the dogs in Tanacross only howled, and this they did at night, howling for ten or fifteen minutes straight, a chain of call-and-response with the wolves way out in the bush.

"What the heck's going on out here?" Mack said, smiling as he opened his door and walked down the steps of his stoop. "You stirring up my dogs, Else? Causing trouble?"

"I'm always causing trouble," Elisabeth said. "Don't you know that by now?"

"I do. I do," Mack said. "And I'll admit it: As long as it's got your name attached to it"—he winked—"trouble doesn't seem so bad."

Elisabeth felt her cheeks flush, and she bowed her head. She was smiling—she couldn't help it—but instantly the air around her and Mack seemed to shift. They were quiet for a beat. Then Mack cleared his throat, and he tapped one foot against the stairs' bottom step.

"So," he said, straightening up, "to what do I owe the pleasure?"

Mack dug around inside for a while. The bulldozer, he said, hadn't been used since last May, and it wasn't something he regularly maintained.

"It's not exactly a Cadillac," he told her. "I change its oil about as often as I take it to a car wash."

Mack's home was more or less a workshop. Tables were piled high with half-completed projects. Bookshelves were crowded with cans of grease, paint, and oil. Sawdust covered the floor like a blanket of snow. On every wall hung rows of tools, wrenches and saws and measuring instruments of all shapes and functions. *Why in the world do you need so many collets?* Elisabeth had asked Mack one of the first times she visited his home. *Why in the world do you know what a collet is?* he had replied, and with that she had reminisced about her father—a tool and die maker with the graceful touch of an artist. Before her sister's disappearance and her father's passing not long after, his workshop behind their home had been one of the mainstays of her and Jacqueline's childhood.

A toolmaking shop was a strange place for children to enjoy, but its strangeness was exactly the reason why their father's shop had been so interesting. It seemed like the laboratory of a wizard or Dr. Frankenstein, a place of tricks and odd little gadgets, a place of invention and, sometimes, a place of mystery. Their father used to make them toys in that shop, and once, when they were eight years old, he made them a doll built from wood and glass and metal pins that held its limbs together. The doll's eyes were wide and unmoving, but when you held it up to the sun or another bright light, they would slowly close as though the brightness was too much to bear. *How does it do that?* Elisabeth had asked. *Magic,* her father said.

"Ta-da!" Mack called out, lifting up a canister of motor oil. He was crouched beside a workbench near the door, and now he rose to his feet. "What's she need this for, anyway?" he said, clomping across the room. Mack swayed stiffly when he walked, hardly bending his knees at all. *Car accident,* he had once explained, and left it at that.

"We're learning about viscosity," Elisabeth said.

"Oh, sure." Mack handed her the canister. "Everybody's got to learn about viscosity."

"Absolutely," Elisabeth said. She smiled a little. "Well, thank you for this. I'll bring it back in a few days."

"Take your time, take your time." Slowly, wincing, Mack lowered himself into a chair beside his stove, a cast-iron Favorite that sat in the middle of the room. "So," he said, "I hear you got a guest."

"Word travels fast."

"Word doesn't have far to go. Sometimes folks know what I'm doing before I've even done it."

"Is that so?" Elisabeth said, feigning an impressed frown. "Well, yes, we've got a guest, and what a guest he is."

She filled him in on all the details—the snoring, the boots on the pillow, the stones that Alfred gulped down like hors d'oeuvres. When she got to the part about spacemen, Mack just shook his head.

"Martians," he said. "I've always hated how nosy they are."

But his joking belied something else. The longer she spoke, the more she saw it: a pinch in Mack's eyes, a shadow of unease. He was judging Alfred, but in that process he was also judging her. Suddenly, Elisabeth didn't want to talk about her guest. Suddenly, she realized that Alfred wasn't the only one being cross-examined. She was, too, and with that realization she felt an unexpected compulsion to defend Alfred's stay— and her decision to allow it.

"Suffice it to say he's an eccentric," she said, hastily coming to an end. "He's an interesting fellow."

"Eccentric?" Mack said. "Is that what you'd call all that?"

Elisabeth shrugged. "I don't know what else to call it. Some people are just a little off-kilter, you know? Especially in the summertime."

"Ain't that the truth?" Mack said, turning his head toward the window. It was eight o'clock at night, but the world outside was awash in a mustard-colored glow. "But honestly," he said, "are you sure this guy should be staying with you?"

"Do I have a choice in that? It's my responsibility, isn't it?"

"Maybe," Mack said. "Maybe. But don't you think these are—I don't know—*exceptional* circumstances?"

"Because of his—"

"Because of everything," Mack said, and he chuckled briefly, though his eyes had no sense of humor in them. "John is out of town, and it's only you and Margaret in that house with the guy. And he's not the most . . ." He shook his head. "Well, he's not the most normal guy, obviously, and on top of that there's his background."

"His background?"

"Yeah, you know."

He stared at her, waiting for a cue, her flicker of understanding, but Elisabeth gave him nothing. Mack wilted. The skin on his face was pocked with acne scars, decades-old marks that made him look older than he really was—thirty-seven, only two years older than John was.

"Okay," he said. "If we're leveling with each other, I'm not sure I'd trust any of them these days."

"Them?"

"Sure," Mack said. "You said it yourself. Where he's from, I mean. They're fanatics, you know."

Ah, Elisabeth thought, *that.* She couldn't help but feel stung. She leaned back on her heels, shifting the oil canister from one hand to the other.

"And I'm not talking about you guys," Mack said, holding up both hands. "Obviously, I'm not. But it's something that's been on my mind. That's all. Especially with John out of town, I just don't know how good this is, Else."

"Well, eccentricities aside, I'm not too concerned about that. Sometimes people just find themselves on the wrong side of a war. That was the case for a lot of people." *Like my entire extended family,* she could have added, *and John's, too.* But she decided against mentioning that. "Besides, the war was a long time ago."

"A long time? I'm talking about now, Else. There's a war going on right now. Don't you remember?"

Elisabeth bobbed her head. "So you think he's, what, spending his weekends at rallies in Nuremberg?"

"I think," Mack said, "that you should simply be careful." He slouched back in his chair. "I'm not telling you to kick the guy out. I'm not telling you your business."

"I don't want him staying with us either, you know. Believe me, I don't."

"I know," Mack said. "I understand the tough position you're in. And again, I'm not telling you your business. I'm not telling you to do anything, really. I'm just saying my bit. I'm saying what's on my mind, one friend to another."

Elisabeth was quiet for a while, thinking. She was studying the tools that lined the walls of Mack's home. Some were rusted and warped—hammers that bent like crippled limbs, saws so tarnished that they looked like strips of bark—but, mixed among those, other tools were gleaming and new, each of their various teeth and chiseled edges still sharp and stiff and strong. No matter. They would all wear away with age. Even if Mack never used them, they would all wear away. Everything did—everything and everyone.

"Well, I appreciate your concern," Elisabeth said. "I appreciate your bit."

But I can take care of myself, she wanted to say, but didn't.

"Good," Mack said. "Thank you."

Slowly, cupping his knees, he stood up, and together they walked to the door.

"Tell Margaret I said hello, okay?"

"I certainly will."

"And tell Delma the same," Mack said.

"I'm sure she'll appreciate that."

Mack reached for the doorknob, but then his hand paused, and his face went slack with seriousness. "Just let me know if you need any help," he said. "I'm not far away. Remember that, will you?"

"I will," Elisabeth said. "And thank you again for the oil."

"That's no trouble," Mack said, smiling as he opened the door, and his eyes were sweet and sad and deeply sincere. "No trouble at all."

CHAPTER 3

It was almost real. She and Jacqueline were sitting in the middle of Mr. Stouffer's cornfield, a rolling swatch of land that stretched for twenty acres behind their home. Facing each other, they sat on the ground in a circular clearing. The corn towered above them, stalks as thick as baseball bats, all of them swaying in the wind with the singular motion of water.

"Drift pin," Jacqueline said, and she held up a tool that resembled a dart. On the ground between them lay an array of other tools, smithing and machining instruments whose names and functions Elisabeth had once learned, in reality, from their father. "Drift pin," Jacqueline repeated, speaking slowly, the way that someone teaches words to an infant.

Elisabeth nodded. "Drift pin."

Jacqueline put the tool back in its row, and Elisabeth watched her sister consider her next selection. In this dream, they were wearing the same clothing: light blue dresses, knee-high socks, canvas shoes, tortoise-shell barrettes clipped in their hair. Even then, a time when they were nearly adolescents, they sometimes dressed exactly the same. They were twins, after all, and matching clothes only added to the novelty.

Jacqueline reached for another tool. "Broach," she said, holding up a narrow flank of metal with angled teeth carved into one side of it.

"Broach," Elisabeth repeated, and her sister set it down.

Now Jacqueline raised a tool that looked like a pair of tweezers—two tapered prongs held together at their hinge by a wide pin. "Calipers," Jacqueline said.

But this time, when Elisabeth tried to speak, the word simply didn't come. She felt as though she was speaking into a vacuum, her words swallowed up before they had even had a chance to form.

"Calipers," Jacqueline said, more insistently now. She bounced her hand, gripping the tool tighter in her fist. "Calipers."

But the word wouldn't come. Elisabeth opened and closed her mouth, her lips popping speechlessly against each other. She could muster nothing more.

Jacqueline sighed. Setting down the tool, she bowed her head. Then she held out her hands, palms down, and Elisabeth saw that they were the hands of an elderly woman: wrinkly and calloused, their veins rising up from her flesh like earthworms.

"I hardly even recognize you now," Jacqueline said, looking up. Though her hands had suddenly aged, her face was still young, eleven years old, always eleven years old.

That was the point in the dream when Elisabeth woke up. She was lying in bed with the sheets pulled up to her chin. Her pillow was damp. Her heart was beating fast. But in spite of the sweat and her racing pulse, she felt very calm. However cryptic her dreams could be, she had come to welcome these visions of her sister. Her dreams had once been distressing; she would wake up with tears streaming down her face, and for days thereafter her teeth would ache from unconscious gnashing. But, since moving to Alaska, Elisabeth had come to appreciate whenever Jacqueline deigned to visit her. The dreams were never long, and they were often sad. But they were all she had left, and because of that she was thankful for them. They brought her back to a place—and a time—that now felt impossibly distant. Elisabeth lay flat on her back, arms outstretched, and she listened to her own breathing. She tried to picture Pennsylvania, and she tried to sleep.

But she couldn't. She would slip into a dream and then slip straight out of it, dreams that weren't as much sleep as momentary visions forgotten the same second they occurred. She awoke with a start each time—twitching, jerking. One moment she was lying on her side. The next, her stomach. The next, her back.

However she lay in bed, she couldn't escape the glow of her window, sunlight that filled every inch of the room with a soft, fiery haze. The Alaskan summer never failed to wear her down. At first, in April and May, the nights were still long enough that she hardly noticed their shortening. Then June came, and bit by bit it pulled the energy out of her. In increments of five minutes, ten minutes, fifteen, she slept less and less, and she carried these minutes through each waking day like weights fixed to her body. By July, she felt her lack of sleep in every labored step she took. It pulsed behind her eyes, a swelling pressure that made her feel as though she might explode. In bed, time didn't flow, but skipped. It was midnight. One o'clock. One forty-five. Sometimes, like tonight, there was no point in even trying. Elisabeth kicked the sheets away at two o'clock, and she pushed herself up.

Even in the summertime, the house was chilly at night, so she wore a quilted dressing gown on top of her pajamas. She spent half an hour at the dining room table, reviewing Margaret's latest work and preparing for the next day's lesson. It was true that she and John had taught Margaret together, but it was also true that Elisabeth had long ago assumed the lion's share of their daughter's education. During the school year, John was busy with the Athabaskan children. Even now, when school was in recess, it seemed as if his time was always occupied with other tasks: clerical duties, repairs, seminars, interim teaching assignments elsewhere in the territory. No matter the time of year, Elisabeth was left with Margaret almost all to herself.

And it was difficult to keep pace with her. Margaret learned her lessons quickly, and she learned them relentlessly. At Margaret's own request, Elisabeth continued to teach her during the summer; Margaret's education hadn't ceased for more than two years straight. They did take it easier in the summer—fewer tests, more tasks—but it still sometimes felt like too much to manage.

Teaching one person was more difficult than teaching entire classrooms of them. That was what Elisabeth had been trained to do. That was what she had *wanted* to do, and that was what she had done before moving to Alaska. For six years, she had taught eighth-grade history and English at Lititz Public School, where John taught arithmetic and biology. It was hard work, and sometimes it made her feel neglectful—they counted on John's mother to care for Margaret during the day—but teaching gave Elisabeth a sense of satisfaction she couldn't deny. She felt that she was doing a job she needed to do, a job she was downright obligated to do. She had graduated at the very top of her class at Franklin and Marshall College, finishing even ahead of John. Elisabeth still shared letters with some of her professors, including Dr. Mueller, who had encouraged her to continue her studies and receive a bachelor's degree instead of just an associate's.

"What a privilege for your daughter to have a teacher as gifted as you," Dr. Mueller had written after they moved to Alaska, "and what a pity it is that the child should have your teaching all to herself."

Elisabeth had blushed when she first read that letter, and she told herself that Dr. Mueller was simply being kind—more than kind. Hyperbolic, really. She was just a novice when it came to teaching, and Dr. Mueller had observed only a handful of her classes. But especially now, especially here, Elisabeth often found herself thinking of that letter, remembering it most often when she was struggling to devise yet another lesson for Margaret, restless little Margaret.

That was the case now. Seated at the dining room table, her books and papers lit by a Coleman gas lantern, Elisabeth was at a loss. She paged through one of her handbooks, then paged through it again, forward and back. She knew that she should devise a lesson of her own, but she just didn't have the energy. Fast asleep, Delma was lying beside her chair, inches from her feet. Every now and then, Delma would shift or sigh, but other than this, the house was quiet. Outside, the world held its breath. The wind didn't blow. The trees didn't rustle. As she had so many times since coming to Alaska, Elisabeth felt the uncanny sensation that she was alone—completely alone, the last person on a desolate earth.

She set to work on Margaret's next spelling test. In the past Elisabeth had always used her own dictionary, but tonight she used Margaret's encyclopedia, her daughter having left the tome at her place at the table. *Braille,* she wrote in her notebook, flipping through pages at random. *Crevasse. Cittern.* Maybe, she thought, they would do a unit on words with two of the same letter side by side, tricky words to spell, even for a child as clever as Margaret.

But soon Elisabeth was just reading the encyclopedia's entries. She couldn't help it. The illustrations caught her tired eyes, and she found herself reading about baize, calcium, Marcus Aurelius. She turned page after page, her eyes drifting from entry to entry the way someone scans a newspaper, the act of learning and the loss of forgetting only half a second separated. She was almost at the end of the encyclopedia when one illustration made her pause—a picture of a pair of calipers—and, in a rush, Elisabeth remembered her dream.

Calipers, Jacqueline had said, teaching her the word. *Calipers.* Repeat after me. But she couldn't, could she? Elisabeth could only move her lips, silent, speechless.

How vivid Jacqueline had looked in that dream—how present, how real. To this day, she could picture her sister with absolute clarity, though she supposed that wasn't surprising. She had only to imagine herself, or someone quite like her, more alike than any other person could ever be.

To the month, twenty years had passed since her sister disappeared. Twenty years a missing child. A stolen child. Twenty years since that summer, that evening in the yard when Jacqueline told her, *I'll come right back,* and never did.

But was she dead? No. Taken, abused, enslaved—Elisabeth could only guess—but not dead. She was certain of it. For a while, her certainty had been unexplainable. It was something that she felt in her bones—her sister was alive, alive, alive—a fact that she felt like heat in a room, something she knew not by a single source but with every inch of her body and every breath that she inhaled.

Then the dreams started, and at once she understood that these were more than merely fantasies. They were proof that she was right. She and Jacqueline were identical twins, and their connection went deeper than appearance or voice. These weren't dreams. They were contact. They were moments in which her sister was reaching out to her, perhaps not literally but at the very least spiritually. Elisabeth was not a religious person; this wasn't an act of God. It was an act of sisterhood, a bond that they had held since birth and held to this day. Her sister was alive, and no one could tell her otherwise. Reaching out, Elisabeth touched the calipers on the page, feeling the tiny ridges of ink on paper, lines so subtle that they were nearly imperceptible. Then, slowly, she closed her eyes.

"Mrs. Pfautz?"

Alfred's voice made her jolt. Elisabeth sat straight, pivoting in her chair and pulling her hand away from the encyclopedia. Alfred was across the room, standing in the hallway near his open bedroom door.

"Alfred," Elisabeth said, and it was all she could do to stop herself from standing up and running from him, strictly on an impulse. "You startled me," she said. "Jesus. You startled me."

But Alfred only hushed her. Walking quickly forward, he hissed—"Shh! shh!"—holding up one hand and pinching his fingers together as if squeezing her lips shut. "Did you hear that?" he said, approaching the table. "Just seconds ago. Did you hear those sounds?"

Alfred was dressed in an undershirt and denim overalls. His hair was disheveled and his eyes were bulging and white, as large as billiard balls. Within the dusky light of the room, Alfred seemed to glow.

"Sounds?" Elisabeth said, still catching her breath. Sitting rigid, she listened. "I don't hear anything."

"But a moment ago," Alfred said. "A moment ago—" He stepped toward the window. His eyes grew wider. His head craned forward. He looked at her. "You didn't hear it?"

No, she certainly hadn't, whatever *it* was. The house had been quiet and was quiet still, silent except for Delma softly grunting, huffy little noises that she made whenever she was curious. Her "houndy humphs," John called them. Delma had raised her head when Alfred first walked into the room, and now she was watching him intently. "No," Elisabeth said. "I didn't hear anything. What did it sound like?"

Alfred stepped closer to the window. "Hammering," he said, lifting back the window's curtain and peering out. His hands were trembling. "Someone was hammering. Just a moment ago. Just outside. The whole house was shaking." Pale with panic, he glanced at her. "You really didn't hear it?"

"Alfred," Elisabeth said, "it's almost three in the morning. Everyone is asleep."

"Not everyone." Alfred swallowed, motionless, still listening. "It was the door," he said, and he dashed across the room, fast enough that the papers in front of Elisabeth briefly lifted, jostled by the rush of his movements. He yanked the door open without a moment's pause—the doors in Tanacross had no locks—but there was only emptiness outside, nothing more than the vacant wooden stoop. A wash of sunlight poured inside the house and the air smelled suddenly sweet, tinged with the Alaskan summer, woodsmoke and damp dirt mixing strangely with the acrid fumes of the Coleman lantern.

"Someone was knocking," Alfred said. "Someone was absolutely pounding."

He took a single step outside, looking right to left. Then, very slowly, as if he had just remembered something long ago forgotten, he bowed his head and walked back inside. His mouth gaped open. His eyes stared down.

"Alfred—" Elisabeth began, but her voice disappeared.

With his arms uncovered to his elbows, Elisabeth noticed something about Alfred that she hadn't seen before: Dozens of scars covered his arms, scars that were ropy and wide. Crisscrossing in a hundred different directions, they rose from his skin in angry red slashes. It looked as though hives of insects were burrowing through his flesh.

"Good God," Elisabeth said. "What happened to your arms?" But immediately she caught herself; immediately she felt ashamed for asking such a thing so bluntly.

No matter. Alfred didn't seem to hear her. He turned away from the door and, still bowing his head, closed it behind him. Then he began to move back across the family room, shuffling—limping—in the direction of the bedrooms.

"I'm sorry, Mrs. Pfautz," he said, breathing harder now. He sounded as if he might break into tears. "I'm so very sorry." Then, not far from the hallway, he paused in midstep, turning his head and staring straight at her. "What can you say about such a thing?" His voice was a breathless whisper. "What can you possibly ever say?"

And with that he shambled away, dragging his feet, and the house was suddenly silent again.

The following day, Alfred acted like a different person. He was quiet and aloof, but more than anything he seemed dejected. His head hung low and his eyes were glassy and distant, the eyes of a much older man. He looked weary and hopeless. He reminded Elisabeth of how her father had looked in the final year of his life.

At breakfast, Alfred said very little, ate very little. Seated at the table across from Margaret, he stared almost constantly at the red leather cover of her encyclopedia, its golden letters glinting in the sunlight pouring through the windows. When Elisabeth asked if he was feeling ill, Alfred only shook his head.

"Not so much ill, no," he told her. "I've just lost my appetite."

He certainly had. Alfred mostly poked at his food—over-easy eggs and cracked wheat—and he drank only a few sips of black coffee. He never mentioned the episode from earlier that morning, and Elisabeth didn't have the nerve to bring it up herself.

"Mrs. Pfautz," Alfred said now, looking up from his food, "I really do appreciate your hospitality." He waited for a second, studying her. "You know that, don't you?"

Elisabeth swallowed a bite of egg. Beside her, Margaret ate as though she wasn't listening to the conversation. Her eyes were trained on Delma, who sat in front of the door, head high, tongue hanging, hot from the heat spreading out from the kitchen and the wood-burning stove.

"Yes," Elisabeth said. "I know that." She made herself smile. "And I appreciate the thanks."

"You're very kind," Alfred said. "Very, very kind, Mrs. Pfautz, so I really do hate to ask for anything else, but I have something more."

Something more, Elisabeth thought, and she realized that she had been expecting *something more* all along, expecting it from the first moment Alfred had spoken to her on the landing strip.

"What is it?" she said, and she tried to seem more concerned than reluctant, more intrigued than apprehensive.

"I need to stay a little while longer," Alfred said. "One of my ailerons isn't working quite right. I could fly with it unrepaired, and that was what I had planned to do, but the more I think of it, the more I'd rather fix it. Not take the chance, you know." He stammered for a second, shaking his head. "I'll need to stay another night, maybe two, if that would be all right." He paused, blinking. "Would that be all right?"

And again Elisabeth felt cornered, as though there was only one answer she could give. But as much as she felt trapped by the obligations of their post, she felt even more trapped by her own recalcitrance. She had dug in her heels with Mack—shrugged away his worries—and in doing so she had already given her answer to Alfred. She had already made her commitment. *Yes, of course. Stay as long as you need to stay. That's fine. Everything is fine.*

"Ailerons," Margaret said, now holding her encyclopedia, "are hinged airfoils located on the trailing edge of aircraft wings. They control lateral balance and are necessary for banking turns."

31

CHAPTER 4

For as long as you can remember, you've talked about running away. But you've never really thought that it would happen.

Jacqueline has a surprise for you. Two surprises, actually, and they both involve *The Plan*. That's what you've always called it. *The Plan*. It's easier to talk about when it's reduced to so little. Two words. It doesn't seem so scary. It doesn't seem so big. And it certainly doesn't seem like something real. It's just *The Plan*, something that you and Jacqueline have talked about all your lives.

But suddenly it seems like it's more than just talk. These surprises are big, whatever they are, and they have to do with running away. Jacqueline has made that clear, but she's offered no further hints. Still, you can hear a nervous tremble in your sister's voice. You can feel the energy fluttering all around her. The excitement. Something is happening, or has happened already.

Dutifully, you await her word to open your eyes. You're sitting on the dusty floor of your father's workshop. Closed eyes or not, you know this place as well as your own bedroom, and you scan the shop in your mind's eye, taking inventory. There are gears the size of bicycle tires above your head. Belts string across the ceiling like party streamers. Hundreds of tools cover the walls. A coal forge stands beside the shop's only window. You're flanked by worktables streaked with grease stains, and an anvil sits on a hickory stump behind you. The air smells thick with oil and shaved metal. You draw a deep breath. Try to relax. Your mouth is dry.

"Is it going to be much longer?" you say.

"Just a minute," Jacqueline says. "Wait a little longer."

She sits down across from you, and then you hear the shuffle of her working. She's setting something between the two of you. Laying something, piecemeal, on the floor. A deck of cards? Books? Magazines?

You wait for a minute, and then your sister is quiet, as if studying the work that she's just completed. Outside, the sun is setting, and the crickets and katydids have begun to rattle. It's July, and the weather is hot, but here inside the shop it's cool.

"Come on," you say. "Let me open my eyes."

"Wait," your sister says. "There's something else. Just wait." And then she's working again, making some final adjustment. "All right," she says. "Open your eyes."

Though it wouldn't make much sense, you expect to see a line of playing cards with naked women on them. Months ago, Jacqueline found a deck of cards like that beneath the pillow on your father's bed. There were naked ladies seated on couches, on stairways, on rocks in the ocean surf, waves breaking in curtains around their shoulders. The aces showed women with their legs spread open, and the jokers showed a woman with a banana held between her breasts.

"Look at how big her nipples are," Jacqueline had said. "And look at how dark."

But when you open your eyes, it's not naked women looking up at you. In two even rows on the floor, Jacqueline has arranged ten stacks of dollar bills. It's the most money you've ever seen, and the sight of it is so surprising that you actually jolt, rearing back your head. Beside it, she's laid a square of paper that reads, in ornamental writing, *For Jacqueline, Meine Hausherrin*. It's beautiful script, practiced and sure of itself, but it's hard to take your eyes away from the rows of money. It's so much money.

"A hundred dollars," your sister says, her eyes gone wide, "and it's *ours*."

You're still for a moment. Stunned. Then you reach out, lift a stack. Your sister smiles, watching you with a kind of awe, as if even she can't quite believe the surprise she's revealed. The money feels crisp. With it closer to your face now, you can smell it. It smells sharp but somehow nice, like a freshly painted room.

"Where did you get this?" you say, glancing at the note.

Jacqueline grins. "A little bird."

"What little bird?"

"What difference does it make? It's ours." She scoots closer and sits up on her knees. "Do you know what we can do with this money?"

You're still marveling at the sight of it. "What?"

"Lots of things," your sister says. "We can buy train tickets. We can run away. We can go on an adventure."

"An adventure?"

She nods.

"Where?"

"Any of the places we've talked about. New York. Los Angeles. Texas." She's talking fast. She's positively bursting. *"Alaska,"* she says. "Anywhere. We can do anything now."

And for the first time you realize that this is no longer just play—not to Jacqueline, it isn't. To her, this is play and something much more—a world of adulthood dizzying in its scope and implication. You draw a deep breath. Chew at the inside of your lip. You lay the money on the floor again, center it in its space in the row. Then you sit back.

"Jacqueline—"

"And I have something else, too," she says.

She springs to her feet and dashes across the workshop. Then she's on her hands and knees, reaching behind the crates your father has stacked in one corner. She returns a moment later with something wrapped in a towel.

"You'll never guess what this is," she says. "Not in a million years."

She hands it to you. It's heavy and firm, the shape and heft of a fire poker, though not quite as long. You unwrap it, and the first thing you see is a golden crown emblazoned with an eagle, wings outstretched.

It's a dagger, and the crown caps the hilt. It's beautiful, more ornate and delicately fashioned than anything you've ever seen before. Its scabbard is wrapped in silver-plated filigree and ribbons, and the hilt is coiled pearloid. Your fingers trace the crown, searching with intention only half conscious, and soon your fingernails are gliding across the eagle, grazing the subtle peaks and paths of its feathers, the hook of its open beak.

"Where is this from?" you say.

"Germany," Jacqueline says. "It's from the war."

But that wasn't what you were asking. "No, I mean, where did you get this?"

"The same little bird."

"What are you talking about? *Who* are you talking about?"

She reaches for the dagger and lifts it gently from your hands. Then she taps one fingernail against its scabbard, studying it as you just did, her eyes tracing over its length and detail. "Just someone I know," Jacqueline says, paying more attention to the dagger than to her words. "A boy."

"What boy?"

"It doesn't matter."

"Why did he give you that?"

She runs one finger over the filigree. "Because I liked it," she says. "Isn't it beautiful?"

"And he gave you the money, too? Why would he do that?"

Jacqueline's face drops. She glowers at you. Her mouth opens and her bottom lip juts out, just an inch. You hate that face—that irritated, "oh, be quiet" face. You hate it because you know it's your face, too. She's annoyed with you, and she's going to scold you, and like so many times before, getting scolded by Jacqueline will feel like getting scolded by your own subconscious.

"Yes, he gave me the money," she says. "I already *told* you that, Elisabeth."

"But why?"

"Because he's kind," Jacqueline says. "He's my friend. He's my *financier*."

She trips over that word, her tongue and cheeks trying too hard, and you can tell that the word isn't her own.

"Jacqueline—"

"Oh, relax," she says, setting the dagger on the floor. "This is incredible, don't you see? This is a miracle. This is *it*."

Her face brightens, and then she's bounding across the workshop, returning to the stack of crates. This time, she comes back with something you recognize: the neatly folded square of your map. *National Roads of These United States,* it reads in bold, black letters across the top, and that's exactly what it is—a map of all forty-eight states and their major roads, which curl across the page like hundreds of interlocking rivers. Late at night, you and Jacqueline like to sit on the floor in your bedroom with the map laid out in front of you. It's printed on a thick piece of paper worn soft with age and attention, and you love how it smells, a scent like wood saturated in rain. With a pair of calipers crafted by your father, Jacqueline will point to places on the map and say, *Here. This is where we'll run away to one day. Here.* She'll point to Dallas, Los Angeles, Seattle, a different place every time. It's thrilling. It's scary. But it's only fantasy, or so you've thought.

"Where should we go?" Jacqueline says now, unfolding the map on one of your father's worktables. She runs both hands over it, flattening the seams. "I want to go to New York," she says, "or Philadelphia. A place with lots of people."

You stand. Join your sister at the table. "But where will we live?"

"We'll live in a hotel. Cities have lots of hotels."

"Hotels are expensive."

"We have money now."

"But that will run out."

Jacqueline waits. Thinks. Then she smiles. "Maybe not."

"You're being cruel, you know."

"What do you mean?"

"Just tell me." You turn to the stacks of dollar bills again, staring in disbelief. It doesn't seem right. It *can't* be right. You feel like a criminal, or at least an accomplice to one. "Tell me who gave you that. You have to. I'm your sister."

Jacqueline sighs, making a show of it. A strand of her hair briefly rises with her breath, and she tucks it back behind one ear. She's making that face again—you can *feel* that face—but then it flashes into something else.

"I'll make you a deal," she says. "I'll tell you all about my little bird if you decide where we'll go."

"Fine," you say, in a hurry. "Chicago."

"No," Jacqueline says. She pivots to face you. "I'm serious. Decide where we'll go, and I'll tell you."

"I did decide. I said Chicago."

"But you weren't being serious." She stares at you, unblinking, and then she steps closer. She takes your hand. "This is it," she says. "*The Plan.* Our plan." She squeezes your hand. Smiles. But it isn't a fun smile. There's something sad in your sister's eyes, and instantly you feel like crying, though you can't explain why. "Tell me," Jacqueline says. "Where are we going, Elisabeth?"

The crickets and katydids are gone. The air feels suddenly colder, and you can feel it stinging like ice inside your nose, your throat, your chest. And all the while, Jacqueline stares at you with eyes that seem brighter now—not their typical blue but a blue so intent that it's nearly white.

The decision is yours. You can answer Jacqueline or not. But if you do, you'll be speaking much more than words. You'll be making a commitment. A bond. With a single word, you can speak a new world into being. A new future.

No, that can't be right. You'll name a city, and it'll make no difference. Jacqueline can't be serious. In her heart, she knows—as you do—that this is only play. Fantasy. Your answer will mean nothing. That weight is not on your shoulders. But still, when you speak, you quiver. The hairs on your arms stand stiff, and the space between your legs goes hot.

"Philadelphia," you say, because it's the first word that you can pluck from the air. An automatic answer. An echo of Jacqueline.

Your sister grins. Then she lets you go and the dazzling ring of sharpened metal bursts through the workshop. The dagger flashes, and like a pirate your sister drives the blade down onto the map. It sticks into the wood of the table and stands upright. She missed the clustered knot of Philadelphia, but by only an inch.

"It's a deal," Jacqueline says, still gripping the hilt.

CHAPTER 5

Despite a cool early morning, that day—the day of the murder—was one of the hottest in Tanacross that Elisabeth could remember. The sun glared down with an almost violent intensity, its light not beams but spears, its shining not warmth but a suffocating pall. Elisabeth's clothes clung to her arms and legs like sodden bandages.

Margaret spent the afternoon swimming with Clara Nez and her mother, Marjorie. The Athabaskans never swam in the Tanana River itself—its currents were much too swift—but, on the handful of days each year when it wasn't too cold for a swim, Glaman Pond was suitable enough. Even so, swimming was hardly a popular pastime. The Athabaskans were not strong swimmers. Why would they be? During most months, the only flowing water in Tanacross lay buried beneath the ice of the river, as swimmable as a channel of lava rushing through a mountain.

Around dinnertime, with the canister of oil in hand, Elisabeth set off for Mack's house, all the while peering up the lane toward the landing strip. Alfred had spent all day working on his plane. He had wheeled it into the middle of the runway, and now the plane was facing northwest, opposite Elisabeth. With its single back wheel so much smaller than the two in front, the plane angled up as though it was always in the motion of taking off.

But it didn't look like the plane would be flying anytime soon. Straddling the engine, Alfred was furiously yanking at something Elisabeth couldn't see. Teddy Granger stood nearby, dressed in a blue jumpsuit and idly puffing a cigarette. At his feet, the ground was littered with pieces of machinery—pistons and coils, shafts and shielding, smaller bits and bolts that glinted in the sunlight like a pocketful of spilled coins.

"Quite an operation over there," Elisabeth told Mack a minute later. She was standing beside his front stoop. Mack was seated on the top step with his back leaned against the door. The canister of oil dangled from one of his hands.

"No fooling," he said. They watched Alfred and Teddy for a little while longer. Then Mack sucked at his teeth. "It's kind of surprising. I guess he was saving up all his energy."

Elisabeth thought about that. "How do you mean?"

"Just about this afternoon. For hours he didn't do but nothing. He just paced around the GD thing." Mack's face went long and he stomped his boots on the stairs, pantomiming the motion of slow, laborious steps. "Just walked and walked around it, one hand scratching at his chin like a professor studying a chalkboard." Mack smiled widely at Elisabeth, as though that analogy would have particular significance to her.

"I see," she said, smiling a little. "Well, maybe he wasn't sure about what all needed to be fixed. He told us this morning that something was wrong with the wings, but I guess he found other parts that needed fixing, too."

"I guess so," Mack said. He thought for a moment, and then he frowned. "Least he's out of your house for now. Better here than there, I suppose."

"Are we really going to talk about that again? You're going to give me the older-brother treatment?"

"Older brother?" Mack said, looking up at her. "Else, I don't look a day over eighteen."

Elisabeth smirked, and they turned their heads to watch Alfred again. Now he was leaning to the side, his right hand darting out as he talked with Teddy. A moment later Teddy was strolling over to the house. The hook of a candy cane was sticking out of his mouth—a trademark of his. No matter the time of year, Teddy was almost always sucking on a candy cane. He ate them slowly, never snapping them between his teeth, each cane melting into a stubby U with ends as sharp as needles. Every few months, Teddy had Mr. Glaser bring him whole boxes of them. Like all of the Athabaskans in Tanacross, Teddy was mostly self-sufficient—he hunted, he trapped, he traded—but he also earned some extra spending money from working in a gold mine up in Chicken.

"Hot as the dark dickens out here," Teddy said, walking up to the stoop. Sweat glistened on his forehead.

"Don't need to tell me twice," Mack said. He glanced at his kennels. "I think my dogs are about to catch fire."

"Burning fur—I wondered what that smell was," Teddy said, and a smile crept onto his face. He turned to Elisabeth and winked. "I assumed it was only Mack's cooking."

Elisabeth laughed. Mack cocked his head.

"And how are you, Mrs. Pfautz?" Teddy asked.

"I'm doing fine. Thank you."

"I hope the old bugger's not giving you and Margaret too much trouble."

"None at all," Elisabeth said, but she couldn't stop herself from glancing down at her feet. "And how's he treating you? You guys sure have some setup over there."

Mack huffed. "Is he fixing the thing or tearing it apart?"

"A little bit of both, I think," Teddy said. He shifted the candy cane from one side of his mouth to the other. He was almost through with it; the cane had been whittled down to a shape as spindly as a wishbone. "Honestly," Teddy said, "I'm really not sure what he's doing. He'll work with one thing, put it back together, and then he'll take it apart again fifteen minutes later. He's messing with the crankshaft for the fourth or fifth time today. Speaking of which"—he turned to Mack—"do you have a set of Robertson bits? He sent me to fetch."

"Maybe," Mack said. Holding both knees, he pushed himself to his feet and headed inside.

Teddy and Elisabeth were quiet for a while. Then, sighing, Teddy wiped one hand across the back of his neck.

"Hot as the dickens," he repeated, staring up at the sun.

Elisabeth folded her arms. "So if he's going around in circles, what all are you doing?" She glanced at Alfred. "It'd be a shame if he's making you just stand around, wasting your time." Elisabeth frowned. "Wasting your talents," she added.

"Oh, I don't mind," Teddy said. "I don't have a whole lot to do this week, and it beats sitting around and reading funny books all day."

"I know how that is," Elisabeth said, but she didn't. There was always something for her to do, and she was old enough now that the idleness of younger people seemed foreign and baffling to her. She watched Teddy draw the last of the cane into his mouth. His lips puckered and pulled at it, tossing the candy from one cheek to the other like a bite of food too hot to chew. Not five seconds later, Teddy pulled another candy cane from the pocket of his shirt. Then Mack opened the door and stepped outside.

"You're lucky I found it," he said. He was carrying a small tackle box in one hand, a thing that reminded Elisabeth of a lunch box.

"Thank you much," Teddy said, reaching out and taking the box. He cradled it beneath one arm and, with both hands working, started to peel the wrapper off the new candy cane. "You all take care," he said, turning back to the landing strip.

"Don't let him boss you too much," Elisabeth said.

But Teddy didn't seem to hear her. He was concentrating on the candy cane, and a moment later he had it freed. He tossed the plastic wrapper away, and it caught in the breeze and fluttered through the air like a sheath of snakeskin.

"He's a big dang kid, that one," Mack said, taking a seat on the top step again.

"Aren't we all?"

"I thought I was your big brother," Mack said. "Now I'm a kid? You've got to get your story straight, Else."

"All right," Elisabeth said. "You're just you. How about that?"

Mack grimaced. "Eh, I don't know if I want to be me either. Being me ain't all that great most of the time."

"I know how that is," Elisabeth said again, automatically, just making conversation, but this time, she realized that she was telling the truth.

Mack knew it, too. He looked up at her for a long moment, and then he reached out for her. He gripped her arm, and at first Elisabeth thought that he was going to pull himself up, that he needed an anchor, but instead he simply held her. Then his hand dropped away, and Mack watched the landing strip once more.

"I've got to get Margaret to bed," Elisabeth said.

"Yeah," Mack told her. "It's about that time, isn't it?"

"I hope you can get some sleep, too."

"I hope I can. I could use it. And I'll tell you what." He looked up at her again, and now he smiled, back to his old self, or some approximation of it. "I'll go on being me if you go on being you. Because I like you being you, Else. I wouldn't have it any other way. So how's that for a deal? Does that sound fair?"

"That sounds fair enough to me," Elisabeth said. "You've got a deal."

"Good," Mack said, and he nodded firmly. "That's all I could ever want."

That night, Elisabeth dreamed that she was wandering through the house—the house here in Tanacross. Up and down its drafty hallways, in and out of the bedrooms, through the kitchen and back again. The layout of the house was the same as it normally was, but it also felt more expansive, and more warped. The hallways seemed to bend. The floorboards were scalloped. The bedrooms buckled at their corners, rooms that stretched so tight they were nearly circles. Still, it was certainly their house. Their pictures hung on the walls. Their books lined the shelves. The hallway was clad in their floral-print wallpaper, and their ironing board lolled open beside the stove in the kitchen.

Elisabeth walked and walked, pacing around with the dubious interest of someone touring a home on the market. The house was peaceful, noiseless, deserted. Then, passing through the living room and into the dining room for the umpteenth time, Elisabeth saw that she wasn't alone. Jacqueline was sitting at the table with a map sprawled out in front of her.

"Where have you been?" Jacqueline said. "I've been waiting for you all this time."

Elisabeth was dumbstruck.

"Well, come on," Jacqueline said. "Let's get started."

She ran her hands across the map, pressing it flatter as Elisabeth approached the table. Although Jacqueline was still a little girl, Elisabeth was the same age that she was now, old enough to be Jacqueline's mother—to be *their* mother, had their mother made it that long. She stopped in front of the table and looked down at the map. It was a map of the world, and it spread across the length of the table. The wiggling borders of countries were marked in thin black lines, but the map was completely unlabeled. It was a teacher's map.

"All right," Jacqueline said, "show me where Korea is," and even though Elisabeth could feel how strange it was to be instructed by a little girl—her sister, no less—she couldn't help but point to Korea.

"Good," Jacqueline said. "Now show me"—her voice hung in the air, trailing along as she considered Elisabeth's next task—"show me Germany."

Elisabeth pointed to Germany.

"Now show me where Papa was born. Do you remember?"

After a second, Elisabeth pointed to the spot where Hamburg was, way down near the bottom of the Jutland Peninsula.

"Close enough," Jacqueline said.

Turkey, Ireland, French Indochina, Brazil; they went on and on. Finally, Jacqueline started asking about states. North Dakota. Arkansas. Oregon. But when Elisabeth was instructed to point at Pennsylvania, Jacqueline just shook her head.

"Try again," she said. "Pennsylvania. Come on. Where's Pennsylvania?"

Elisabeth pointed again. Jacqueline only sighed. "One more time," she said.

But before Elisabeth had a chance to try again, someone knocked on the front door. Both of them turned their heads.

"Too late," Jacqueline said, and then she frowned. The knocking continued, louder now, and scattered. It sounded as if a hundred different people were knocking on a hundred different spots in the house: the roof; the windows; even beneath their feet, noises that resonated up from the root cellar. Each of the knocks rapped quickly three times, then paused, then rapped again. Too frightened to think straight, Elisabeth kept pointing to Pennsylvania. Her finger tapped the paper of the map so hard that it left an indentation.

"No," Jacqueline said, shaking her head. "That's not it," and then her shaking grew more violent. Her entire body oscillated until she was only a blur, streaks of foggy motion like the image of a person who moves while being photographed. Horrified, Elisabeth took a step back. Then she opened her eyes.

"Mama, Mama," Margaret was saying, but at first, still half-asleep, Elisabeth mistook her for Jacqueline.

"What's happening?" she said, and she meant that question for her sister, though it was Margaret who answered it.

"Mr. Granger is here," she said.

Margaret. Her daughter. In Alaska. Elisabeth sat up, and her stupor began to fade. "What?"

"Mr. Granger," Margaret repeated, stepping away from the bed. "He's in the kitchen. Him and Mr. Nilak. They told me to wake you up." She was silent for a second. Then, quizzically, "Why didn't you answer the door?"

CHAPTER 6

What had happened, Teddy told her, was this: About an hour earlier, Alfred had bludgeoned Mack with a hook wrench, and now Mack was dead.

"If he put up a fight," Teddy said, his voice catching in his throat, "it sure didn't last long. Alfred doesn't have a mark on him. Not one mark. And it was savage, Else. Absolutely savage. I'm telling you. I saw Mack, and this was"—his eyes glazed over—"this was really something else."

"He just about bashed his goddamn head off," Daniel Nilak said, taking one step toward the table. Daniel was one of Mack's many nephews. Heavyset and seventeen years old, he had never been particularly friendly with them, and now a tenor of rage boomed in his voice. "His goddamn brains are all over the landing strip. Why did—"

"Cool it," Teddy said, lifting one hand.

"What was that Kraut doing here?" Daniel said.

"I said cool off," Teddy told him, and he turned in his seat, raising his palm and pushing air at Daniel. "Let's all just calm down."

Seated at the kitchen table across from Teddy, Elisabeth watched and listened in silence. It was just after one o'clock in the morning, and the skin around her eyes felt puffy from sleep. Sitting there, taking it all in, she felt as though she was still partly dreaming. She thought of the warping hallways, the contorted rooms, the recessed floorboards. The kitchen table looked huge and surreal, and Teddy seemed to be sitting very far away.

You're in shock, she told herself, but she didn't know if that was true. Maybe she was calm because of just the opposite; maybe she had expected this from Alfred all along. And what if she had? Way down deep, was the calm she felt something like relief? *It could have been us,* she thought more than once. *It could have happened to us,* and she was thankful that it hadn't, but giving thanks had never felt so shameful.

Because, Mack. Dear God, it had happened to Mack, and that was hardly any better than it happening to them. Mack was dead, and the horror of how it had happened was so extreme that Elisabeth couldn't even cry. She just sat there, blinking and breathing and a little bit dizzy.

"But why did he do it?" she finally said. "What did Alfred say?"

"He said they got into an argument."

"Over what?"

"Cards," Teddy said. "A hand of rummy. I left Alfred around seven o'clock, and at some point after that Mack started helping him in my stead. Then they started playing cards, and then it happened. Buddy Luke heard the commotion when he was going to the toilet out back behind his place, and so he went running. But by then it was over." Teddy closed his eyes, rubbing at his forehead. "Thing is, I just don't get it. I've known Mack all my life, and he wasn't the gambling kind."

"And he wasn't the cheating kind," Daniel added gruffly, crossing his arms.

"No, he wasn't," Teddy said. "I don't understand it."

A log shifted in the fire of the stove, hissing and popping as it fell.

"And what happens now?" Elisabeth said.

"Buddy Luke's already radioed Fairbanks. They're flying in some folks from the city to take him away."

"And where is Alfred?"

"Buddy and Henry Isaac have him up in the big cache on the south side. Henry's keeping an eye on him." Teddy sighed, scooting forward an inch or two. "In the time he was here, did he ever say anything about Mack? Did he talk about him at all?"

"No," Elisabeth said, "not that I can remember. Honestly, he didn't really talk to us much. The first day he just slept, and then all yesterday he was working on the plane." She leaned back in her seat. "I don't know what to say," she told him, which was true.

They were silent. Then Teddy cleared his throat, reaching up and running his fingers across the top button of his shirt. It was mother-of-pearl, nicer than the other buttons, and even in the dimness of the kitchen it gleamed like a tiny moon.

"There is one other thing," he said. "Another reason why we came here to tell you this."

Elisabeth lowered her chin. "What is it?"

"Well, it's just that"—Teddy shifted in his seat—"well, he asked about you."

"He asked about me?"

"He wants to talk to you. He *really* wants to talk to you."

"About what?"

"I don't know," Teddy said, "but he wouldn't quit about it. He went on and on asking for you. Screaming for you. Over and over. Outside of the basics, it was just about the only thing he said to us." Teddy swept one hand through his hair and, briefly, his bangs stood up in a swooping wave. "He tried to get over here."

"Over *here*? Our house?"

Teddy nodded. "He had a fight with Henry about it. They tussled some. Him and Buddy. So they—" Teddy started fiddling again with the top button of his shirt. For once, he had no candy cane to toy with, and his hands seemed restless. "Well, they restrained him. They had to. But still he wouldn't quit about it. So I told him I'd come over here and ask if you'd be willing to talk to him. It was the only way he'd quiet down. He was waking the whole *keey* up."

Turning her head, Elisabeth stared through the window above the sink. And there it was: that ever-present wall of trees, a suffocating blend of green and gray and dirty brown that was closing around them like a clenching fist. Tanacross felt smaller than ever before—smaller and infinitely more isolated. They were a colony at the bottom of the sea. They were a speck of civilization on Mars. And they were all trapped here together. Then those words of Alfred's came back to her—*the wilds*—and Elisabeth hated herself for thinking of them. She turned back to Teddy.

"Did he say what he wants to talk about?"

Teddy shook his head. "But I'm hoping you can get some more information out of him."

"What do you mean?"

"He's lying about the fight," Daniel said. "He's a goddamn liar, and we want to know what really happened."

"If he's lying to you," Elisabeth said, "why would he tell me the truth?"

"Because he's your *friend*," Daniel said, and he glowered as he said that word, *friend*, as if he needed to make it any clearer how he felt about her right now.

"We're not *friends*," she said, almost spitting as she spoke. "I didn't want him here. I didn't ask for him to stay. I had an obligation. I didn't—"

"Okay, okay," Teddy said, pumping his hands. "I get that. I know that, even if Daniel doesn't," and he glared at Daniel over his shoulder. "But the point is, we don't know what he wants to talk to you about, and we'd like to find out. That's all." He sat back heavily, sighing as he went. "Even so, I mean it when I say this: You don't have to do this if you don't want to."

"Do what?"

"Talk to him."

"It sounds like you're insisting."

"I don't mean to. I'd be lying if I said I didn't want to know what happened, but at the same time I know what we're asking. Else"—and now Teddy wasn't watching her as he spoke—"he's gone loopy, and I'm not sure if it's safe for you to be around him. We told him that we'd come and talk to you, and we're doing that now, but we didn't promise him that you'd come, and you don't have to. It's your decision—it really is—and if you don't want to go, that's understandable."

Yes, it would be, and yes, it was her decision, but in the pause that followed Elisabeth knew what she would do. Of course she would visit Alfred. Already, she knew that there was no sensible explanation for what he had done—no good reason, no cause—but she had to hear what Alfred would say, however deranged it might be. She had already lost one person without any closure whatsoever; she wouldn't lose Mack like that, too. Elisabeth turned her head and looked at the window again. The trees seemed even closer now, as if they were inching forward every minute, consuming her, engulfing her.

"All right," Elisabeth said, and she looked at Teddy. Then she pushed her chair away from the table.

CHAPTER 7

You never knew your mother, but you know your vision of her as well as you know any real person. When you close your eyes at night and wait for sleep, you can see her smile. You can hear her laugh. You can smell her perfume, and you can feel her touch on your face, her fingers running through your hair. You've thought of these things so often, and so vividly, that they might as well be real. To you, they are real.

You have entire fantasies about her. Nothing heroic. Nothing larger-than-life. You fantasize about the mundane, because the mundane is easier to believe. You have a fantasy of going grocery shopping with her. In another, you visit the beach in Maryland, chitchat with a woman your mother happens to know from high school. You have fantasies of her taking your temperature. Walking with you to school. Reading books to you at bedtime.

But these are only dreams. The more often you dream them, the clearer they become, but they're all make-believe. In real life, your mother died from chest cancer when you and your sister were four years old. In real life, it's only you and Jacqueline and Papa. That's the way it is, and that's the way it always will be.

"I'm not raising children," Papa's told you. "This family has no time for children."

He treats you and your sister like adults. You have been taught—trained—to think of yourself, Jacqueline, and your father as a team. You and your sister maintain the house, cooking and cleaning and ironing and doing all the things grown women do. You've known how to make schnitzel and potpie since you were six, and you've known how to sew since you were five.

Not only that: You help with your father's business, too. He's the best tool and die maker in Lititz, and you and Jacqueline help him run his shop. You fetch for him. You run errands. You return tools to their places on the wall. You sweep filings off the floor. You oil the machinery, the punches and plates and spools and springs. You manage his appointments, and you maintain a careful ledger of the orders that come from them. He even lets you manage the payments and receipts, though your father delegates this task to you and you alone.

"You're the favorite," Jacqueline has said more than once. "You're the favorite, and I'm number two. I'm number poo."

You roll your eyes. Sigh at her. You tell her, "No, no, no. I'm good at arithmetic. That's all. Papa loves us just the same. We're a team, remember? And every member of a team is just as important as the next."

But, really, you *are* the favorite child, and both of you know it. Jacqueline wants your comfort, which you're happy to give, but the truth is that Papa acts sweeter and kinder and more patient with you, and he trusts you more, too.

"You got all your mama's good sense," Aunt Ethel once told you, "and you didn't leave any for Jacqueline."

Your sister talks back. She glowers. She scowls. She lies. She *acts out,* as your auntie puts it. Once, she tried to shoot an apple off Cousin Charlie's head with a Daisy BB gun, and she nicked a chunk of flesh off the top of his ear. Another time, she got mad at Papa during dinner, and instead of cleaning up like normal, she hurled the dishes through the open kitchen window, shattering a dozen pieces of china. She cusses, she sings in the bathtub, she sasses your teacher at school, she slaps girls in the mouth when they're cruel to her and kicks boys in the crotch when they bully her. Once, you and Jacqueline and Jesse Rhiner were messing around in the woods, and Jacqueline stomped on a dead opossum and sprayed its rotten guts all over Jesse's legs. That's the kind of thing she does.

And your father's patience goes only so far. He may treat you like a grown-up. He doesn't check your homework or force you to bed. He trusts you with the shopping and going to town. But your sister toes the line, and he can't let her go completely unpunished, not always. Sometimes, he grounds her. Other times, he gives her more chores.

"He treats us like his servants," Jacqueline has huffed. "His personal maids."

"No, he doesn't."

"If Mama were here, she wouldn't let him treat us like this."

She says that a lot. "If Mama were here." For you, your mother is a vision. Your imaginary paradise. But for Jacqueline, your mother is her defense. She's a make-believe avenger.

"With Mama," she says, "our lives wouldn't be like this. She'd put Papa in his place, and we wouldn't be prisoners."

"We're not prisoners now," you say.

But Jacqueline doesn't hear you.

Your sister will never admit how lucky she is. Papa never hits her, not even when she screams in his face or throws dishes out the window. His papa used to beat him senseless, and he says that he has no wish to do anything like that to his own children. He's huge—six foot something and about as wide as a doorway—but he's gentle and calm. The worst he ever does is sass your sister back.

"I'm going to call the police on you," she threatened him once, "and tell them about that whisky bottle in your bedroom."

"Go ahead," he told her. "After talking with you, they'll probably want a drink, too."

"I wish I could just vanish," she told him another time. "I wish someone would kidnap me."

"Once they get to know you," Papa said, "they'd bring you right back."

She deserves every bit of sass he gives her. Or almost every bit. Sometimes, especially when he drinks from that bedroom bottle, he says things that make you hold your breath, things that twist your heart even though they're not aimed at you.

"Goddamn it, Jacky," he said the night she took off part of Cousin Charlie's ear. "You could have shot his eye out."

"We were playing," she protested. "I didn't—"

"You didn't what?" he snapped. "You didn't *think*. You didn't think because you're stupid. Do you understand that, Jacky?"

But your sister was silent.

"Then I'll repeat it," your father said. "You're stupid. You're a stupid little girl who doesn't think. You're a dumb disappointment."

And later that evening, after your sister went to bed crying, your father said something more.

"Else," he told you, and from his seat at the kitchen table he reached for your hand. "You're the good one," he said. "Don't ever think otherwise."

You stared at him, and you couldn't think of anything to say. But he didn't want you to say anything. His hand dropped weakly from yours, and he turned away.

You know he shouldn't say such things, but you also know this: A lot of people would agree with him. You and Jacqueline are twins, two of a kind, and people think of you as a set. And when they think of you together, they think of you as the better half. The kind one. The polite one. The good one.

But they don't understand what you do: Jacqueline isn't bad—she's fun. Despite her sass and scowls and short temper, you wouldn't want her any other way. Her mischief makes your life worth living. She's adventurous. She's brave. She's exciting. The good one? Your papa has it backward. In truth, you wish that you could be more like Jacqueline and less like yourself.

But at least you can tag along. You may not be her, but you can be with her. You love your sister, and she loves you. Your mother may be dead and one day Papa will be, too, but you'll always have Jacqueline, and the simple knowledge of that is enough to comfort you when you're scared, to make you happy when you're sad.

"We're the real team," Jacqueline has told you. "Not the three of us. The two of us. Me and you."

Maybe she's right. You were born into this world together, and you've been together ever since. That's all that's ever mattered. That's all that ever will.

So you play along. When Jacqueline unfolds your map, you kneel above it with her, and your fingers trace in unison over the roads of New York, Ohio, Nebraska, California.

"Where should we go?" she'll ask. "Where will we be happy?"

We're happy now would be your real answer.

But instead you smile, and you fantasize. You point to a destination, and you dream.

CHAPTER 8

Although all the meat had been removed at the start of summer, the cache still smelled like cooking rawhide, a scent so powerful that it made Elisabeth's eyes water when she first stepped inside. The open door cast a wide blue block across the middle of the floor, but other than this, the cache was dimly lit. It was humid inside, as cool and dank as a cave.

Alfred sat in a chair against the back wall. His arms and legs were bound to his seat with thick winds of rope. The block of light slipping through the door didn't quite reach his legs, so he sat in relative darkness. Still, Elisabeth could see him well enough. His eyes were wide and sallow. His face was covered in a scrim of peppery stubble.

And his clothes—Elisabeth felt sick just looking at them. His shirt was stained with spatters of blood, and in certain places the fabric hung more loosely, wet, as if someone with dyed red fingertips had pinched him there. She could see blood even on his pants, and on the tips of his boots. In a flash, she imagined it as clear as a strip of film: Alfred beating Mack with the hook wrench; Alfred stomping on his face, his head, his throat. Her knees felt weak, but Alfred looked calm. He stared straight at her. He was very still.

"I'll be right here, Mrs. Pfautz," Henry said. He was standing behind her. "I'll be here the whole time."

"No," Alfred said. "You'll have to wait outside. I want to speak to Mrs. Pfautz alone."

Henry stepped forward. "I'm staying here. I'm guarding you."

Alfred glanced down at himself, exasperated. "I'm not going anywhere," he said. "I can't move."

"That doesn't matter," Henry told him. "It's for Mrs. Pfautz's safety."

His insistence seemed fair enough. Alfred was a killer, and who could tell what else he might be capable of? But in spite of that, Elisabeth wasn't afraid of him. It wasn't the ropes that bound him or the shotgun that hung by Henry's side. Elisabeth's fearlessness came from that brief exchange she and Alfred had shared on the landing strip: *I'm always comfortable with my countrymen,* he had told her. In Alfred's mind, Elisabeth was his ally. She was his attorney behind closed doors. She could only guess what he might do in different circumstances, but Alfred wouldn't hurt her today, not here.

And besides, she wanted the truth. The uncensored, candid truth. That was what she had come for, and she wouldn't get it with Henry here.

"It's all right," Elisabeth said. "I can be alone with him. It's okay."

"It's not okay," Henry said, "not with me. I'm looking after you, Mrs. Pfautz."

Elisabeth chewed at the inside of her bottom lip, thinking.

"How about this?" she said. "Stand outside. Leave the door open, I mean, and you can watch us the entire time." She glanced at Alfred, surprised to find that, of all things, she was seeking his approval.

"Yes," Alfred said. "Stand outside. That would be fine."

"Mrs. Pfautz—"

"It really is okay," Elisabeth said, and she tried to sound as self-assured as she could. Her teacher's voice. "Trust me."

Henry watched her for a second. Then, sighing, he lowered his head and turned to leave. The cache rested on four stilts that raised it ten feet off the ground, far from the reach of bears and wolverines. Its steps were wide and steep, not so much steps as rungs of a ladder. Slowly, Henry climbed to the ground and paced away. He stopped about fifteen feet from the cache and turned to face them.

"A little farther," Alfred said, pointing with his chin.

Henry rolled his eyes. He walked a few feet more, then set his boots firmly in place. They sank in the grassy mud. "This is as far as I'm going," he told them.

"Fine," Alfred said. "That's fine," and, a little wearily, he turned his eyes up to Elisabeth.

They were quiet. Elisabeth stood to Alfred's left, five or six feet away from him.

"Thank you for seeing me," he said. "I appreciate—"

She spat in his face. Alfred flinched, turning his head, closing his eyes, and in that flinch Elisabeth felt something terrible and true.

"Elisabeth—"

She stepped forward, and she spat on him again, even fiercer this time. She was shaking. Balled into fists, her fingers ached. Everything ached.

"Will you let me speak?" Alfred said. And then, gravely, "I have something to tell you."

And admittedly, she wanted to hear it. Taut with fury and grief, she turned away from him, and she made herself breathe. She studied the walls of the cache. They were built from aspen logs, and the spaces between the wood glowed with narrow bands of twilight. Dust was swirling through the air and, cast against the walls' glowing backdrop, it looked as if the cache were filled with undulating flames.

"Elisabeth?"

She breathed.

"Elisabeth. Please listen to me."

"You have one minute," she said, facing him again. "You have one minute to tell me about what happened."

When she said that, her stomach felt suddenly light, tingling as if she might get sick. She thought of Mack. *What happened,* she had said, and it sounded so innocuous, so small. But it wasn't, and as Elisabeth listened to herself talk, she felt again that she was stuck between waking and sleep, stuck in some limbo that wasn't quite real but wasn't quite a dream. She felt dizzy, but she did her best to seem calm. If she looked at all unnerved, Alfred didn't seem to notice.

"I think you're mistaken about something," he said. "This isn't about Mack."

"I came here to talk about Mack," Elisabeth said, "and if that's not the topic, then I'm not going to stay."

Now Alfred smiled, though it wasn't malicious. It was a bashful smile, almost coy. "You'll want to stay for this," he said. "I promise you."

"Tell me why you did it."

Alfred sat straighter. "Cards. An argument. Didn't Teddy and the boy tell you?"

"They told me you're lying."

"They would think that, wouldn't they?"

"Are you?"

Alfred watched her. "Do *you* think I'm lying? Tell me the truth, because that's what this is all about: you and me getting to know each other. Just a little. Today is our first step toward the truth, so tell me what you're thinking."

"I think you're lying, yes," Elisabeth said. "Mack wasn't a gambler, and he wasn't a cheat, and he wasn't a fighter. I think you killed him in cold blood, but I want to hear the reason why. The real reason."

"All right," Alfred said. "I'll tell you why I did it." A pause. An agonizing second. "I was protecting you. There was an argument, yes, but ultimately this was a thing I did for reasons beyond that. I was protecting you from him."

"I doubt that very much."

"I don't want to talk about this anymore," Alfred said. "Telling you what happened to the Indian would be a waste of breath."

"Call him by his name," Elisabeth said, and a quiver of rage shot through her. She clenched her teeth. Her toes curled in her shoes. But Alfred paid her no attention, and he continued.

"I brought you here," he told her, "to talk about one thing, and one thing only." He fluttered his eyes as if he were waking from a heavy sleep. "I want to talk about her, Elisabeth. You know who I mean."

In an instant, her heart was pounding. Every muscle in her body tensed.

"Elisabeth—"

"Stop," she said. It was all she could muster. But he ignored her.

"We need to start working together," Alfred said, "and together we can find her."

"I told you to stop."

"Jacqueline," Alfred said. His head hung low. His eyes glowed white. His mouth gaped open. "I know things about Jacqueline."

Elisabeth steadied herself. She closed her eyes. She waited a long while. *He's baiting you,* she told herself. *He's torturing you.* The rational part of her mind knew exactly what he wanted. *Jacqueline?* he wanted her to say, raising one hand to her mouth like a woman in a melodrama. *How do you know about my sister?*

And she knew she couldn't give him the satisfaction. Never mind that she hadn't told him anything about her sister. There were plenty of explanations for that: Margaret, Mack, one of the photographs scattered throughout their house, some of them neatly labeled with Jacqueline's name beneath her image. The part of Elisabeth that implored her to be sensible was working at full speed: *He's baiting you. He's trying to get at you.* She knew that she should leave the cache. She knew that she shouldn't even entertain this. Her sister? She wasn't going to talk about her sister, not with this man, and not in these circumstances.

But of course, she couldn't leave. However powerful her inclination for skepticism, it was nothing compared to her desire for hope. Already a thing was thrashing inside her, a thing that Alfred was waking and now might never sleep again.

"I bet you dream about her," Alfred said, "don't you?"

Elisabeth opened her eyes.

"I dream about her, too," he said. "I dream about her every night, which is to say I dream about you, too." He lifted his chin. "I know how it feels, Elisabeth. How it feels to be so utterly alone. These woods"—he was staring at the north wall of the cache, and now he narrowed his eyes as if he could see straight through it—"these woods eat you up, don't they? They trap you and squeeze you and shut you off from the world. Do you know what I'm talking about?"

She did. She knew exactly what he meant. There was a trail that stretched from their yard into the woods, snaking its way up and around Glaman Pond. An offshoot of the trail led even farther than that, a trail that the Athabaskans used for hunting. It extended through the forest until finally, half a mile out, it petered away and left only the bush.

Sometimes, John went hunting with the other men, and once, just for fun, Elisabeth walked with them until the trail came to an end. It was November, early winter, and the woods were already filled with snow. The trees weren't very large in Alaska, but the snow made them look thicker and more imposing. Their branches sagged with clumps of snow and ice that merged into the branches of other trees around them, the entire forest linking arms. In Pennsylvania, the woods were wide and easy to traverse, but here the woods swallowed you up, every burdened tree leaning this way or that way as though the whole forest was collapsing on top of you. Standing at the end of the trail, watching John and the other men slink away, Elisabeth had been shocked at how quickly they disappeared altogether—how suddenly, almost instantly, she was standing by herself.

"That's why people like you and me come to Alaska," Alfred said. "We come here because we feel alone, and in our weakness we want to surrender ourselves to that loneliness. We want to be lost, and what easier place to be lost than Alaska?" He swallowed, bowing his head. "But you can't give in to that temptation. It's easy to feel alone, and it's easy to surrender, but I'm here to tell you the truth."

Her voice was a raspy whisper. "What truth?"

"That you are not alone," Alfred said. "I am here for you, Elisabeth, and I want to help you."

She watched him. "What do you know about my sister?"

"I know that she's alive."

"How?"

He took a breath. A single breath. "Because I was involved in her disappearance."

She couldn't move. She couldn't think. She could only stare at Alfred Seidel, and he stared right back.

"I lived in Lititz at the time it happened," he said. "It was shortly after I came to America. I was there, and I was involved."

"Then tell me where she is," Elisabeth said.

"It's not that simple. I told you that today was going to be the first *step* toward the truth. It's nothing more than that. It's only the start."

"What does that mean?"

"It means I won't tell you anything more than what I've said already. It means I can't tell you everything I know, not in one sitting."

"Why not?"

"Because if I do," Alfred said, and he slumped, staring up at her with a look of desperation and fear and unmistakable tenderness, "you'll have no more use for me, and then I'll be alone again."

CHAPTER 9

Jacqueline's "little bird" is hardly little. He's a grown man—Jacqueline says that he turned nineteen in March—and his name is Jacob Joseph.

"Is he one of Papa's friends?" you say.

"No, he's one of *my* friends," Jacqueline says.

The two of you are kneeling on the floor of your father's workshop, collecting the money that your sister arranged into stacks only minutes before. But now you pause, sitting up on your knees.

"But he's a grown-up," you say. "Why does he want to be friends with you?"

You don't mean for that to sound insulting, but that's how the words come out. And now Jacqueline stops working, too. She glares at you, smoothly balling her fists in her lap.

"You don't get it," she says, like a snob, lifting up her chin. "I knew you wouldn't get it. Jacob's like a big brother. He's nice. He's smart. He's like a fun big brother."

"And he gives you money?"

"Sometimes," Jacqueline says. "He's rich. I've been helping him around his house, and sometimes he gives me money."

"You mean, you're doing chores for him?"

"No. I *help* him. I'm his feminine presence in the house."

"His feminine presence?"

"Yes, you know. I cook for him sometimes, but other times we just talk, or he shows me things. He's terribly interesting."

He's a native German, your sister explains, a recent immigrant who fought for the German Empire in the war. And not only that—he's royalty.

"He was a war hero," Jacqueline says, "and a prince, or something like that. But after the war, his castle was taken away from his family, and he came to the United States."

"A castle?" You scrunch up your face.

"I've seen a picture of it," your sister says. "It's real."

"But people don't really live in castles, dummy. That's all made up."

"It's not," Jacqueline shouts, "and I'm not a dummy. I didn't believe it either, but I've seen pictures, and I've seen his medals, and I can tell it's all true. And then there's this." She holds up two handfuls of dollar bills. "Jacob just *gave* this to me. Like it was nothing. He's rich. He's royalty. He has boxes and boxes of money. A whole basement of it."

You sit straighter, and for a moment you and Jacqueline just watch each other. "Boxes of money?" you say. "Honest?"

"Yes, honest," Jacqueline says. She's working again, and her voice is soft. "Cross my heart and hope to die."

For the rest of the day, you think about Jacob, turning him over and over in your mind. *The Plan* is forgotten, or at least it pauses for a moment. You ask one question after another, and Jacqueline answers each one.

You're cutting onions for a pot roast.

"Does he live all alone?"

Jacqueline is cutting carrots.

"Most of the time. But he has relatives in New York City."

You're cleaning dishes at the sink.

"How did you meet him?"

Jacqueline is drying a coffee cup.

"At the hardware store. I was buying copper filings for Papa, and Jacob was buying something, too. A hammer or something."

"Where was I?"

"Baking pies with Auntie."

You're dumping trash in the woods.

"What does he do for work?"

Jacqueline kicks a glass bottle.

"He doesn't have to work. He's rich."

You're spreading coffee grounds over the garden out back.

"Why haven't I met him?"

Jacqueline wipes her hands on her apron.

"Because he doesn't ever come over."

"Then when do you see him?"

"A little bit at a time. I go to his house sometimes when I run errands. And sometimes he writes me letters that he leaves behind the workshop."

You're scrubbing Papa's shirts.

"Why does he live all alone? Why isn't he married?"

Jacqueline is scrubbing socks.

"He *is* married. He's handsome and rich and smart as the dickens. But his wife is still in the old country."

You're watching fireflies.

"You've actually seen boxes of money? Whole boxes of it?"

Jacqueline is jamming a stick against the ground.

"Yes."

"How many times have you been to his house?"

"I haven't kept track. A bunch."

You're brushing your sister's hair.

"Where does he live?"

Jacqueline sighs.

"In a house on Shenk Lane."

You're lying next to each other on the hardwood floor. Embracing.

"Can I meet him?"

Jacqueline closes her eyes.

"I'll ask, but he's a very private person."

Throughout all of the answers that Jacqueline has given, that's been a theme: Jacob likes to keep to himself. He lives alone. He doesn't work. He doesn't socialize. He has no friends, it seems, apart from your sister— his *feminine presence*. And he's in Lititz only temporarily. His wife has yet to leave Germany, but her immigration is underway, and when she arrives he'll move to New York City and join her.

"And she's marvelous," Jacqueline tells you the following day. "Marvelous and beautiful and wonderful in every way."

You're hanging laundry on the line out back. "You've met her?"

"No, but I've heard all about her. I've heard oodles." Jacqueline steps closer, nudging you playfully with her shoulder. "Want to see a picture of her?"

And the woman she shows you is indeed beautiful. She wears a fur capelet and a flat-brimmed hat, one adorned with a blooming flower the size of a saucer. Silver earrings dangle beside her jawline like drops of falling water. Her head is turned three-quarters to the side, and her nose is long and narrow. Her eyes look kind, and her lips bend with a faint smile. She looks dignified. Proud, but not pompous. She looks, you must admit, like royalty. But even more than that, she looks like someone else, and you realize who after a minute of thinking. The slant of her nose. The shape of her lips. The posture. The way her hair is crimped around her ears. She looks like your mother.

"Isn't she beautiful?" Jacqueline says.

She takes back the picture and cradles it in both hands, as though it's something delicate and small. An injured animal. A broken toy.

"Yes," you say, fighting the lump in your throat. "She's beautiful."

"And Jacob says she'd love to meet me. He's certain of it."

"Jacqueline," you say, but you don't know how to finish.

You stand up from your seat on the edge of your sister's bed. Jacqueline is standing by the window, still studying the sepia portrait in her hands. Outside, it's dark, and above the cornfields fireflies strobe, a rippling sea of winking gold. How can you ask the thing you need to ask? How can you say it without Jacqueline getting upset?

"Can I—" And you struggle with the words for a moment, but finally your tongue feels stronger. You know how to get at what you need to ask. "You said that Jacob sends you letters?"

Jacqueline looks up at you. "Yes. Sometimes."

"Can I read them?"

"Why?"

"Because he sounds amazing. This is *all* amazing."

She considers your question, but then she leans away from you. "No, they're private." She walks to her vanity table—a piece of furniture that belonged to your mother—and she slips the photograph into its center drawer. "I've already said too much."

"About what?"

"About everything," Jacqueline says. "I shouldn't have told you about Jacob at all. He told me this is a secret."

"What's a secret?"

"Everything."

You shake your head. "But why does it have to be a secret? What is there to hide?"

"The money," Jacqueline says. "I don't want Papa to know about the money."

"Why not?"

"Because he'll take it for himself."

"Did Jacob tell you that?"

And you can see from her face that, yes, he did. He's encouraged her to keep this a secret. To keep everything a secret.

"Don't you think this is strange?" you say. "If he's so nice, if he's like a big brother, why doesn't he make friends with us all? He's a grown-up. He could be friends with Papa."

"But he's *my* friend," Jacqueline says. "I don't want him to be friends with Papa."

And that's all you can take. You have to ask her directly, even if it makes her upset. Even if it makes her hate you. "Jacqueline," you say, "are you telling me the truth about Jacob?"

She sits down on the stool in front of the vanity. "What do you mean?"

"Is he—" Just say it. However ridiculous it sounds. "Is he your boyfriend?"

She frowns. Takes instant offense. "No, he's not my boyfriend. What are you talking about?"

"It's just that—"

"It's just what?" Jacqueline says.

"Well, why did Jacob give you so much money?"

"Because he's kind," she says. "And he's rich. You saw the dagger. You saw the money."

That you did. The dagger, you know, is wrapped in its towel beneath Jacqueline's bed, and the money is hidden in a hatbox beside it. A hundred dollars. That's more money than your father charges for his most expensive tool, and who knows how much the dagger is worth?

However much is too much. It's strange, and Jacob is strange, too— you know that in your bones—this grown man who gives your sister money and sends her notes and tells her to keep secrets.

"Does he give money to other people, too?" you say. "Does he give it to church? Or to his neighbors?"

"I don't know," Jacqueline says. "I don't think so."

"Then why did he give it to you?"

"Because I'm his friend."

"Yes, but I've never given my friends a hundred dollars."

"That's because we're poor, Else."

"We're not poor," you say, more angrily than you intended.

"Compared to Jacob we are. That's what he said."

"Then fits on him," you say. "Fits on this whole stupid thing." Your face and neck flush with heat.

"Fine," Jacqueline says, crossing her arms over her chest. "Then I guess you don't want to meet him after all."

"I don't. Not anymore." But you do. Of course you do. In a way, you feel it's your obligation. Your face softens. "Did he really say that?"

Jacqueline watches you, her arms still locked. She's debating whether she should keep on fighting. "Sort of," she says. "But he wasn't trying to be mean."

"Well, fine. So, can I meet him or not?"

Jacqueline relaxes. "Maybe," she says. "Or maybe not. I don't know."

"But will you ask him?"

She thinks. And finally, she lowers her arms, and she turns away from you. "Yes," she says. "I'll ask him. But I'm not making any promises."

CHAPTER 10

Alfred held firmly to his word: He didn't tell Elisabeth anything else that day, no matter her insistence. At three o'clock in the morning, the police arrived in two planes, and when they left, Elisabeth went with them. She spent the next four hours at the police station in Fairbanks, stretched out on a cot that they set up for her in a bathroom.

And she cried. Finally, in the private darkness of the bathroom, she let it all wash over her, and she let herself break down. Elisabeth had never been one for weeping, but when she did, she did it only in the dark, only when she felt truly hidden, when even she couldn't see what she was doing. Exhausted, her nerves as brittle as glass, she cried for an hour straight.

She was thinking of Mack. She was feeling the weight of what had happened: that she had lost her closest friend in Tanacross, and one of the closest friends she had ever had. And she had lost him tragically. Brutally.

"His goddamn brains . . ." Daniel had said. "His goddamn brains . . ."

Again and again, she let herself imagine it. She forced herself. She saw Mack's ruined face. She heard his screaming. She saw Alfred's wild eyes. She saw pools of blood. She heard the dull smack of metal hitting bone.

Had something like that happened over cards? No. It had been over her, though she couldn't guess the reason. *I was protecting you,* Alfred had said, and that may have been the truth as he saw it, but it wasn't the whole truth. Elisabeth was sure of that. She was missing something. For now, the picture wasn't clear.

But the simple fact remained: It was she who had let him stay in Tanacross. Whatever Alfred's motive, she was at the center of this. And in that way she was guilty. Because of her, Mack was gone. And for that, she cried.

But as much as she felt guilt and grief, Elisabeth felt shame in equal measure. Because over and over, no matter how concertedly she tried to think of Mack, she thought of her sister even more. Mack was dead, yet he wasn't even the foremost person in her thoughts. How could he be?

After all, Alfred *was* involved in her sister's disappearance. She knew it through and through. She felt it like heat, and already her mind was racing with what *involved* could mean. She wasn't stupid, and she wasn't forgetful, not when it came to that summer. For twenty years, she had lived with the clues. The medals. The dagger. The money. The plan to run away. An older man—a German, no less. *Involved* could mean anything, but when it came to Alfred Seidel and her sister's disappearance, it meant one of two things: Either Alfred knew the person who took her, or he was the one who had done the taking. After twenty years of nothing, she was one step closer to finding her sister, and she'd be damned if she didn't get closer still.

And wasn't that marvelous? Bitterly, shamefully marvelous? Sorrow, guilt, joy, disgrace: She felt it all, until at last she was lying silently in the dark, staring up at the black-and-white-tiled ceiling in a state of exhausted bewilderment. Then, a knock on the door.

"Mrs. Pfautz," a voice said. "The detective is ready for you."

His name was Sam York. Briefly, she had spoken with him in Tanacross, but they had ridden different planes to Fairbanks: York and Alfred—and Mack—had been in one plane, and Elisabeth and two deputies had been in another. After a short drive from Ladd Army Airfield, York and Alfred had disappeared into the depths of the station, and Elisabeth was offered the cot.

Now she sat in York's office. The room was a hurricane of papers, manila folders, and notes tacked to the walls. On his desk sat an old-fashioned candlestick phone, flanked by a steel coffeepot and an ashtray blooming with dozens of cigarette butts. York sat behind his desk, and Elisabeth stared at him in a daze. It was nine o'clock in the morning, and the sun was blasting through the windows.

Lanky and narrow shouldered, it was easy to see the man that York had once been. Lithe. Lean. A man like a lightweight boxer—quick on his feet but also clever, the kind of man whose slightest movement was artful and cunning. But at this middle point of his life, age had started overtaking him. He had a bulbous, oval belly and a roll of stubble-covered fat beneath his chin, additions still so new that he was clearly unadjusted to their presence on his body. When he moved, he lumbered; when he sat, he fidgeted. Whatever sense of canniness he'd once possessed was now replaced with an almost painful appearance of unease.

"Sorry you've been waiting so long," York said. "Busy night."

"You mean morning."

"Yes," York said, glancing at the window. "I guess I do."

"Do you always work through the early morning?"

"Just in the summer." He shrugged. "What's the point of sleeping?"

He could have smiled, but he didn't. He wasn't joking. He looked down at the papers in front of him, a sprawl of typewritten loose-leaf and handwritten notes torn out from a pad.

"What did Alfred tell you?" Elisabeth said.

York was quiet for a second. "Can you be more specific?"

"What did Alfred tell you about the murder?"

"We can get to that in a minute," York said, picking up a pencil, "but first I was hoping you'd help me get a few things straight. Standard procedure, you know." He smiled, faintly, and he flipped open a new page in his notebook. "For starters, I understand that Mr. Seidel had been visiting you."

"Not visiting, but he was staying with us, yes."

"I don't follow. You mean he—"

72

"Our house has a guest room," Elisabeth said, "and I felt obligated to help him. I wish I hadn't. Obviously."

"Help him how?"

"He said he needed sleep. He said he was exhausted."

York was scribbling rapidly. "Why didn't he stay with someone else?"

"My husband works for the OIA. Our house is owned by the government. It's the school, and it's our home, and it's also a—" She couldn't find the right word. "It's not a hotel, exactly. It's not like we charge any money for the room. But it's the place in town where visitors stay. Government visitors. And he asked to stay."

And so I let him, she almost added, but Elisabeth stopped herself short. She couldn't bring herself to say those words. She felt sick even thinking them. She had let this happen, and she could have stopped it had she tried. It wasn't the first time she had let something horrible come to pass. First her sister, and now—

No, don't think like that. Don't get caught up. Think about what you can do. Where you can go from here. Jacqueline. Alfred knew about Jacqueline. Think of that. Go forward.

"And when did Mr. Seidel arrive?" York said.

"Tuesday."

"Was he agitated at all?"

"No. I told you, he was tired. He slept." Then Alfred's voice came back to her. *You really didn't hear it? Just a moment ago. Just outside.* "Well," she said, "actually, he woke up briefly in the middle of the night. He had some sort of nightmare. He thought he heard someone knocking on the door. But then he went back to sleep."

"And the following day . . ."

"He worked on his plane. Repairs." She crossed her legs. "Don't you already know all this?"

"Just trying to make sure I have everything right," York said, glancing up at her for the briefest moment. "And Mr. Sanford helped him with his plane?"

"Yes."

"Did Mr. Seidel ever talk about Mr. Sanford? How did they know each other?"

"They didn't. And, no, there was no talk about Mack. Not to me."

"And what about the war?"

"What about it?"

York looked up. "Did Mr. Seidel talk about the war in Europe?"

"No," Elisabeth said, "but he told us about his service in the Great War. He told us"—she cocked her head—"he said some strange things."

"But did he mention anything about the war today?"

"No."

York scribbled. "What about politics? Did he talk about politics?"

"What does this have to do with Mack?"

"I'm just doing my job," York said. "I'm trying to understand."

"Understand what?"

York went on with his scribbling. "If Mr. Seidel's politics or heritage have anything to do with what happened."

"Why in the world would that be the case?"

"Again, I'm just doing my job. I'm trying to cover all the bases."

"And that's wonderful, thank you," Elisabeth said, "but can you answer my question now?"

Still scribbling. "About what?"

"What did Alfred tell you?"

"A number of things."

"Did he tell you why he did it?"

Now, finally, York set his pencil down, and he sat back in his chair. "Yes. He told me they fought over a game of cards."

"Do you believe that?"

He thought for a moment, frowning. "I suppose I do, yes."

"Then why are you asking questions about the war?"

"Procedure," York said. "Due diligence."

"Well, you're asking the wrong questions. I can tell you that. You're stuck on the wrong topic."

"All right, Mrs. Pfautz," York said, lifting his pencil again. "Why do *you* think Alfred murdered Mr. Sanford?"

"I don't know why he did it. That's *your* job, remember?"

"May I ask why you're being so difficult?"

Exhaustion. Frustration. Twenty years of missing answers. But she only blinked, sighing, and she tried to remove the bite in her voice. "He's not telling the truth," Elisabeth said. "There's something more going on, and it hasn't got anything to do with the war. Did he tell you about my sister?"

"Yes, he did."

"And what did he say?"

"He implicated himself in your sister's disappearance." York shuffled through his papers. "Jacqueline Metzger, was it? Lititz, Pennsylvania?"

"Yes," Elisabeth said. "But it wasn't just a disappearance. She was taken."

"By who?"

"Someone she knew," Elisabeth said. "Someone she thought was her friend." *And I let it happen. I made it happen.* But Elisabeth gritted her teeth and pushed those thoughts away. *Look forward, not back. Move. Make things right.* "She had come to know someone, and I don't know exactly who that someone was. But he's the one who took her."

"That's not what it says here."

"What does it say?"

York set one finger on a page, his hand moving in time as he read. "That no one was ever charged. That no arrests were made. Searchers found nothing. That Miss Metzger disappeared."

"Children don't disappear," Elisabeth said. "Children are taken, and my sister was taken, and Alfred knows something about that. Maybe everything."

"You're saying—"

"I'm saying he was involved. He either took her himself, or he knows the person who did. One of those two. He was *involved*. He was there."

York bobbed his head, flipping through papers. "That's actually why we've had you waiting so long, Mrs. Pfautz. We've been making some calls. We've been in touch with the Lancaster County Police Department,

and with a few other folks, too. Time zones can be convenient sometimes."
He scratched the side of his head. "But I'm still confused: What all does
your sister's disappearance have to do with Mr. Sanford's murder?"

"I don't know," Elisabeth said. "That's something you'll have to tell me. "

Now Sam York leaned his full weight back in his chair. It creaked,
springs stretching as it went, and York made a steeple with his hands.
His eyes turned down, and suddenly it showed how tired he was.

"Mr. Seidel had nothing to do with your sister," York said.

The room felt very small, and very quiet. She could hear her own
heartbeat. She could smell the stink of Sam York's breath. She felt dizzy.
"What?"

"With a thing like this," York said, "we look into immigration records. Just an hour ago I was on the phone with New York. Your sister
went missing in 1921, correct?"

Her silence confirmed it.

"Well, Mr. Seidel immigrated to the United States in 1929, so he
couldn't have been responsible for that."

"Involved," Elisabeth said. "He told me *involved*. I don't care what
year he came over. He could have been visiting. He could have had relatives in the area. He could have been going by a different name. Something. He was involved."

"He's toying with you," York said in his own version of the teacher's
voice, stern and uncompromising, the chilly voice of authority. "I'm going on sixteen years in this job, and I know it when I see it. You might
be surprised, but people do this all the time. They like to be big shots.
They do something that'll send them up the creek, and so they figure,
'Why not? I'll tack some other stuff on top.' Murder, rape"—he gestured
at the papers on his desk—"missing kids. These things are trophies to
them. Badges of honor. And if they know they're getting sent away forever, they try to collect as many as they can."

"That's not true. . . ."

"Just because a guy says he did something doesn't mean he actually
did it."

And the plain simplicity of that made her pause. York was right: She was making a leap. For a time, her sister's disappearance had been talked about in every corner of southeastern Pennsylvania. Her photograph had cycled through newspapers, post offices, courthouses, and telephone poles. Alfred could have seen her picture on their walls in Tanacross and recognized Jacqueline from years before. He was a murderer, and perhaps he was a liar, too. Maybe it was all as simple as that.

But it wasn't. There was something here. Something more. How did she know? Instinct. Her deepest core. But what drove her certainty was a force even greater than that. *I bet you dream about her,* Alfred had said. *Don't you? I dream about her, too.* That wasn't just Alfred talking. It was the universe, and it was her sister. Elisabeth believed him about his dreaming, and she believed in the connection between her dreams and his. Her sister was speaking to them both, bringing them together.

But she couldn't tell York that, could she? Elisabeth imagined his smile—a wry, pitying grin. Thinly veiled loathing. She had seen that smile from John, from strangers, from countless other men. Always men. And she would see it from York if she said a thing like that.

"All I'm asking," Elisabeth told him, "is that you look into this. All I'm asking is that you do your job."

"I do my job every day, Mrs. Pfautz, and I'll keep on doing it until it's done. I'm sorry about what you've been through. I really am. And of course I'll look into this, but I'm telling you now that I'm not going to find anything."

There was no use in going on. She was wasting her time. Elisabeth stood, and she started for the door.

"Every effort will be made to investigate Mr. Seidel's claim," York said. "But I'm just being realistic. I'm telling you what I think."

She turned. "He *said* he was involved. He confessed. What else would you call that?"

"Fine," York said, "and I confess to the murder of Thelma Todd. Me, and about a hundred other guys who have never even set foot in California. See? Someone confessing a crime doesn't mean it's a true confession.

It might just mean they're an asshole looking for laughs." He blinked. "Pardon the language."

"But this isn't Thelma Todd," Elisabeth said. "This is my sister, and this is a man who—"

"I'll say it again," York told her. "We're going to look into it. I never said we wouldn't. But the guy isn't telling us anything more about your sister, and I'm guessing that's not going to change. But we'll see. We'll keep trying with him, and we'll look into it on our end, too. What more do you want me to do?"

"Nothing," Elisabeth said. "This has all been very helpful," and she opened the door and let it slam shut behind her.

She already knew where this would take them: nowhere. York would get nothing more out of Alfred, and he would get nothing from an *investigation*, whatever that meant. Her sister's disappearance was twenty years gone. If the police in Lititz couldn't find anything at the time it happened, there was no way that police halfway around the world would find something two decades after the fact, all the more if they doubted Alfred's involvement in the first place.

But York was wrong about Alfred. His instinct wasn't as keen as hers, not when it came to her sister. Nobody's was. Alfred was involved, and Elisabeth was going to find out exactly how, and exactly what he knew. Bursting through the station doors and standing in the bright Alaskan sun, Elisabeth felt as if her entire life had been leading to this moment. Every dream she had ever had about Jacqueline, every inchoate feeling that had told her, *Yes, your sister's alive,* had been leading squarely to Alfred Seidel. She had failed her sister once before. She had made this happen, and she had carried the guilt of that like a stone in her stomach. It haunted her. It ruined her.

But now she would make amends. She wouldn't fail Jacqueline again. She had been waiting for Alfred Seidel since she was eleven years old, and now he was here. She was going to find out how he had been involved, and then she was going to find her sister. Elisabeth stood in the sunlight for a long while. She closed her eyes, but she had never felt so awake.

CHAPTER 11

You expect an excuse. You expect the answer—somehow, for some reason—to be *No, he doesn't want to meet you*. But then, as you and Jacqueline are walking to Black's Market for flour and milk, your sister takes you by the arm and steers you north.

"Now you'll see he isn't strange," she says, pulling you close and whispering, though there isn't any need to whisper. The afternoon is bright and busy and oblivious. "Just be nice, okay?"

You're surprised, really. Astonished by the detour. But then something else, too: You're excited. You're nervous, of course, but mostly you're excited—fear and anxiety and adventure boiling together in your stomach. Your head feels light, and you can't help but smile.

"This is marvelous," you say, not intending to sound so much like Jacqueline. Or maybe you are. Your sister smiles back, and the two of you walk a little faster.

You take Water Street over the creek, and then you're only a few blocks away. You cut through the Brenners' woods and hop over Willie Parlow's fence, slinking and ducking all the way. There's no need to whisper, and there's no need to sneak, but you're doing something secret, and it feels right and good and fun to whisper and sneak and carry on like bandits. Finally, you turn onto Shenk Lane, and almost immediately Jacqueline leads you down the alleyway between two houses.

"He said to come in the back," she tells you. "And he said to come at eleven. What time is it now?"

"I don't know." You look up at the sun, but you've never been good at that, not like Papa. "It must be eleven," you say, trying to sound sure of yourself. "Maybe a little later."

Jacob's house is small and white, two stories, taller than it is wide. Hardly the kind of house where royalty would live. It's a city house, as your father calls it, one that's likely only two bedrooms, much different from the broad, welcoming farmhouses that stand on the outskirts of town, where you live. The backyard is a narrow patch of overgrown grass, pocked in the center with the charred oval of a firepit. You can tell that it's been used recently. Blackened cans and warped glass bottles spill out from it, and among the trash there's a single scorched glove splayed out on the grass as if it's crawling away.

"Well, come on," Jacqueline says, waving one hand at you. She's standing at the top of the back stoop.

You bound up the steps and join her. She knocks on the door's little window, and the two of you wait. The house is dark and quiet, and beyond the glass pane you can see a kitchen. The ghostly white curves of an icebox. The intimidating darkness of a stove. Your sister knocks again, and you wait, but no one comes. She turns the knob and opens the door an inch.

"Hello?" she calls.

"Jacky—"

"Hush." Now she pushes the door wider, and she leans inside. "Hello?" she calls again. "It's Jacqueline." And after a few seconds of silence she opens the door completely and steps inside.

"Wait," you say.

"It's fine, Elisabeth. He's expecting us." From her place inside the house, your sister stares down at you, but her face isn't scornful. It's not the

"Oh, be quiet" glower looking back at you. Instead, she smiles—warm, motherly—and she offers you her hand. "This will be fun," she says. "Aren't you excited?"

And you have to admit: yes. Yes, yes, yes, yes, yes. This *is* exciting. You *are* having fun. How could you not be? You smile back, and you take her hand, stepping inside. The door closes heavily behind you.

The house is very quiet, very dark, and despite its appearance on the outside, it now seems strangely massive. Without light or the presence of lives being lived, the house feels positively cavernous. For a time, holding hands, you and Jacqueline stand by the doorway and take it all in. The kitchen is to your left, and to your right is a hallway. A closed door stands in front of you. The basement, you guess. Faintly, you can smell the scent of something rich and smoky—bacon, perhaps, or breakfast sausage— but mostly the house smells stale. Shafts of sunlight lean into the kitchen, and they sparkle with galaxies of dust.

"Hello?" Jacqueline calls again. She lets go of your hand and starts down the hallway.

No voices call back. You follow your sister, but you move much more slowly than she does, walking as if you're moving through water. You lift your hand, trailing your fingers along the walls as you walk. They're plain white plaster pimpled with bumps, and the texture tickles your skin.

The hallway ends at the front door, and to the right it opens up into a living room. Your sister goes left, still searching, but you're content to explore the house on your own. In all its quiet, the house feels frozen in time. It's gloomy, but it's peaceful, too, and you feel the odd desire to lie down on the floor, close your eyes, and go to sleep.

But you keep moving. You turn the corner—a chunk is missing from the plaster where the hallway comes to an end—and you step into the living room. It's sparsely furnished. In front of the fireplace, two uphol- stered armchairs sit on either side of a table, and a matching couch stands against the opposite wall. An enormous oak footlocker looms in one corner, and a wooden chair is set beside it. The room is small, but its sparseness makes it feel large and lonely. Only one decoration hangs on the walls: a calligraphic illustration nailed into the plaster above the fireplace.

You walk to it. About the size of an open newspaper and drawn in plain black ink, it's an illustration of two birds perched on a branch, their bodies entwined like a pair of hooking fingers. The illustration's lines are long and sweepingly elegant; the birds are one continuous stroke, looping and curling into form. Hundreds of quick, patterned embellishments surround them, lines as thin as the single barbs of a feather. Flowers bloom at the birds' feet, and butterflies alight on their beaks. Near the bottom is a single line of inscription: *Brüder in der Blüte.* Like the note with the money, the inscription is in cursive, but these letters are shaky and uncertain of themselves. They quiver. They're still learning to take shape. You step closer to the illustration, reaching out—you want to touch those quivering lines, to feel them if they're able to be felt—but then your sister is standing beside you, and you draw back your hand.

"He's not here," she says. Her eyes are glassy, not even looking at you, and her voice sounds weary and defeated. "I can't believe he's not here. He said he would be."

"Where could he be?"

"I don't know." She looks up at the illustration, but her eyes are still lost in thought. "He said he'd be here."

"Maybe he'll be back in a minute." You sit down on one of the armchairs. "Maybe we should wait. Let's wait."

"But Papa thinks we're at the market. We're already going to be late making lunch. He's already going to give us the dickens for dawdling."

"That's true." You fold your hands in your lap. "Yes, maybe."

But then Jacqueline's despair disappears, and she smiles at you. "Want to see the money?"

It's a dirt basement. You can tell that from the moment Jacqueline opens the door. It washes over you—the thick, rank smell of sheltered dirt—and the air on your face feels cool and damp.

"Just you wait," Jacqueline says, starting down the steps. "Just you wait to see this. You won't believe your eyes."

And there it is again: that churn of excitement in your belly, a spark that Jacqueline can light like no one else. But as you move down the steps, you feel a stir of dread, too, as if you're descending not into a basement but into a tomb. An open grave.

"Aren't there any lights?" you say.

"No, but there are windows. Half windows. You can see well enough." And as your sister plunges ahead, undaunted, you can't help but follow her.

She's right: The basement isn't entirely dark, but it still takes your eyes a moment to adjust. When they do, what you see at first is rather ordinary. The walls are piled stone veined with condensation, and half a dozen vertical beams buttress the house above. The floor isn't wet, but it's been wet in the recent past, and it's rutted with footprints. The soil is absolutely trampled, as if many feet have worked many hours in this small, dark space.

You and Jacqueline pause at the bottom of the steps, letting your eyes adjust, getting your bearings, and then you see what you've come for: In the basement's farthest corner, dozens of cardboard boxes are stacked tall and deep. Wooden pallets raise them several inches off the ground. Jacqueline strides to the corner without hesitation.

"Well, come on," she says. "See for yourself."

The dried footprints are so numerous that the floor is uneven, and twice the toes of your shoes catch in the darkness and you nearly stumble. But then you're beside your sister, and she's lowering one of the boxes to the ground. Kneeling, she opens it wide, and sure enough: The box is filled to its top with row upon row of paper money.

But it's not American money: It's German. The bills are all the same. *Reichsbanknote*, they read across the top, and then centered beneath that, *50 Mark*. The left side of each bill depicts a farmer sharpening a scythe, and the right depicts a factory man with a hammer against his shoulder. You reach down and lift a block of the bills, which are loose but surprisingly crisp in the dankness of the basement.

"This is German money," you say.

"Yes. Jacob is German. I told you that."

"But I thought it was United States money. Like the money in the hatbox."

"It doesn't make a difference," Jacqueline says. "Money is money. It's all the same. This is a fortune. Look." She stands and takes down another box. More bills, only these are *100 Mark*. "Money is money," she says again. "People trade German money for American money all the time. It's still a fortune."

Yes, it certainly is. You step back, trying to get a better measure of the piled boxes. There must be a hundred of them, maybe more. You've never seen such a thing, not even at the big bank downtown. *Boxes and boxes of money,* Jacqueline had said, and she was telling the truth. Years from now, you'll know that this money is almost worthless—you'll see the photographs of German people papering their walls with this money, hauling wheelbarrows of it to the market—but today, in this basement, you think that Jacob must be the richest person in town. You feel like a princess who's found the dragon's gold. It's stunning, and for a time you just stand there, motionless, your mouth hanging open very slightly.

"And that's not all," Jacqueline says. She stands on her toes, opening another box. More money, *100 Mark* bills again, but that's not what she's looking for. She moves on to another box, then another after that. And finally she makes a little noise—*ah!*—and she takes down a box and places it at your feet.

"Remember what I said about the war?"

This box is smaller than the others, but it's brimming with medals and ribbons and sterling tokens. You kneel and remove one, a chocolate-colored medal depicting a helmet and two crossed daggers. In the box, another catches your eye: a bronze, angled cross anchored by a jewel-studded crown.

"They're like treasure, aren't they?" Jacqueline says. She turns away from you and roots around in the boxes again. "I told you this is incredible, didn't I? Didn't I say that?"

"Yes."

Gently, you shift aside the medals on top. And beneath them, another bronze cross, and another pair of daggers intersecting a helmet. There seem to be multiples of everything. Awards in abundance. You reach for an angled cross, but then your hand slides to something else: a slim, silver case with etchings of ivy and leaves crawling around its edges. It's a cigarette case, and among the medals and ribbons, it seems misplaced.

Misplaced, though beautiful in its own right. It's heavy—real silver—and even in the dimness of the basement, it shines like captured sunlight. For a moment, you simply hold it. Feel its cool weight digging softly at your palm. Then you press the dimpled button on its side, and the case clicks open.

It's filled with pictures of the marvelous woman. A dozen of them are held together by a hinged clasp, each portrait about the size of the one that Jacqueline has. The woman is posing with flowers. She's seated in a garden. She's overlooking a picturesque mountain range. She's holding an umbrella at a beach. She's turning her eyes bashfully away from the camera. In one portrait, she holds a baby on her lap. In another, she sets one hand on a carriage.

And as you look at her, a wave of spite shivers through you. She's wonderful. She truly is. She's marvelous, as much a treasure as the money or the medals. It's absurd for one person to have so much. Wealth. Renown. A marvelous woman captured in a cigarette case. And what does he do with it all? Shovel it away in a dank cellar and stick his tongue out. At whom? At you and your sister—and at your father.

We're poor, Else. That's what Jacob said.

Thinking of that makes the hair on your neck stand stiff, and you squeeze the cigarette case as if you're trying to crush it like a coin on railroad tracks. Its edges bite into your skin. *We're poor, Else. We're poor.* You're hearing those words, and you're looking at the marvelous woman, and you feel like hurling the cigarette case against the wall. But instead you relax, and without really thinking about it, you snap the case shut and drop it into the pocket at your hip. Jacqueline doesn't notice.

"We're really late," you say, lifting the box of ribbons and medals. You put it back with the other boxes.

"But do you see?" Jacqueline says. "I was telling you the truth."

"Yes, you were."

"There's a fortune down here. A hundred dollars is nothing to him."

You can't argue with that, but it's all still strange. If anything, Jacob seems like even more of a mystery now—Jacob and his basement bank vault.

But you don't want to think about that now. You want to leave this place. You want to run. You're sweating, and you want to be back home.

"It's a fortune," you say. "You were telling the truth," and your sister seems content with that.

The whole way home, you can feel the cigarette case in your pocket. It bounces heavily as you move. It tugs at you. Taps against your thigh.

But you feel no shame in having taken it. That night, after Jacqueline and Papa have both gone to bed, you hold it in the darkness of your bedroom, and you feel strong and wicked and good.

PART

2

CHAPTER 12

September 1941

The day that the first letter arrived was bright but brisk. Though the sky was clear and the sun was strong, a frigid chill consumed every slanting stretch of shade, winter creeping closer one shadow at a time.

Elisabeth and John were out back cutting wood. John was still dressed in the clothes he wore to teach—brown brogue wing tips, high-waisted trousers, and a blue button-up shirt, though he'd taken off his tie. It was strange to see him cutting wood in his dress clothes, clothes that he usually pampered with the care and attention of a man preparing for his wedding. He believed that teaching was as much about appearance as it was instruction, as much about the semblance of authority as it was the skills that actually created it. And although Elisabeth wouldn't disagree in that regard, at times John's fastidiousness seemed to verge on obsession.

All the more reason why it had been so strange to watch him march straight to the back, straight for the woodpile. Strange, but not especially surprising. John was working off some tension. Today was the third day of school, and already things had begun to sour. On Monday, during dinner, he had mentioned that two of his students had been pulled out of class at the last minute. Then, yesterday, two more students had followed: a second-grader and a third-grader, two sisters. Then, today, just minutes before John finished teaching, Elisabeth had found a note from Gladys Thomas on the floor beside the front door.

Mr. Fautz, it had said, *I am writing to withdrawn Little Joe from your class. Thank you for your instruction, but we will no longer need it. Good afternoon.*

It had said nothing more—no explanation, no elaboration—though John insisted that her reason was clear enough.

"You know why," he told Elisabeth now, setting a log in place on the chopping block. "It's the same old thing. It's not difficult to figure out, is it?"

It wasn't, or at least it wasn't difficult to guess what John was assuming. In the six weeks that had passed since Mack's murder, Tanacross had changed. People joked with them less. Talked with them less. They were invited to fewer lunches and dinners, and fewer children came knocking on their door in search of Margaret. The air itself felt heavier, as if all the gravity in town had grown more intense. People still greeted them, still nodded or waved as they passed in the street, but there was distance in everyone's eyes, leeriness in every smile.

"But people don't blame you for anything," Teddy had reassured Elisabeth just the week before. "It isn't like that, Else. What happened to Mack was a thing someone else did, and you had no part to play in it. Everyone knows that." But the softness in his voice and the sweetness in his eyes betrayed his own words, and Elisabeth knew that he was only being polite.

Still, she wanted to believe him. And, naïvely, or perhaps just stubbornly, she tried to.

John, on the other hand, was not so optimistic. In fact, he was quick to assume one additional reason for the shift in the Tanacross air.

"Let's just say this," he had told Elisabeth one night as they were lying in bed, oceans of inches between their resting bodies. "I'd bet dollars to doughnuts no one would bat an eye at us if our last name was Martin or Bennett or Anderson."

That, she knew, was what he was talking about now. But again Elisabeth tried to be optimistic. Again she tried to keep a good face, despite her own nagging doubts.

"I really don't think it's that," she said.

"Oh, it isn't?"

John lifted the ax and brought it down in a clean arc. The log seemed to burst more than split, its two crescent halves flying off in either direction.

"It's happening all over the country," he said, standing straight again. "I read they've been burning German furniture stores in Cleveland." With the back of one hand, he wiped a skim of sweat from his forehead. "I'm sure everyone in town is expecting us to start goose-stepping any second now. *Heil*, Tom," he mimicked, waving one hand and grinning vapidly. "*Heil*, Mary. How you doing today? *Heil* there."

"Stop it," Elisabeth said. "Just stop."

"Watch," John said. "The second that the bombs start falling on New York, we'll be run out of town. We'll be lucky if we're not lynched. Forget the fact that I'll be shipping off to Berlin with all the others. We're the enemy, Else, or people think we are."

"Well, fine," Elisabeth said, moving to pick up the split pieces of wood. "If you really think that's what's happening, then let's think about what we can do to change it. How can we *change* things? What can we *do?*"

"For one thing," John said, raising his eyebrows, reaching for another log, "we should stop letting psychotics stay at our house."

And just like that, they were at it again. Never mind that it was Alfred alone who had done the thing he had done. Never mind that it could have been Elisabeth and Margaret in place of Mack. And never mind that it had been John who left them behind that week, John whose job had brought them to Alaska and obliged Elisabeth to host a stranger. Somehow, despite it all, when John talked about Alfred, he talked in a way that assigned the fault to her. *You could have turned him down,* he had said once. *You're lucky he didn't come after you,* he'd said another time. It always came back to that. *You,* he'd say. *You* could have done this. *You* should have done that.

"Ah," Elisabeth said, tossing pieces of split wood onto the pile. "So it's my fault you're losing students. I see."

"Is that what I said?"

"It's what you implied."

"It's what you *thought,*" John said, snapping at her. He beat two fingers against his temple. "It's what you *heard.* It's what you wanted to hear. I said *we.* I said *we.*"

"But what you meant was *me.* What you meant was that I'm the cause of all our problems, because you want someone to blame other than yourself."

"Brilliant analysis," John said, leaning his weight against the ax and glancing off to the side. "We've found Dr. Freud's successor, but I'd really prefer it if you didn't tell me my own thoughts. I can think for myself, actually, as much as that might surprise you. I know what I meant. And I know the cause for all this well enough."

"This?"

"Yes, this," John said, and now he propped the ax against one leg and gestured all around him, both hands waving at the world as if he had suddenly gone blind. "This," he said, "this. People looking at us funny. Treating us funny. What are we talking about, Else? Isn't that what we're talking about?"

"Fine, yes," Elisabeth said. "You don't have to be—" And she stammered for a moment, fumbling for the right word.

"Don't have to be what?" John said, centering another log. "Please, darling, speak your mind."

You don't have to be such an ass about it, she wanted to say, but then Elisabeth stopped herself. "You don't have to be so dramatic," she said. "Besides, I'm really not sure it's that at all. Maybe there's no rhyme or reason to why you're losing students."

"Then it's what? Coincidence?" John swung the ax again, harder now, and the log split into three uneven parts. Its bark came loose and dropped away like a flank of peeling skin. "I bet I'll lose three more students yet, maybe four—who knows?"

"Well, what's the difference?" Elisabeth said. "What does it matter, really?" She paced around the yard, gathering up the splintered wood and cradling it in her arms. "Your class has several students fewer now, and that's good, don't you think? It'll be that much easier to instruct them all. In a way, it's a fine thing to happen, no matter the cause."

John was silent.

"Isn't it?" Elisabeth said. "Am I wrong?"

John had set another log in place, and now he was leaning against it with both arms, his head hanging low, his body bent forward. For a second, Elisabeth thought that he had hurt himself, but then he stared up at her. His lips were slack; his eyes were wide, his cheeks flushed with redness. Elisabeth had seen this face before, seen it a thousand different times, though it had taken two or three years of marriage for it to make its first appearance. He wanted to erupt, but instead he was restraining himself, and he was keen to make a show of it. *You're lucky,* this expression seemed to say.

That was its intended message, but Elisabeth had long ago learned to steel herself when she saw this face, and now the only thing she could see was its artifice, a face that was nothing more than a petty little act. *Don't look at me like that,* she always wanted to tell him. *You look stupid.* But she held her tongue time and time again. Why? She couldn't quite say, though she knew that it wasn't because she feared his reaction, not as she once had. If he was going to hit her, let him hit her. She wouldn't even flinch at it. She wouldn't give him that.

"Just drop it," John said, speaking slowly and tightly, three separate sentences crammed into one. *Just. Drop. It.* He pushed himself upright again, no longer looking at her.

"I'm only trying to help," Elisabeth said. *I'm a teacher, too,* she could have added. *Or I used to be, before we moved here.* But then she didn't.

Why bother? Why say a thing that would leave her accused of baiting him? They'd go on for another ten minutes if she said a thing like that, and Elisabeth didn't have the will or a reason to continue any longer than they already had.

Perhaps John didn't either. He was quiet, and a few moments later a familiar purr was driving through the air. The mail plane, Mr. Glaser's plane, back to its usual routine. In a rush, the plane's distant drone made Elisabeth think of summers back home, of Junes and Julys defined by the relentless buzz of insects in the grass and trees. The summers in Alaska had their own orchestras of droning insects, but here that noise was different than it was in Pennsylvania—raspier and shriller—and the simple knowledge of this difference made Elisabeth feel suddenly, immensely close to John, if only because he would know this difference, too.

Then, just as soon as the moment had come, the moment had gone. John took a step away from the stump, and he raised the ax for another strike.

"Could you please just get the mail?" he said.

In six short weeks, this was what Elisabeth had come to associate with the mail and Mr. Glaser: failure, frustration, one dead end followed by another. She had spent the last month and a half feverishly searching for details about Alfred Seidel's past. With every free minute of every passing day, she wrote letters, wired messages, scoured page after page of assorted documents. She was searching for any connection between Alfred and her sister, and she knew that this search could be conducted in one way only: by piecing together as much information about Alfred himself as she could. She didn't believe what Sam York had told her about Alfred's immigration record. Sanctioned or unsanctioned, permanent or temporary, he had been living in Pennsylvania in 1921. This was more than a hunch. This was fate itself.

But she needed more. She wanted to know where Alfred had lived and when, what he had done for work, who his friends and cousins and siblings had once been or still were. She'd spent each of the past five weekends in Fairbanks—Walter Glaser was happy to accept a little money for toting her around—and soon the staff at the Fairbanks Emerald Hotel knew her as well as one of their own bellboys.

Yes, hello, she would say, hunched over a telephone in the Emerald's stuffy call room. *I was hoping you could tell me what your library has as far as newspapers go.*

Which newspapers do you mean? was always the response.

Regional papers.

You'll have to be more specific. The Lancaster Inquirer? *The* Intelligencer Journal?

Anything you've got.

Well, just come on in and we—

That's very good, Elisabeth would say, as kindly as she could manage, *but I'm afraid I can't come in. You see, I'm some miles away. I'm doing research for a historical project. What kind of archives do you have?*

How far back do you need?

At least twenty years.

Oh my, the voice would say. *I'll have to check. Can you hold on a minute?*

Certainly.

And so on. She called Philadelphia and Lancaster County libraries, colleges, Masonic lodges, courthouses, and police stations. She called Lititz-area restaurants, hotels, banks, and doctors' offices. She perused entire years' worth of local newspapers, her eyes keenly scanning for the last name Seidel. Surely, she thought, if he'd been there, someone must have known him. Yet every Seidel she spoke with said one of two things:

No Alfreds in this family, least not in that generation.

Or:

Why, yes. Would you like to speak with him now?

Dead ends, one after another. Of course, she also wrote Alfred himself, and twice she tried to visit him in jail. Both times she had been turned away.

"He's in keep lock," she was told.

"For what?"

"Infractions."

The prison's receptionists gave no clarifications. Whatever the reason for the lockdown, Elisabeth could only assume that Alfred's unresponsiveness through mail was related. She had written him four separate times, each letter with its own tone and tenor—one pleading earnestly for answers, one spitefully, one menacingly, one ruefully, each of them manipulative and cunning in its own way—but the letters had proven as futile as her own methodical detective work.

York, as Elisabeth expected, gave her almost nothing. He confirmed with the territory's postal service when Alfred had started working for them—1939—but beyond that, York had gleaned nothing about Alfred's past. He clung to his assertion that Alfred was merely posturing, citing again and again the supposed immigration record. John, naturally, agreed with York's conclusion.

"The guy's getting off on it," John had told her. "It's a power thing. He's toying with you, and it's pleasuring him. You're pleasuring him."

And there it was again. *You*, he had said. *You*.

But for all her discouragement, Elisabeth was undeterred. Alfred was involved. He knew something. Perhaps he knew everything. She had waited twenty years for answers; a few months of setbacks weren't going to sap her in the least. She was driven. She was tireless. She slept only a handful of hours each night, and her lessons with Margaret dwindled to almost nothing.

"Can I come with you to Fairbanks?" her daughter asked.

"No, I'll be working on my project."

"Can we do that lesson on volcanoes today?"

"No, sweetie. I've got to work on my project."

That was what she called it, her *project*, as if all this research was nothing more than some stuffy bit of genealogy, hardly a thing that a child would enjoy. And although it did pain her to tell Margaret no—day after day, lesson after lesson—in truth it stung Elisabeth only briefly.

She had to work. She had to sacrifice. For the first time in many years, she had to use her time for herself.

Elisabeth was getting close to a breakthrough; she could feel it. She dreamed about her sister almost every night now, though her dreams were always the same: She saw herself chasing Jacqueline through a vast, golden wheat field. She cut through the paintbrush grains like a swimmer through water, legs pumping, arms reaching desperately forward. Yet her sister stayed always in front of her, ten stubborn feet that Elisabeth couldn't close no matter how hard she ran. Finally, never breaking her stride, Jacqueline would glance over her shoulder and smile, and in that implicit way that dreams work, Elisabeth would realize that this was all a game, not an anguished chase but a simple bit of fun between the two of them.

Come and get me, her sister seemed to say. *Just keep running.*

And so she did.

By the time that Elisabeth reached the landing strip, Mr. Glaser had already wheeled his plane around to take off. The box of mail sat on the gravel of the runway, the air around it swirling with a mist of sparkling dust. More often than not, Mr. Glaser's deliveries went exactly like this; he would land and unpack his cargo without a second to spare, and then he'd be gone again, no rest, no cigarette, no chitchat. When Elisabeth planned on flying out of town with him, she had to wait with her bags on the landing strip. If she didn't head him off, he'd fly away without her. He had always been hasty, but recently his deliveries had become more frequent—in August, the post office had arranged for twice-weekly visits in lieu of once every Monday—and Elisabeth guessed that Mr. Glaser's stringent efficiency had something to do with this.

From a distance, Elisabeth watched his plane pulling noisily away, its tires pelting gravel and dirt in every direction. Then it started climbing, and the plane was gone in half a minute more. Elisabeth walked forward and began sorting through the delivery.

The box was filled with only paper mail today—no packages or cans or specialty orders of any kind—and what mail the town had received didn't amount to much. Two letters for Teddy; three for Mary Alexander; five for Father Ingraham and his wife, Rita; a copy of the National Bellas Hess catalogue thrown in for good measure. On the cover, a husband and wife—smiles wide, shoes shining, clothes crisp, waists narrow, shoulders broad—were pushing a stroller down a tree-lined city street. Their feet, Elisabeth noticed, weren't even touching the ground. Through fault or design, the pair was actually floating down the sidewalk. Arm in arm half an inch above the ground, they were literally walking on air. Though she couldn't say why, the illustration filled Elisabeth with contempt. She dropped it back in the box and reached for the last few envelopes.

Skimming through them, Elisabeth moved her eyes quickly, hardly reading the addresses at all. She had written to the Immigration and Naturalization Service some weeks ago, hoping to gather more information about Alfred's wartime service in Germany, and with every delivery she expected a response and was invariably disappointed.

She flipped through the envelopes so hastily, so presumptuously, that she almost missed it altogether: a slim letter the size of a postcard. It was adorned with crisp, leaning script and a decorative flourish beneath the address. *Elisabeth Metzger Pfautz,* it read. *Tanacross, Alaska,* and the return address—a stamp of purple ink—read *Territory of Alaska Penitentiary System, 3500 Winston Avenue, Fairbanks, AK.*

Floating, Elisabeth watched her hands split the envelope open.

CHAPTER 13

My dearest Elisabeth,

First, an apology: I know   you have been attempting to reach me, and I have wanted to respond, but   until now   I have been unable. I   deeply regret this, and I sincerely apologize. I am   an unwelcome man in this cage. My fellow   prisoners   hate me, and fear me,   and they have not   taken well to me. My captors neither. Our kind — yours and mine — is not welcome in   this land anymore. Perhaps we never were.   And day and   night, my captors and fellow   prisoners pit themselves   against me, and often they send me   away without light   or food   or even water, and certainly without human contact   as gentle and good as yours.

But, for now, I am   free. I received all your letters at once, and I relished each one. Even the third one? you're wondering.   Even the one in which you're so angry?

Yes, Elisabeth,   even that one.

You can be angry with me. You can   insult   me and threaten me and   abuse me,   and I'll never hold it against you.   I don't blame you for such feelings. I understand them,   and I understand you.

Let me write that again: I understand you, Elisabeth Pfautz. And I know that, deep down,   you understand me, too. You may not realize   it yet,   but the   Truth   is that you and   I are Gleichgesinnte.   Kindred spirits,   one and   the same. You   will know   this, Elisabeth,   in time.

I have a proposition   for you. What I told you in   the cache I'll tell you again: I cannot   reveal everything I know about your sister   in a single sitting or conversation   or letter. Why not?   It's very simple: I am desperately alone, and in   my own selfish way I want to ensure our   correspondence for as   long as possible. We have to cooperate, Elisabeth.   All I want is to talk to you.   I want to see your writing,   to read your words, to feel your   presence. Selfish, yes, but is that really so awful?   It's human, Elisabeth. I am flesh   and blood and bone, and I need you.

And you need me, too. You want the same things that I do.   You want   to feel connected. You want to carry on with me for   as long as you   can. Yes, you want to   be reunited with your   sister, and I will   help you do just that.   You want to know what happened,   and I will help you   know just   that. But you also want a kinship much larger   than yourself   and even Jacqueline, and in   that respect   I will help you,   too.   I will provide.

I am here for you.

My proposition   is very simple: I am going to ask   you for three gifts, and for each gift you deliver,   I will take you one step closer to Jacqueline. I will reunite you,   incrementally,   with your sister, until at last   you and she are together again   in the flesh and blood.

But a caveat comes   with my offer: You cannot involve the police. If you involve them in our exchange,   that exchange   is over. These are   my slavers, Elisabeth, and they   are not to be   trusted. This is a matter   between you and me.   This is a matter   be-

*tween   Countrymen. You are   my sister, my lover, and my
daughter,   and I do not think it's   unreasonable to ask for this to
be a private matter.
I await your   acceptance or declination   of my offer.*

*Yours sincerely,
Alfred H. K. Seidel*

She read the letter four times. Her hands quaking, she pored over every word. She sat on the edge of her bed, and she felt like a woman sitting on the edge of a bridge, ready to drop and fall away. Fall into what, she didn't know. But she was teetering.

An exchange. A cooperation. Three gifts. Reunited with Jacqueline. Elisabeth could only guess what *gifts* Alfred might want from her, but she was certain that they wouldn't be gifts she'd enjoy giving.

It's a power thing, she remembered John saying. *It's pleasuring him.*

And she couldn't disagree. *My sister, my lover,* he had written. She had a vision of Alfred clutching her letters in his cell, one hand gripping the paper as the other hand pumped at his waist. *You wicked little cunt,* she had crackled in her third letter, a phrase by far the worst thing she had ever put in writing, and now she imagined Alfred reading that phrase over and over again. *Little cunt,* she heard him murmur, sweat glistening, right hand working. Perhaps just the sight of those words was thrilling for him. Perhaps this exchange would be, too.

And then there was this: There was no guarantee that she could trust him. Even she would acknowledge that. If correspondence with her was what Alfred wanted, he might simply string her along. On a dime, he would change the terms of their agreement. He would ask for more. He would give his word and then go back on it without a moment's hesitation. He might toy with her for months on end.

But she also knew this: Already, she was making progress. She held the letter, and her eyes traced its script. His handwriting. Beautiful.

Elegant. All his own. In the weeks before her disappearance, Jacqueline's *little bird* wrote her letters, and although those notes had been destroyed long ago, Elisabeth still remembered their penmanship. How fine it was. How precise. She couldn't be certain without a side-by-side comparison, but she felt as if she had something. Not evidence, perhaps. But the possibility of evidence. A lead.

And in time, she would gather even more. Would she comply? Would she respond? Absolutely. What choice did she have? Should she go behind Alfred's back and involve York and the police? No. Even without Alfred's warning, that wasn't something she would do quite yet. For now, at this early juncture, this was something that she had to manage. That was the best way to think about it, she decided—a thing to be managed, a matter of business—and it was something she would manage without any help from York and his deputies. She didn't need them. She could get her own answers. Her own leads.

In fact, she could start right away. Perhaps she didn't have to say yes or no quite yet. She had to be coy. If he was going to play a game with her, then she had to play one, too. She took a seat at the vanity beside the bed and set down a sheet of blank paper. *First,* Elisabeth wrote, *I need to know you're not toying with me. You talk about proof, but I don't have any proof that I can trust you in the first place. Prove to me that your "involvement" isn't all a fabrication.*

She didn't sign the letter. She stuffed it into an envelope and filled out the address. Then she held the envelope in her hands for a long while.

"This is the right thing to do," she whispered. "Just keep running. Just keep running."

CHAPTER 14

Two days after visiting Jacob's house, Jacqueline wakes you in the middle of the night. You open your eyes, and she's standing over you in the dark.

"Emergency meeting," she whispers. Her voice is roiling with excitement. "Meet me at the base in five minutes."

Before you can speak, Jacqueline bounces away. You sit up. Rub the sleep from your eyes. Then you take the cigarette case from its place beneath your pillow, and you move it back to its hiding spot. You've cut an inches-long slit in the fabric of your mattress, and the case drops neatly between the springs.

Jacqueline is already waiting when you step into your father's workshop. She's kneeling on the floor in her nightgown, the fabric billowing around her like a cloud. An oil lantern sits on one of the worktables, and the walls of the shop ripple with dancing yellow light.

"It's happening," Jacqueline says. "It's really going to happen."

"What is?" But you're afraid you already know the answer.

"The Plan," your sister says. "Look at what I've got." From beneath the canopy of her nightgown, she lifts two orange cards about the size of

dollar bills. NEW YORK, SUSQUEHANNA & WESTERN CO., they read. Train tickets. "All we have to do is get to Lancaster," she says. "The train leaves from there. It leaves on Friday."

Friday. That's four days away. You step forward. Your legs feel weak.

"You bought train tickets?" you say.

"Jacob bought them for us. But they don't go to Philadelphia. They go to New York."

"Jacqueline—"

"And I know that's not what we agreed on," your sister says, pushing herself to her feet, "but listen." She sets the tickets on the worktable and walks forward, taking your hands. "Jacob's wife arrives in New York this week, and we're going to meet her. Isn't that wonderful? We're going to stay with her and Jacob."

"What are you talking about?"

"In New York," she repeats, as if you hadn't heard her the first time. "We're going to stay with them for a little while, just at first, and then we can go to Philadelphia like we agreed."

"When did you decide this?"

"Today," Jacqueline says. "I got a note from Jacob. And the tickets. He's invited us on a holiday. We've never been on a holiday."

"We never talked about this."

"I know, but I wanted—"

"I'm not going to New York with some strangers," you say, yanking your hands away from her. You don't feel shaky anymore. You feel angry. You feel tired. "I'm not going, and you can't either."

"What do you mean?"

"You're not thinking," you say, trying to ignore how much you sound like your father. "We can't do this."

"Why not? Of course we can." She grabs the tickets from the table. Holds them up in front of your face. "And we have money, too. We have lots of money."

"I don't care," you say. "We could have a million dollars, and I still wouldn't run away to New York with you. I wouldn't let you run away either."

"But we made a *deal*."

"To go to Philadelphia," you say, as if you had planned on honoring that deal all along.

And your sister seems to believe that. She trusts in your devotion. Your word. She straightens. Squares her shoulders. She puts the tickets back down, and she takes a deep breath.

"We *will* go to Philadelphia," she says. "But first, New York."

"Why should we?"

"Don't you want to go on an adventure?"

"But why are we meeting Jacob's wife all of a sudden?"

"Because, why not? Don't you want to meet her?"

"No. I don't want to do any of this. I want to stay here, with Papa."

At that, she turns away from you. She stomps across the workshop, balling her fists and beating them against her thighs. "I knew you wouldn't really do this," she says, whirling back around at you. "You're a baby, Elisabeth. You're a coward."

"And you're stupid," you say. "You're a stupid little girl."

She rushes at you, both hands whipping, but you catch one of her wrists and the other crashes bluntly—almost painlessly—into the solid part of your upper arm. You push her away, and you storm toward the door.

"Don't leave," your sister cries. Her voice is trembling. She's on the verge of tears. "Just wait. Please."

And you do. You turn around. You're panting, and you're angry, but you wait for her to speak.

"I can't—" she says. "I can't go without you. I don't want to. Please, Else. Please go with me. You told me you would."

"But we can't leave Papa."

"Why not?"

"Because we just can't." *We're a family,* you want to say. *We're a team,* but you know how little that would mean to Jacqueline. "It's just not allowed," you tell her. "It's illegal."

"What's illegal?"

"Running away. We'll get in trouble. It's an awful thing to do."

"We're not running away," Jacqueline says. "We would be staying with Jacob and his wife."

"This isn't right. I don't like this."

She lowers her head. Her shoulders sag.

"Why is Jacob doing this?" you say. "Buying us train tickets. Giving you money. What is going on?"

But Jacqueline doesn't answer you. She's staring down at the floor. Her hair glints in the dim light.

"And why didn't he meet us?" you say. "Why wasn't he there when we—"

"Did you take something from Jacob's house?"

The suddenness of the question—and the question itself—catches you off guard. You're silent.

"Tell me the truth," Jacqueline says. She raises her head. Watches you. And suddenly, bathed in the jaundiced light of the lantern, her face looks deeply tired. The skin beneath her eyes is swollen and dark, and her lips are dry. It looks as if she hasn't slept in days. "Did you take something from the basement?" she says. "Something from one of the boxes?"

"No," comes the answer.

"You're lying. You took something, didn't you?"

"Jacky, I don't know what you're talking about."

She watches you awhile, measuring your answer, but then she blinks and turns away.

"If you're not going with me," she says, "then I'm going by myself."

"You're not."

"Says who?"

"Says me." You try to sound strong, but you've never been the strong one, and you can hear how thin your own authority sounds.

Jacqueline can hear it, too. She scowls at you, tightening her lips, and in that moment you've never felt so distant from her.

"I'm going," she says, "because I want to, and because I said I was going to."

"Then I'm going to tell on you."

"No, you're not."

"I am."

But she's unfazed by your threat. She grabs the tickets from the table and pushes past you, opening the workshop door and stepping into the yard. The insects are buzzing in the fields, and the air is warm and wet. It smells like rain.

"Jacqueline," you say, watching her walk across the lawn. "Jacqueline!"

But she doesn't look back at you. She marches toward the house, and her footsteps leave a trail of prints in the dew-covered grass.

Friday. You have until Friday to stop this. And you will. Starting here, starting now, you have to be the tough one. You have to be the strong one. You've never felt so small and so alone, but you clench your teeth and shut your eyes and try to feel in control.

CHAPTER 15

Elisabeth didn't have to wait long for Alfred's response; a second letter arrived the following Monday, just one week after the first.

Elisabeth had spent the past few days in a trance of busywork. The contact she had finally made with Alfred gave way to a lapse in her obsessive detective work—after six straight weeks, she allowed herself to breathe—but, as soon as she tried to relax, she found that she couldn't. Like the grief-stricken trading a fit of weeping for a fit of frantic housework, Elisabeth occupied herself in other ways. She caught up on planning for Margaret's lessons. She treated the outhouse with a new layer of hydrated lime, and she dumped a week's worth of trash in the woods. She patched clothing for the winter. She cooked. She cleaned. She walked Delma four times a day. With the energy of a drug-addled manic, she cut an entire cord of wood by herself.

Currently, she was rushing around the kitchen. Margaret's birthday was the next week, and Elisabeth had decided that she would celebrate with a strawberry whipped cream cake. But summers in Tanacross posed some difficulties when it came to baking cakes. In the winter, the entire town was refrigerated, but in the summertime, eggs and cream and fruit spoiled fast. To complicate matters further, baking in the wood-burning stove could be difficult; last year, she had botched two cakes before finally succeeding, and it was purely a serendipitous mistake that Mr. Glaser had delivered enough butter and eggs for Elisabeth to make a third. And those were simple pound cakes. A strawberry whipped cream cake, she knew, would be a different matter altogether.

"If cream cakes are so difficult," John had asked the night before, "why in the world are you making one?"

"Because it'd be nice," she had said. "It's an old family recipe."

She could have gone on to say that it was the same cake her aunt Ethel used to bake for her and Jacqueline's birthday, but she didn't feel like mentioning that. Frankly, it made her feel kind of hokey, yet even worse, Elisabeth knew that explaining the root of her motivation would render it so pedestrian that she might never bake a cream cake again.

So she had left it at that. After surveying the kitchen, she jotted down her order for Mr. Glaser: one pound of flour, half a pound of butter, four pints of strawberries, a bag of lemons, vanilla extract, a dozen eggs, heavy whipping cream, and, finally, mascarpone.

"Masca—what?" Mr. Glaser said, staring down at the list. "I don't even know what that is."

They were facing each other on the landing strip. She had headed him off. The mail she wanted so desperately to peruse now sat in a box on the gravel between them.

"It's a soft, creamy cheese," Elisabeth said, but Mr. Glaser only blinked at her. Then she added, a little stupidly, "It's from Italy."

Mr. Glaser shook his head. He couldn't have been much older than Alfred—late forties, early fifties—but his face was fat and he wore a moustache as large and unruly as the tail of a squirrel. Together, these features made for the look of a man who could have been her grandfather.

"I'm not sure you remember," Mr. Glaser said, and his moustache drooped into the crescent of a frown, "we're in Alaska. I think you've got as much chance of finding this cheese as you do a dodo egg."

But he promised that he would see what he could do. The grocer in Fairbanks, he said, sometimes ordered items from Seattle, and who knew what sort of things might turn up in Seattle? Elisabeth paid him, thanked him, waved good-bye as his plane gathered speed down the runway. Then she set to doing what she had waited to do all day, and soon she was holding an envelope with that familiar sweeping script.

It was beautiful handwriting—it truly was—and, as Elisabeth opened the envelope with one finger, she heard her aunt Ethel's voice echoing through the channels of her mind. *If you really want to know a man,* she had told Elisabeth when she was a teenager, *look at his penmanship. You can learn all you need to know by the shape of a man's letters: if he's kind, if he's graceful, if he's a cheat,* and she had said that last word with an extra snap—*cheat*—drawing it out as if it contained entire volumes of implications, a world of womanly information that Elisabeth, in her youth, had simply yet to grasp. Then, blinking, she shook the memory away, and the letter was open a moment later.

Proof. She had asked for proof that he wasn't leading her on, and the note inside the envelope addressed just that—and one thing more.

Your proof is waiting in my aeroplane. And if it meets your satisfaction, let's begin our exchange. Send me your body: a photograph, a lock of hair, and a portrait in your own hand. For that, I'll bring you one step closer to your sister. But first, your proof. Look in the aeroplane.

Did he know that she'd be reading his letter on the landing strip? Because she lifted her eyes and then, as if on cue, she was staring at it: Alfred's Fairchild 71. Since the day after the murder, it had sat in a ditch between the landing strip and the wild bush beyond. Months ago, in an attempt to move the plane to an impound lot in Fairbanks, the police had flown in a mechanic—a haggard, stooping old man who was missing his lower jaw from war or disease or God. What was left of it dangled by his neck like the snood of a turkey, and for a whole afternoon he had pinched and rubbed at that dangle, pacing around the plane and, on occasion, glancing at its engine. He couldn't fix it. Alfred had disassembled too much.

So the plane couldn't fly, and instead it stayed in Tanacross. Elisabeth was walking to it now. As she moved, she glanced all around her, scanning the area for watchful eyes, but the north side of Tanacross was surprisingly desolate. Briefly, and inadvertently, Elisabeth looked at Mack's chicken-wire kennels, which now sat silent and abandoned. A twist of guilt and grief squeezed at her stomach, and she looked away, walking faster.

The plane was locked. She tried both doors of the cockpit, and then she tested the big sliding panel that opened the cabin. Tight as tight could get. She even tested the windows, but only one was capable of opening and its lock felt as secure as the doors'. Peering through the cupped circle of her hands, Elisabeth looked inside the cockpit, and soon her eyes adjusted to the shadowed dimness within. Gauges. Dials. Meters. The cracking leather of the pilot's seat. The shaft of the control column, its twin grips as smooth as ossified antlers. The crooked elbows of cigarette butts. Discarded matchbooks. Drifts of ash, dirt, dust. A few papers spread haphazardly across the floor and, centered atop the instrument panel and mounted on a wooden peg, the skull of a wolverine gazed through the darkness. Its mouth opened wide, and its incisors shined so brightly that they looked wet, as if the animal's jaws might spring back to life at any moment and clamp mercilessly shut.

Elisabeth stepped back. Then she walked around the plane, testing its doors once more for good measure. Finally, she pulled a rock from the dirt beside the landing strip, and she steadied herself beside the pilot-side window.

It's going to be loud, she told herself. *It's going to be an explosion.*

But it wasn't. The glass split, and it fell to pieces like broken ice. Elisabeth reached inside and felt around the door, and soon she had it: the little lever that released the lock. She pulled the door open and, carefully angling around the scattered glass, she moved inside.

At a glance, there wasn't much she hadn't already seen. The papers littered on the floor were nothing much: records of deliveries, a sprawling list of towns and times that dated back to May, each line written in Alfred's elegant print. Free of its final delivery, the cabin was entirely empty. Crouching, she searched it nonetheless, but found nothing.

Proof, she thought. *Your proof is waiting in my aeroplane.*

But what exactly was she looking for? Elisabeth made her way back to the cockpit. And, sitting down in the passenger seat, she noticed something that she hadn't seen before: a small compartment near the bottom of the instrument panel. About the size of a magazine, the compartment had a small latch that Elisabeth released with the lightest tug. Maps—dozens of them, each neatly folded—and, beneath them all, there was also something else: an iron lump that at first Elisabeth didn't recognize.

Then she was holding it in her hands: an old-fashioned compass, a pair of calipers. And there, etched into the metal near the pin, were the initials of the designer and forger of the compass: *H. F. Metzger, Lititz, Penn.* Her father's name.

John was unswayed by the compass's significance, to say the least.

"Your father's compass," he repeated, holding it in one hand. His voice was flat, dubiously puzzling through her words as if a child had just reported something strange and only semicomprehensible. "You mean your father actually used this?"

"No, he made it," Elisabeth said, and she pointed at his name. "This is his work. It's from his shop."

"And you smashed a window of the plane?" John said, looking at her now. "Are you serious, Else?"

"What?"

"You smashed a window?"

"You're missing the point," Elisabeth said. They were standing on the stoop behind the house. A minute earlier, Elisabeth had pulled John out of his class. She had told him about the letter, but she hadn't mentioned Alfred's proposition or the first pair of notes they had exchanged.

She had mentioned only the compass, and now she snatched it back from him. "This is evidence," she said, wagging the compass in John's face. "And that's not the only thing. You remember my sister's *little bird*? Alfred's handwriting is similar."

"Similar, or the same?"

"I can't be sure," Elisabeth said. "But remember the connections to the war, too. That dagger my sister had—"

"Was standard-issue if you fought in the war," John said. "They're not exactly rarities. My uncle Adalard has one, and he uses it to chop vegetables."

"Fine, but it's still a connection. It's a commonality."

"What's your point?"

"My point is that this is all adding up. Alfred's handwriting. His service in the war. It fits with the person who took my sister."

"A person who's a veteran and has nice handwriting." John made a face at her. "You're right, Else—that really narrows it down."

"Don't talk to me like that. This isn't nothing. This is something." She lifted her hand, still clutching the compass. "This is proof."

"Of what?"

"That he was *involved*," she said. "Never mind about the handwriting and the war. Let's just say that's coincidence. Even if it is, he still had my father's compass. He's still connected. He knows something more. He's telling the truth about that, at least. Do you really think this is all—"

"He could have gotten the compass anywhere."

"Not anywhere. Lititz."

"He could have gotten it secondhand. It could have come with the plane itself."

"Then how would he have known this is my father's name?"

And, for a second, that did seem to win John over. Then his lips soured, and he shook his head.

"Else—"

"Stop. Whatever it is you're going to say, just stop it."

He started to turn. "I'm going back. Thanks for the break. Very helpful."

"Am I being unrealistic? I'm not stupid. I'm not crazy."

"No, but you should let the police deal with this."

"Why?"

He stared at her. "Because they're the police. This is what they do."

"I'm *dealing* with this," Elisabeth said, "and I've found more in a week than they have in two months. I'm not sure how it all fits together yet, but it's adding up to something."

"Tell me specifically: What does this prove?"

"That he's not just toying with me. That he knows something."

"That's not specific. What does this *prove*, Else? That he murdered your sister? It's a thing your father made, and the other stuff is just conjecture. They're presumptions."

"They're leads," Elisabeth said, and she hated how plucky that made her sound. Cartoonish. She felt like the heroine in a radio program.

"Okay," John said, and now he faced her straight on. He slipped his hands into his pockets and walked toward her. "I'm going to say this as your husband: Let the police handle this. Pass on the compass if you want to—that's fair—but then stay out of it. Enough is enough. You've obsessed about this plenty, Else, and Christ knows I've been patient with you. You've let Alfred get to you just like I said he intended to do, and now you're grasping at straws. Here's the truth—"

"The truth—" Elisabeth began, but John's voice rose above hers.

"Here's the truth," he boomed. "You're failing me as a wife, and you're failing Margaret as a mother. Think about that. Are you listening? Are you hearing me?" He stepped forward as if challenging her to a fight, and out of instinct, she stepped back. As much as she would hate herself for it later, she retreated. "It's been two months," John said. "Two months of flying to Fairbanks, wasting money, wasting time, playing the fool." He spat that word. *Fool.* "This has taken up too much of your time. Drop it. For God's sake, just drop it," and in a rush, he stormed inside the school, slamming the door behind him.

CHAPTER 16

Fuck him. And fuck Sam York. She wasn't letting this go. But she was rattled. John could do that to her.

"Listen," Elisabeth said, whispering to herself. She was sitting on the edge of her bed, staring down at her feet. She waited for a moment, and then she said the word again. "Listen."

Even when she was a child, that word had been a sort of mantra for her. Very often, when she was alone, it was easy for Elisabeth to let her mind consume itself with nightmarish fantasies, waking visions that would take hold of her almost instantaneously. At night, she would be alone in her bedroom and sense that someone was watching her just beyond the window, and in five seconds flat she could see the glint of a man's eyes, the soft curves of his motionless limbs. Other times, she would be walking home late from school after an evening of work on the yearbook, and suddenly she would imagine an inhuman figure loping through the cornfield beside her, a thing that moved on all fours, crooked knees and bony elbows pumping furiously as it scuttled like a crab through the cornstalks. The field swaying in the wind became its motion; the scurry of an animal became its knuckles troweling through the dirt.

They were nothing more than fantasies, but the rush of their creation and the vividness of her imagination made these visions so potent that the terror they delivered was immediate and absolute. She would feel impelled to break into a run, and occasionally she did, but in time Elisabeth learned to quell these visions with that single word. *Listen,* she would tell herself, and it would help her calm down. Gather herself. *Listen. There's the sound of crickets. There's the throttle of a car. Listen. There's Uncle Harry snoring. Listen.*

"Listen," she told herself again, still staring at her feet. "Just listen," and she did. At first she noticed very little, but then she heard the stiff, rhythmic beat of someone cutting wood. Then she heard the suck and sigh of her own breathing, the faint tick of Delma's claws as she traipsed through the living room. *Listen.* Someone laughed in the distance. *Listen.* A group of children hurried down the road, whooping as they played hoop and stick. *Listen. Just listen.* She closed her eyes. She tried to relax.

She would write Alfred back in spite of John; it was all as simple as that. She was on the cusp of something. The verge of a breakthrough. The handwriting. The compass. The dagger from the war. These pieces were adding up to something, though Elisabeth wasn't yet sure what that something was. Alfred was involved. She believed that. She didn't need to take his word for it; she had the proof right here. More pieces of the puzzle were what she needed now. Until she knew what *involved* really meant, she needed more information. And she would get that from Alfred. Only Alfred. John? She didn't need him for anything.

But she knew that he was right about Margaret, and that was what had shaken her. Yes, in these past few weeks of endless work, Elisabeth had neglected her—Margaret, her only daughter, her pride and joy and greatest triumph, the most important person in her life.

The most important person in her life? Really, was she? Elisabeth stared at the backs of her open hands, searching the crests of her veins and the parched earth of her dry skin as though she might find an answer there. These were Jacqueline's hands she was looking at. Jacqueline's flesh and gray-blue blood. That was true, wasn't it? In a sense? Today, her sister's hands would look more or less identical to hers. Elisabeth often thought about things like that—all the similarities that she and her sister would still share. She hadn't seen her sister in twenty years, but they would recognize each other immediately. They would know each other because they *were* each other, and not many sisters could say that.

The resonance of the calipers was not lost on Elisabeth. It wasn't simply that this tool was of her father's making. He had made many instruments throughout his career—saws and drills and hammers and punches and picks. It could have been anything in Alfred's plane, but it wasn't just anything. It was a compass. A pair of calipers. Jacqueline was speaking to her. Reaching for her. She remembered her sister's voice from that dream weeks ago. *Calipers,* Jacqueline had said. *Calipers,* and with that she had meant so much more. *Come find me.*

And Elisabeth would. She'd be damned if she didn't. And that meant, for the time being, that Margaret would have to wait. In six weeks, she had already made sacrifices. She had skimped on Margaret's education. She had paid her daughter less and less attention, both as a teacher and as a mother. And going forward, Elisabeth could only guess what other sacrifices she might have to make.

But these sacrifices—past and present and future—were sacrifices worth making. Her sister or her daughter? Ultimately? She couldn't say, but for now, her sister. Margaret could wait. She had to. Elisabeth stood, crossed the room, took a seat at the small vanity in the corner.

A photograph, a lock of hair, and a self-drawn portrait. That was what he wanted.

First, she cut her hair. She pinched a few inches' worth between two fingers, and she clipped it loose with a pair of sewing scissors. She fastened the hair with a wind of white thread. Then she leaned to the side and pulled an album of photographs from a nearby bookshelf. She chose a picture of her and John, one that he would never miss, a forgettable shot John's mother had snapped outside of a Lancaster diner two months before they left for Alaska. Elisabeth had dressed up for the occasion—a town-tailored rayon crepe dress, feather-trimmed sleeves, finger waves in her hair—but she and John had fought in the car on the way to the restaurant, and their dinner had been marred by lengthy spells of brooding silence. John's mother, however, had been oblivious.

"Let's get a picture of the lovebirds," she had said in the parking lot. "Cuddle up, you two," but only their shoulders had touched, and their smiles were like winces.

Now Elisabeth cut the picture in half, leaving only the image of herself. *I asked for a photograph of you,* she imagined Alfred writing if she did anything otherwise, *not a photograph of you and your husband.* She set the picture and the lock of hair aside.

Then she set to work on sketching an illustration of herself. With the hard cover of a book as her board, she sketched an outline of her head and shoulders, and soon she was filling in the details—the contours, the shading. Against the paper, she held her pencil at an angle as though it were a stick of charcoal. Continually, she raised her eyes to study her reflection in the vanity mirror.

She had never been skilled at drawing. She had taken two classes in high school, lessons that had been agonizing at the time, twenty twitching students sketching pots of flowers or arrangements of fruit as their geriatric teacher droned on about ratio and form. Circling them like a weary tiger, he'd tap his cane against the boys' bottoms when he caught them slouching. With the girls, he'd do the same, only he'd tickle. Elisabeth's illustrations never turned out well. Her apples looked like warts. Her flowers seemed to wilt.

Her skills hadn't improved in the intervening years. Her self-portrait was barely recognizable. The more details she added, the less it became. The woman in the illustration was a mass of smudges and shadows. It seemed to be a portrait of a person submerged in dark water.

But a portrait was all he had asked for, not an accurate portrait necessarily, nor a skillful one. She guessed that accuracy was beside the point. The point was control—he wanted her following his orders. That, and he wanted something he could use to *gratify* himself. Elisabeth picked up the photograph again, and she made herself think of that now. She saw him in his cell, hunched like an animal in one corner. He held her photograph in his left hand, and he held it close to his face, close enough to see it in all its detail, close enough even to smell it, to taste it. Pulling up the side of her skirt and then pulling aside her underwear, Elisabeth stuffed the photograph between her legs, and she rubbed it against herself like a piece of bath tissue.

"I hope you choke on it," she said, slipping the photograph, hair, and folded illustration into an envelope. Then she retrieved another sheet of paper.

Let's begin, she wrote, and in fluid cursive she signed her full name— *Elisabeth Helene Metzger Pfautz*—and in doing so she couldn't help but feel like she was signing some contract with the devil himself.

CHAPTER 17

Tuesday and Wednesday pass, and you and Jacqueline keep your distance. You barely speak. You carry on with your chores, and many of these you undertake together, but you and your sister work side by side in silence. Neither of you attempts a reconciliation. When your chores are done for the day, Jacqueline locks herself in her bedroom. You spend time in the woods. You crack branches against trees. You tie the stems of leaves together. You hurl stones against larger rocks and watch them splinter. You think, and you worry.

But you never tattle. You know that you should, and you want to, but you don't. You hate to prove your sister right, and her challenge echoes through your mind. *You won't,* she told you. *You won't.* That alone makes tattling almost worth doing.

But you still feel a sense of obligation to keep *The Plan* a secret. Your dedication to Jacqueline goes beyond honor or oath. It's ingrained in you. It's habit. You're faithful in a way that's almost involuntary. Again and again, you consider the possibility of tattling, but as soon as it enters your thoughts, you brush it away.

So you don't tattle, but that doesn't mean you're powerless. There's one thing that you can do, and you've always known that you could do it. The hatbox beneath her bed. The money. The train tickets. If Jacqueline refuses to change her mind, if she's truly bent on going through with this, then you know what you have to do, and you won't feel the least bit sorry for having done it. It's her fault for putting you in this position.

But getting to the hatbox is easier thought of than done. Surely, Jacqueline knows what you must be planning, and she protects her bedroom like a guard protecting a bank. Though the two of you rarely speak, she's always a few feet away. She's watching you. Listening. She's waiting for you to try something. The days pass, and you never have your chance.

Until, suddenly, you do. On Thursday morning, your father walks into the kitchen while you and Jacqueline are washing dishes, and he claps his hands together.

"I'm driving to Ephrata," he says, "and, Jacky, you're going with me."

You both turn from the sink. Your hands drip foam on the floor.

"What?" Jacqueline says. "Why?"

"Do you remember Mr. Helmer?"

"No."

"He's a die maker, and he's going out of business. I'm buying a press and a set of molds from him."

"But why do I have to go?"

"Because," your father says, placing either hand on Jacqueline's shoulders, "I think it would be nice."

"Take Elisabeth."

"Elisabeth's staying here."

"That's not fair," your sister says, her voice jumping up half an octave. "Why am I going but not her?"

"Because the two of you need some time apart," your father says, looking first at Jacqueline and then at you. "I don't know what's going on, but an errand would do us all some good." He turns to walk out of the kitchen. "We're leaving in half an hour."

She whines. She protests. She tries to bargain. But your father is stubborn, and in time, to your surprise, Jacqueline relents.

"Don't go in my bedroom," she hisses as she walks toward the door. She's as angry as she's ever been—angrier, even, than the night in the workshop earlier that week. You're surprised that she doesn't spit at you as she passes. But you say nothing in return. You don't grin or glare or poke your tongue out. You let her go.

You wait a few minutes for good measure. You stand by the living room window and watch Papa crank his screenside truck. It rattles to life, and you wave at Papa and Jacqueline as the truck rumbles away. Then you're alone. You retrieve a grocery bag from the kitchen, and you head upstairs.

The bedrooms lock from the inside, but not from the outside. You push Jacqueline's door open and stand in the hallway for a minute, looking in. It occurs to you: You've never gone into her bedroom like this. You've never sneaked behind her back. You feel like a traitor. You feel disloyal.

And you're frightened, too—not by the possibility of Jacqueline running away, but by the reality of what she'll do when you stop her. She'll be furious. She'll hit you. She'll never forgive you. Despite it all, you're still not certain that she'll really even do it, and if she doesn't, what then? This will be for nothing. And imagine her fury in that case.

But you've got to do it, and once you step inside her bedroom, you move faster and more easily. You move with purpose. You crouch on the floor beside her bed, and you reach. There's the dagger wrapped in its towel. And there—there's the hatbox. You leave the dagger where it lies, and you slide the hatbox out from underneath the bed.

It's empty. The tickets and money are gone. But you're not surprised. Wouldn't you have done the same? You know your sister as well as you know yourself, and you expected her to take extra precautions. After all, she knows you, too.

What she doesn't know is this: You're no dummy. You've got her figured out. You know about a second place where she hides things: the vanity that used to belong to your mother. It has three drawers—one in the middle, and two in the sides, and the drawers in either side pull out if you lift them from their tracks. There's just enough space behind them to hide something. Before the vanity was kept in Jacqueline's room, it was kept in yours; the two of you have agreed to share it, passing it back and forth in yearlong intervals. When you had the vanity to yourself, you liked to hide knickknacks and notes from boys behind the drawers, not because they needed hiding, but because it was fun to have a secret place all your own. And when you noticed one recent afternoon that the right-side drawer was slightly crooked, not quite on its track, you knew that Jacqueline had discovered the same thing about the vanity that you had.

Carefully, you remove the right drawer. It sticks for a moment, as if something is holding it back, and when it finally comes free, you see what that something is: dollar bills caught in the track. You pull them out, and in a minute more you have the rest of the money, all one hundred dollars, heaped on Jacqueline's bed. She's stashed the tickets with the money, and you take those, too, but after you've loaded the money and the tickets into your grocery bag, you pause for a second and think.

The other drawer. What's she hiding there? You've got what you came for, but you can't help but look. You remove the left drawer, and in the narrow cavity it conceals, Jacqueline has hidden a dozen folded papers. The letters from Jacob.

His penmanship is, perhaps, the nicest you've ever seen. That's the first thing you notice. Swift and elegant, perfectly lined and evenly spaced, it reminds you of your teacher's writing, and Miss Heidelman claims that she still practices lines on the chalkboard every morning before school. For a moment, you just hold the letters and study their grace, but then you start reading.

She sounds like a dope, one reads.

If she talked to me like that, reads another, *I'd slap her teeth out. She deserves it.*

That's you they're talking about. You're the dope. You're the one who deserves to get her teeth slapped out. Of course, you're not the letters' only focus. Mostly, Jacob boasts about Germany. About wealth. He brags about his wife, her beauty, her kindness. Endlessly, he praises your sister, calling her brilliant and beautiful and brave. He knows all about *The Plan*, and in his letters he responds to it with enthusiasm, soothing your sister's doubts and driving her forward. But among all the boasting and praise, in almost every letter he writes about you, too, responding in kind to the unspecified things that your sister has said about you. They've even got a nickname for you.

And when it comes to Booby Beth, one paragraph reads, *don't listen to her. She sounds about as fun as a boiled egg, and about as smart, too.*

The first time I meet her, reads another, *I'll tell Booby just what you suggested, but if she starts to cry, try not to laugh.*

That's the last thing you read. You crumple the page in your fists, and then you're shoveling all the letters into the grocery bag, heaping them on top of the money and the tickets. You replace the drawers, but before you leave, you open the vanity's center drawer, too, and you snatch up the photograph of Jacob's wife. You take the dagger while you're at it, and then you retrieve the cigarette case hidden in your room. You rip out its portraits without lifting the clasp, and you toss the pictures into your bag with the money and the tickets.

The dagger and the cigarette case come first. Your arms want to work. You want to break something. In your father's workshop, you take a pair of tongs and a straight-peen hammer from the wall, and you set the case on the anvil. It doesn't take much. The metal is thin and malleable. *Friendly,* your father calls it. You hold it steady with the tongs, and you strike it again and again, until at last it's as thin as a buffalo nickel and cracked around the edges, the clustered ivy nothing more than trampled smears.

The dagger is tougher, less *friendly,* but with effort it warps all the same. You keep it in the scabbard and start at the bottom, flattening the blade and its sheath inch by inch. The filigree goes smooth; the ribbons spread flat. Then you hammer the grip. The pearloid shatters instantly, showering the workshop with crystalline shards. One nicks your open eye, but this only emboldens you, and soon you're hammering the grip with breathless ferocity. You gasp for air through your open mouth. Your arms burn. Your back sweats. Twice, you miss the grip entirely and hit the anvil instead, and sparks spurt through the air. But you keep hammering, until at last the grip is a mangled, twisted waste.

You hide the dagger and the cigarette case behind the crates in the corner. Then you step outside, and you circle around to the back of your father's workshop. You pile the money together, just like you would paper and kindling, and soon the bills are caught and smoking.

They burn quickly. The flames eat them up like they're newsprint, but you've got plenty to stoke the fire with. When the money's all gone, you feed the fire with the train tickets and Jacob's notes, two at a time, those beautiful loops and lines all burning to ash. Finally, you add the pictures of Jacob's wife. At first they only curl, but then the fire engulfs the lot of them, and the marvelous woman is gone, vanished a dozen times over into a soup of crackling bubbles.

You watch the fire die away, and then you spread the heap of ashes with your foot. Slivers of the money and corners of the notes litter the grass, and you're glad that they do. You don't want the fire to eat up everything. You want bits and pieces. You want your sister to see this. You want her to know that you really did it—that you're not playing some trick on her—but mostly you want slivers and shards because you know that they will make it hurt more. You know that something left behind is worse than nothing left behind.

With two fingers, you lift one triangle of blackened paper, and you let it flutter back to the grass. You close your eyes for a minute. You breathe the acrid smell of smoke, and you listen to the birds singing across the yard. The wind gently blows, and it feels good against your damp skin. Your heart is racing. Your hands ache. But you feel triumphant, better than you have all week.

And yet, you feel like crying. You stand in the shadow of your father's workshop, and you fight the lump that's growing in your throat, the tightness in your chest. You wish your sister were here. You wish that none of this had ever happened. You wish that you and Jacqueline were together again, and you feel an uncanny sense of terror that she and your father will never return from Ephrata.

"Listen," you say, and you shut your eyes tighter. "Just listen."

The katydids are chattering. *Listen.* The wind whistles past your ears. *Listen.* There's the rumble of a car struggling up the hill around the corner, and there's the sound of your breath, your pulse in each ear. *Listen. Just listen.* That's all you have to do. Take it in, and calm yourself down.

Your sister and papa will return. Everything is fine. What you're feeling is from the work you've just done. The exertion of it. The work has made your head go funny. You're being unreasonable. Your sister and papa will come back from Ephrata, and then—then Jacqueline will see what you've done.

But she'll forgive you. She has to. In time, everything will be as it once was.

CHAPTER 18

Margaret's twelfth birthday came, and the strawberry whipped cream cake was not well received.

"I don't even like strawberries," Margaret said. "Don't you know that?" And without taking so much as an appraising bite, she scrunched up her face and added, "It's too sweet. It's ick."

In unblinking silence, every eye in the room was watching Elisabeth, which meant that all of Tanacross was watching her, too. Only a handful of families had turned out—five families, to be exact, a total of sixteen people—but Elisabeth knew well enough that these couples and their children were scouts of a kind. By tomorrow afternoon, the entire town would know every detail of this get-together, but only one detail would stick. The spoiled child. The haughty white girl. The daughter for whom nothing was good enough, and wasn't a daughter the product of her mother?

The Athabaskans loved rich food. They ate butter like candy, chunks of fat like vitamins. Once, Elisabeth saw a boy and his father eating Crisco like a tub of ice cream. In far-flung Alaska, a strawberry cream cake was nothing short of an unparalleled delicacy. Margaret's reaction was tantamount to spitting in Elisabeth's face. Spitting in all of their faces. Elisabeth traded a look with John. Then she pulled out a chair and took a seat.

"This is the cake I made," she told Margaret, "and it'll have to do. You can eat it, or you can sit there and be rude. That's all there is to it."

And in the end, Margaret did eat a piece of the cake, chewing glumly, as if the frosting were made of sand. Everyone else seemed to love the dessert; Elisabeth had made enough for twenty guests, and what little cake remained after the initial round was quickly consumed.

If there was one saving grace to the party, it was Margaret's gratitude when it came to opening gifts. With the exception of Deborah Denny and her mother—who had gifted Margaret a pair of traditional beaded mittens, *deshoz jeyh*—every guest gave her a book, and Margaret was thrilled with them all.

"*Tsíndá'ęę,*" she told them. *Thank you very much.* "*Tsíndá'ęę de'ishłęę.*" *I'm grateful.*

And at least to Elisabeth's blunt ears, Margaret spoke as smoothly as a native speaker, and her words sounded sincere. Elisabeth had to choke back an unexpected surge of tears.

The party lasted through the late afternoon, and it wasn't until eight o'clock that night that Elisabeth realized she had neglected to retrieve the mail. It was Thursday, the second and final delivery day of the week, but somehow that fact had escaped her. Cooking and preparing for the party had been distraction enough, and then there was the odd way that summertime days in Alaska all blended together. When the sun barely set—when it dipped beneath the horizon one minute only to rise again the next—it was easy to mix days up. The first summer they had spent in Tanacross, Elisabeth had x-ed out the days on her calendar with the diligence of a prisoner notching weeks into the plaster of his cell. It was the only way that she could keep things straight.

John was busy grading in the spare bedroom. With her head resting on Delma like a pillow, Margaret lay reading on the living room floor.

Neither of them noticed Elisabeth leave. Crossing the town in a hurry, she felt like a woman sneaking out for a tryst, which she supposed—in a way—she was.

The box of mail still sat on the landing strip. A wealth of packages and crates sat beside it, deliveries of food and clothing and gifts for an upcoming potlatch in honor of Mack. For weeks now, the Sanford family had received shipments of goods just like this. On Monday, the delivery had been large enough that it took Mr. Glaser and Henry Isaac—a second cousin of Mack's—nearly half an hour to unload it all.

"Those are for the potlatch, too?" Elisabeth had asked, nodding at a massive wooden crate stamped with a block of text that read WINCHESTER REPEATING ARMS CO. WCF .30, in fat black letters.

"The potlatch? No," Henry said, deadly serious. "These are for killing Nips." Then he and Mr. Glaser had burst into laughter.

Elisabeth was glad that today's box of mail was largely lost among the bigger packages, and she was even more relieved to find that, in spite of the time, the box was still stuffed with catalogues and envelopes. She wasn't the only person who had forgotten to check the delivery, and Elisabeth counted her blessings for that. Had a solitary letter been waiting in the crate, one embellished with Alfred's florid script, that wouldn't have looked good. It didn't look good regardless, but among a mix of magazines and other envelopes, Elisabeth's mail blended in. Or she hoped it did.

And indeed a letter from Alfred was waiting for her. She could hardly resist tearing it open right away, but first she hurried back to the house and took a seat on a stump by the woodpile, where the angle of the yard and the formidable stack of aspen logs hid her from the street and onlooking windows. She began to read.

Darling Elisabeth,

I received your package.   *To say I am pleased*   *with your*
continued correspondence, and   *with the items you enclosed,*   *would*

be an understatement.   I am ecstatic,   truly. I can   think of no
finer way   to put it.

Do   you know what that word means?   Ecstatic.

Yes, of course   you do — you're a brilliant woman — but do
you   know its origin? The prison has a tattered old dictionary,
and I looked it up. It comes   from   the Greek   word eksta-
sis, which means entrancement to the point   of insanity.

Isn't that marvelous?   It is marvelous, Elisabeth,   because
that is   precisely how   I felt when I   received your items.
They enraptured me. They took   me to a place of   belonging
and beauty,   and you were   there with me.   I am buried alone
in the depths of this cage,   but with your gifts I   am with you,
not only   in thought but in   body now, too.

Can you hear me speaking to you in your sleep?   Each night as
I fall away, I whisper to you, and I know that   I am reaching you,
if only   in your dreams. You are two   hundred miles away,
but know   that I am lying there beside you, and I am talking.   I
am reaching you,   Elisabeth Helene Metzger Pfautz. I am penetrat-
ing your mind.

And that is how   I know you   are in trouble. Elisabeth: I
worry about you. The woman in your portrait—she's drowning,
isn't she? And the   woman   in your photograph   —   she's
weeping. You are crying out   in anguish, but your   husband
and your family   and your Indians cannot hear you.   But I
can. I hope you remember that,   always.

You have spoiled me,   Elisabeth. You have   lavished me with
generosity,   and now   words and ink and printed paper are not
enough.   Here's the next   part of our exchange, the second
gift I want from you:

Your mind.

I want you to visit me in Fairbanks.

I want to see you in the flesh.

I want to hear your voice.

Come alone, and in exchange   I'll bring you one step   closer to your sister.

The date   is 16 September. I am waiting.   And in the interim, I will be whispering.

Yours sincerely,
Alfred H. K. Seidel

P.S.
I did not forget my end   of the bargain.   In exchange   for the package you sent, I offer you   my own first gift.   I've already delivered it, you see.   It is hanging in   Margaret's closet.

Elisabeth lifted her eyes, and an icy coolness took hold of her. Then she stood, and she walked around the house and opened the front door. In the living room, Margaret was still lying in the same spot: supine, legs sprawled across the floor, Delma breathing gently beneath her head. She was reading *Little House in the Big Woods*—a gift from Elisabeth and John, along with the next three letters of the encyclopedia—and she was wearing the same white dress that she had worn to the party. A beautiful dress, one with pink lilies embroidered around the shoulders. It was a hand-me-down, but for the past few months, it had fit Margaret perfectly.

And why wouldn't it? It had been Elisabeth's dress when she was a child, and her adolescent self and Margaret were almost exactly the same height and build. She and Margaret, and Jacqueline, too. Elisabeth stepped forward, and Margaret looked up.

"What, Mama?" Margaret said, lifting her eyes and lowering her book. "What is it?"

But Elisabeth just shook her head.

"It's nothing," she told her. "Never mind," and she made herself turn and walk out of the room.

But it wasn't *nothing*. The dress was Jacqueline's, and Elisabeth confirmed as much later that night, after Margaret and John had both
gone to bed.

She pulled the dress out of Margaret's hamper, and she sat with it at
the kitchen table. To keep their clothing sorted out, their father would
stitch her and Jacqueline's separate initials into the fabric of their dresses
and skirts. He insisted on doing this even when Elisabeth and Jacqueline
were older—older and more skilled at sewing than he was. His stub-
bornness and the untimely death of their mother had forced their father
to learn certain skills. Embroidery and sewing were among them,
though he wasn't especially talented at either. His stitched letters resembled the handwriting of a child—blocky and inelegant and invariably
lopsided—but those letters were still clear enough to read.

Elisabeth was looking at three of them now. *JGM*—Jacqueline Gabriela Metzger—stitched on the inner backside of the dress's skirt. Elisabeth ran her thumb across the stitching, feeling the thread, closing her
eyes. She had plenty of clothes from her childhood, and that was why she
hadn't singled out the dress as anything unusual.

But in fact this dress was the only article of her sister's clothing still
in existence. A year after Jacqueline's disappearance, their father had
destroyed her entire wardrobe. Elisabeth was a senior in high school
before she ever thought to ask her aunt Ethel about the clothes' absence.
Her father was dead by then, and she was living with Ethel and her
uncle Harry. In cleaning the house one idle Sunday, Elisabeth came
across six boxes of her childhood clothing—intended hand-me-downs—
and immediately she noticed that there were no boxes of Jacqueline's
clothes. Why not?

"Your father gathered everything up," her aunt explained, "and he
burned it all." And when Elisabeth had asked why he'd ever do such a
thing, her aunt had simply said, "Drink," though of course Elisabeth
understood that it was much more than that. Losing a loved one was

terrible, but losing a loved one and having some hope of that person's return was something entirely different—and entirely worse. That was why her father had burned Jacqueline's clothing. Bitterness comes easily from the things you have lost, but more easily still from the things you have lost but not lost completely.

So all her sister's clothing had been destroyed, yet here was this dress. Here, because of Alfred, was the single surviving piece of Jacqueline's wardrobe. *Her body*, Alfred had asked for, and in exchange, what he had given Elisabeth was her sister's body. She saw the symmetry of it right away. Their mutual gifts.

But how—how had he gotten it? That was the important thing. There was one simple explanation, and again Elisabeth felt that icy coolness sweeping through her when she thought of it: The dress had been the dress that her sister was wearing when she disappeared.

Wasn't that the only explanation? The only possibility? It was, but Elisabeth wracked her mind, and for the life of her, she couldn't remember with certainty what her sister had been wearing the day she disappeared. She had been wearing a dress, and it was white, but she and Jacqueline had owned at least a dozen white dresses, and she couldn't remember the details or design of the one in question. MISSING GIRL, the signs and tabloid advertisements had all read. BLONDE. ELEVEN YEARS OLD. GERMANIC. TALL FOR HER AGE. TALKY. LAST SEEN WEARING A WHITE COTTON DRESS. JACQUELINE METZGER. BRING OUR GIRL HOME. There had been no specifics, not that Elisabeth could recall.

And God, how she wished there had been. She sat at the kitchen table, and she rubbed at her temples. *White dress. Your sister. The year of all years. The smell of summer. Think.* But she couldn't remember. It was too far away. She couldn't be sure.

But she didn't have to be. That was all beside the point. This was Jacqueline's dress, and that meant one thing: Alfred had known Jacqueline—or their family—after she had disappeared. This was more than a lead. There was no chance for coincidences here. This was bona fide proof of his involvement, and perhaps something more. Elisabeth searched every inch of the dress's fabric, looking for stains, marks of any kind. There was nothing, but in studying its seams and wear and tear, what Elisabeth noticed most about the dress was how the fabric felt—how soft it was, and how sheer. It had the feeling of a dress that had been worn and washed many times.

And yet how many times could Jacqueline have worn it? How long would it have fit her before she disappeared? A year, at most? And it wasn't as if the dress was one that Jacqueline had worn frequently before her disappearance; Elisabeth would have remembered it otherwise. Margaret either. Today was just the second or third time that Margaret had worn the dress, partial as she was to more rugged clothing: canvas skirts, knee-high socks, thick cotton shirts. But this dress—this was a dress that had been worn dozens and dozens of times. Well used. Well taken care of. Lived in.

I want you to visit me in Fairbanks, Alfred had written. He wanted to talk with her, one-on-one.

Nothing would please her more. Just keep running? To hell with running. She was sprinting now.

CHAPTER 19

Mack's potlatch was held that Sunday and, with it, Elisabeth and John faced a difficult decision. They could attend the potlatch and risk being unwelcome guests, or they could avoid it altogether and risk offending Mack's memory and the entire town along with it. Elisabeth wanted their family to attend. John felt otherwise.

"It's an Athabaskan function," he said. "We'd be out of place."

But that wasn't entirely true. They had been to a handful of these events in the past, and they had never felt unwelcome. Then again, they were always out of place to some degree in Tanacross, and even more it was clear that this was going to be an event much different from the other potlatches that they had attended.

For one thing, the scale of Mack's potlatch seemed large enough for a town two or three times the size of Tanacross. There were boxes of gifts and guns and food, but as it turned out, those were just the beginning. The Sanford family made dozens of blankets, mittens, hats, necklaces, tunics, and *ts'enîin tl'ŭul'*—beaded slings for carrying babies—a quantity of gifts that must have entailed almost round-the-clock work since Mack's murder.

Peering out the living room window, John was watching some of that work right now. It was just before noon, and Henry Isaac was busy draping all the soon-to-be-gifted blankets and clothes on the beams of a makeshift fence near the banks of the Tanana River. The effect was a bending sprawl of color as long as several houses. Nearby, Daniel Nilak and his two older brothers were constructing a kind of open-air pavilion, complete with a patchwork floor made of teal linoleum that they had flown in from Fairbanks.

"There's no way we can go to this," John said, stepping away from the window. "It'll be awful. Everyone will be glaring at us the whole time. We'll ruin the whole thing."

"We have to go," Elisabeth insisted. "We'll stand out like sore thumbs if we're not there."

"Then we'll be sore thumbs. To hell with it."

"Think of what our absence would say. It'd be totally disrespectful to Mack, and wasn't Mack our friend? Isn't that reason enough to attend? This is his funeral, for God's sake. His Athabaskan funeral. Think of what we'll imply if we don't attend. It'll look like we're admitting fault for what happened. It'll look like we're standing by Alfred, not Mack."

John paced across the room, clicking his teeth as if he were chewing food, an old habit of his that Elisabeth had always found irritating. "We're not the most popular folks in town right now," he said.

"And we'll be even less popular if we don't show up," Elisabeth told him, but she really didn't have to. She could tell that John was already starting to waffle.

Around five o'clock, the shooting began. A volley of shots cut through the air, followed closely by another, then another after that. On cue, people started shuffling outside and, with Margaret in tow, John and Elisabeth followed suit. The shots went on for five more minutes, and soon Elisabeth was standing with everyone else in front of their source: Daniel, his brothers, Henry, and several of Mack's other cousins and nephews were lined up along the river, each of them firing a gleaming new rifle into the air and over the water.

From the looks of it, the entire town was in attendance. Even the Ingrahams were there, despite how much they kept to themselves, and it was especially surprising to see Rita. Although Father Ingraham rarely traveled, Rita spent entire months at a time in Juneau, absences that suited Elisabeth and everyone else in town well enough. Rita wasn't exactly well liked. She was condescending and unapologetically blunt, a bad combination, and during her many years in town she had managed to offend almost everyone at one point or another. *Oh, but think nothing of it,* she would often add on the heels of some muted insult. *What I feel is only what I feel.* Once, she scolded Elisabeth for letting Margaret read so much, saying that little girls who read too much grew up to be either bachelorette librarians or pompous schoolteachers.

"Oh, but think nothing of it," Rita had added, true to form. "What I feel is only what I feel."

"What I feel," Elisabeth had told John later that evening, "is that you're a nasty old bitch."

But tonight, at first, Elisabeth did her best to be the friendly neighbor. When she and Rita spotted each other in the crowd outside of the pavilion, Elisabeth was all smiles. Rita had been out of town since late May. Thank God she hadn't been in Tanacross in July, and thank God she had returned only a few days ago. Mack's murder would have been the gossiping event of her life, but it was difficult to gossip through once-a-week letters shared only with your buttoned-up husband. Even if Rita had sent messages to other folks in town, Elisabeth doubted that she received many replies.

And if Rita wished to gossip now, she wasn't letting on. She and Elisabeth chatted about their sleep, the sun, the war in Europe. Everything, it seemed, but the murder. They talked about Rita's new granddaughter—"Cute," she said, "but a bit too fat, even for a baby"—which had been the occasion for her recent stint away from town. Only when the conversation began to dwindle did Mack come up, and even then, they avoided direct references to what had happened.

"I won't pretend I knew him very well," Rita said, glancing off to the side and taking a survey of who might be listening. Then she leaned forward and added, crooking her jaw, "I know he wasn't much of a churchgoing man, so of course there's that," and it was easy to understand from her tone that this charge was aimed also at Elisabeth and John; they attended Father Ingraham's services about once a month, if that. *Pfautz,* she remembered Rita saying the first time they met. *Is that Jewish?* And Elisabeth had told her that, no, it was simply German. *Ah,* Rita had said, and the face she made in response was very similar to the one she was making now, a face unafraid to show its casual disdain, its haughty disapproval.

"What say we all sit together?" Rita said.

And Elisabeth paused for a second, and replied, without thinking or filtering, "I would, but I'd rather not listen to your bullshit for the whole night," and a second later she and John and Margaret were shuffling inside the pavilion while Rita stood dumbstruck behind them.

Let her gossip. If anything, that single sentence would do more to endear them to the town than anything else in the whole three years they had lived here.

The day had already cooled off, and the air inside the pavilion was sweet and thick. Four separate bonfires surrounded the enclosure, filling the space overhead with wisps of ribboning smoke. Moving in one slowly shifting motion, the crowd arranged itself into rows that formed six concentric squares, everyone facing the center of the pavilion. When the crowd sat down, knives and forks and ceramic cups and bowls were passed from person to person, and a minute after that everyone was knocking their bowls against the linoleum floor, a torrent of clattering noise that sounded like driving rain. Grinning, enthralled with the potlatch already, Margaret joined in.

"Stop it," John said, reaching out and snatching at her wrist. But, really, who was he to stop her? Why should they seem any more out of place than they already were? Elisabeth picked up her bowl and clasped it, unmoving, in her hands. She wasn't sure what to do, so she just sat there.

Massive kettles of tea began moving through the crowd. Each person—Elisabeth and John included—doled out one cup at a time, drank it quickly, then waited for the next kettle to come around. All the while, Elisabeth expected the eyes to start falling on them. She expected to hear murmurs, the furtive whispering of judgment and doubt. But nothing ever came. The kettles moved, and people talked and nodded happily among themselves. Elisabeth felt no twinge of awkwardness in the air. She had no sense that they weren't welcome. Not yet.

After the third kettle of tea had been served, the music began, and with it some of the older people in the crowd rose to their feet and began to sing, their voices breathless wails that sounded to Elisabeth like melodic weeping. As they sang, they danced. Men and women laid down their cups and then stood, breaking into song before they had even left their rows. Most of the young people remained sitting, but in time a few joined the chorus—Kira Denali, Clarence Sanford, Big Paul Elmer, Mary Mabel Mildred—all of them noticeably stiffer than the older dancers, stiffer and, Elisabeth could tell, less sincere.

"Care to dance, Else?"

Teddy was standing above her, smiling as he bowed cordially.

Elisabeth feigned a little laugh, though she wasn't sure if she should be laughing at all. Perhaps he was serious. "I wouldn't know the first thing about it," she said. "I couldn't keep up."

Teddy shook hands with John and exchanged a quick greeting. Then he was sitting down beside them. "Oh, I'm sure you could manage," he told Elisabeth. "The dancing is like"—he thought for a second, turning his head toward the center of the floor—"well, it's like painting or drawing, that's all, and you can draw, can't you?"

She thought of her self-portrait from only days before. *She's drowning, isn't she?*

"Stick figures," Elisabeth said. "Not much more than that."

Teddy laughed. "Well, I'm sure they're brilliant stick figures, Else. I'm sure you're the Michelangelo of stick figures." His attention trailed off. He was listening to the music, watching the dancers again. "Yeah,"

139

he finally added, "Mack was a hell of a guy." Teddy laughed, though it wasn't as much a laugh as a sigh, a single jolt that moved his entire body. He smiled, shaking his head. "This may look like a big deal, but it could never be big enough. It could never do him justice."

That almost broke Elisabeth down. She had braced herself for this potlatch—she had sworn that she would keep a good face, not free of sadness necessarily, though at least free of weakness—but Teddy's remark made her chest go tight. Because, of course, he was right. Nothing could ever give Mack what he deserved. The world owed Mack something more than dying on the landing strip. Something better than that, something justified. But that wasn't this world. This was a world of hook wrenches. A world of murder and hatred and dying in the dust. A world of disappearing children.

Her eyes were throbbing. It was all she could do to keep herself from crying, however sensible crying would be, tonight of all nights. The singers wailed. The crowd beat their cups against the ground. Around the fires, men and women were leaning forward to singe their hair, and the breeze was sharp now with the bitter smell of burning. Dusk was fast overtaking the sky, its shroud of thickening blue creeping up from the horizon, and against the fires' heaving light the distant trees seemed to slope ever closer with a life of their own. Elisabeth stared down at the floor. She closed her eyes. She tried to breathe.

Then there was Teddy's voice cutting through it all, and his words were soft and easy once again.

"And how about you, sweetheart?" he said, speaking to Margaret. "Do you want to dance?"

"No," Margaret said. "I can't draw either," and Teddy laughed.

The potlatch went on. Dancing, singing, music, kettle after kettle of tea, round after round of food, dumplings and caribou and salmon punctuated strangely with the food that the Sanford family had flown in from the city—glazed ham, oranges, pineapples, ice cream, Hershey's chocolate bars.

"A taste of home," John said, snapping off a piece of the candy between his teeth. "But I would have preferred some Wilbur's."

The singing never ceased, but in time the melodies shifted in tone and temper. Doleful songs gave way to lighter music, and soon the potlatch felt very different from the way it had begun. At no one's concentrated direction, it became a celebration—a raucous, convivial party. By eight o'clock, the air was as rich with laughter and chattering voices as it was with singing. Despite the tears that had hung in Elisabeth's eyes only hours before, the night began to melt away with talk and food; she spoke at length with Henry and Kira and half a dozen others, conversations coming comfortably and naturally. Maybe, Elisabeth thought, John's sense of things was wrong. Maybe both of them were wrong. There was no hint of wariness in anyone's eyes, no note of hesitance in anyone's voice. No one seemed to treat her any differently than they had before the summer, before the war, before Alfred. Unexpectedly, Elisabeth found that she was having a wonderful time.

Then, winding back to her original seat, she saw that the same couldn't be said for John. She had been away for only a few minutes, but now John was sitting with both hands balled beneath his chin. His eyes stared off to the side. His lips faintly grimaced. Later, Elisabeth would remember Daniel Nilak walking heavy-footed in the opposite direction, but for the moment, he was simply one more swaying body within the crowd, one more person among so many.

"Ready?" John said, looking up at her.

"Ready for what?"

"To leave."

"It's still early," Elisabeth said, and then—reaching for a joke, just a little one—she smiled. "You haven't even asked me to dance yet."

But John was having none of it.

"Else," he said, "we should go." He turned to the side and pointed at Margaret with his chin. She was leaning her head against his arm. She had dozed off.

"Oh," Elisabeth said, and she took a step back. "Well, we at least need to get in line before we go."

"What line?"

"The receiving line."

John stood, and Margaret, blinking sleepily, rose beside him. "I don't think I want any gifts," John said. "I don't think we need any gifts."

"Well, yes, but it'd be rude if we didn't accept something. It's part of this whole"—she searched for the right word—"tradition."

Silent, John watched her for a moment. Then, rolling his eyes, he took Margaret's hand.

The receiving line was actually two separate lines: the first for men and their Winchester rifles; the second for women and everything else. Although the night was still young—one of Henry's brothers had told Elisabeth that the potlatch would last well into the morning—a number of families had already begun to gather around the lines, though the men's line seemed to move much quicker. John split off from Elisabeth and Margaret, and it wasn't five minutes later when he returned, one hand clasping the tall profile of a new .30-30 rifle. Its stock was solid wood, but its barrel and the loop of its lever twinkled like polished glass in the light of the nearby fires.

"There you go," John said, and he held the rifle high, lifting it up like a cheap trophy won at a carnival. "I got my gun now, so if you don't mind, I'm heading back."

"Don't you want to wait here with us?" Elisabeth said. She looked at the line in front of her. "I don't think it should take much longer."

"I don't know." He sighed, rubbing his eyes with two fingers. "Really, Else, I'm tired. I'm done. I'd like to go home."

"What's wrong? What do you—"

"I just want to go home, and I think that you should, too."

"What? Seriously. What's wrong?"

"We can't talk about it now," John said, and to his credit, he controlled his voice. He rubbed one hand against his forehead, closing his eyes. "We'll have to talk about it later. Just get this done and meet me back at the house, okay?"

"Well, fine," Elisabeth said. "That's fine," and she was going to say something more, but John was already turning. Without saying good-bye, he was gone, weaving his way back through the crowd in the direction of the house.

The school, the OIA, some throwaway conversation in which he'd found some reason for offense. Elisabeth cycled through a litany of possible reasons for John's sour mood, anything and everything but herself or Alfred. She had enjoyed herself tonight—she truly had—and that enjoyment had been possible in part because she had felt so comfortable. She had told herself, over and over, *You see? Everything's all right. No one's talking about you behind your back. Everything's just the way it used to be.* She didn't want to believe otherwise. She tried not to think about it.

She and Margaret stood in line for five minutes more. Henry's sister, a stout young woman named Anna Addams, was posted at the front of the line. She and Elisabeth chatted for a short while, but whenever Elisabeth mentioned anything about the potlatch—the food, the dancing, anything at all—Anna would lower her eyes and grow immediately reticent. She would smile and nod at whatever brief thing Elisabeth was saying, but other than that, she would barely react at all. After one last bout of silence in the conversation, Anna turned and started sorting through the piles of gifts behind her, and a moment later she was pushing a tower of folded blankets and clothes into Elisabeth's arms. Before Elisabeth could even thank her, Anna was already speaking with the next person in line.

Standing off to the side, Elisabeth gave Margaret an armful of items, and together they began to walk home. But as they passed one of the bonfires, something caught Elisabeth's eye: an odd shape lying within the flames, a bulky chunk of metal that glowed as red as a split tomato. With Margaret still following her, Elisabeth stepped closer to the fire, and then she saw what the strange shape was: the vise that Mack had kept bolted to his worktable. The table itself had already been eaten up by the fire.

She stood there for a second, watching the vise gently pulsate with heat, and it didn't take long for her to notice other things within the fire as well, other shapes, other objects. The remains of a dough box blazed bright and hot. Dancing with flames, a sickle of wood burned like a massive matchstick, and Elisabeth quickly realized that this was one runner of a rocking chair, the rest of it collapsing into ashes close by. Straggles of clothing were strewn everywhere at the foot of the fire. Leather belts and hide coats crackled with a sound like radio static. Plates, bowls, traps, knives, guns, tools, tools, tools: the fire teemed with everything Mack had once owned. Near the center of the fire, a heap of metal picture frames smoldered like coals. The photos that they had once held were nothing more than blooms of curling char.

"Mama," Margaret said, and Elisabeth felt a tug on her hand. "Are we going home now?"

But before she could answer, there was shouting, screaming, a burst of commotion. It came from behind them, from the midst of the pavilion, and at once all the talking and singing ceased. Elisabeth and Margaret were squeezing through the crowd a second later, and then they were standing with John near the far corner of the floor.

John's hair was wild and rough. The collar of his shirt was askew. Daniel Nilak lay on the ground two feet away. His eyes and nose were streaked with blood, and his head was turned to the side just an inch too far. With a life of their own, his hands and feet twisted, and his arms began to thrash. Then his whole body shook, convulsing with the first throes of a seizure as all of Tanacross watched.

CHAPTER 20

Words had been exchanged, a punch or two thrown. Then John had hit Daniel with the butt of his rifle. That was all it took, all that was needed to leave Daniel slowly thrashing on the ground, his eyes wide open yet stripped of all consciousness. Almost two hours passed before the medical crew arrived from Fairbanks, and by then Daniel was barely breathing. Blood still trailed from his nose, and this came to mix with a thick, tawny fluid that dripped like brewing coffee from one nostril.

"I didn't even hit him that hard," John told her an hour later. He was slumped forward on the couch. His arms were propped up on either knee. "Honestly, he just kind of"—John shook his head—"fell into it or something. I barely did anything more than just lift the stupid thing. He rushed at me and then, boom, he was on the ground."

And what, Elisabeth asked, had happened? Now that they were alone, away from the crowd, away from the commotion and the panic and all the eager listening ears, what in the world had actually happened?

She wished she hadn't asked. More than that, she wished she could blink out of existence entirely. Because what had happened was this: The whole town knew about the letters, photograph and lock of hair and all.

At the potlatch, sharing one last cigarette with Henry and Daniel and a circle of others, John had said that they were leaving. He had said that Margaret was tired, and Elisabeth was, too. And then Daniel had remarked, "I guess that means Alfred is back in town. I *bet* she's tired."

That was the line that had started it. And, laughing, Daniel had taunted John with the vaguest of details: love letters exchanged, a secret affair, clippings of her hair. Someone had seen her letters in the box, and had read snatches of their text through the semitransparency of the envelopes.

And so she had to own up to it all. She told John about the letters, about her and Alfred's *exchange*, about the dress. Stammering, shaking in chilly anticipation of John turning on her and letting loose, Elisabeth even told him about the queer spacing in Alfred's letters, how each sentence seemed to have a little something missing.

"But there's nothing more to the letters than that," Elisabeth said. She was choking back tears. "I swear to God. There's no—" She didn't even want to say the word. She didn't even want to acknowledge it. But she had to. "There's no *affair*. That's absolutely not true. I'm using him. I'm trying to find my sister."

John had been facing the window as she spoke, but now he turned and paced across the room. He held his head stiffly upright, his lips as tight as a fist. When he stopped, they were standing toe-to-toe.

"I knew it wasn't true," John said, "because honestly, who would want a stupid bitch like you?"

He turned away, started for the hallway. But then he looked back at her.

"You fucked us, Else," he said. "You fucked us all. You may as well add Alfred while you're at it. Maybe you haven't already, but see if I care. What difference does it make now?"

And then he was gone.

She slept in the guest room that night, and the next few days flitted past her in a dreamy rush. She never left the house, not even to cut wood in the backyard. She couldn't face the town. The day after the potlatch, the police flew into Tanacross to take a report on the incident. By then, John had a dark shiner that had swollen his eyelid almost completely shut. Daniel, it seemed, had thrown the first punch. The shiner stretched across John's cheek and partway up his forehead. The police officer from Fairbanks laughed when he saw it.

"Looks like he got you, too," the officer said, chuckling as he pulled a notepad from one pocket.

His name was Jeff Hubbell—two *B*s, two *L*s, he said, "like the ball-player." He was one of York's lieutenants, and he spoke with John for all of ten minutes. If his investigation had been any more lax, there would have been no investigation at all.

"Charges?" Hubbell scoffed at that, hissing air through his lips as he reared back his head. "No, I don't think so. I talked with a few other folks, and they all said he's the one that started the damn thing. Even if he hadn't"—Hubbell clapped his notebook shut—"I mean, Christ, it's just one Indian."

An Indian, he assured them, who'd probably be fine.

"More or less fine," Hubbell said. "I saw him just this morning," but he didn't add anything more than that. His plane was charging down the runway a few minutes later, and that was the last they ever heard from him.

It was hard to imagine how John's class proceeded in the days following the potlatch, but Elisabeth knew well enough to let that topic rest until John himself brought it up. He never did. They barely spoke at all until Wednesday afternoon, when he walked into the living room with an announcement.

"I just spoke with the OIA on the radio," he said. "They want to talk with me more in Fairbanks."

"Fairbanks?" Elisabeth said, looking up from her spot on the couch. A week-old copy of the *New York Times* was spread across her lap.

AMERICAN MERCHANT SHIP TORPEDOED: 24 DEAD, its headline read. "They want to talk in person?"

"In person."

"When?"

"Friday."

"This Friday?"

"This Friday," John said.

That doesn't sound good, Elisabeth almost blurted out, but she caught herself. No, it didn't sound good. Why state the obvious? John walked across the room. He sat down on the other side of the couch, one cushion between them.

"I think we may as well take advantage of this," he said.

"Of what?" Elisabeth said, surprised to hear him still thinking of them as a *we,* as a unit.

"The trip," John told her. "The OIA is flying in Friday morning to pick me up, and I think that you and Margaret should come with me. We could stay in the city through the weekend, and we could probably get a lot done."

Of course she was already thinking of Alfred's letter. Of course she was thinking of her chance to see him in person. But she did her best to forget about that for now, and to contain her enthusiasm.

But John was right: If they went with him to Fairbanks, they could probably get a few things done that needed doing. Margaret hadn't been to a doctor in almost four months, and she hadn't seen a dentist in nearly a year.

And then there was the promise of simply getting out of town for a few days. They all could use that, and undoubtedly John was thinking the same thing.

"It'll be a good break," he said. "For everyone, I mean." He sat back heavily, chewed at his bottom lip. "I'll probably have a chance to visit him. I should probably do that."

"Daniel?" Elisabeth said. "You know where he's staying?"

"There's only one hospital, and Henry gave me his room number."

"And you're sure that's a good idea?"

"No," John said, "but I should probably do it anyway."

"What does Henry think of all this?"

"Visiting Daniel?"

"Everything," Elisabeth said. "The fight. The situation." She swallowed. "Everything in general."

"I only talked to him a little bit, and he was very"—John shifted his shoulders, rolling them as if he had an itch in the middle of his back—"he was polite. He didn't say much. He didn't need to. Honestly, what's he going to tell me? *Don't worry. Everything's okay?* They're talking about us, Else. They're talking about us and Alfred, and it's humiliating."

They both slumped in their seats, and they were silent. No anger was left in John's voice; he spoke with weary sobriety. And in the absence of his anger Elisabeth felt more keenly what she had done to him. She had humiliated him. That was the word he had used, *humiliating*, and at once she felt like the most awful person in the world.

"Honest to God," John said, "I didn't want to hurt him. Daniel's a prick, but I didn't mean to do that."

"I know."

"It's just one of those things. One of those freak things, you know? I never thought I'd hurt him so badly. I really didn't."

"I know."

"Told Henry as much, too."

"And what did he say?"

"He said he believed me." And again John flailed a little, rolling his shoulders. "And he said that other people aren't so sure." Reaching up with both hands, he rubbed his face. "I don't know how we can fix this, Else. I don't know what to do."

But Elisabeth knew what to do, at least for the time being. She knew that she should sidle up to him, take him in her arms. She knew that she should tell him, pulling him close, *It's all my fault, and I'm sorry. But I swear I'll do you right from now on. Everything will be okay. We're still one family, and that's all that matters. Us, not them, not anyone else. We'll work through this one way or another.*

That was what she was supposed to say—she the wife, the voice of comfort, the voice of humility, the obliging breast to sleep on. She could feel it in the air, John's expectation, his manifest and clearly desperate need, but Elisabeth didn't say a single word. They sat in silence, the blue Alaskan afternoon as thick as water all around them, and soon Elisabeth felt as if she were sitting next to a person she had never even met before. Finally, John stood up and left without speaking, and only then did Elisabeth feel like herself again.

CHAPTER 21

Your father and sister return from Ephrata later that afternoon, and the three of you have dinner. Cold sliced ham. Creamed potatoes. Rolls and coffee. After eating, your father walks to the hardware store downtown while you and Jacqueline wash up.

And all the while, your sister says nothing about the missing money and notes and tickets. She must have checked on them—after returning from Ephrata, she promptly went to her room—and you wonder if she's secretly relieved. Perhaps you'll never speak of it. Perhaps *The Plan* and Jacob and everything else will be forgotten. Perhaps, years from now, this will all seem like some kind of dream.

But you want a fight. You want this to be over, but you want to end it yourself. Your skin crawls with nervous energy. Your lips are cold and dry. Once, in the silence of clearing plates from the table, you almost start laughing, not from humor but from nerves. After washing up, you go to your room and sit on your bed, and you feel like jumping out the window.

"Jacqueline," you whisper, though you know she can't hear you. "I'm waiting for you. I'm right here. I'm waiting."

And then the wait is over. Jacqueline pushes open your door, and she takes a single step inside your bedroom.

"Where are they?" she says.

You stand. "Where do you think?"

"Tell me. The money and the dagger and the tickets—"

"And the letters?"

"They're mine," Jacqueline says. "Where are they?"

"I read the things that Jacob wrote about me. What have you been telling him?"

"The truth. That you're a baby, and that you're awful."

"How am I awful?" you say, and you can't control your voice anymore. Tears are boiling in your eyes. Your words tremble. "What have I done wrong?"

"You're—"

"I'm your sister," you say, and then you're sobbing, tears streaking down your cheeks and itching your chin. "We're supposed to be a team. You're my best friend. You're supposed to love me."

Your sister is crying, too. She holds her face in her hands, and her shoulders quake and bounce. But it doesn't feel good, watching her cry. It doesn't make you feel any better. It makes you angry, and you step forward and shove her on both shoulders.

"The workshop," you say.

Jacqueline stares at you. Aghast. She doesn't move.

"Your things are behind the workshop," you say, pushing her again. She nearly falls backward. "Go get them."

She stares for a second longer. Then she turns and bounds down the staircase. You follow her, but you take your time. You move slowly. The stairs seem very steep. The ceilings seem high. Outside, the world glows pink and blue as the afternoon recedes. Across the yard, your sister is already behind the workshop. She's kneeling beside the ashes.

"This is a joke," she says, looking up as you approach. Her eyes are dry. Her face is calm. "You didn't really burn them."

"I did," you say. "The money. The tickets. The *letters*." You glower—

you this time, not her—and it feels good. "Everything. I burned it all up. It's gone."

Jacqueline stands.

"The photograph, too," you say. "I took it from the vanity. You can tell Jacob, for all I care. I hope you do."

"Else—"

"And also," you say, "I did take something from the basement." Now you walk around to the front of the workshop. The ruined cigarette case and the dagger are waiting behind the crates. You take them outside and drop them on the grass by your sister's feet. "There were pictures of her inside that case," you say, "and I burned them up along with the one that you had. I smashed the case flat. The dagger, too."

"There were pictures?" Jacqueline sinks to the lawn. She picks up the cigarette case. Cradles it in her hands. It doesn't shine anymore. It's scuffed and broken, more gray than silver. "This is really it?" she says. "You took this from Jacob's house?"

"Yes."

But Jacqueline doesn't yell. She doesn't cry. She doesn't pounce at you. She stands, the cigarette case still balanced in both hands, and she turns her head to look at you. Mischief flickers in her eyes. "He's going to be really mad."

"Good."

"You shouldn't have done that."

"But I did. And I don't give a lick if Jacob's mad. His wife, neither."

"She's not his wife," she says, sighing the words more than speaking them. "At least, she isn't anymore. She's passed away. The baby, too." She closes her eyes. Shakes her head. But she's not annoyed with you. She's annoyed with herself. "Jacob lied to me," she says. "He lied about a lot of things."

So you were right. You were right all along. You sensed that something was strange about Jacob, and your instinct was correct.

But still, you struggle with it, here in the moment. You're stunned. Momentarily, you're speechless, and the reason why is very simple: No matter how certain you were about Jacob, you could never quite believe it, because you're so uncertain about yourself.

"The woman in the photo?" you say, still working through it. "He lied about—"

"He lied about everything," Jacqueline says. "His name's not even Jacob. He's a liar, and I hate him." She's turning the cigarette case over and over in her palms. "We have to get rid of this."

"Why did he lie?"

"We can melt it," she says, not hearing your question, or more likely, not caring. "We can melt them both." She grabs the dagger from the lawn and starts for the workshop. "Help me get a fire going."

"Wait—"

But she doesn't. You have to jog around the workshop to catch up with her. Jacqueline is already inside, loading coal into the forge. The ruined case and dagger sit beside it on the floor.

"When will Papa be back, do you think?"

"That's not going to work," you say. "They're silver and steel. It'll take hours."

"Hours?"

"Yes."

"Really?"

"Yes, really." You step forward. "What else did Jacob lie to you about?"

"I don't want to tell you," Jacqueline says.

"Why not?"

"Because you'll say I'm stupid."

"I won't."

In either hand, she lifts the cigarette case and the dagger off the floor. Then she thinks. She sizes you up. "He just—" she begins, but her lips pinch shut. She holds her chin a little higher. "I don't want to tell you, okay? We had an argument—that's all."

"When?"

"Last night. I went to his house."

"You snuck out?"

"I sneak out every night." Jacqueline shakes her head, looking back at the forge. "*Hours?* Really?"

"Yes," you tell her. "But why—"

"Then I'll get rid of them some other way. I know where I can go."

"Stop," you say, and now you press a hand against her chest. "What is going on?"

"He's going to be furious—that's what," Jacqueline says. "And he's coming over to get his things back."

You tense. "He is?"

"Yes. They both are."

"They *both?* Who else is coming?"

"It doesn't matter," she says. "The point is, Jacob will be here soon, and I'm getting rid of these." She sidles around you, stepping into the yard in the direction of the house. "But I'm glad you did it," she says, as if it's an afterthought, whirling around to face you again. "I really am. The money, too. I don't want his money. I don't want any of his silly stuff."

She drops the cigarette case and the dagger as she says that, and she walks forward. She reaches for you, and instinctively, you take her hands. This is your sister, your only sister. Your reflection. Your other half.

"I'm sorry about the letters," she says.

"What did you tell him?"

"I don't know. Things."

"What things?"

"Lots of things," Jacqueline says. "I was angry at you."

"Why? What did I do?"

"Nothing."

"Then why were you mad at me?"

"Because I—" Jacqueline looks up at the sky. The watery roses of clouds. "Because I'm mean," she says. "We can't both be the good one."

You lower your head. Somehow, when she says that, you feel ashamed.

"But I am sorry," Jacqueline says. "I really am."

"Do you still want to run away?"

"I don't know." Her voice peters away. Then she drops your hands, and she bends to pick up the cigarette case and dagger from the grass. "First, we have to get rid of these. He'll be here soon."

She walks back to the workshop and retrieves a leather satchel. It's made for holding a set of tongs, but it fits the dagger perfectly, and Jacqueline drops the case in, too. She slings it over one shoulder.

"Where are you going?" you say.

"I'm going to hide these."

"Where?"

"A secret place."

"Just hide them here," you say. There are shovels in the garden. Picks and trowels and spades. "We can bury them."

"I am going to bury them," Jacqueline says. "But not here. Somewhere else."

"Then I'll go with you."

"No, you have to stay."

"Why?"

"Because," Jacqueline says, and she grins, beaming with power and mischief, "my place is a secret, and secrets are fun."

The adventurous one. The exciting one. When she tells you that— *secrets are fun*—you smile. Because it's true: They are. You close your eyes, just for a second, and in that moment Jacqueline leans forward and kisses you on the cheek. It's a strange thing for her to do, a thing that a grown-up might do. Your aunt. Your big cousin Ella. But Jacqueline has never kissed you before, and you can't quite tell if the oddness of it is upsetting or nice or some strange mix of the two.

"I'll come right back," she says. "It won't take long," and then you watch her cross the lawn, and go. For minutes after, her touch still lingers on your cheek, the chilly dampness of her lips settling on your skin until at last you wipe the mark away with the back of one hand.

CHAPTER 22

Fairbanks, as it happened, had been Elisabeth's first impression of Alaska. They had flown from Philadelphia to Chicago, then from Chicago to Denver, then from Denver to Seattle, and then finally— *finally*, after more than twenty hours of airports and airplanes and deafening propeller engines—from Seattle to Alaska. They touched down in Fairbanks on a Friday just like this one, and were set to fly into Tanacross that Sunday.

Fairbanks. The largest city in the interior. That was what she had known about it, and that was the fact that had shaped her expectations. She expected a city not too dissimilar from Pittsburgh: gritty and industrial, certainly, but a city not without its share of energy and verve and hard-nosed charm. Perhaps, she thought, before setting out for Tanacross, the three of them could catch a movie—Clark Gable's *Test Pilot* had just come out—and afterward, perhaps they could do a bit of shopping. They could pick up a few things for the new house. John's post with the Office of Indian Affairs had filled them with an almost childish sense of hope and enthusiasm. It had seemed serendipitous when John first secured the job: One morning he saw the ad affixed to the em-

ployment board in the post office; then three days after that he inter-
viewed by phone; then the day after that he had an offer in hand. Their
lives were going to be an adventure, and adventures always ended happily, didn't they?

Their arrival in Fairbanks was Elisabeth's first indication that Alaska
had a tendency of defeating expectations in all their varied forms. In her
mind, she had seen Pittsburgh; in reality, Fairbanks wasn't much larger
than Lititz, and any vestige of its vitality had long ago worn away. The
streets were wide and nearly free of cars. Paved sidewalks petered out at
random into pitted lanes of dirt. The city's only movie theater had recently burned to the ground, and they were told it would be months
until the new one would be finished. It didn't seem justified to call Fairbanks a city. If Fairbanks was a city, Pittsburgh was a world-class
metropolis.

Since then, however, Fairbanks had grown, not in truth but in its
impression. Each time they visited, the city felt richer and livelier and
vastly more inviting than it had that distant afternoon when they first
arrived. There were drugstores, grocery stores, doctors, dentists, restaurants. There was electricity. There were toilets that flushed and showers
that rained hot water. But this time, more than any luxury, the thing that
Elisabeth relished was the presence of strangers—guarded, hurried
strangers. She was far from Tanacross, and she was anonymous here. No
one was watching her, judging her, gossiping about her. They stayed at
the Emerald Hotel, and when a young man in the lobby snubbed Elisabeth's perfunctory smile, she felt an unexpected flutter of delight in her
stomach.

John set out immediately for his meeting with the OIA, an office of
which was housed in the basement of a building on the east side of town.
He wore a snappy bound-edge Mallory hat and his best navy blue suit,
its double breast fitted with amber buttons that shined like winking eyes.
In the past, these clothes had always granted him a look of suave self-
assurance, Humphrey Bogart meets investment banker. But today, his
suit seemed to fail him. John's skin looked soft and pale. His eyes were

tired. He exuded a sense of disgruntled resignation; he reminded Elisabeth of a man standing up in court to hear a verdict that was all but assured. *Let's just get this goddamn thing over with, shall we?*

"Good luck," Elisabeth told him, but neither of them could manage even to smile.

For the past few days, Elisabeth had dreaded this meeting with the OIA almost as much as John had. It wasn't just the possibility of John losing his job. What was the worst that could happen in that regard? They would move back to Lititz or somewhere near it—Lancaster, maybe, or Ephrata—and if push came to shove and no easy jobs could be found, they could always fall back on John's parents or her own aunt and uncle. After three years of their living abroad, John's mother would be thrilled at the idea of sharing the same roof with her granddaughter. *Mein Schätzchen,* she called Margaret. *My little treasure.*

So unemployment be damned. That she could manage. But Alfred? She could only imagine how he'd react to the news of an imminent move back to Pennsylvania, but if his letters were any indication, he wouldn't take to it kindly. If the second "gift" he wanted was an in-person meeting, what would be the third? A whole series of meetings? Something even . . . more than that? Whatever he planned on asking for, it wouldn't likely be something she could offer from four thousand miles away.

And another wrinkle: Wouldn't Elisabeth's moving away from Alaska give Alfred more leverage? *If you leave the territory, our exchange is over. It's me or John. Choose one.* That didn't seem far-fetched. Alfred wanted her near him. He wanted her contact and her attention, and she had no idea how much longer he'd keep demanding it—or how much longer she'd let him. But one thing was for sure: If John lost his job, time would be of the essence.

But maybe, even if he was fired, time would still be on her side. Surely, the OIA couldn't find a replacement right away. Surely, they would let him finish the school year. But for now, all she could do was wait for answers. Elisabeth tried her best to forget all the variables, and she tried to forget the real reason she was here—to meet Alfred in person, and God only knew what that would entail. She pushed these things from her mind, and instead she tried to concentrate on the ostensible reason why she was here: to run errands with Margaret.

First, the doctor's office—Margaret quizzed him about the Hippocratic oath—and then the two of them found their way to a Sears & Roebuck, the only department store within walking distance of the hotel.

"What do you think of this one?" Elisabeth asked, reaching for a gray, adolescent-sized cardigan that hung within a row of identical copies. She glanced at the price tag—six dollars, a veritable bargain—and then she held it up against her own body, modeling the sweater with a sultry smile. The tapered sleeves barely reached her forearms. "It's mohair. It's fancy."

"What's mohair?"

"It's wool from a special kind of goat. A silky, long-haired goat."

And the face Margaret made in response was so adult—so sneeringly judgmental—that for a second she hardly recognized her own daughter.

"No, thank you," Margaret said, turning to another rack. "Can I just browse around by myself for a while?"

Elisabeth found a seat and sulked. What little energy she had managed to muster seemed to dribble out from her toes. It was just one remark, and it wasn't even all that nasty, but it hit Elisabeth hard all the same. She could see, in flashes, the woman her daughter was becoming. A year ago, Margaret would have reached out for the mohair, kneaded it between her fingers. *I've always admired goats,* she would have said, or something just like that, something stilted and erudite but childish all the same.

But lately, sneers and skeptical eyebrows were more common than ingenuous charm. It wasn't just that Margaret was getting older. Kids get sassier, especially with their parents. But Elisabeth had already lost one eleven-year-old best friend, and it pinched her somewhere deep and tender that she was now losing another. *Gleichgesinnte* no more.

Waiting for Margaret at the dentist's office half an hour later, Elisabeth didn't even have the energy to read. She slouched in her chair and closed her eyes. An hour after that, they were walking into their hotel room, and Elisabeth planned on going straight to bed for a nap.

But John was waiting for them, pacing around the room. His collar and tie were already undone, and he had tossed his hat on the bed. When he saw them he rushed forward, smiling widely, bursting with all the energy Elisabeth didn't have.

The OIA had been upset about the fight with Daniel Nilak, no doubt about that. Technically, they had even given John an injunction, though this was nothing more than a brief record of the event in his personnel file. They chatted about the fight and jotted down John's summary of the incident, but the main topic they had wanted to discuss was something else entirely. They had offered him a new job, a teaching post right here in Fairbanks.

"There's a school at Ladd," John explained, Ladd Army Airfield, the base that they had flown into only hours before. "It's a high school for the kids of military officers. Army brats, you know? It's tiny, but one of the math-and-science teachers is moving down to Juneau, so a spot just opened up. Or it will open up, I mean."

"When?"

"Two months," John said. "End of November."

"This other teacher's not finishing the school year?"

"He's sick." John shrugged. "He's jumping ship on them."

"And you were there to take his spot."

"And I was there to take his spot," John said. "They weren't too happy about the fight, but they said they've been looking at my curriculum, and they thought I'd be a good fit for the post. Mix that with the fact that they know Tanacross isn't exactly the perfect place for me to be teaching anymore, and bingo, the job was mine." His eyes grew wider, going glassy. "The squeaky wheel, Else. It really is true. The squeaky wheel."

The pay, John said, would be a little less than the post in Tanacross, but there was one major benefit of the job at Ladd.

"I'd be rendered an essential employee," John told her. "All the teachers on the base are essential employees."

"What does that mean?"

"It means, if we really do get involved in Europe, I wouldn't be conscriped."

What could she say to that? What could she say to all of this? *Wonderful. Fantastic. That's absolutely fantastic.* And it was fantastic, of course, but that had less to do with John and more to do with Alfred.

Fairbanks. They were moving to Fairbanks. Away from Tanacross and all its judgment and gossip, but, more important, closer to Alfred and all his secrets and promise. Not only that—telephones, telegraphs, post offices that delivered mail more than twice a week. Her involvement with Alfred was going to get easier, and answers were going to come faster. John talked and talked, but the more he went on, the less Elisabeth listened.

She was stunned—not surprised, really, but stunned. Her head felt heavy on her shoulders. Her hands felt swollen. She felt drunk, so much so that the next thing she did wasn't as much a conscious action as it was a thing she simply *did*, an action like movement in a dream, inevitable and easy. She stood, or rather, she felt herself stand. John was in the middle of a sentence, but, blinking, he went silent.

"Sorry," Elisabeth said. "I don't mean to cut you off, but I've got to go."

She wanted to move. She wanted to *do*. She wanted to start—or restart—her work this very minute. And she would. But John just blinked at her, confused.

"What?" he said. "Go where?"

"A doctor's appointment," Elisabeth replied, and hearing that surprised even her.

"Oh," John said. "Sorry." He glanced at his wrist. "This late? It's almost five o'clock. It's almost dinnertime."

"It's a lady's doctor," Elisabeth said, "you know," and even though this wasn't exactly an explanation, John nodded as if it was.

"Sure," he said. "No, I mean—" He stopped himself and, briefly, a perplexed sort of sternness crept into his face. But then he shook it away. "All right. Okay. That's fine. Let's just eat when you get back, all right? We can talk more then." He even managed to smile. "We'll celebrate."

"Yes," Elisabeth said. "Absolutely," and then she had her purse slung over one shoulder and her hand was reaching for the door.

"Do you have a car service?" she asked a young man at the front desk.

"A car service?" he said. "Like a—"

"A taxi. Are there any taxis around here?"

"Oh, a taxi, sure." But then the flash of understanding immediately vanished from the man's face. "Well, no. We don't have a taxi or anything like that, no."

"Is there a—"

"Well, actually, there's a mechanic down the street," the man said. "Elmer's Oil. That's Elmer Whitlock's shop. He's got a car that he sometimes—"

"Left or right?" Elisabeth said. She was already halfway to the door.

"Left," the man said. "Left, left. Tell him Artie sent you."

"Can it wait?" Elmer asked her two minutes later. He was tall and skeletally thin. Although he wasn't dressed like a mechanic—he wore slacks and an orange button-up shirt—his hands were thick with calluses and covered in dirt and oil.

"Honestly, it's something I'd like to take care of right now," Elisabeth told him. "I can pay whatever you like." She reached for her purse. "What do you usually charge for rides? I'll double it."

"No, no," Elmer said, shaking his head. "You don't need to pay me anything extra. It's no big deal. I just wondered if it could wait. I'm just a lazy good-for-nothing." He smiled and started loping toward a nearby car—a rusty red DeSoto with only one working headlight. The other dangled by a wire like a chunk of bait at the end of a fishing line. "Well, come on," Elmer said, waving her along. "Come on. Come on. Let's get on with it, then."

Any hint of annoyance in his voice seemed to disappear as soon as they were driving.

"So, the pen, huh?" Elmer said. He grinned widely and glanced at her in the rearview mirror. "Got a brother-in-law locked in there myself. Ain't nothing to be ashamed of, you know. Just one of those things, is all," and as he said that, Elisabeth understood that Elmer had assumed she was visiting her husband or, at the least, a relative. Why shouldn't he? And, for that matter, why should she correct him? It was easier just to go along with it.

"Sure," she said. "Nothing to be ashamed of."

Still smiling, Elmer glanced at her again in the mirror. "He know a Bill Leighton? Lived in Portland way back when? Fat guy. Big, huge, fat guy."

"I really don't know."

"Ah, no problem. That's okay."

The car's radio was softly playing, and for a moment they listened to Glenn Miller's "Chattanooga Choo Choo" in silence. *"Dinner in the diner. / Nothing could be finer / Than to have your ham and eggs in Carolina."* The car bumped down a little ways, and now Elisabeth saw that they were driving on dirt. Clouds of dust swirled around them.

"Well," Elmer said, shifting the car into a lower gear, "if you see a Lieutenant Reid when you're checking in, tell him I said hello. That bum still owes me ten bucks for some work I did on his truck." He laughed. "Tell him I'm calling the cops on him, all right?"

Elisabeth had never visited a prison before, let alone any prison large enough to be called a penitentiary. Something about that word seemed impressive. Intimidating. She pictured row upon row of barbed-wire fences. She pictured guard towers. Spotlights. Rifles poised to break into sniper fire at a moment's notice. She pictured a modern-day fortress.

In fact, the Fairbanks penitentiary wasn't any larger than some high schools Elisabeth had seen—and it wasn't much more fortified either.

After a quick exchange at a shabby guardhouse, they passed through two gates and then pulled into a circle drive. The penitentiary was four stories high on its west side, one story tall on its east.

"Can you wait here?" Elisabeth said, leaning forward.

"How long will it take?"

"I really don't know. Just keep the meter running."

"The meter?" Elmer said, but then he shook his head and slouched lower in his seat. "All right, sure," he said, grinning. "I'll keep the meter running."

Hours, she thought as she pushed the door open. *They probably have visiting hours,* and she certainly didn't know what they were. She had never gotten that far. In the past, when she had called to inquire about visiting Alfred, the conversations had been quick and short on details. Alfred was locked down, so there wasn't any need for her to know about visiting hours. Now that she realized her mistake, she felt certain that they would turn her away.

But, after winding through hundreds of feet of chilly hallways, she found herself standing in front of a man who, with his wilting eyelids and frowning lips, didn't seem to give a damn about anything. If the penitentiary did have visiting hours, he probably wasn't even aware of them.

"Sign here," he said, pointing to a spot on a form that he slid across his desk.

Gray-haired and monstrously overweight, he reminded her of an aging walrus she had once seen at the Philadelphia Zoo, a creature whose only activity in life seemed to be laboriously gasping for breath.

"Now sign here," he said, pointing to another spot. He never even asked for proof of her identification.

She waited for ten minutes. She sat alone in the visitation room: a dim, drafty box lit only by a row of naked light bulbs and a pair of windows fifteen feet above the ground and flush against the ceiling's paneling. Near one corner of the room was a windowless door. COURTYARD, an uneven line of letters read above it, and Elisabeth could tell from its skewed proportions that the letter *O* was a zero. With ten chairs placed on either side of it, the room's only furnishing was a narrow table, its surface tattooed with hundreds of carvings: names and initials and crossed hearts of the people who had once sat here in the drafty dreariness. People like her. But despite the etched remains of measureless longing and love before her, Elisabeth was alone, and she felt that as deeply as ever.

She sat near the middle of the table, hands folded flat in her lap. She was thinking of Alfred as he had looked on that day in July, that day in the cache. Captured. Cornered. Slick skin. Feverish eyes. A killer, and a conspirator. That was the man she expected to walk through the door and sit down across from her.

But that man wasn't here. A guard pushed open the door, and there Alfred was, leisurely strolling toward her. His hair looked soft and recently washed. His cheeks and chin were neatly shaved. His clothes looked crisp—a plain blue collared shirt and beige cotton pants with two small pockets in the front. He looked content and utterly at ease. No shackles wreathed his hands or feet. His eyes seemed to sparkle even in the feeble light of the room.

"Elisabeth," he exclaimed, walking toward her. He beamed, and his smile was so genuine, so filled with pure delight, that it was all Elisabeth could do not to smile back. Alfred pulled out the chair across from hers. "You got my letter, I presume?"

CHAPTER 23

Elisabeth sat stiff, Alfred watching her from his seat across the table. He was calm. His eyes were bright and eager.

"Yes," she said. "I got your letter. It came last Thursday."

Alfred smiled, and he leaned forward a little, clasping his hands in front of him. "So," he said, "this is my gift. This is my visit."

"This is your visit."

Bashful, he bowed his head, taking his eyes off Elisabeth for the first time since he had walked into the room. "I'm so glad you're here," he said, grinning like a boy talking to his crush. "This is wonderful. Thank you."

"Why?"

He cocked his head.

"Why is it wonderful?" Elisabeth said. "Why are you so"—she knew the right word, but she didn't want to say it—"enamored of me?"

"Is that how I've come across?"

You've come across like a psychotic, she wanted to say, but she didn't. She held herself back. Why? Because she was afraid of him, partly, afraid of how he might react. It was well within the realm of possibility that he would reach across this table and slap her, throttle her, burst forth with some fit of rage as intense as the fits of passion he had shown in his letters. She wasn't stupid: His letters were the work of a man unhinged. And what could she expect from a man unhinged? Anything. Anything and everything.

But, beyond that, somewhere else deep inside her, she didn't want to reveal her true reaction to his letters because she didn't want to hurt his feelings. Part of her, a very small part, felt like a girl who just didn't like a boy as much as he liked her. And that made her feel a little sad.

"'Enamored' is one way to put it," she finally said.

"I'd say more like"—he leaned back—"protective of you. Do I love you? I *have* love for you, if that's the same thing. But I believe you're misinterpreting my words for lust. I don't lust for you, Elisabeth, but I do care for you. Very, very much."

"And why is that? You barely know me."

At that he laughed, wagged a finger at her. "I know you well, my dear. Better than you realize. Do you remember the word I used in my letter?"

"*Gleichgesinnte.*"

"Yes," Alfred said. "And that's exactly what we are. We're kindred. We have a lot in common, you and I."

"You're talking about my sister?"

"Not in the way that you mean," Alfred said, crossing his arms over his chest, "but we do share a similarity in that regard. Do you know that I lost a sibling as well? A brother. A twin, actually. Did you know that?"

"No."

"It's not the same as you and Jacqueline, but it's similar. My brother died when we were six years old. Typhoid. There was a terrible epidemic in Munich that year. Six years old, but I remember him very well. Yet more, I *feel* him. I feel his presence to this day, but just barely. And I imagine it's very much the same thing you've felt since Jacqueline disappeared. A kind of"—he raised one hand and, thinking through his words, circled it in the air—"a kind of *grasping*. It's not a void, exactly.

It's not an absence, is it? Because your sister and my brother have never really left us. They're still part of us, and they always will be. They're still with us. But then again, they're not. And so the result is like . . . it's like when you distantly hear music. Or when you *think* you hear music, and you listen very closely, but you can't be sure that you're hearing anything at all. Your sister still feels present, but barely beyond your fingertips. That's what it's like, isn't it? Distant music. That's what it's like for all the wretched people like us. Isn't that right?"

It was. How she felt about her sister was very different from how she felt about her mother or her father or, for that matter, how she felt about Mack. These people were gone, utterly wiped off the face of the earth, but her sister—her sister stared back at her every time she looked into the mirror. It wasn't just that she believed Jacqueline was still alive. And it wasn't just that she believed they would one day be together again. It was something deeper. It was because they were sisters, and because they were twins. They were split from the same substance. They were themselves, and they would be forever. Elisabeth knew exactly what Alfred meant.

But she didn't feel like admitting it.

"It feels something like that," she said.

But Alfred only smiled. His whole face widened. Then, in a rush, he leaned forward again. "So, tell me," he said. "What would you like to talk about?"

"Several things."

"Such as?"

She hardly knew where to start, or how to start. But she knew that she had to be careful. She didn't want him getting defensive—and she didn't want to give away too much. She didn't want to reveal what she already knew. She needed to draw him in. Intrigue him. She needed to play the game.

"I'd like to know more about you," she said.

"There's a lot to learn."

She smiled. "Tell me more about your time in Germany."

"What would you like to know?"

"I'd like to know about your service in the war," Elisabeth said. "You were a pilot, correct?"

"Correct."

"Were you decorated?" *Slow down,* she thought. *Ease your way into it.* But she couldn't help herself. She was thinking about the box of ribbons and medals. So many medals.

"Decorated?" Alfred said. "You're asking if I killed a lot of Englishmen?"

"I suppose I am."

"You sound like one of the other prisoners here," Alfred said. "Next you're going to ask if I support Herr Hitler. Are you going to try to slit my throat, too?"

"Has someone really tried to slit your throat?"

Alfred lowered his eyes. "We're not very popular these days," he said. "Countrymen, you know."

"No, I guess we aren't. But I'm not talking about the war today. I'm talking about the old one."

"Why do you care how many Englishmen I killed?"

She was still. She gave him nothing. "Just curious."

And, to her surprise, that was good enough for Alfred. He thought for a moment, scratching a spot on his cheek. "Well, I'd love to impress you," he said, "but if we're being honest, my greatest achievement was getting through the war alive. My skill wasn't killing. My skill was surviving." He leaned forward. "Much like yours."

"How do you mean?"

"I mean your whole life. You're a survivor, Elisabeth. You persevere. You keep going, despite so much tragedy. We're very much alike in that way, you and me."

"Is that right?"

"I think so," Alfred said. "My parents, an aunt, two uncles"—he squared his shoulders, setting both hands on his knees—"all gone. Three years was all it took for me. You're not the only orphan here."

"How did they die?"

"How do you think? You asked about the war, and I'm telling you about it. My parents died during the Turnip Winter, my mother's sister from the pandemic, and my uncles were killed in Ypres. That war took everyone from me."

"Not your brother."

He froze, and for a moment Elisabeth thought that she had hurt him. Perhaps she meant to. But then Alfred smiled, and his eyes seemed to flicker.

"That's true," he said. "Not my brother." He relaxed. "But the point remains: You and I have many things in common. We're survivors, Elisabeth. You and me, and Jacqueline, too. Survivors all."

"I wish you'd stop doing that."

"Doing what?"

"Speaking in ambiguities about my sister," Elisabeth said. "You act like this is all a game to you."

"It isn't."

"Then why aren't you giving me answers about her?"

"Because," Alfred said, "you aren't asking the right questions. I told you we could talk about anything, and you're asking me about the war. Honestly, of all things, you'd like to talk about the *war*?"

Now Elisabeth crossed her arms over her chest. She had to restrain herself from raising her voice. "All right," she said. "Then let's talk about why you killed Mack. Or about how you were involved in what happened to my sister. How does that sound?"

"That sounds fine," Alfred said. "By all means, let's talk about Mack and Jacqueline."

"Then let's start with the first."

Alfred sighed. "I did what I did because Mack was going to keep you from me, and I couldn't let that happen for either your sake or mine."

"What do you mean by that?"

"What don't you understand?"

"How was he going to keep me from you?"

"He was going to . . . pollute our relationship. If I hadn't done what I did, this conversation wouldn't be happening. You and I, we wouldn't be talking about Jacqueline, and I wouldn't be setting you on the path to finding her. You wouldn't have let me, because you wouldn't have had a chance. Mack would have kept you from me. I would have been cut off from you."

"You're still speaking in ambiguities."

"If these are ambiguities, then ambiguities are all you're going to get." But then Alfred frowned, shrugging one shoulder. "For now."

She shook it off. She had to move. She had to investigate.

"And my sister," she said. "What do you mean by 'involved'?"

"I mean just that. I played a part in her disappearance. It's quite fair to say I was involved, yes."

"You mean, you took her?"

"No, no, no," Alfred said, "I did not," but then he paused, and all the air in the room seemed to disappear. "But I know the person who did. And I know where I can find him today. And I know that Jacqueline is alive, and so I know that we can find her together."

"Then give me his name," Elisabeth said. "Tell me who took my sister."

"A young man," Alfred said, "who claimed to be her friend. But he wasn't. He tricked her, and he took her."

Elisabeth stared. Stony. Unblinking. Unyielding. Yet her chest was heaving, and a throb was pulsing behind her eyes. Jacqueline's *little bird*. It was all fitting together. She wasn't crazy. She wasn't a fool. The pieces fit.

"But why did he take her?" Elisabeth said. "What did he do to her?"

"He held her captive. He kept her under lock and key." Alfred turned his head, and his cheek glowed icy blue against the light coming through the window. "And as far as what he did to her, you don't want to hear me say it, but you know well enough what he did."

Her hands were quaking in her lap. She clutched them beneath the table.

"What is his name?" she said.

"I can't tell you that."

"Why not?"

"Because I can't—"

"You can," Elisabeth said, snapping at him. "You can tell me everything, but you're yanking me around instead. You're torturing me. You're leading—"

"I know, I know," Alfred said, holding up his palms, "and I'm sorry, but you need to stay calm, Elisabeth. You need to trust me."

"Why should I? Why should I believe any of this? Do you know what the police think? They think you're a huckster. They don't believe your confession. They think you're toying with me."

"I'm sure they do," Alfred said.

"The compass. Tell me how you had it."

"I bought it," Alfred said. "After the war, I flew crop-dusting planes in Lancaster County, and I bought it from your father. He was—"

"What year?"

"What year was what?"

"What year did you buy the compass from my father?"

"I don't know exactly. Probably sometime in 'nineteen or 'twenty, not long after I—"

"Your immigration record says you came here in 1929," Elisabeth said flatly. "So now tell me why I should trust anything you say."

Alfred slumped forward, narrowing his eyes. "My record says what?"

"It says," she repeated, "that you came here from Germany in 1929, ten years after my sister disappeared."

"That's plainly wrong. That's a mistake."

"The police don't think it is."

"The police," Alfred said, turning now in his seat, crossing one jaunty leg over the other, "should not be dealt with. I already told you that. Don't listen to a word they say, Elisabeth. *They're* the hucksters. They have their own agenda. All they want is to corrupt you. They want to split us apart. This is very important. You cannot speak with them about these matters or trust them in the least. They want—"

"So if your immigration record is wrong, when did you come over?"

"The summer of 1919," Alfred said, "and that's God's honest truth. I flew crop-dusting planes in Lancaster County. I knew your father well. I'd call us friends, even. Frequently I saw him at Kohler's Haus on Juniper Lane. Do you remember that place? A restaurant and contraband tavern. Augie Kohler owned it. Your father and I met there, and some months later I bought a number of tools and instruments from him, the compass among them."

Yes, she was familiar with Kohler's Haus on Juniper Lane. During her childhood, it had been a Lititz institution, and it was openly known—among adults, among children, even among the police—as one of the few places to buy a glass of beer, despite the ban on alcohol. And she remembered Augie Kohler vividly: a sweet, heavyset old man with an ages-old burn on his face, a patch of puckered skin around his lips that made him look as if he was always chewing something sour. The whole town had mourned him when he finally passed away when Elisabeth was in high school, and his restaurant closed immediately thereafter. Viktor Kohler, his only son, lived in Des Moines and had no interest in carrying on the family business. Still, knowing just how popular Kohler's Haus had been, Elisabeth had reached out to Viktor in Iowa.

"Seidel?" he had said. "Was he a fat man? Blond haired?"

No, not blond, but he could have been fat, for all she knew. And then Viktor had sighed. He worked as a sales-and-loan manager at a bank, and she had felt then how beneath him this phone call was, how beneath him and how completely uninterested he was in anything she had to say.

"My father knew a lot of people, Mrs. Pfautz," he had told her, "and he probably knew this fellow Seidel, but I can't say for sure. Now, is there anything else?"

"And my father," she said to Alfred now, "did he know the man who took my sister?"

"I believe he did," Alfred said. "Lititz is hardly a large place."

"And this man," she said. She couldn't let it go. She wouldn't. "What did he look like?"

"Elisabeth—"

"You have to tell me something more."

"I can't."

"Then tell me why you can't. Tell me that, at least."

"Please, Elisabeth—"

"You can't control me like this," she said, and now she stood. With a clattering slam, she pushed her chair beneath the table. "If what you want is my company, if what you want so desperately is my unrelenting attention, then here's what's going to happen: I'm going to walk out of this room and never come back unless you give me something more. The man who took my sister. Tell me about him."

Alfred hung his head. "He's a fellow German."

"Everyone is German. Tell me something more."

"He's my age. Mid-forties."

"Does he have relatives in Lititz?"

"I don't believe so."

"Does he have friends?"

"Unlikely," Alfred said. "He kept to himself."

"And what is his name?"

"Elisabeth—"

"Where does he live? In Pennsylvania?"

Alfred studied her. "No."

"Then where?"

"Please, sit back down—"

"What does he do for a living? How did he know my sister? Did he know me, too?"

"I've already told you, you have to trust that I—"

"But you still haven't told me *why* I should trust you." She hovered over him, bracing her arms on the table. She wasn't scared anymore. An energy palpitated all around her, and in its current she felt fearless. Not invincible, certainly. Not beyond harm. It was just that she no longer

cared about what harm might come to her. If Alfred snapped and strangled her atop this very table, what difference would it make? This—her
sister, finding out about her sister—was all that mattered to her now.

But Alfred was unintimidated. He stared back at her with the shimmering eyes of a madman, a killer, a prophet.

"You should trust me," he said, "because I'm the only one who really
loves you." He let that settle in the air, and then he went on. "Your husband, your family, your Indians, even Margaret. What do you really
mean to them? Have you asked yourself that? I don't blame you if you
haven't, because the answer is difficult to bear. To your husband, you're
a servant. To your family, you're a footnote. An orphaned child. And
Margaret? There's love there, perhaps, but how does a child's love com-
pare to a parent's? It's nothing." He swept one hand through the air as if
batting away a fly. "It's primordial. It's vacuous love. It's as meaningful as
a baby's clutching. Strictly instinctive. But my love—" He sat straighter,
looking up at her, and Elisabeth didn't shy away. Across the table, they
were speaking so close that they almost touched. "My love is the truest
love you've ever had." Alfred moved even closer. "The truest, that is,
since your sister's." He sat back. "Now, aren't you going to ask about *my*
gift to you?"

She eased away.

"My gift," Alfred said. "Our exchange. You kept your end of the
bargain, visiting me here today, and now I'm going to keep mine."

But before he had a chance to continue, the door to the visitation
room swung open and a guard stepped inside, a mousy young man who
couldn't have been older than twenty. On cue, Alfred stood.

"Wait—" Elisabeth said.

"I'm sorry," the guard told her, "but it's already a quarter till six.
Dinner's almost over." He walked to the table. Alfred extended his arms,
and the guard reached for a pair of handcuffs that hung on his belt. "We
have very strict mealtimes," he said, and for a moment he looked as
though he would say something more, but then he simply clasped the
handcuffs around Alfred's wrists.

"I'm sorry we've run out of time," Alfred said, jostling as the guard tightened the cuffs, "but let me say that I still enjoyed this immensely."

"We're not done yet—"

"Relax," Alfred told her, and he smiled. "I'm not shortchanging you." With the guard lightly pressing at his back, Alfred reached into one pocket of his pants, his hands moving in unison though only the right grasped at the pocket's contents. He pulled out a small beige envelope— the kind that a greeting card might come in—and, turning to the side, he laid it flat on the table. "This," he said, "is my thanks to you," and again he smiled. "Stay in touch, darling."

Then he was gone, walking with the guard out of the room and down the hallway beyond. Elisabeth waited for their footsteps to recede completely before she stepped forward and reached for the envelope. It was unsealed, and she could feel that the envelope was old, its paper not beige—not originally—but rather yellowed with age. It contained a single photograph: a picture of Jacqueline.

She stood outdoors. The sun shined brightly. Overgrown grass reached up to her knees. Behind her, a cherry tree shined in the daylight, exploding so brilliantly that its unpicked fruit glowed like a cluster of stars. Jacqueline wore a plain white dress and stared straight at the camera, unsmiling but not angry. She just looked calm. Composed. Her arms hung loosely at her sides, and her fingers were curled very slightly. Elisabeth stood with the photo for what felt like whole minutes— motionless, her hands pulling the picture as taut as the skin of a drum— though it took only one glance for her to realize that this was a photo she had never seen before, one in which Jacqueline looked not eleven but thirteen or fourteen, at least.

CHAPTER 24

You are alone. You sit on the top stair of the front stoop, and you wait for your sister to return. You try to stay calm. You close your eyes and listen. You study your breath.

But it's difficult to concentrate. You're thinking of Jacob. Again and again, your mind starts racing, and you hear your sister's warning. *He's coming over to get his things back.* He'll be here any moment. You can feel it. You brace yourself for a confrontation, and you wish that your father were here to protect you. From what? From everything. Jacob and so much more. You hug your knees against your chest and wish that this would all go away. You close your eyes, forcing back tears, and you try not to feel so alone.

Then, suddenly, you aren't. You hear soft footsteps on the grass, and the chilly shadow of a figure passes over you. But when you open your eyes, it isn't Jacob or Jacqueline who's standing on the lawn. It's your father. He holds a small paper bag in one hand, and he slips the other hand into his pocket. He smiles.

"Just the girl I was looking for," he says. He walks forward. Takes a seat beside you on the stoop. "Nice evening, isn't it? Good time for a walk."

"Yes."

You should tell him. You should talk to him. Now. Finally. Tell him what's happening. But the words aren't coming. Your tongue feels thick and fat, and you're quiet. You swallow. Bow your head. You're glad that your father is here, but now that he is, you wish that you could disappear. You wish that you could go upstairs, climb in bed, and go to sleep.

"You know," your father says, "I always wanted daughters."

You look up at him.

"Some people think that's odd," he says. "Most men want sons. They want little copies of themselves." He puffs up his chest in a mocking imitation, squaring his shoulders and sitting straighter. "They want strong hands for the farm. They want more of what's in the mirror." He slouches, waving one hand through the air. *Pff.* "Fits to that," he says. "I wanted daughters, and I always knew that's what I'd get. Honestly. I knew it." He smiles, and then he touches your cheek as if rubbing away a splotch of food. "Of course, I didn't know I'd get two, not at the same time, but that suited me very well."

For a while, the two of you are silent. How long has your sister been gone? Twenty minutes? Thirty? It's nearly seven o'clock. What could be taking her so long? But the yard is empty, and there's no sight of her coming up the road in the distance. You stare down at your feet. Your palms still burn from your work with the hammer, and you can feel how the web between your thumb and index finger will soon blister and break.

Tell him, you think. *Just tell him,* but your father's voice comes before you can speak.

"I have something for you," he says. He opens the paper bag and removes a silver chain held together with a clasp. It shines in the early evening light like a trickle of floating water. "I wasn't at the hardware store," he says. "I was at the jewelry store. I bought a pair of chains because I've made you something. You and Jacqueline both." He pauses for a second, waiting for your reaction. His face drops. "Try to contain your excitement, please."

"I'm sorry," you say. "It's just—" But that's all you can manage for now.

Your father doesn't sense your anxiety, or perhaps he mistakes it for something else. He waves one hand again, brushing the awkwardness away.

"You'll be pleased to know," he says, "that I spoke with your aunt about this, and she told me it's very nice. Elegant, she said. I hope you'll agree."

With two fingers, he reaches into his shirt pocket and retrieves a silver locket, an oval of metal the size of an almond shell. He strings the chain through the locket's hoop, and then he holds out the necklace for you to take.

It's beautiful. More beautiful than the stolen cigarette case or the medals or anything else you've ever seen. Polished to a dazzling shine, its face is decorated with a hairline etching of a tree. Its roots mirror its tangled branches, and in this way the tree is a reflection of itself, a study in symmetry. This time next week, overcome with grief, you'll hurl the locket into the Susquehanna River. But for now, it's here. You hold the locket in your hand, and it's marvelous and beautiful and new. A treasure.

"Open it," your father says.

There's a picture of Jacqueline inside. It's a portrait from last summer, when your father took you and your sister to a photography studio in Lancaster. Jacqueline wears a dark dress with a lacy pinafore, and her hair is curled into ringlets. She stares straight into the camera, and she doesn't smile.

"I made one for your sister, too," your father says. From his shirt pocket he retrieves a second locket, one with the same etching of the double-image tree. Snapping the locket open, he shows you the portrait inside: a photograph of you, identical in style and composition to the photograph of your sister. "At first," he says, stringing the other chain through the locket's hoop, "I was going to put portraits of your mother inside. But the more I thought of it, the more I liked this better." He clasps the chain and then palms the locket, staring down at your picture in the middle of his hand. "Your mother is gone," he says. "What's the point of carrying her around on your neck?" He looks at you. "But your sister," he says. "You'll always have your sister."

You're breathing harder now. Your shoulders ache. The locket is like a burning coal in your hand. Already, you know that something is wrong. Already, you know that your life has changed. But it's only a feeling—a gathering premonition of dread—and you watch your father in a kind of daze. A shaking, terrible daze.

"I don't like it when the two of you fight," he says. "I don't know what's going on, and it's not my business to know, but I hope you resolve it soon." His hand closes around the locket, and it clicks shut in his palm. He sets his elbows on either knee, and he stares out across the yard. "Think about it," he says, dropping Jacqueline's necklace into his shirt pocket. "Your sister will know you longer than anyone else. I've known you since you were born, but someday you'll outlive me. I'll be gone, Else, but you'll still have your sister. And the years will march on, and you'll have a husband and children and grandchildren, but none of them will ever know you for as long as your own sister. She'll be your oldest friend. Your friend since the moment you were born. That's why siblings are so special."

And now you're crying. Softly, silently, tears are streaming down your face, and you lower your head to your knees. Your father puts his hand on your back and rubs your shoulders.

"It's you and her, Else. I know you know that, and I know your troubles now are only in passing, but it's good to remind you sometimes. It's you and her. You're a team. I told your sister the same thing earlier this afternoon."

Then something happens. The air seems to settle and cool, and your father's hand pauses against your back. Everything has changed, and now he's sensing it, too. He draws back his hand, and he's quiet. He's watching you. Thinking. Feeling.

"Where is your sister?" he says. You can hear the concern in his voice, his first revelation that something is terribly wrong. And when you don't answer, his voice hardens, and he leans in closer. "Else," he says. "Where is Jacqueline?"

The Brenners' woods. The ravine south of town. The quarry off Penn Valley Road. In a few days, they'll search them all, every man and trained hound in Lititz scouring the terrain like threshers cutting through a field.

But they'll never find her, and they'll never find the cigarette case or the dagger or the satchel. They'll search Jacob's house, too, but the house—even now—is empty. It's owned by an elderly couple named Diehl, and they'll explain that they had it leased to a man named Cullum who was months behind on his rent. Was he German? No, he had come from Georgia, or perhaps Mississippi. They'll say they've never heard of anyone named Jacob Joseph, and despite your sister's warning, no one will come to the house that night.

"You should have told me," your father will say. By then, he'll know about *The Plan*. About the money. Everything. And you won't be the "good one" anymore. You'll be the girl who should have said something. The girl who let this happen. The dumb disappointment. "You should have told me," your father will say, again and again. "Why didn't you tell me?"

Why? Because you're a child. Just a child. Frightened and uncertain and still grappling with life and all its shifting demands. But that answer won't be good enough. Not for him, and especially not for you.

"An errand," you tell him now. You lift your head, your cheeks still streaked with tears. "She went to town on an errand."

"Where?"

You try to think of something. The market. The post office. Something. But you only shrug.

Slowly, your father stands. He watches the yard. Then he turns and walks up the stoop, but he pauses by the door and looks back at you.

"Go find her," he says.

You're shaking. Your mouth is dry. The wind is blowing through your hair.

"Else," your father says. "Go find your sister right now."

And after a moment, you feel yourself stand. Your head is light and your feet are weak, but you rise, clasping the locket in your fist.

"All right," you say. "Okay."

You step onto the grass, and then you start walking. You have no direction, no sense of where you'll search, but you're moving, and it feels good. With each step, your legs feel stronger. You cross the lawn and step into the road, and then you're moving faster. Go forward. Move. Find her.

And as your legs start running, you know that you will. You don't know where you'll find her, and you don't know what will happen when you do, but you know that you'll be together again soon. You sense it. You feel it. The dusk is growing. The sky is darkening. But that doesn't matter. Your legs push you forward, and you run. You're going to find your sister. You're going to find Jacqueline.

CHAPTER 25

When she said it all out loud, she felt a little foolish. The "ex-change," breaking into Alfred's plane, the dress, the visit to the penitentiary—everything sounded slightly ridiculous, but even worse, everything was asterisked by its previous secrecy. The fact that she had mentioned none of this to Sam York until tonight seemed suddenly strange and, she knew, more than a little bit childish. From the second she set off on a rambling summary of it all, she felt like a kid coming clean to a parent about some minor piece of mischief.

But pangs of embarrassment and forfeitures of pride were beside the point now. Beyond the chagrin that her synopsis delivered, Elisabeth felt mostly vindication and an unabating sense of resolution.

"You're sure you've never seen it before?" York said. "And you're sure that it's your sister, and that she's older than eleven in the photograph? You're *sure*?"

"I'm positive," Elisabeth said, clenching the picture so hard that it flexed in the middle. Her hand bounced in time with her words. *I'm. Positive.*

And, to his credit, Sam York seemed to believe her. They were seated on either side of his cluttered desk, and now he nodded solemnly, wrote something down in his notebook. Perhaps Elisabeth had underestimated him, but York seemed nothing if not serious. Sympathetic, even. There were no patronizing grins. No "Oh, tut-tuts" of condescension. He listened to her, and he seemed to listen carefully.

"And this dress," he said, "you're sure about that, too? That it was Jacqueline's?"

"It has my father's stitching in it," she told him. "He sewed our initials into all of our clothes, and the dress has my sister's initials."

"It actually says 'JM'?"

"'JGM.' Jacqueline Gabriela Metzger."

Another nod. Another note. Then he looked up. "Couldn't you have had it all these years?"

"No," Elisabeth said. "My father destroyed all of Jacqueline's clothes. Alfred's had it all this time, and he slipped it into Margaret's closet while he was staying with us."

"But why would he do that?" York said. "And why now?" but these questions weren't judgmental. They weren't skeptical. He was thinking out loud—genuinely trying to resolve his own line of thinking and, perhaps for the first time, genuinely asking for Elisabeth's opinion.

"He's said he killed Mack because Mack was going to 'keep him from me.' I don't know what that means exactly, but it shows you just how much he wants my attention. I think he killed Mack and knew he was going to jail. He knew he was going away, and so he opened up about all this as a way to keep me under his thumb."

York set his pencil down, and his eyes scanned up to the ceiling in thought. "But he must have placed the dress in Margaret's closet before the murder. When could he have done that?"

"We went out while he was sleeping," Elisabeth said. "Just for a little bit. He could have done it then."

"All right," York said, "but why? Was he planning Mr. Sanford's murder all along?"

"I don't know," Elisabeth said, "but I don't think so. It doesn't all make sense yet, but I don't think he's been planning our 'exchange' for very long. He likes seeing me, and when he did what he did to Mack, it forced him into a corner. I think that's why he opened up about my sister. He wanted to give me a reason to stay in touch with him."

But she knew there was another possibility: that Alfred had opened up about her sister because he truly wanted to reunite them. There was no doubt that other forces impelled him. Yes, he wanted to force his way into seeing her, and of course there were motives at work that she didn't fully understand yet, particularly when it came to Mack's murder. But those things aside, perhaps there wasn't much more to this than what Alfred himself had claimed: Perhaps he cared about her and wanted to help. Perhaps it was all as simple as that.

York finished jotting another note, and then, easing back in his chair, he set his pencil down and looked up at her. "This is quite a development," he said, "but if we're being honest, it's still not much. There's a lot of—"

"Are you kidding me?"

He raised one hand. "There's a lot that depends on you, Mrs. Pfautz. There's a lot of trust you need to carry. We have to trust that you're right about your sister's age in the picture. We have to trust—"

"But the dress—"

"Having someone's dress doesn't mean you murdered that person."

"We're not talking about murder," Elisabeth said. "We're talking about *involvement*. We're talking about Alfred knowing more. We're talking about this being proof that he's not leading me on."

"All right," York said, "*but*, I was going to say"—and he bounced his hand at her—"*but*, this is all still enough, by far, to begin a formal investigation."

"Meaning?"

"Meaning I'm going to get back in touch with the police in Lancaster County, inform them of all this, have them reopen the file on your sister's disappearance, and then we're going to carry this to a conclusion, if we can."

"And what exactly were you doing before? You once told me you'd 'look into this.'"

"Yes," York said, "and I did, but that was just poking around. I was following up, you see, but we weren't—"

"You weren't doing squat," Elisabeth said, as bluntly as she could, "but now you're telling me you will."

He lowered his chin, just an inch. Then he smiled politely, making a show of it. "That's right."

"Well, that's just grand," Elisabeth said, "but I don't want an investigation."

"Sorry?"

"What I want," Elisabeth said, "is to know where my sister is, and that means getting more information out of Alfred. I'm not done yet. There are more pieces here. More to learn."

"Just let us go forward from here, Mrs. Pfautz."

"By all means," she said. "Go ahead. Please. Open your investigation. Start looking. Start doing your work. It's about time, and God knows this is all I've wanted from you since the beginning. But as for me, I'm going to do my work, too. I'm going straight to the source."

"And so will we, if need—"

"No," Elisabeth said, "no, no, no. I told you the second I sat down, Alfred can't know about this."

York stared at her.

"Are you hearing me?" Elisabeth said. "He was very clear about—"

"You don't need to repeat yourself."

"I think I do." She sat forward. "Don't mention *any* of this to Alfred. Don't go to him. That's critically important. Let me handle him."

And there it was, at last—the patronizing smile, the narrowed eyes filled with imperious pity.

"We're not partners, Mrs. Pfautz," York said. "I told you we'll open an investigation, but that doesn't mean you're a part of it."

"I am part of it," Elisabeth said. *You goddamn prick. You goddamn, god-awful prick.* "I've been part of it from the start."

"Then now is the time to take a step away."

She stood.

"You'll only make things worse," York said to her back. "Trust me."

Trust me, she heard Alfred saying again, *because I'm the only one who really loves you.*

"What I said before still stands," York said. "Involved or not, he's fleecing you. He's a grifter. And now you're trying to switch it up on him. You're trying to play him. But do you know the one thing every grifter hates? Getting grifted. He's going to catch on to you, and you're going to muck everything up."

She turned around, glowering at him.

"You think I'm a fool," she said, and she took a single step forward. "You think I'm a silly little child." She looked him up and down, and her hands clenched at her sides. "Well, I'm not, and I'm not going to *muck* anything up. So please, stay out of *my* way. It's for the best." She turned, but then she glared again over her shoulder. "Trust me."

CHAPTER 26

Elisabeth slept better that night than she had in weeks, months, years. She slept a black, engulfing sleep, devoid of dreams and music. In the morning, she felt as though she had been asleep for a decade. She lay flat on her back and stared up at the wrinkled plaster ceiling, and she smiled at nothing in particular.

The day got worse from there. They skipped breakfast, and John went alone to visit Daniel Nilak in the hospital. Then he met them for lunch—root beers and roast beef sandwiches at the malt shop across from the hotel—and while Margaret used the bathroom, John told her about his visit.

He had spent an hour at the hospital, but it didn't take Elisabeth more than a second to discern that it hadn't gone well. Opening the door and walking into the restaurant, John had looked tired. He looked as if he was coming from a funeral, so much so that Elisabeth's first thought was *He's dead. Daniel has died.* Well, he hadn't, not quite.

"But will he be able to walk?" Elisabeth asked.

"Sort of," John said. "He'll need crutches for the rest of his life. Like, polio crutches, I mean. He doesn't have much feeling in his legs."

And was he mad? Had he screamed at John when he walked through the door? Had he spat in his face?

"No," John said. "He wasn't mad. He was just"—John sighed—"he was mostly just sad. That's the best way I can put it."

"Sad?"

John nodded. "He told me his whole body feels different now. He told me he hated his life. He said he wanted to die, but at the same time he said he prays to God every night that he'll keep on living, because he's terrified of what else dying might be like. That's what he said. What *else* it might be like, like he's died some already. He's in traction, you know. He can barely move."

And then, John said, as if the whole situation wasn't awful enough already, Daniel had started to cry. Slowly, "horrifically," he cried.

"And what did you do?" Elisabeth asked.

"I just sat there," John said. "I sat there and watched him."

And now they were here, sitting together at the malt shop like a couple on their first date. Margaret came prancing back to the table.

"Daddy, my dearest," she exclaimed, embracing him. "How wonderful of you to join us."

They ran a few more errands; Margaret insisted on finding a bookstore, and after that they shopped for a new set of kitchen knives at the Sears & Roebuck. Then Elisabeth set into motion the thing she had waited to do all day.

"Another?" John asked. "Is it anything serious?"

"No, no," Elisabeth assured him. They were pacing through aisles of mixing bowls, cups, and platters, everything softly shining as if the whole store were made of ice. "It's just a follow-up for yesterday." Then, after a moment, because it made it sound more official, she told him, "It's standard procedure."

And that was good enough—or intimidating enough—for John. He dropped it. She was riding in Elmer Whitlock's limping DeSoto not half an hour later.

"Didn't get your fill yesterday, huh?" he asked her, grinning into the rearview mirror.

"Something like that."

"I get it," he said. "I get it." He lit a cigarette and rolled his window down halfway. The car filled with smoke and dusty air. Fairbanks smelled much different than Tanacross did—saltier and staler, as if the city rested on the edge of a rank, tepid ocean. "What's your fella's name, anyhow?" Elmer asked. "I probably know the guy."

Her mind raced through possible answers and explanations. But then it twitched into speaking, and what she said was, "Alfred." After a pause, "Alfred Shaw."

Elmer exhaled a spear of smoke, puzzling in the rearview mirror. "Shaw," he said. "Don't know no Alfred Shaw. He related to Tall Tom Shaw? Big Tagish fella? Used to work at the Ester camp over west?"

"I don't believe so."

He shrugged. "Well, still. Probably know him. I'm just stupid's all." Elmer smiled again into the mirror. "Old age'll do that to you. Old age and other stuff." He winked, patting his breast pocket, and Elisabeth heard the faint sloshing of a flask. She smiled back.

If the Walrus remembered her from yesterday, he didn't let on. They went through the same paperwork, filled out the same forms, and then she was waiting again in the drafty room with its massive wooden table and its matching rows of chairs. The day before, Alfred had left so quickly that they hadn't discussed a crucial topic: his third and final "gift." She had kept her end of the bargain, visiting him in Fairbanks, and he had kept his end, too, delivering the photograph. Now it was time for the next step.

And what that step was, she honestly couldn't guess. But as she sat there, waiting for Alfred to walk through the door, an odd realization crept up on her: She was excited. Not only for getting closer to her sister, but for the sheer anticipation of Alfred's next request. She dreaded it, partly, but in dread there was also a brand of exhilaration. The past three years felt to her now like some singular bout of stasis. Alaska had trapped her, frozen her. But now she had thawed, and her blood was flowing, and her heart was beating, and she was moving. Perhaps Alfred would ask for something horrible. But horror was better than nothing at all. And for that, she was excited. Positively giddy.

Somewhere down the hallway, a door opened and shut, and then Alfred and a guard were strolling up to the room. The guard unlocked the metal door at the front of the room and held it open for Alfred like a bellhop.

"Twenty minutes," he said, and exchanged a single glance with Elisabeth. Then the door shut and latched behind him, and she and Alfred were alone.

"I wasn't expecting you," Alfred said. He stood staring at her, thirty feet away. "What a pleasant surprise," but his voice belied his words. He spoke flatly, and there was a sharpness in his eyes that Elisabeth hadn't seen since that morning on the landing strip when he had asked to stay the night.

"We weren't finished yesterday," Elisabeth said. "So I thought I'd pay you another visit."

He slipped his hands into his pockets, ambling forward. "My next gift, you mean. Our third and final."

"That's right."

He nodded, kept walking. He stopped by the seat across from hers, though he didn't sit down. He leaned forward, resting both hands on the top rail of the chair. "I guess you liked the photograph, then? It was acceptable?"

"In what sense?"

"As my gift. My thanks for your visit. It was up to snuff?"

"You could say that," Elisabeth told him. Then, staring him down, "Where did you get it?"

Nothing. No reaction. No movement. "From a friend."

"And this friend—that's where you got the dress, too?"

"Correct."

"And the name of that friend?"

"That's for me to know. Not you."

"We're still going to do this? Speak in ambiguities?"

He pushed his weight off the chair, turned away from her, and walked toward the windows that shined overhead. "I can't see the sky from my cell."

"The photograph and the dress," Elisabeth repeated. "Where did you get them?"

"We're not talking about that anymore," he snapped, whipping his head around. His eyes were pinched with fury, and a strand of hair hung in front of one eye like a bending claw. He stepped toward the table and began rolling up his left sleeve. "The sky," he said, struggling to control his voice, "is very important to me. I know some people are afraid of flying, but they're misguided. They think the sky is full of peril and danger, but they're wrong. It's the earth you've got to worry about. The hard, unforgiving earth."

The scars on his left arm were revealed now, and again Elisabeth had trouble taking her eyes away from them. It seemed that there were even more of them now, and they looked thicker and darker, like veins turned inside out.

"When I'm flying is the only time I ever feel truly at ease," Alfred said, rolling up the right sleeve. "The sky is freedom. It's possibilities, not peril. That's why they keep me in my windowless cell. That's why they keep me from seeing the sky. They're trying to break me down. To rob me even of hope. It's one of only two cells," he said, "just two cells in the entire prison without a window. The other houses a mute idiot who tears his own clothes off. That's how highly my captors think of me here."

He was pacing around the table now, hooking toward Elisabeth. Instinctively, she pushed her chair away from him as he approached, and then she stood, bracing herself for whatever was coming next. Alfred held his arms straight up, which were bare now to the elbows.

"You asked me about my service," he said, still walking toward her. "I was talented at surviving, but it wasn't always easy." She moved back, step after step, but Alfred kept coming, and in a second more their bodies were only inches apart. "These," he said, still holding up his arms, "were the primary decorations I received from the war. My plane went down, and I woke up in a pool of glass and splinters and blood. You can't tell with my clothes on, but my whole body is covered in scars. I was cut to pieces. I would have rather died. The ground," he said, "the ground is the most dangerous part of flying, Elisabeth, and the most punishing."

He lowered his arms now and looked down at her body, his gaze as thick on her as smoke. Then he raised his eyes.

"Get on your knees," he said.

She stepped back.

"You're mistaken about something," he said, matching her every movement. "You think you have the upper hand, but you do not. You have no leverage over me. You have no control. It's me, Elisabeth," and with that he came so close that they finally touched, her breasts flattening against him. "It's me who controls this relationship."

Silence, and now she wasn't retreating. She stood squarely against him.

"Your knees," he said. "Get down on your knees."

Her heart was beating. Her blood was flowing. She had thawed. She was moving. And then she was easing down to the floor, despite every rational thought in her mind. She stared at Alfred's arms, which hung loosely beside him. His scars reached out for her.

"Sometimes," he said, "they bleed." He stared down at her. "After they pulled me from the glass, they took me to a camp in Frith Hill. They didn't treat my wounds as they should have. We did terrible things to the English, Elisabeth, and a few of them paid us back in kind." He rotated his arms, palms facing out. "Like your sister," he said, "I do not take well to captivity, and I do not take well to any man who holds me captive, English or Alaskan." He closed his fists and scowled at her, fury teeming in his eyes. Elisabeth couldn't move. She was frozen. Captured. "I know you spoke to the police," Alfred said. "I told you not to, but you spoke to them anyway."

She was back on her feet in an instant, but then Alfred had her by the neck, his right hand clamping around her like the jaws of a striking snake.

"What did I tell you?" he said, pushing her back. "What did I say?"

She slammed against a wall, and then he was squeezing her neck even harder, the arch of his hand pressing up toward the base of her skull. She thrashed against him, but already she was weak, and she could feel for the first time how powerful he was. She beat her hands against his arm, but his tensing flesh felt as stiff and strong as stone.

"I told you," he said. "I told you not to speak to them. I told you to keep this between us. Between countrymen."

His breath was hot on her face. He was leaning so close to her. Elisabeth flailed against the wall, but she couldn't break away from him, and she couldn't breathe. She couldn't muster the lightest gasp. He was crushing her.

"Tell me you spoke to them," Alfred said. "Admit you disobeyed me. Say 'Yes.' Say 'Yes.'"

And she wanted so desperately to say that word. She would admit fault—she'd admit anything—if that was what it took for him to loosen his grip around her neck. But she couldn't breathe, and she couldn't speak. There was sound escaping from her throat, but this was only the rasping of life leaving her body. She felt her heels rise off the ground. Perhaps he was lifting her, or perhaps she was losing consciousness. But his grip never loosened.

"Say it," he repeated. "Say, 'Yes, I betrayed you.'"

Even tighter now. His fingers were digging deep into her neck. She closed her eyes, and darkness enveloped her. She heard nothing. Felt nothing. Then she was braced on her hands and knees, her forehead touching the cold concrete floor. She was racked with shaking, fighting for air through a fit of coughing. Alfred still stood over her.

"And what else did I tell you?" he said. "I told you that if you went to the police, our exchange would be over. And it is." He knelt down next to her, though Elisabeth could see his form only vaguely. The world was still coming back to her, and her eyes were clouded with mucus and tears. Alfred loomed beside her like a shadow. "Are you listening to me?" he said, his voice as tender as a parent's. "Elisabeth, darling, do you hear me?"

And then she was running toward the door, pounding on it with both fists. The door was open a moment later, and Elisabeth fled so urgently down the hallway that she didn't see the guards gaping at her or hear their puzzled questions. A moment later she was outside, and the sun was on her face, and the Fairbanks air had never tasted so bitter. It burned in her throat like acid.

CHAPTER 27

A clerical error—that was what York called it. For a second time, he had contacted the Immigration and Naturalization Service, and thanks to Elisabeth's own persistence in contacting them about Alfred, they had already looked further into their records, discovered a discrepancy, and corrected it accordingly. Alfred had been telling the truth about the year of his immigration. He had come to the United States in 1919, not 1929, and he had moved straight from New York to Lancaster County. He had been living in Lititz at the time of Jacqueline's disappearance.

Not only that: He had kidnapped her, and he had murdered her. The signed confession sat on York's desk.

Elisabeth's first reaction wasn't fury. She didn't rage at York, not when he detailed his meeting with Alfred and his revelation of the compass and the picture and the dress, not even when he announced— triumphantly—the confession.

No, at first Elisabeth broke down, and she cried. She felt as weak as a baby, though not because of the bruises already spreading across her neck, hidden for the time with a layer of hastily applied concealer. She was weak with despair and frustration, but even more she was weak with the possibility of Alfred never speaking to her again. She sat across from York and listened to his deadpan summary of it all, and she cried. She sobbed into both hands.

"This is difficult, I know," York said, totally oblivious. "And I realize it wasn't exactly what you wanted, but isn't it something?"

She didn't answer him.

"Mrs. Pfautz—"

Across the desk, he offered her a tissue.

"Mrs. Pfautz, your sister—"

"My sister," she shouted. "My sister—" but she couldn't go on. She was getting carried away with herself, and she just couldn't help it. A noodle of mucus hung from her face, but what did appearances matter now? Let him see what he had done to her. Let him see how he had broken her down.

"This is a lot to process, I know," York said. "But you have to understand—"

"What happened to the grifter?" Elisabeth said. "What happened to him toying with me? Now you believe anything he says?"

"The facts have changed. The evidence has changed."

"He's lying," she said. "He's doing this to spite you. Are you really this stupid?"

Nothing.

"I told you," Elisabeth said, and she pounded her fists against her head like a madwoman. "I told you not to talk to him. My sister isn't dead, and Alfred didn't kill her. But he knows what happened to her, and he was going to tell me everything, but now it's all ruined."

"You have to calm down, Mrs. Pfautz."

But she was sobbing and couldn't stop it, and she had never felt so close to the brink of losing her mind. She cried, and Sam York stared at her in silent terror as she pounded her fists against her head. And again and again, rising through the hurried horror of her thoughts, she saw Alfred's scars. She saw them bleeding, and she understood why they would, for some things are irrevocable and cannot ever heal, no matter the effort or bandage or balm.

PART

3

CHAPTER 28

January 1942

The official story: Alfred H. K. Seidel had kidnapped Jacqueline with the intent of holding her for ransom. As the search for the young girl escalated, however, Seidel grew increasingly nervous, and he abandoned his plan altogether and murdered her in cold blood. He strangled her with a belt, tied rocks to her arms and legs, and then dumped her body in the Susquehanna River some fifty miles south of town. All these years later, a bald sense of guilt had driven him to confession. His trial for the unrelated murder of Mack Sanford was postponed until June, and his arraignment for the murder of Jacqueline Gabriela Metzger would be scheduled shortly thereafter.

Alfred was a ruthless killer. Sam York was a hero. The family of the girl wept in relief and bittersweet catharsis. Elisabeth read a dozen newspaper articles about the crime and the confession, and each one took the same angle and lingered on the same details. The rocks. The belt. A decades-long mystery solved. Each newspaper, too, reached out to Elisabeth for comment, and she told them all the same thing.

"I have no statement on Alfred Seidel or my sister's disappearance."

Why bother? If she stirred the pot, what difference would it make?

She would be ignored, or she would be treated as if she was deranged. She and Jacqueline and their entire family would draw even more attention to themselves, and it was outsider attention that had gotten her into this fix in the first place. So she deferred. She curtly declined. Besides, her uncle and aunt gave the papers all they wanted.

"He's a beast," her aunt Ethel was quoted as saying in the *Lancaster Herald*. "He's a vile degenerate, and may God alone have mercy on him."

Even with all its drama and hyperbole, Elisabeth didn't doubt that Ethel really said that. The two of them spoke just days after Alfred's confession, her aunt in fits of tears.

"It's over," she wept into the telephone. "It's really over."

"Yes," Elisabeth told her, "it is."

Though she didn't want it to be, despite what had happened. Alfred had nearly killed her, yes. He had proven himself to be exactly what Elisabeth had always feared: a true psychotic, a man who wasn't safe to be around for a single second.

But she had come too far. She couldn't give up now. If Alfred was a wild animal, then she was his handler, and no handler would be deterred by a brush with the animal's teeth. There was still so much she didn't know, so much she felt unsure about. Her sister was alive—she trusted that—but had Alfred been telling her the truth apart from this? *A fellow German,* he had told her. *My age. Kept to himself,* and that seemed like a real possibility, one that meshed with the mysteries of that summer twenty years past.

But did she believe him absolutely? No, not yet, not by a long shot. Perhaps he was mingling facts with fiction. Perhaps Alfred and the *little bird* were one and the same. The evidence was there—his service in the war, his handwriting, the dress, the photograph—but Elisabeth knew that she needed more: more information, more time, more of everything. And she wanted to press on, however cautiously, but Alfred wasn't returning her letters. She wrote him a dozen times. She telephoned. She visited the penitentiary in person. Yet always she heard nothing, or was turned away.

"He's not seeing visitors," the Walrus told her.

But she kept on trying, and the months flitted by. October, November, December. First the quick autumn, then the long winter. It came on as it always did—so fast and intense that it seemed almost unnatural. Had it really been *this* cold last year? That didn't seem possible. But it had been, and it was, though their new home made the weather more manageable.

The house in Fairbanks was nice. Four bedrooms, one and a half bathrooms, big kitchen, fully furnished. The living room came with a Zenith console radio, and the emerald Formica kitchen countertops were seas of gleaming perfection. The couch was wrapped in a gorgeous Dorothy Draper slipcover, and the bathtub had a white swan painted onto its pink linoleum tiles. Their neighborhood was just outside of Ladd, and their home was a perfect copy of the houses on either side of it. Each had its own fenced-in yard, but theirs had something extra, too: a plywood work shed, the handiwork of the man who had lived there before them, an army colonel who practiced woodworking.

In the weeks just after the move, Elisabeth spent entire hours at a time in that work shed. It had a small fireplace, but she never kept it lit. Dressed in her boots and parka, she liked to sit in the winter darkness and feel the icy cold enveloping her. The ceaseless light of the summertime had given way to a night that was never far away. The sun rose at ten o'clock in the morning, and it set shortly after four. In years past, the Alaskan winter had always been a challenge for her. If the summer was a season for rattled nerves and fits of brittle sleeplessness, the winter was just the opposite. January and February weren't so much months as bouts of soporific depression. In the summer, Elisabeth would go to sleep with the expectation of waking too soon. In the winter, she would sleep with the expectation of never waking at all.

But this winter was different. The darkness still sapped her energy, but there was also some comfort in that—some semblance of tranquility that she had never before found in the winter's frigid darkness. Sitting in the work shed out back, she liked to feel the cold creeping through her clothes and spreading across her skin. She liked to watch the dissipating clouds of her breath, plumes of air that seemed to sparkle as they floated above her head.

But more than anything else, she liked to watch the work shed itself. Apart from a single stool and a scarred pine table, the work shed was empty—or almost empty. Through some trick of condensation or smoke from the fireplace, the walls of the work shed were lined with the shadows of the tools that had once hung on them. Chisels, dowels, jigs, clamps, marking knives, countersinks, burnishers, and saws, dozens of saws. She would sit and study their ghosts, ticking off their names one by one, over and over again.

She had the time for this in Fairbanks. A week before their move, the school at Ladd had offered to take in Margaret when the January term began, and John and Elisabeth had eagerly accepted. Between the arrangement's convenience and John's own insistence that declining the offer would be rude, it seemed as though they had no choice in the matter. So, just like that, Elisabeth's teaching days came to a close.

As for John's own teaching, his first few weeks were unhurried and nearly carefree. Then the Japanese attacked Hawaii, and everything changed. Listening to the president's address, the three of them sat around the radio in the living room, huddling together as if for warmth, as if some creeping coldness would soon freeze them all to the core.

"The people of the United States have already formed their opinions and well understand the implications to the very life and safety of our nation," Roosevelt told them. "Hostilities exist. There is no blinking at the fact that our people, our territory, and our interests are in grave danger. With confidence in our armed forces, with the unbounding determination of our people, we will gain the inevitable triumph—so help us God."

John stood and switched it off.

"I hope we burn them all alive," he said, "women and children and all."

In a seeming instant, Fairbanks changed. Transport planes and heavy bombers rumbled overhead. Jeeps and half-track carriers clamored down the roads. Soldiers were everywhere, young and old alike, men who rushed around with worry in their eyes but joy in their smiles, frightened of the war but happy for its purpose. By the looks of the commotion that now defined Fairbanks, you might have thought that the Japanese were only miles away and closing quickly, and indeed Elisabeth heard almost constant chatter about the possibility of an invasion.

"Let 'em come," she overheard a man saying one night at the grocery store. "We'll string 'em up by their rotten buckteeth."

Fairbanks's population swelled, and Ladd was at the center of its growth. By Christmas, the school was bustling with students; by New Year's, it was teeming.

"That's the thing about military men," John told her. "Most of them have enough kids to raise their own standing armies."

For the January term, John was assigned three periods of eleventh-grade biology, three periods of tenth-grade mathematics, and two periods of ninth-grade English. He was inundated with work. Some days, he stayed so late at the school that Elisabeth thought he might be sleeping there. When he did come home, he poured himself a drink, ate a cold dinner, and went silently to bed. In Tanacross, Margaret and John were never far away. In Fairbanks, Elisabeth hardly ever saw them.

And although she would never admit as much out loud, she found that she didn't really miss them. Part of her did; most of her didn't. It wasn't that she reveled in her newfound independence. It was just that she didn't think of John and Margaret, not when they were away. Planes and trucks thundered all around her, but she barely even heard them. The radio droned with endless updates about the war, but more often than not, the places and names and battles and numbers rolled right off her. She thought of Alfred. She thought of her sister. She thought of Pennsylvania. And sometimes, when she was lucky, she didn't think of anything at all. She sat in the work shed. She watched her breath. She studied the shadows on the wall.

"Dovetail saw," she would whisper, and the air felt cold enough to freeze her heart. "Fretsaw. Backsaw. Bucksaw. Bow saw."

It was around that time—the January term, midwinter—when Margaret started acting strange. She had taken the move to Fairbanks in stride, or so at least it seemed. When John and Elisabeth had asked her how she felt about enrolling at Ladd, Margaret had shrugged.

"That's fine," she told them, and then quizzically tilted her head. "But who is Ladd Airfield named after?"

If there had been a response more typical for Margaret, Elisabeth couldn't guess it. *She'll be fine,* Elisabeth had thought. In all likelihood, Margaret would thrive in her new environment. She was placed in a sixth-grade class, though her composition skills, arithmetic, and background in science were more in tune with a seventh- or even eighth-grade curriculum. She was more than adequately prepared in terms of her background, and when it came to making friends, Elisabeth had felt certain that Margaret wouldn't flounder. Her intellectual curiosity had always lent itself to a brand of friendly effervescence; in Tanacross, she had been just as keen to learn about hurricanes or the life cycle of jellyfish as she was to share that knowledge with other children. *Yes,* Elisabeth thought. *She'll certainly be fine.*

But almost straightaway, Margaret changed. She was quieter, but it wasn't this alone that seemed strange. It was the mood of her quietness, the feel of it. Margaret's reticence was weighty and foreboding. Her silence had all the tension of someone lost in thought on the heels of an argument. Once, the two of them were reading together in the living room, and Elisabeth noticed that Margaret's eyes weren't even moving. Her gaze was fixed on a page of her dog-eared cryptogram book, but she was sitting in motionless detachment like a person stuck in time. Even her blinking seemed to cease.

"What are you thinking about?" Elisabeth asked her.

"Leopards," Margaret told her, but somehow Elisabeth sensed that this was a lie, not Margaret herself but a careful impersonation of her.

Her schoolwork had its own peculiarities. Her teacher gave frequent quizzes in math and spelling, and Margaret's results were almost always the same: one or two answers shy of perfect. That was fine, naturally, but her mistakes were so out of step with her other answers that Elisabeth had to wonder if they were intentional. On one vocabulary test, Margaret spelled every word flawlessly but one—*crystal*, which she spelled *krystelle*. The following week was more of the same. Every answer was perfect but *calligraphy*, which Margaret spelled *kayligrafy*.

She was reaching out, Elisabeth guessed. She was pleading for more attention, more love, more something. And that seemed to make sense, the blame for which lay squarely on Elisabeth's own shoulders. But when she confronted Margaret plainly about the quizzes, she swore that her mistakes were genuine, and she promised that everything at school was fine, perfectly fine. And was she making friends?

"Scads," Margaret said. "Scores and scads."

Then, early one morning, Elisabeth awoke to go to the bathroom and noticed that a light was shining from the hallway. She poked her head outside the door and saw that the light was coming from Margaret's bedroom. At first, she didn't think anything of it. After three years in Tanacross, they were all still getting reacquainted with things like electricity and running water. They forgot to flush toilets and turn off light switches, and more than once Elisabeth had briefly scolded herself for neglecting to stoke the fire in the kitchen, only to remember that their stove was now electric.

Yawning, she pushed Margaret's door open and reached for the switch on the wall. Then she glanced at Margaret's bed, and she saw that her daughter was gone. She padded down the hallway, presuming that a light would be on in the bathroom. It wasn't. *The kitchen, then,* Elisabeth thought, but Margaret wasn't there either. The refrigerator softly hummed and ticked, but the kitchen was dark and cold. Elisabeth paced through the house, not panicked, not yet, but she couldn't find Margaret anywhere. It wasn't until she circled through the kitchen again and walked past the back door that she noticed Delma and a solitary figure standing in the shimmering white expanse of the backyard. Margaret was still wearing her pajamas and slippers, but she was wearing nothing to sufficiently fortify her against the cold—no parka, no gloves, no scarves. It was nearly two o'clock in the morning. The thermometer that hung outside the door read twenty-five degrees below zero.

For a second, the sight of Margaret was so surprising that Elisabeth just stood there in shock, staring. Then she almost screamed. She dove for the door, yanked it open, and rushed out in her bare feet, never thinking to pull on shoes. No matter. She didn't even feel the snow and ice beneath her. With all of her strength, she grabbed Margaret from behind and heaved her up with both arms, flinging Margaret and herself back inside the house as if the entire yard were on fire, a deadly burning field. For all intents and purposes, it was.

She screamed some garbled approximation of *Oh God* as she slammed the door behind them, nearly clipping Delma's nose in the process. Then she and Margaret were tangled up together on the floor, and she was pulling Margaret closer to her. Margaret's skin—her legs, her ankles, her feet—felt soft but icy cold.

"What are you doing?" Elisabeth shouted. She pulled off Margaret's right slipper and tucked her foot beneath her arm—*Wrap, don't rub,* she had learned about frostbite when they first moved to Alaska—but Margaret jerked her foot away.

"Stop it," Margaret said. "Get off me. We were only out there a second."

She scooted back. She was scowling, angrier than she had been in years. Elisabeth was stunned. It was more than the abruptness of Margaret's resistance, and it was more than just her words. What surprised Elisabeth was Margaret's tone, which had all the scathing maturity of a girl much older than twelve. With her face pinched into a glower, she even looked older than twelve, as though the person that Elisabeth had pulled inside the house was a different girl than the one who had walked out of it only moments before.

And Elisabeth could see that it had been only moments. There was no trace of frosty whiteness on Margaret's skin.

"Are you—"

"I'm fine," Margaret snapped. "I was out there for just a minute."

Elisabeth shivered. "But why weren't you wearing anything?"

"I was looking at the northern lights," Margaret said.

"But why in God's name weren't you wearing anything?" Elisabeth repeated, raising her voice, and again she reached out for her. Margaret pulled away, standing now.

"I'm fine," she said, holding up both hands and splaying her fingers open as though that proved something. "I wasn't going to freeze to death. I'm not an idiot."

And before Elisabeth had a chance to respond, Margaret turned and stormed away. John was standing in the darkened kitchen nearby, but for the time, he said nothing. Elisabeth sat by the door for a minute more, feeling distinctly like she had just woken up from a dream.

CHAPTER 29

Weeks passed. The winter pressed on. Margaret's aloofness continued, but there was nothing else alarming that went with it, not after the early-morning episode when Elisabeth had found her outside. If anything, Margaret's days seemed comfortably bland. On Monday, Wednesday, and Friday, she'd return from school around three o'clock, play with her puzzle book or listen to the radio for an hour, eat dinner, help with the dishes, walk Delma. Then she'd start her homework, and it was eight or even nine o'clock before she was finished. Tuesdays and Thursdays were more or less the same, but Margaret stayed a little later at school; she had joined an after-hours jewelry-making club, and she often came home with colorful beaded necklaces, bracelets, and clip-on earrings.

"I made an orca," she declared one afternoon, holding up a necklace with a beaded pendant the size of a fist. The blocky figure of a whale was breaching above a row of cobalt blue waves. "An Athabaskan lady came by and showed us how to do it."

"That's wonderful," Elisabeth told her. "That's beautiful."

She was getting along all right, Elisabeth thought. Perhaps what she had said about her "scads" of friends wasn't far from the truth. She rarely mentioned other children by name, and she never brought any girlfriends to the house, but Elisabeth didn't find much cause for concern in that. Margaret was still fitting in, after all—she was still, Elisabeth could only assume, one of the "new girls"—but if her willingness to join an extracurricular club was any sign of things to come, Margaret was hardly being antisocial. All things considered, in light of the winter and the war and the move and everything that went with it, she was holding up rather well.

Then Elisabeth learned that she wasn't. One afternoon in early February, she received a phone call from Catherine Curry, Margaret's schoolteacher. There had been an *incident*—her word—and Margaret had been at the center of it.

"She's still here," Curry told her. "She's serving her detention right now."

Elisabeth went through the motions—the sighs, the apologies, the shaking of heads, the *tsk-tsk* of ticking tongues. Curry, for her part, wasn't exactly sympathetic. She was terse, and her report of the incident was vague to the point of being mysterious. When Elisabeth asked what had happened, Curry just paused for a moment and said, "It really would be best if we talked about this in person."

"Oh," Elisabeth said. "Yes, that's fine, but I'd really—"

"Are you free right now?" Curry asked. "You live just down the bend, don't you?"

"We do," Elisabeth said, *the bend* being local shorthand for the neighborhood adjacent to the airfield. Elisabeth had never understood the term; the neighborhood was nothing more than a straight-shot main street with ten avenues on either side of it.

"Excellent," Curry said. "Can you be here in, say, half an hour?"

It took her a little while to get John on the phone. The upper school secretary placed her on hold for several minutes, then a second hold for several minutes more, then a third hold after that. Finally, John came on the line. He sounded winded and, Elisabeth could tell, more than slightly annoyed.

"And what did she say this is all about?" he asked.

"She wouldn't tell me."

"She must have said something."

"She didn't. She was very unspecific."

John groaned. "Well, did she say how long this would take?"

"No," Elisabeth said. "I told you, she was very unclear about the whole thing. I don't know what else to say, but I thought you should be there, too. You're not teaching now, right?"

"I'm not, but that doesn't mean I'm not busy."

"All right," Elisabeth said, "but surely you can spare a few minutes."

"A few minutes, maybe, but Else, I've got a hell of a lot to do." He exhaled in a tight burst; he was smoking a cigarette. They were quiet for a moment. Then, "Listen, can't you just handle this?"

"Of course I can handle it," Elisabeth said, "but I thought it'd be nice for you to be there. Don't you think so?"

"Nice?"

"Yes, nice," Elisabeth said. "This is part of keeping up appearances. This is part of being a parent."

"Thank you," John said, and paused for effect. "I had forgotten what it means to be a parent, though I did think that my working all the time and supporting this family night and day had a little something to do with it."

"Why are we even fighting about this? I just thought that you would want to know your daughter's in some trouble at school. Don't you care to know that?"

"I do," John said. "I do care to know that, and now I'm well informed. Thank you."

"You're welcome," Elisabeth said, and it came off sounding even nastier than she had intended.

"But, again," John told her, speaking slowly, the voice he might have used with an aggravating child, "it'd be nice if you could handle this."

"You're two minutes away," Elisabeth said. "You're one hallway and one courtyard away. Is this really too much to ask?"

"It is," John said. "In a way, yes, it is."

"It's not."

"It is," John said, more adamantly now. "And, frankly, all of this is a lot to bear, too."

"*This?*"

"This."

"*This* what?"

"Your badgering me. Your pestering me. I don't know if you've noticed, but I'm not exactly dripping with free time these days. I've got lesson planning, Else. I've got grading to do. I've got mountains and mountains of grading."

She made herself breathe. "In the time we've been talking," she said, "we could have met with Catherine Curry."

"Maybe," John said, "but that's beside the point."

"And what *is* the point, then?"

"The point," he said, snapping now, "is that this is something I'd like you to handle. This is something you *should* handle. You have your job, and I have mine. Now let me do mine, and I'll let you do yours."

"That's a shit thing to say," Elisabeth told him. "She's your child, too, you know, and it's a little disconcerting that I should have to tell you that."

"It's a shit thing, Else, that you sit around all day and do nothing. It's a shit thing that you don't take care of your daughter. You, not me. You."

It was all she could do to say good-bye, all she could do to keep herself from hurling the phone against the wall. "Good-bye," she said, or heard herself say, and she slammed the receiver on its cradle. Her fingers clenched. Her toes curled divots in her shoes.

Catherine Curry wasn't much older than Elisabeth, and perhaps was even younger. She was small and very thin—her collarbone jutted out so fiercely that it looked as if it were trying to break free of her—and a single curl of gray eddied through her otherwise uninteresting hair, a streak of sham sagacity that she was undoubtedly extremely proud of.

Elisabeth had met her only once before. Shortly after moving but prior to the start of the January term, Margaret undertook a battery of tests administered by Curry, the sum of which was aimed at assessing her readiness for the fifth grade. Margaret had passed everything with ease, including a brief geography test.

"It's an absolute wonder," Curry had said, shaking her head, leafing through her papers. "She's a smart one—I'll give her that. I don't know how she managed it," and although her remarks were likely made in innocence, Elisabeth had taken some offense at them. Not once had Curry acknowledged her instruction. Not once had she said, *My goodness. You must have been doing something right these past three years.* And hadn't she? Margaret was gifted—that much was clear—but surely Elisabeth's teaching deserved some degree of credit. She didn't need the validation, but the total disregard of Margaret's stint of homeschooling seemed to be a condemnation of it. *I don't know how she managed it.* When Curry had said that, Elisabeth just nodded.

"It's a miracle, all right," she had said, as dry as she could manage.

The school's windows were poorly insulated, and the classroom was as chilly as a catacomb. Elisabeth had expected Margaret to be waiting with Curry—she imagined Margaret banished to a corner, or perhaps writing lines on the chalkboard—but Margaret was nowhere to be seen. It was only Curry at her desk. A porcelain hula girl stood sentinel beside a stack of papers.

"Thanks for coming in so quickly," Curry said, flashing an effete smile.

The *incident*, she explained, had occurred only hours before. Shortly after lunch, Margaret had asked to use the bathroom.

"We have a hall pass," Curry said. "One student at a time."

But Margaret didn't readily return. When fifteen minutes had passed, Curry sent another student to the girls' room to check on her.

"And, surprise," Curry said, "Margaret was gone. I had the students take up some silent reading, and I checked on her myself. I went from bathroom to bathroom, up and down the hallway. No Margaret. Then

I noticed that her parka was missing from its hook." Curry gestured at the door. "Each student hangs up their things in the morning, and each student has their own hook in the hallway. Now, you can imagine my alarm when I saw that all of Margaret's things were missing. Her parka, her scarves, everything. For ten minutes, your daughter had a whole team of us almost losing our minds." Curry leaned forward now, clasping her hands on the desk. "I don't think I need to tell you this, Mrs. Pfautz, but our students don't often play hooky. They're military children, they're *obedient* children, and a thing like this just doesn't happen here, let alone what happened next."

Elisabeth lowered her eyes. "What happened next? Where was Margaret?"

Again the affected smile, the pretense of civility. Curry leaned back.

"She was halfway to the airfield itself. She had gone clear through the courtyard, clear through the upper school, and down the service road after that. If you can believe it, she even passed through a guard station. Goodness knows how she managed that. A patrol finally stopped her and brought her back, kicking and screaming." She added a little flourish here, *kicking and screaming*, dragging out the words as though they were an insult—to Margaret, yes, but an insult aimed mostly at Elisabeth.

"Kicking and screaming?"

Curry nodded. "Margaret's always been such a quiet child. I've thought all this time that she's a sweet little girl. 'I've got a little poet in my class,' I told a girlfriend the other day. That's why this was so disappointing. She kicked. She screamed. She fought. She cursed."

"She cursed?"

"She called me a 'stinking bitch,'" Curry said, and the surprise of that phrase—delivered with all its naked bluntness—was jarring enough that Elisabeth literally flinched.

"*Margaret* said that?"

"She did," Curry told her. "And, to say the least, I didn't appreciate it."

"Miss Curry—" Elisabeth began, but Curry leaned quickly forward again.

"This is a problem," she said. "This is a big problem, and you'll have to excuse me for saying so, but I think that problem starts with you."

Elisabeth felt her face flush. "Me?"

"Yes," Curry said. "What else do you make of all this?"

"I'm not quite sure what you mean. You're asking—"

"This is a stressful time for everyone," Curry said. "Believe me, I understand that. There are lots of things going on right now, and that's especially true when you're living in an army installation. And on top of that, I know fully well that Margaret is still adjusting to a new city, but none of that excuses this, not as I see it. I don't know what kind of child you've been raising, but the child I saw today has no place at this school."

"I don't disagree. I'm not—"

"And make no mistake," Curry said. "This is the child that *you've* been raising. It doesn't take a genius to understand why children act out. They act out because of bad parents. Boys act out because of bad fathers, and girls act out because of bad mothers."

"Or bad teachers," Elisabeth said, so instantaneously that she couldn't give it a second thought before speaking. The heat in her cheeks wasn't just from embarrassment. A knot of defiance was swelling inside her.

"Excuse me?"

"What did you miss?"

"Mrs. Pfautz—"

"Wait a moment," Elisabeth said. "You've interrupted me quite a bit, so now it's time for me to talk. And first of all, I'll say again that I'm sorry for this."

"I'm not sure if you said it a first time."

"Well, in any case, I am," Elisabeth said, "but I'm not going to sit here in silence while you berate me."

"I don't know why you're being so difficult, but it's definitely not—"

"I'll tell you why I'm being difficult," Elisabeth said, folding her arms in her lap. She was a picture of placidity, but her heart was pounding and her eyes could hardly see straight. "You called me here this afternoon because my daughter did something reckless," Elisabeth said, "something dangerous, even. And obviously, you're right: There's no excuse for it, and there's certainly no excuse for what Margaret said to you and did to you. And, once again, I'm terribly sorry for everything that happened. But beyond that, I'm not exactly sure why you've called me here today. That's why I'm being difficult. I'm not sure how this is being productive. You're venting, I suppose, and I admit you can't be blamed for that, but if venting is all this boils down to, then I'd like to be on my way."

"Venting? Have you listened to a word I've said?"

"I've listened to them all."

"Your daughter," Curry told her, speaking forcefully now, "played hooky on an army airfield in the dead of winter and then did everything short of spitting in her teacher's face. You say I'm berating you, Mrs. Pfautz, but all I'm trying to do is help you. I'm trying to help you rein in this daughter of yours."

"I believe I'm in control of that. Thank you."

"Clearly, you are not."

"You have your job, and I have mine," Elisabeth said, though she didn't mean to quote John, not at first anyhow. "Let me do my job," she said, "and I'll let you do yours. How does that sound? Does that sound fair?"

"And what is my job?" Curry said. "Getting called a 'stinking bitch'?"

"Taking care of your students," Elisabeth said. "From one teacher to another, I can tell you that the problem isn't always at home."

Did she mean this? Did she believe it? To some extent, yes, though admittedly Elisabeth wasn't sure what exactly she thought, not right now. Her jaw ached. Her neck was burning. She wanted only to put an end to this meeting, to stand up and leave without so much as glancing behind her. *This is something you should handle,* John had told her, and for better or worse, that was what she was doing. Elisabeth stood, and Catherine Curry looked up at her, pale with fury.

"One more time," Curry said, and she raised a solitary finger. "If she acts out like this just one more time, she's not welcome back in this school. I don't have all the sway in these things, but I have enough."

"She won't," Elisabeth said, turning for the door, so dizzy with blood rushing to her head that her steps almost staggered.

Margaret was now sitting outside of an office at the end of the hallway. She was staring down at her shoes, but as Elisabeth swiftly approached, Margaret raised her head.

"Mama," she began, but Elisabeth caught her cheek before she could say anything more. She slapped her—not hard, but hard enough. Margaret froze.

"What in the hell is wrong with you?" Elisabeth said, and she grabbed her daughter by the wrist and started walking again.

CHAPTER 30

W hat followed was easily one of the worst nights of Elisabeth's
recent life. First, there was Margaret. Every trace of the quiet
intellectual had vanished, and the person who had replaced her was an
infuriated little hellion who Elisabeth could scarcely have imagined. After they left the school, not a minute passed before they were at each
other's throats.

"And where in the world did you think you were going?" Elisabeth
said. "What were you doing at the airfield?"

"I was trying to leave."

"To leave?" Elisabeth shifted her eyes between her daughter and the
road. They were driving home in their battered blue Plymouth, a secondhand sedan from Elmer's Oil. "To leave where? To *go* where?"

"To go anywhere," Margaret shouted. "I hate Alaska, I hate this city,
I hate this place, and I especially hate you."

Elisabeth slammed on the brakes then, skidding to the side of the
road. They were on the edge of their neighborhood, and the snow-lined
street glowed in the dusk. "I don't care what you hate or who you hate,"
Elisabeth said. "You *don't* leave school, and you *don't* do what you did

today." She leaned closer to Margaret. "And what exactly were you going to do, board an aircraft bomber on its way to Tokyo? Did you think about this, Margaret? Did you think for one second?"

Margaret glowered at her. "I didn't know what I was doing, and I didn't care. Anything would be better than staying here. Anything would be better than staying with you."

"You'd better watch it," Elisabeth said, and she did her best to sound intimidating, though the part of the intimidating mother was starkly unfamiliar to her.

"Or what?" Margaret said. "You'll slap me again?"

And that meant she had to do it—Elisabeth slapped her, hard this time, and she didn't even regret it. "You're acting like a brat," she said.

"You're acting like a bitch!" Margaret shouted, and in a flash she was out the door and running down the street as if her life depended on it. Elisabeth caught up with her a moment later, and then they were tussling with each other like two children fighting in a schoolyard.

It went on and on. They were squaring off in the living room. They were squaring off in Margaret's bedroom. But wherever they were and whatever was said, it all came down to the same few things: Margaret hated Alaska. She hated Fairbanks. She hated the winter. She wanted to leave. To leave for where was never said in any concrete terms. She simply wanted to *leave*, as though that word was a destination in itself.

"You don't get it," she shouted. "My plan wasn't any plan at all. *That* was the point. *That* was the plan."

Elisabeth's blood went cold when she heard those words put together. *The plan.* She couldn't deny it: She felt like she was trapped in a shouting match with Jacqueline. She felt like she was a child again, like she was back in her father's workshop, weathering her sister's scowl. How had this happened? *When* had this happened? As she stared her daughter down, stunned into temporary silence, Elisabeth felt as if she was looking at someone new, not her daughter but her niece—her sister's haunted legacy.

Then John came home, and the night was a new kind of terrible.

Since their phone call earlier that day, he had heard about Margaret's escapade—of course he had; the entire school was probably talking about it—and Elisabeth could tell right away from his early arrival home that this would be a night they'd all remember for the rest of their lives. Margaret surely knew it, too. However quick she had been to fight back in the car, she was even quicker to surrender to John. For ten minutes Elisabeth sat out back in the work shed, though she could hear it all clear enough: Margaret crying, Margaret shrieking, the steady thwack of the belt—steady but not entirely rhythmic, because who could beat a child for ten minutes straight with any kind of even tempo?

"Fretsaw," Elisabeth whispered, closing her eyes, "backsaw, bucksaw," but the longer she tried to distract herself, the more clearly she heard her daughter's cries.

She spent the night on the couch, braced for an escape attempt that never came. She didn't sleep, and by the morning her nerves were like glass. She felt as if she might literally fall to pieces, as if she might crumble into a cloud of twinkling dust at any moment. John and Margaret awoke, dressed, and left for school without eating breakfast. No one spoke. They slipped on their boots and coats and scarves, and then they were gone without saying good-bye, and the house was quiet, and Elisabeth traded the couch for the kitchen table. She made herself a cup of coffee but didn't drink a single sip.

Of course, this was all her fault. *It doesn't take a genius,* Curry had said, and even though it had incensed her at the time, Elisabeth agreed with her now. Since moving to Fairbanks, she hadn't altogether neglected Margaret, but perhaps the diversion of her attention—and, admittedly, her heart—had been enough to set Margaret off. Surely, that was it. Curry was right. Whose fault could it otherwise be?

Flagging attention. Flagging support. Flagging love. That was what had done it. That, and Margaret getting older. Each year of raising her had been more difficult than the last, and this year wasn't shaping up to be any exception. Raising children was strange like that: One year, you felt stretched to your limit, but a year after that you felt stretched even more, realizing only then what an easy life your past self had owned. There had been a time when Margaret seemed like an extension of Elisabeth's own body. She fed her when she was hungry. She changed her when she needed changing. She taught her when her mind was willing. And in all of these efforts, there was no discussion or debate. When it came to the day-to-day of living life, Elisabeth had reared Margaret unconsciously and without self-doubt. She simply did. She simply functioned.

But now she was lost. Never mind that Margaret was already pulling away from her intellectually. Never mind that she could no longer help with Margaret's mathematics, and never mind that Margaret could read a book three times as fast as she could and with far greater retention. She was lost in ways that went beyond the intellect. She didn't know how to help Margaret anymore, not as she once had.

But what really stung Elisabeth went even deeper than this. What stung her was bearing witness to Margaret not only growing up, but growing embittered. Inherent in childhood is a degree of enlightenment—everything is fascinating and new, and life is beautiful. Elisabeth could once make Margaret double over in laughter with the slightest effort. Hiding her face in her hands. Peeking out from a corner. Singing like Louis Armstrong.

But now Margaret was getting older, and each year of her life brought her closer to adulthood and all its diminished joy. Now, Margaret scoffed at her. Margaret scoffed at a lot of things, and she would for the rest of her life. Never again would she have such easy fascination with the world. Never again would she be as elementally happy as she was when she was a child. What stung Elisabeth was the realization that Margaret would never know herself as she once had, because what is adulthood if not year upon year of putting up walls, of distancing yourself from your very own being? And that was awful to witness in the life of your child. Awful, but inevitable.

Really, what could she do? Plaster up the windows in Margaret's room? Fasten all the doors with dead bolts? Escort Margaret to and from school, the dining room, the bathroom? If she fought back, that would make matters worse. And if she did nothing? That would let it happen. Margaret was stronger and smarter—yes, smarter, admit it— than she was. If Margaret wanted to run away, she wouldn't fail a second time. She would succeed, at least to some extent, and Elisabeth had no wish to discover what extent that would be.

How, then, could she fix this? How could she stop it from happening? Simple: She had to do better. She had to be a better mother, a better woman, a better person. *Do your job. Be the parent you're supposed to be.* She had to be friends with her daughter again, but did Margaret want to be her friend? She didn't know anymore.

The phone was ringing. The noise of it came to Elisabeth like life intruding on a dream, and at first she heard the ringing but somehow wasn't fully aware of it. Then she was—*Oh, the phone; that's what that is*—and in a moment more she was holding the receiver against her ear, blinking sleepily.

"Yes. Hello?"

A voice came stiff and secretarial. "Hold, please."

And then something she hadn't expected in the least: a familiar voice, gentle and fluid. Sharp consonants. Breathy vowels.

"Do you still want to know what I want?"

She was silent. What felt like entire minutes passed.

"The third gift," Alfred said. "Our final exchange. Do you still want to know what I want?"

She tried to speak, but her throat was dry. She swallowed. She steadied herself. "That all depends."

"On what?"

"On whether or not I can trust you."

"We've already been through this, haven't we?"

"We have," Elisabeth said, "but then you tried to kill me."

A long sigh. Weariness. Somehow, she could tell that he was hanging his head. In shame? In frustration? In irritation?

"I'm sorry," Alfred said. "I can't excuse what I did that afternoon, but you should know that I'm sorry."

"*Sorry* doesn't mean that I can trust you. *Sorry* doesn't mean that you won't do it again, or that you won't succeed the next time."

"I won't do it again."

"Why did you do it the first time?"

"I lost control. I was angry. I felt betrayed. I felt very hurt by you."

"And what if I hurt you again?"

"I still won't do what I did. I swear on my—"

"Don't swear on anything," Elisabeth said. "It means nothing to me."

She closed her eyes, rubbed one thumb against her forehead. Then she reached for a pack of cigarettes in the drawer of the telephone table. Viceroys. Filter tips. John's cigarettes. They were better for your teeth, John claimed, and teeth were something that John had always felt self-conscious about, so Elisabeth felt inclined to believe him. She lit one, but mostly she just held it in her hand, twists of smoke curling through the air. She hoped it might relax her, and it did. There was something contemplative about watching smoke. Something in the way it moved. So easily. So sure of itself.

"Why are you calling me now?" she said. "I've been trying to reach you for months, and you've stonewalled me. Why the sudden change?"

"Because this is not a rash decision. That's why you can trust me, and that's why you can feel safe: because this is something I've thought a lot about, and calling you now is not something I've taken lightly. I considered reaching out right away. I considered apologizing that very day. But I needed to think things through, and now I have. I'm more certain than I've ever been before: I need you, Elisabeth, and you need me. I'm not the only one."

"What does that mean?"

"Your sister. Jacqueline needs you, too. She needs *us*. Let's finish this."

Now she smoked. She took a long drag and held it in, letting it pinch at her lungs. She leaned her head against the wall.

"What is it you want?"

"Come to the prison and talk with me."

"That's what you want? That's the third gift?"

"No," Alfred said, "but I'll tell you what I want if you come to the prison."

"Tell me over the phone."

"I'll tell you in person."

"But why in the world should I see you in person?" Elisabeth said. She pulled on the cigarette again. "You tried to murder me. You tried—"

"If it's your safety you're worried about, we can take certain measures to help you feel at ease."

"Certain measures."

"A guard can watch us. How would you feel about that?"

"You're missing the point."

"And you," Alfred said, "are being coy. You *want* to visit me, Elisabeth. You want to know the third thing. You're playing hard to get."

And that was true, or close to the truth. She was testing him. Feeling him out. But she did want to move forward. Despite it all, she truly did. There was a night not long ago when she had lain awake in bed and contemplated her recklessness in corresponding with Alfred. The man had tried to kill her, and yet she still pursued him, and she knew that their relationship wasn't over. There was something suicidal about her behavior, about her willingness to carry on with Alfred, not only in the way that she toyed with her own destruction but also in the compulsion that drove her to do so. She couldn't quit, no matter the risk. She was sick. Deranged. But in acknowledging her sickness she had come to accept it and, perhaps, to embrace it. Alfred was right: She wanted to visit him. In a way, there was nothing she wanted more.

"And this third thing," she said, "what happens if I decline? Let's say I don't want to give you what you want."

"Then you don't have to give it. You can turn and walk away."

"And you'll shrug it off? You won't care in the least?"

"Of course I'll care, but your decisions are your own."

"You're not answering the heart of what I'm asking you."

"Then ask it more directly."

She sucked on the cigarette. Smoke stung her eyes. "If I say no to whatever it is you want, will you kill me?"

A pause. Contemplation as thick as the smoke hanging in the air.

"No," Alfred told her, "but you'll never see your sister again," and he hung up the phone.

CHAPTER 31

She stood, crossed the room, and lay down on the floor. And she lay there for a long while, smoking cigarettes and thinking. The radio played idly, and slowly Elisabeth came to listen to it. A familiar song was playing—Cliff Edwards' "I'll See You in My Dreams."

> *Lonely days are long.*
> *Twilight sings a song*
> *Of the happiness that used to be.*
> *Soon my eyes will close.*
> *And I'll find repose.*
> *And in dreams you're always near to me.*

"I love you, Else. You know that, don't you?"

She was hearing John's voice, and then she was hearing her own, watching her younger self nod in sleepy contentment.

"Yes," she said. "I know that. And I love you, too."

March 1930. A few months before their marriage. A year and a half before Margaret was born. She and John were seated beside each other on the tumbledown love seat that he and his roommate owned. A record was playing. Cliff Edwards. The very same song.

I'll see you in my dreams.
Hold you in my dreams.
Someone took you out of my arms.
Still I feel the thrill of your charms.

And she really had loved him. He was funny, sweet, sympathetic. He was kind to his mother. He was happy around children. When he smiled, his ears wiggled and rose, a thing she found deeply endearing. And God, was he smart. Not counting English, John spoke three languages—German, French, and Italian—and he was working on a fourth, Mandarin, of all things. He wanted to express himself, he had told her, and it took more than one language for him to feel adequately expressive. He wrote poetry back then—of course he did—and she was a sucker for it.

But that night another man was showing himself. Not some diffident poet but a man more presumptuous. They kissed. Her hand was on his knee. They kissed and kissed.

"Touch it," he said, their lips finally parting. He took her hand, shifted it from his knee to his lap. "Feel me, Else. Touch it."

"Touch it," Jacqueline told her. They were lying together in Jacqueline's bed, and their pajama bottoms were pulled down around their thighs. It was summer 1920, a year before she disappeared. "Touch me," Jacqueline said, and she took Elisabeth's hand and moved it to her wanting. "It's all right. We're the same. We're twins." Jacqueline closed her eyes. "It feels nice."

Yes, it did. It felt like nothing Elisabeth had experienced until then and nothing she had experienced since. To this day, she didn't regret it. She felt no shame. After all, they were only children, but there was also truth in what Jacqueline had told her. Their bodies felt different, but not much different. They were the same, and for that reason Elisabeth had not been afraid to do what she had done, and she wasn't afraid to think of it now.

"Am I afraid of it?" Mack said. "No, not in the least."

They were sitting on either side of Mack's table, the stove pulsing warmth beside them. Margaret was sleeping in an armchair across the room. She and Elisabeth had visited Mack to have dinner and learn about machinery. Gears. Mechanisms. The movement of many-jointed parts. But now Elisabeth and Mack were speaking in whispers, and they were talking about death.

"Why should I be afraid of it?" Mack said, smiling faintly.

They were drinking whisky. The Athabaskans in Tanacross drank—that was no secret—but they did it almost exclusively in private. Mack and Elisabeth were like family, and the whisky they shared that night was an unspoken but unmistakable indication of this. Elisabeth tossed the last of hers back, wincing a little. It was December, but the whisky and the stove made her feel as warm as if it were the midst of summer.

"What if you go to hell?" Elisabeth said, grinning. "What if God smites you because of your wicked ways?" She tapped her empty glass. "Your indulgences?"

"If hell's full of whisky drinkers," Mack said, "it'll be a fine place indeed."

And then, perfectly naturally, he reached across the table and took her hand. She didn't balk at it. His hand was thick and warm, a hand brailled with calluses that belied the gentleness of its grip and the tenderness of his intent. Elisabeth smiled, and she held him, and she felt more at peace in that moment than she had in many years. But her cheeks did flush. She bowed her head.

"And what about you?" Mack said. "You afraid of dying?"

"No," Elisabeth told him. She thought for a little bit. "I'm scared of what it might feel like. I'm scared of it like I was scared of childbirth. But in itself?" She looked up at him now. "No, I guess I'm not."

"Why not?"

She shrugged. Smiled mischievously. "Well, hopefully," she said, "you'll be dead long before me, so at least I'll have you waiting for me in the afterlife."

"With open arms," Mack said, and he winked, lifting his glass with his free hand.

She should have kissed him then. It was what she had wanted to do, and there was no doubt in her mind that Mack would have kissed her back. But she didn't. She wasn't brave enough. And as she came back to the present, the air thick with fetid cigarette smoke, she heard Cliff Edwards still crooning through her living room.

Lips that once were mine.
Tender eyes that shine.
They will light my way tonight.
I'll see you in my dreams.

Her eyes stung with tears, and it seemed to her then—as it had many times before—that her whole life was a series of lost loves. Maybe that was everyone's life. Love was often like that: the wrong moments embraced, the right moments rebuffed or all too fleeting. Yet there was nothing she could do but keep going, keep striving, and convince herself that she wouldn't let another opportunity pass her by.

"Just keep running," Elisabeth whispered, if only to hear her own voice. She stared up at the ceiling. "Just keep running." And then she pushed herself up.

That afternoon, the prison's visitation room was positively frigid. It had been drafty before, but now the air seemed to pass through the walls as if they were sieves, and the sweet smell of winter hung wetly in Elisabeth's nose. She kept her parka on, and she held her hands firmly in her pockets.

The wait was even longer than before; thirty minutes passed without explanation. She would have been warmer had she stood up and paced, but she preferred sitting down. She felt safer that way—impervious as a rock in her sedentariness. Elisabeth sat there, and she studied the names and initials and dates that scored every inch of the table in front of her. She hadn't paid the etchings much mind before, but now she lost herself in them, following their bends and curves as if studying a vast, meandering maze—trying to find her way out. Near the center of the table, someone had carved *Relax: You'll be dead soon.* Somehow, it made her smile.

"What's funny?"

She looked up. Alfred was standing in the open doorway. Behind him, a guard nodded at Elisabeth—the same mouse of a man who had taken Alfred to dinner months before—and then he left the room, shutting the door behind him, closing them in. Elisabeth didn't move. Alfred walked forward.

"You were smiling a moment ago," he said. "Tell me what's funny." And then, so stiff that it sounded slightly sweet, "I'd like to smile, too."

"Relax," Elisabeth said. "You'll be dead soon."

Alfred recoiled. "What?"

"It's carved into the table." She let herself glance away from him for a second, pointing with her eyes at the carving.

Alfred walked to the other side of the table, scanning its runes as he went. Then he saw it—she could tell from the way that his eyes settled and focused—but he didn't smile. He gave a little shrug.

"Well, I guess that's true," he said. He pulled out a chair and sat down. "Not especially amusing, but true."

They were silent. They watched each other. Then Elisabeth raised her chin. "Are you afraid of dying?"

Alfred considered the question for a few seconds, and then he answered firmly, "Yes."

She hadn't expected that. "Why?"

"Because I don't believe in God, and I don't believe in the afterlife. This is all we've got"—he held up his arms—"and for that reason I'm afraid to lose it."

"That's exactly why I'm not afraid to lose it," Elisabeth said. "If there's nothing after this life, why be afraid? You won't know you've lost it at all."

"That's true," Alfred said. "I'm not suggesting it's rational. It's instinctive. It's just how I feel."

"So, in the war, when you woke up in the wreckage, you were afraid of dying?"

"Of course," Alfred said. "I woke up crying, I was so scared."

"I can't imagine you crying."

"I don't do it very often. I'm like you."

Elisabeth stared him down. "How do you mean?"

"Well, you don't cry very much, do you?"

"No."

"And when you do cry, you cry alone, in all but the most extreme circumstances. Because being alone is the only time you feel comfortable enough to do it. Isn't that right?"

"I suppose it is," and she couldn't help but feel impressed by the accuracy of his assumption—impressed, and vaguely unsettled.

Now Alfred crossed one leg over the other, leaning back, getting comfortable. "Why do you think that is?" he said. "Why do you hold back when you're around other people?"

Because it feels too intimate, she could have told him, *more intimate than anything, even sex, and I have no one I feel intimate with,* but she bit her tongue.

"It's just something I never did much growing up," she said. "We were taught to keep a stiff upper lip. My family wasn't very emotional."

"Your father, you mean. Your mother—she died when you were very young, correct?"

"How did you know that?"

"Lititz is a small town," Alfred said, "and you were something of a celebrity, weren't you?"

That she was, and in the worst way possible. As a child, she had been the town's sob story. The little girl for whom tragedy never ended. First, her mother, when she and Jacqueline were only four years old. Cancer of the chest. Two beautiful girls left behind by the most important person in their lives. Imagine the heartbreak. The outpouring of sympathies.

Elisabeth didn't recall much from that year, but she remembered the food. The town must have fed them for a year straight, because who wouldn't want to feed this stricken family? This man and his two darling daughters. Motherless. Abandoned.

And it didn't end there. Six years later, Jacqueline disappeared, and dear God, what attention that had brought. Newspaper articles. Reports on the radio. Every telephone pole in Lititz plastered with pictures of Jacqueline's face, and with that Elisabeth's face, too. For years, people would see her in town and report the sighting to the police, believing she was her sister. The agony of losing Jacqueline was endless, and the food was, too. A continuous parade of optimists and well-wishers came to the door, and this time Elisabeth remembered their gifts vividly—sauerbraten and schnitzels and tray upon tray of dessert. To this day, she hated shoofly pie, not for how much of it she ate but for how ubiquitous it had been in her kitchen, and how little she had desired to taste it.

Then, the final coffin nail: Just three years after Jacqueline, she lost her father to the bottle. Viral hepatitis, ostensibly, but she and everyone else in town knew the truth of what caused his body to fail him. And they knew the sad reality of Elisabeth's young life: Her whole family was dead and gone by the time she was fourteen years old. At that point, the well-wishers only shook their heads from afar, but Elisabeth still saw the pity in their eyes, and she suffered through their fortified, reassuring smiles. *Quiet: Here comes the Metzger girl. You know about her, don't you?* Yes, Lititz was a small town, and for a time she had been the most pitied girl in Lancaster County.

"You could say that," Elisabeth told Alfred. "There were certainly many people who felt sorry for me."

"And how did that make you feel? Did the attention comfort you?"

"No. I hated the attention."

"Why?"

"Because I hated people feeling sorry for me."

"But why?"

She thought about that. "I suppose—" she said, still working through it. "I suppose because pity seems presumptuous to me."

"How so?"

"People didn't trust that I could manage my grief on my own. It felt like they thought I needed their help, as if their feeling sorry for me would help me cope." She reached out, traced one finger along a pair of initials. *L. W.* "It didn't. Being pitied made me feel worse. I felt patronized."

Alfred nodded. "I understand completely. And I'd add one other thing about pity: It's self-centered. *Pity* is the kind way of phrasing what those people felt for you, but the truth of what they felt was envy."

"Envy?"

Another nod, slow and thoughtful. "We claim to pity people like you—people, especially children, whose lives are filled with tragedy—but deep inside we're also envious. Tragedy is a spectacle, isn't it? It draws attention to the victim, and all humans desire attention and envy those who have it." He turned his head and looked up at the window. "I'm speaking from experience, of course."

"Your brother."

"That's right."

"What was his name?"

The briefest pause. "Heinrich."

"And you say he died when you were six years old?"

"Correct."

"Must have been hard," Elisabeth said, sucking at her teeth, "but I bet you got a lot of free food out of it, at least."

Alfred laughed, and the echoing boisterousness of it was enough to make Elisabeth smile.

"From our neighbors, you mean?" Alfred said. "Yes, that's true. They had to do something for us, so they cooked and cooked." He was still chuckling. "I was fat for years thanks to my dead brother."

"I never ate a bite of anything anyone gave us."

"What a missed opportunity," Alfred said. "The people of Lititz know their way around a kitchen. That reminds me." He angled to the side now, reaching for a pocket, and then he set a folded piece of paper on the table. "I have something for you."

"Is this about my sister?" Elisabeth said. "Or our—"

"Can we just relax for a minute longer?" Alfred asked. "Can we be friends again, just for a little while?"

We were never friends. But again she bit her tongue, not only to avoid confrontation, but also because she wanted to see what Alfred was giving her. She couldn't resist.

"It's a gift for you," Alfred said. "It's not *the* gift. This is outside of our exchange. But it's something I wanted to give you." He tapped it two quick times. *Tup. Tup.* "Open it."

She expected half a dozen different things. Another letter. A threat. An impassioned love note. A single cryptic word designed to peck at her. But as Elisabeth unfolded the paper, she saw that Alfred had offered her a drawing: jumbled lines of dark ink that stared through the backside of the paper like a thousand inverted shadows. With each fold she undid, the picture came more into order, and soon she was looking at an illustration of downtown Lititz, Pennsylvania.

It was like a photograph. The fork of Main Street, the row of brick homes on the corner of Broad Street, the molded columns of Lititz Springs Bank, everything rendered in perfect detail. Elisabeth couldn't help but smile.

"You drew this?"

Alfred nodded, not proudly, but not entirely modestly either.

"I didn't know you could draw like this."

"Why would you?"

"Well," Elisabeth said, "still. It's surprising. That's all." She stared at the illustration. Even the leaves in the trees were finely detailed, each with its own network of veins, lines so thin that they were nearly invisible. The streets were free of people, but somehow Lititz looked thriving and full of life. "It's wonderful," Elisabeth said, and it was.

"Thank you."

They were quiet.

"How long did this take?"

"It took a good bit," Alfred said, squirming in his chair, "but time is something I have, needless to say."

"Well, it really is quite good. I could never do something like this."

"Why not?"

"Because I just couldn't. Drawing has never been one of my strong suits. You saw my self-portrait."

"I love your self-portrait. I have it hanging in my cell. It's across from my bed. I admire it every day."

She laughed. "What's to admire?"

"The expression of it. Your composition."

"It's nothing," Elisabeth said, and she looked again at Alfred's picture. "This—*this*—is really something. This is out of my range."

Alfred was leaning sideways, reaching for a back pocket. He pulled out a second piece of folded paper. "Do you have a pencil?"

"No," Elisabeth said.

His face went blank. "You don't carry a pencil with you? Not even a pen?"

"No, I meant I'm not going to draw anything, if that's what you're hoping for."

"It is."

"Well, I'm not."

"Come on," Alfred said, wriggling his fingers like a blackjack player asking for another hit. "Get your pencil," and when she didn't immediately reach for her purse, his head fell to one side and his lips went flat. "Loosen up, Elisabeth. For God's sake."

Rolling her eyes, she had her pencil a moment later.

"Give it to me," Alfred said, and she did. He unfolded the paper and turned it over—she caught only a glimpse of an incomplete illustration, the outline of a fountain—and then Alfred was sketching hurriedly on the paper's blank side. He bent so close to the table that his nose nearly touched the paper. "I mentioned Kohler's Haus when we spoke some time ago," he said. "Do you remember it? A little restaurant and pub in Lititz. A man named—"

"I know Kohler's Haus, yes."

"Good." His hand jumped around the page. "And how well do you recall it? The building, I mean. I know it closed some time ago, but the building is still there. Can you picture it?"

"Of course," Elisabeth said, "and this is all very cute—"

"—But nothing," Alfred said, and now he pushed the piece of paper across the table. He had drawn a rough sketch of Kohler's Haus, complete with the sidewalk and the ghostly outline of a stoop but little more than that. "Fill in the blanks," he said.

"There are a lot of blanks."

"Yes, but I can't do everything for you."

Elisabeth reached for the pencil, but then she paused. "I really am terrible at this."

"Then you'll draw something terrible," Alfred said. "I'd still like to see it." Leaning forward, he swept his hand around the page. "Give it windows, a doorway, a sign, bricks, trees, whatever else you remember."

"I'm not sure I remember it in that kind of detail."

"Then make it up," Alfred said. "That's all this is—just making things up, filling in the blanks. Accuracy is beside the point."

So she started to draw. In the interest of speed and her own fragile ego, she tried to keep it simple, mimicking Alfred's rough lines as closely as she could. Above the door she sketched a sign—a wooden slab that had hung by ropes from two wrought-iron posts—and then she started outlining the windows.

"I think there was a little window above the sign," she said, "like, a decorative window, but I really can't remember." She looked up at Alfred. "Was there?"

"It doesn't matter. If you remember it, then draw it."

"But I don't remember it. That's my point."

"Then *don't* draw the window," Alfred said. "For goodness' sake, Elisabeth, just put something down, would you?"

They sat in silence for ten minutes, Elisabeth working all the while. She was hesitant at first—hesitant and sharply aware of Alfred watching her—but soon her heart was beating slower and she made herself focus. The pencil scratched against the page and her hand moved with a life of its own, the life of many distant years, the life of memory and hazy recollection. And when she finally finished, or when she had done enough to feel justified in giving up, the place that she had drawn wasn't exactly Kohler's Haus but it wasn't something else either. It was a place part new, part old, part truth, part fantasy. Like a dream.

"Not bad," Alfred said, staring down at the drawing. He turned it toward himself, studying it for a second longer. "You could have done worse."

"Gosh, *thank you*," Elisabeth said. "That's about the nicest thing anyone's ever told me."

Alfred frowned. "What would you like me to say?"

"I'm only kidding," Elisabeth said. "I know it's not very good. I told you it wouldn't be good."

"No, no," Alfred said, "it is good. I only meant that you could have done better with your choices."

"What choices?"

"The things you made up. The blanks you filled in. You let yourself go for a little while, but you could have done more." He studied it again, and now he smiled—warmly, the smile of a sympathetic teacher. "But it is good, Elisabeth. Honestly, it is." He slid it back to her. "I hope you finish it."

And although she knew that she wouldn't, Elisabeth told him, staring down like a child, "Maybe I will."

She folded the incomplete illustration, and she did the same with Alfred's picture of Lititz, slipping both of them and the pencil into her purse. Then she gathered herself, and she tried to sound as official as she could.

"Now we need to talk," she said. "You called me here to talk about my sister, and the last part of our exchange."

"Yes," Alfred said, "absolutely"—and he pushed his chair back and stood—"but would you mind if we talked outside? In the courtyard, I mean."

He didn't wait for her approval. He crossed the room and called for the guard through the barred window in the door. The guard and Alfred exchanged a few words, and a moment later the Mouse was unlocking the courtyard's sliding door—a wall-sized flank of metal that opened from the bottom to the top like a mechanic's garage.

"Just ten more minutes," the Mouse told them. "You've already gone a little long," and he left them again.

The courtyard wasn't much to look at: thirty by thirty feet of plain snow. No trees, no bushes, no frills of any kind. Wreathed in rusting barbed wire, twenty-foot concrete walls enclosed the space. In the corners and along the top, the concrete was crumbling to pieces like dry bread. The courtyard was reasonably well shoveled, though only a foot of snow was piled against the walls. There should have been more.

"What did they do with the rest of it?" Elisabeth asked, pointing with her chin. They were walking side by side in an uneven circle.

"The rest of what?"

"The snow. Where do they pile it?"

"Oh, they have us haul it away," Alfred said. "They trade work for time outside." In lieu of a coat, the guard had given him a pair of tattered mittens and a wool blanket, which Alfred held tightly around his body. It was five degrees that afternoon, cold, but not as punishing as it could have been, especially here in the courtyard, where the walls blocked much of the wind. "On designated days," Alfred said, "two trash bins of snow gets you five minutes of free time out here. That's the going rate."

"That seems like a fair trade."

"Fair enough," Alfred said, "but I'm one of the few prisoners who ever takes them up on it. Most of the others seem content to stay indoors. I think for Alaskans, prison is a fine vacation. Free heat."

They walked another circuit in silence. It was snowing now, and Alfred's brown hair sparkled with flecks of wetness. He reminded her of someone then, but she couldn't quite place it. Her uncle? Her father?

"So," Alfred said, "our exchange. We'll talk that through, but first we must discuss another matter."

"Which is?"

"Trust."

"You already made your pitch on the phone—"

"No, no," Alfred said. "I'm not talking about why you should trust me. I'm talking about why *I* should trust *you*. That's what this exchange is all about, but after you involved the police, I don't know if I can trust you again. You have to earn my trust again, just as I have to earn—"

"What is it you want?" Elisabeth said, unafraid to show her annoyance. "I'm tired of speaking in these grandiose statements. Just tell me, plainly. What do you want?"

In two quick steps, Alfred was in front of her. But he didn't reach for her. He only stood there. His hands still clutched his blanket, and his eyes shined as wild and electric as they had in Tanacross those many months ago. *Someone was knocking. Someone was absolutely pounding.*

"I want Margaret to visit me," Alfred said. "Alone."

"Margaret?"

He nodded. "Your daughter, Margaret."

"Why?"

"I won't tell you," Alfred said. "That's between me and Margaret."

The snow was picking up. It nipped at her eyes, stung her cheeks and chin. "You have to tell me what you're—"

"I won't explain why," Alfred said. "That's part of the exchange. We're establishing trust again, and you have to trust me. Margaret," he said again, stepping closer now. "I want Margaret to visit me here, alone."

"I don't think I can do that."

"Why?"

"Because it's asking too much."

"Why?"

"Because I don't—"

"Because you don't trust me," Alfred said, "but you *will*. You'll see. I'll *make* you see."

"That doesn't sound very reassuring."

"If I sound brusque, forgive me. But this is what I want. It's very simple: Margaret, here, alone. Twenty minutes. That's all. You can wait for us in the lobby down the hall from the visitation room."

"Down the hall and on the other side of a locked door."

"That's right," Alfred said.

"And will a guard—"

"No guards. No you. Just me and her. Twenty minutes. Trust me," and as he said that, the faintest quiver of a smile dashed across his face. "No harm will come to your daughter."

She turned away from him and paced through the gathering snow. *We're establishing trust again,* but the plainness of that trivialized the true stakes at hand. Whoever had taken her sister was a swindler, and a slaver, and a monster. And for all Elisabeth knew, that person was Alfred. At the least, he was a killer. At the most, he was something much worse.

She could never do it. She couldn't implicate her daughter. Shutting herself inside this place with Alfred was one thing. Shutting Margaret away was another.

And yet, and yet. She had to ask. She had to know.

"What's your end of the bargain?"

"I'll lead you to Jacqueline in the flesh and blood."

"No more abstractions," she said, facing him again, "not even that much. My sister, Jacqueline Metzger: She's alive and well?"

"Alive and well."

She stepped forward. "And the man. A German. Your age. Tell me more about him, and how you know him."

"After Margaret visits me."

She steeled herself. "You know, sometimes I very seriously doubt this altogether."

"Doubt what?"

"This story you're spinning," Elisabeth said. "Do you know what a reasonable person might think?" The handwriting. The medals. The little bird. *He's handsome,* her sister had told her once. "A reasonable person might think that you're the one who took Jacqueline."

"I did not take your sister. On my honor, I swear it."

"I told you that means nothing to me."

"And I'm sorry to hear that. But it doesn't change the fact: I did not take your sister, Elisabeth. I did not."

"But you know the person who did," Elisabeth said.

"Yes."

"And what is your relationship with him? Are you related to him?"

He was shaking his head. "No more of this," Alfred told her, "not before I meet with Margaret. I can't tell you any more about how I know what I know."

"Then what can you tell me?"

"That your sister is alive and well."

"And this man," Elisabeth said, "she's free of him now?"

"Not exactly. I told you that she's not *captive* anymore."

"Meaning?"

"Meaning that her situation has changed," Alfred said, watching her fixedly. "Your sister is living with this man as his wife. She's still a captive, so to speak, but not like she used to be."

"And this man, you know where he lives?"

"Yes."

"But why hasn't Jacqueline contacted me? Why hasn't she contacted anyone for help?"

"I don't know exactly," Alfred said, "but soon you can ask her yourself." He glanced down at her waist. "Is something wrong with your arm?"

She was holding her right arm strangely: palm down, tight against her body, arched over her stomach. She used to stand that way when she was pregnant with Margaret, when she'd had a swelling belly to rest her arm on. Unconsciously, she had posed that way now, and only when Alfred pointed it out did Elisabeth realize it. She dropped her arm, brushed off his question.

"And what about your confession?" she said. "Are you going to re-scind it?"

"Let me deal with that. The confession is a minor detail now." He looked up, facing the falling snow straight on. "I dreamed of you last night," he said, "and I dreamed of Jacqueline, too. I saw the two of you together in a field—a huge, sweeping field—and you were holding hands, and you were together, and you were happy."

He looked at her, and then he walked forward. He let his blanket rest on his shoulders, and he took off his mittens, reaching for her. She didn't recoil. He took her hands, and his flesh felt soft and warm. Even through her gloves, she could feel his hands burning like flatirons in her own.

"I'm going to reunite you and your sister," he said. "You have my word, whether you want it or not. Your reunion is coming, Elisabeth, but first you've got to trust me." Gently, he squeezed her hands. "We're *Gleichgesinnte*, you and me. Kindred." He smiled. "We're the same. We're twins."

And with that the Mouse rattled open the door to the courtyard, and the visit was finished. She didn't agree to Alfred's exchange, but she didn't decline it either, not to Alfred, and not to herself.

"It was good to see you," Alfred said, looking back at her as he paced away. Then he smiled, and he lifted his chin, speaking over his shoulder. "Please tell Margaret I said hello."

CHAPTER 32

S he sat in the work shed for an hour that night. Drifting clouds had poured snow on Fairbanks all afternoon, but for now, the sky was clear and the moon shined with bright sterility. The yard was very quiet, and the space inside the work shed was quieter still.

Elisabeth was studying Alfred's illustration. It lay open on the pine table. Its creases were almost flattened from the cold or the damp or a combination of the two, but one stubborn ridge refused to lie flat. It stretched across the paper's middle, and the entire page sat up in the shape of a pyramid. Every few minutes Elisabeth would run her hand down the crease, but the fold reared up time and time again. Lititz, it seemed, was reaching for her.

She was thinking of something that had happened when she was a child. In the autumn of 1919, when she and Jacqueline were nine years old, her sister nearly died of influenza. The sickness started slowly, and at first their father hardly worried, but soon Jacqueline was battling a fever that refused to drop. She cried. She hallucinated. At times, she tore at her sheets with the bewildered mania of a trapped animal, slapped and scratched at her own face.

And all the while, Elisabeth stayed by her sister's bed. It seemed unfair that Jacqueline should have to suffer alone. It seemed that she, Elisabeth, should be sick as well, and in all the time she stayed with her sister, part of her hoped that she would come down with the sickness, too. But she never did.

"Miss Hunnefield is not a doctor," Elisabeth's father told her, "but she's like one. She's a nurse."

He couldn't afford a doctor, so their father had sent for this woman instead—a prim, older lady with gunmetal gray hair and a dimpled chin cavernous enough to swallow the tip of your pinkie. As she worked, she had an odd habit of ticking her tongue against her teeth, as if gentle chiding would scold her patients' diseases into healing. She fussed around Jacqueline for thirty minutes, and finally she tied a handkerchief tightly around Jacqueline's left arm.

"What are you doing?" Elisabeth's father asked, standing in the hallway outside of the bedroom. Elisabeth was seated on a stool beside the nightstand.

"I'm drawing blood," Miss Hunnefield told him.

"Why?"

"To purify her."

Elisabeth's father stepped into the room. "You're bloodletting?"

"Yes."

"Do doctors still do that?"

Miss Hunnefield stared up at him. "I'm not a doctor," she said. "And bloodletting is a vital part of the healing process. Your daughter's sickness resides in her blood. We must purify her, therefore, in part through a medication I'll provide, and in part through drawing blood. Drawing it, and then replacing it."

She reached into a handbag near her feet, and she placed a small wooden rack on the nightstand. It held four glass vials.

"I'll draw four tubes of blood, let your daughter rest for an hour, and then I'll return three tubes to her body," Miss Hunnefield explained. "Then you're to give her four of these a day for the next five days." She set a bottle of pills on the nightstand. *Spencer & Clayton Cure All*, the label read, and it featured a fantastical illustration of a man grappling with a snake. "Do you have any other questions before I begin?"

Her father did not, and Elisabeth watched Miss Hunnefield draw four vials of Jacqueline's blood, corking each tube when it was full. She set three of the vials in the rack, and the fourth she dropped into a wicker dustbin beneath the bed.

"We have to let her rest now," Miss Hunnefield said. "One hour, and by then the drawn blood will be distilled and free of the influenza. But, darling"—she turned to Elisabeth—"will you please stay here with her? Your breath will help clarify the air, all the more because you're sisters."

Yes, sisters. Of course her breath would help clarify the air, and of course she would stay. Elisabeth had even slept in the room the night before, curled up on the hardwood floor in a nest of blankets. She had no plans to leave Jacqueline. Not ever.

And as soon as her father and Miss Hunnefield left the room, Elisabeth crouched and reached for the dustbin beneath the bed. The vial was still faintly warm, like milk still fresh in a bucket, and for a moment Elisabeth simply held the tube, rolling it around in her palm. The blood moved strangely—not sloshing but shifting, sliding around inside the vial with slow, weighty listlessness. Finally, Elisabeth uncorked the tube, and without hesitation she tipped back her head and drank. How sweet it had tasted, even sweeter than she had imagined, like the glycerin of a cherry pie.

And at last, she came down with it. A few days later, the sickness hit her, and for a week she fought and sweated through it. Jacqueline was still recovering from her own, and their father pushed their beds together and let them sleep in the same room.

What bittersweet pleasure she had taken in that illness—what pleasure, and what pride. She could tell that Jacqueline took pleasure in her sickness, too. Not with spite or maliciousness; it simply felt right for them to suffer together, and to suffer for each other. To Elisabeth's mind, and to Jacqueline's as well, it was only natural. They were one and the same. Kindred, then and forever. If one of them suffered, both of them suffered.

"M ama?" Margaret said now, and the sound of her voice made Elisabeth open her eyes. With her elbow propped on the table, she had drifted into an uneasy sleep. Margaret was standing outside the open door of the work shed, dressed in her parka and boots.

"There's my girl," Elisabeth said, as though she had expected her all along. She extended one hand, and Margaret walked forward. They embraced, and the touch of Margaret's head against her breasts almost pulled Elisabeth back to sleep. Then Margaret spoke.

"I'm sorry I called you a name," she said. "I'm sorry I fought with you."

The episode at school and their subsequent fight seemed so long ago, but it was only yesterday. God, was it really? Time was moving so slowly these days, and yet so quickly.

"I'm sorry, too," Elisabeth said.

They were quiet for a while, and neither of them moved. With Margaret standing and Elisabeth on the stool, they held each other as if the full power of the cold had rushed inside the work shed and frozen them instantly in place. Elisabeth closed her eyes.

"I don't really hate you," Margaret said.

"I know."

"And I'm sorry I made Papa hit me."

Elisabeth nodded. "I know." A lump caught in her throat like the pit of a peach, but she forced herself to swallow, hoping that her voice would stay steady with what she had to say next. "You—" she began. "You're not going to run away from me, are you?"

And even though Margaret answered almost immediately, the air inside the work shed seemed to shudder, a force that Elisabeth felt in her bones.

"No," Margaret said, "I won't," and she pulled away. She stood facing her now, and there was something in Margaret's expression that re-minded Elisabeth of Alfred, a certain keenness in her lips, an intensity in her gaze. "What happened to Jacqueline?" she said.

Elisabeth watched her. "You know what happened," and that was true, though Margaret knew only the basics. The outline.

"She disappeared," Margaret said. "The whole town looked for her, but they couldn't find her."

Elisabeth nodded.

"But where did she go? Why did she run away, and why didn't she come back?"

I don't know, Elisabeth almost said, but she stopped herself. What *did* she know? Or rather, what did she believe? "She didn't come back," Elisabeth said, "because she wasn't able."

"What do you mean?"

"She didn't run away, exactly. She was taken."

"Who took her?"

She was only speaking to her daughter, and she was speaking of things—details, shading—that even she couldn't know for sure. And yet, Elisabeth felt in that moment that her words would be a commit-ment to something, as if whatever she spoke would be codified as the truth. And sure enough, when she finally spoke, that was what it felt like. The truth. The facts, and of all people, she had gotten those facts from a person who had nearly killed her.

"A man," Elisabeth said. "A man who tricked her into thinking he was her friend."

"What was his name?"

"I don't know."

"Why did he take her?"

Elisabeth swallowed. "Because he wanted to hurt her."

"You mean he wanted to rape her?"

She couldn't help but look away when Margaret said that. *Yes* was the answer. *Undoubtedly, yes,* but it wasn't the answer that crushed her. It was

Margaret's question, and the very fact that she had known to ask it. And yet, was she really surprised? Margaret was twelve years old, and in those years—somewhere, somehow—she had read, had heard, had come to know that word and all its meaning. She had gone through some terrible rite of passage. This horrifying life, it came for everyone. Elisabeth lifted her eyes, and she nodded, but Margaret didn't flinch.

"Did he kill her, too?" she said.

And again Elisabeth felt as if she was bringing the truth into being, and this time she answered even more quickly, and more firmly.

"No," she said. "She's alive."

"But where is she? Is she okay?"

"I don't know, but I'm trying to figure that out."

Margaret stepped closer. "You're looking for her." She glanced at the table. "That's what you've been doing all this time, right?"

"That's right. And I can find her if I keep looking. I'm certain I can."

"We can search for her together," Margaret said. She was working hard to restrain herself, but the trembling giddiness in her voice was unmistakable. "I can help you, Mama. We can be a team. We can solve the mystery."

But Elisabeth only shook her head. She was dealing with a madman. A murderer. Would she bet her life that he could help her? Yes, but would she bet Margaret's life, too?

She couldn't. There had to be another way. A compromise. Alfred was playing a game with her, and she had to devise a new set of rules. Elisabeth reached out, pulled her daughter close again. She held her tightly against her body, and she wished that she could cling to this child forever.

"No," Elisabeth said, closing her eyes. "This is something I have to do by myself," but again the air in the work shed seemed to shudder.

CHAPTER 33

Sacrifice. Suffering. And more specifically, suffering together. If what Alfred claimed was true, then she had failed her sister beyond measure. She didn't like imagining the awful things that Jacqueline must have endured, but like the intruding fantasies of Mack's murder, Elisabeth couldn't help herself. And as Jacqueline had suffered through her entire adolescence and adulthood, what had Elisabeth been doing? Going to school. Earning her associate's degree. Getting married. Raising Margaret. Living life with peacefulness and ease. The tranquility with which she had passed through life now felt like something to be ashamed of, but Elisabeth had every intention of evening the scales, however fractionally. In fact, she would start today.

"Where's Margaret?"

Alfred was standing just inside the door to the visitation room. Elisabeth was seated, but now she stood.

"She's not here. I didn't bring her with me."

"Then we can't—"

"Hear me out," Elisabeth said. "I brought something for you."

She held it out for him to take: a pearloid photo album as thick as a dictionary. It held hundreds of pictures, spanning Elisabeth's childhood through just last month. Alfred walked forward, and he took it. For a minute, in silence, he thumbed through the album, but his eyes stayed narrow with skepticism and displeasure.

"Is this supposed to be a substitute for what I requested?"

"No," Elisabeth said, "but I'm hoping it's a start."

She stepped closer to him, feeling light on her feet. She had been drinking. Before leaving the house that afternoon, she had drunk four glasses of Kentucky Tavern whisky, each of them diluted only with ice. As she tossed back the final glass, she realized that Kentucky Tavern had been the brand she once drank with Mack, and something far fiercer than the whisky burned inside her throat. But she made herself forget about that now.

"I want to talk about this," she said. "I want to work out a different exchange."

If he already sensed what she was getting at, Alfred didn't let on. He closed the album and set it down on the table.

"I made myself very clear."

"You did."

"There's no room for negotiating."

"We're just talking."

"There's nothing more to talk about."

"Please," Elisabeth said. Gingerly, like a girl taking the hand of her date at a dance, she reached for him. And Alfred didn't shy away. She pulled him to the row of chairs, and they sat. "There's got to be something else we can do."

"There's not. I've made this very simple for you. It's Margaret visiting me here, or it's nothing."

"I don't like the police any more than you do," Elisabeth said. "Believe me: I'm not going to talk to them about anything. Truly, that's the last thing I'd do. If this is really a matter of trust, you can trust me absolutely when it comes to the police."

But Alfred only shook his head. "Margaret," he repeated. "Margaret has to visit me."

"I can't tell Margaret what to do, not when it comes to a thing like this. Even if I agreed to this, it's not my decision to make. It should be hers."

"Then let her make the decision. She's not a child anymore. Tell her what's going on, and tell her what I asked for."

She brushed that off. "What more would you want?" She pushed the album toward him. "You can have that, and you can have anything else you want." *Anything.* "I'll give you a hundred more photographs of my-self. A thousand. I'll visit you every day, if you'd like that. I'll bring you food, alcohol, cigarettes, money, if it has any value here. Just tell me what you want, what *else* you want, and I'll give it to you."

And then he was on her. He lunged forward and kissed her, hard, and she kissed him back. Their teeth knocked together. They pushed and pulled. He tasted like rawhide, and his breath felt as hot and wet as steam from a kettle. His hand was in her hair, and when he tensed his fingers, he pulled at her scalp, and she couldn't deny that what she felt was more pleasure than pain. But just as quickly as Alfred had moved in, he moved away from her.

"This was what you planned," he said, still gripping her hair, "wasn't it?"

"Yes."

"This is what you're offering."

"Yes."

They were kissing again, and something even more than that—grappling awkwardly with each other, groping and pushing and heaving. Her chair slid sideways, and she almost toppled to the floor. Somehow, she stood, but he stayed on top of her, and together they stumbled across the room, Alfred pushing forward as she wheeled back, the two of them entangled all the while. She slammed against the room's farthest wall, the same that he had pinned her against when he throttled her, but today Elisabeth felt no fear or panic. She wanted this. She wanted to give him whatever he wished to take, if that would keep them going.

"You'll come here every day," Alfred said.

"Yes."

His left hand was clamped around her breast. His other troweled her hair.

"You'll give me anything I want."

"Anything you want."

They staggered to the corner of the room. His hips were against hers, and she could feel him pressing at her. They kissed. Deliriously, savagely, they kissed.

"You'll give me photographs. You'll give me drawings."

"Yes."

"And you'll give me anything else I ask for. As it suits me, on a whim."

"Yes."

And now his hand tensed harder in her hair, and pain darted down her neck and spine. He pulled her head back, and he held his forehead against hers like a ram locking horns with a rival.

"You could do all of that," he said, "and it still wouldn't be enough."

He let her go. Turned away.

"This is what you want," she said, breathing heavily. Her lips stung, and her scalp was throbbing. "I don't care what you say about lust and love. I *know* this is what you want. The drawing. The photograph. The lock of hair. This is what you've wanted for months. Isn't that right?"

He was silent. His back was turned to her. He wiped one wrist against his mouth.

"You dream of me," Elisabeth said. "You're *obsessed* with me." She rushed forward, grabbing at his arm. "You want this."

He swung around, yanking his arm away from her. "But you don't."

"That's not true."

"This is beneath you, Elisabeth. You're whoring yourself."

She slapped him. And when he only stared at her, glowering down from inches above, she slapped him again. But he didn't move. He didn't lift a finger at her.

He was right. Even Elisabeth could admit that. Whoring was exactly what she was doing, or what she was prepared to do. Yet she was failing at even that, and her frustration made her want success all the more. She stepped forward, pressing herself against him.

"Do you want this?" she said. "Yes or no?"

His eyes seemed to soften. His lips relaxed. His jaw loosened. "Yes."

She turned her hand and opened her palm, and she grabbed him. He was hard, and as she touched him, he got harder still, pulsing in her clutching fist. She squeezed, strong enough that it surely hurt, but only the briefest shadow of pain passed across Alfred's face.

"This is mine," Elisabeth said, and as she leaned forward to kiss him, she thought that she had won. But again he pulled back. She squeezed even harder, but he slipped away from her. He crossed the room, pounded his first three times on the door.

"Margaret," he said. "Twenty minutes alone with her."

"Don't you fucking leave—"

But the guard was already opening the door. A different guard this time, the Walrus, and he stood there gawking at her, sallow eyes that Elisabeth could feel crawling over her skin like a rash.

"Don't visit me again without Margaret," Alfred said. "If you come here alone, I won't even bother coming out of my cell."

He turned and left the room. The Walrus followed.

"Alfred," Elisabeth shouted. "Alfred!"

But he was gone, and she was alone. She realized then why the Walrus had been staring: Alfred had ripped loose one of the buttons on her flannel blouse, and her shirt was flapping open. She pinched it closed, but the blouse sagged open again, and in a fit Elisabeth yanked her whole blouse apart, its buttons springing loose and casting through the air like sparks from a fire. She stayed there for a minute longer, the room's bitter drafts churning coolly against her naked stomach and chest, covered only by her brassiere. Then she put on her parka, and she buttoned it tight.

CHAPTER 34

If Margaret said no, Elisabeth wouldn't force her. That—*that*—was a line she wouldn't cross. But once she had made the decision to ask, Elisabeth found that it was very easy to justify the proposition. There would be guards everywhere, she told herself. Not in the visitation room, no, but just outside of it. One shout away. Fifty steps. Maybe less.

And she herself would be sitting outside the room. The door's barred window would allow her to hear the rise and fall of their conversation, perhaps even entire words. If there was a power more perceptive than a mother's sense of hearing, Elisabeth didn't know it, and her hearing that afternoon would be more acute than ever before. Maybe, if she went about it the right way, she could even have the door unlocked, unbeknown to Alfred. It locked from the outside with a key, so all she had to do was speak to the guard as he exited the room. With the door latched but unlocked, she could rush in at a moment's notice. Perhaps this whole ordeal wasn't as dangerous as Elisabeth had first assumed.

And then there was the matter of letting Margaret make her own decision. How often had she remarked about Margaret's maturity? Her intelligence. *Let her make the decision,* Alfred had argued, and that wasn't such an absurd thing to suggest. Margaret wasn't stupid, and she wasn't incapable. Just the opposite: Margaret was one of the smartest and most capable people that Elisabeth had ever known. She wouldn't force her. She truly wouldn't. She would let Margaret decide for herself, and if there was one thing that Margaret wanted in this life most immediately, it was the chance to make decisions for herself. She craved responsibility. Agency.

And in that way, maybe this would bring them closer together. Elisabeth thought of the other night when she had confided in Margaret about her sister. Wasn't that the single best thing she had done for their relationship in months? It had made her feel closer to Margaret, and she knew that Margaret felt the same way. Remember: Margaret had wanted to help. Why? *To solve the mystery,* but what that really meant was that she wanted to be closer to her mother, and that's precisely what this would do. The episode at school had been an episode rooted in loneliness. But now—now they would be a team. They would be friends. They would be confidantes. They would solve the mystery, and they would solve it together. She couldn't fight against Margaret, but perhaps she could work with her. Perhaps this was exactly what needed to happen.

"Of course I'll do it!" Margaret swooned. "You can count on me, Mama."

They were sitting in Margaret's bedroom, Elisabeth in her desk chair, Margaret seated on the edge of her bed. The door was closed, and John had already gone to bed, exhausted from another grueling day at the base. Elisabeth had explained everything—or almost everything. She didn't tell Margaret about the episode in September, her brush with the lion's teeth. But she wanted to be sure that Margaret had a sense of it. She wanted her daughter to make an informed decision.

"Take this seriously," she said. "I want you to really think about what you're doing. Mr. Seidel—"

"I'm not scared of Mr. Seidel," Margaret said. "I know what he did to Mr. Sanford, but I don't care." She sat back, leaning on her hands, smiling smugly. "I could be his daughter. That's what he told me."

Elisabeth puzzled at that. "When did he say that?"

"When he stayed with us." She bounced closer to the edge of the mattress. "I can't wait to meet Jacqueline. She'll look just like you, right?"

"You're getting ahead of yourself. I want you to really—"

"What's Mr. Seidel going to talk to me about?"

Elisabeth sat back. "I honestly don't know, but I think talking is beside the point. He'll probably just ask you about school and Fairbanks and other little things. I think he just wants to see you." *This is all a game to him, and you're the ante.* That would have been the easiest way to put it, and the most honest. "He's lonely," Elisabeth told her instead, "and this visit will mean a lot to him. It'll be a favor, understand, so he'll do us a favor in return."

"He'll tell you where the man is living. The man who kidnapped Jacqueline."

"Yes."

She jumped to her feet, and then she flung herself back down on the bed, bobbing with excitement. "This is amazing," she said. "I feel like Monsieur Poirot!"

"Okay, okay," Elisabeth said. "Be quiet now, all right?"

And then she explained, just to be clear, that this was something to be kept strictly between the two of them.

"This is our secret," she said. "You absolutely can't tell Papa about this."

"Why not?"

She worked through it for a second. "Because it'll worry him."

"But there's nothing to worry about," Margaret said. "I'm not scared of Mr. Seidel, and you'll be there the whole time."

"No, no," Elisabeth said. Had she really failed to make that clear? Or had Margaret not listened? "I'll be there with you at the prison, but not in the visitation room. You'll be meeting Mr. Seidel alone."

Margaret's face went slack. "Oh."

"But I'll be right around the corner. I'll be right outside the room, and if anything goes wrong, I'll be there in a heartbeat."

Even that felt too ominous. *If anything goes wrong.* Then again, she had wanted Margaret to make an informed decision, and now she understood the situation in all its gravity. But after a moment, she dismissed it.

"I'm still not scared," Margaret said. She grinned, positively glowed. "We're a team, Mama. I won't let you down."

Elisabeth lay in bed for an hour that night. She was sleeping in the guest room—she hadn't shared a bed with John since Tanacross—and the bedroom was as dark as a tomb, illuminated only by a single shuttered window. She was chewing her lips. Kneading the sheets in her fists. Was she really willing to trust Alfred? She could still turn back. She could call off the whole thing.

But, yes, truly, in her deepest core, she thought that she could trust him. She convinced herself of it. She could trust him because she trusted Jacqueline. She believed in their connection. Alfred's dream was no coincidence. A huge, sweeping field, he had told her. The two of them holding hands. *Come and get me,* Jacqueline had beckoned in her own unceasing dreams, and Alfred's visions were proof positive that her own desperate reaching would finally find its mark, not in dreams but in true life.

It was all preposterous, she knew. Dreams. Visions. A universal connection. This wasn't like her. She was a sensible woman. A rational woman. But the connection between her and Jacqueline went beyond the senses. Their connection could not be explained in rational terms, but that didn't mean it wasn't real.

Why, then, couldn't she fall asleep? Why couldn't she relax? Nerves, she told herself. It was just nerves. She lay blinking in the dark, but sleep never found her, and with it neither did her sister.

CHAPTER 35

Saturday. Margaret was free from school, and John was grading in his office at the base. It had snowed the night before, and the world was a muted wash of white. Smothered in fresh powder, everything looked tighter. The world seemed to be drawing a long breath.

They were silent in the car, but Margaret didn't appear to be nervous. Hers was the silence of concentration. She was an athlete braced for the big one. The debutante at the top of the stairs. She felt confident and unintimidated, or so Elisabeth hoped, all the more because of the exchange they had shared before setting out.

"Put this in the pocket inside your parka," Elisabeth had told her, and she had given Margaret a hunting knife clasped in a leather sheath. Eight inches long and razor sharp, its handle was carved from the antler of a caribou. It had been a gift from Mack. "Just in case," Elisabeth had added, and they both ignored the implications of that.

"I thought it'd be bigger," Margaret said now. They were walking inside the prison, and Margaret was glancing all around her.

"I know. I thought the same thing."

"Where are the watchtowers? And the patrols?"

"They're all inside, I guess."

She mulled that over. "That's the most important thing, I suppose."

"Yes," Elisabeth said, "I suppose it is."

She had to fill out some extra paperwork for Margaret, and Margaret had to sign a separate record book. *Juveniles,* its cover read in flaking gold print, and there were only a handful of entries above her own. As always, the Walrus processed them, accepting their paperwork without even reading what they'd written. But he was more chipper than Elisabeth had ever seen him. He grinned with the warmth of a saint as he watched Margaret fill out her record.

"Looks just like him," he told Elisabeth, and she could have corrected him, but instead she merely smiled.

Saturday, it seemed, was the most popular day of the week for visitations. Two other prisoners were seated at either end of the table: a wizened Negro and an Indian boy no older than eighteen. The Negro man was speaking to a pair of well-dressed women approximately Elisabeth's age. Daughters, she assumed, or perhaps even granddaughters. The women spoke at a normal volume, but the man spoke so bashfully that Elisabeth couldn't hear him from even ten feet away. The Indian boy was talking to his mother in a weary, wavering dialect of Athabaskan. It was similar to but different from the Tanacross dialect, and Elisabeth could only partially comprehend it. She understood just one sentence in its entirety.

"Don't let them see you crying," the boy's mother told him.

They waited for twenty minutes. And then, finally, the lock clicked open and the door swung wide, and Alfred was with them. Elisabeth had expected elation. *Margaret, my dear,* she imagined him booming, and would she stop the embrace he'd surely attempt?

But as he approached them, and as Elisabeth and Margaret rose to their feet like gracious diplomats, Alfred solemnly shook his head.

"You'll have to come back another time," he said.

Elisabeth's mouth fell open. "What do you mean? Why?"

"I wanted to meet Margaret alone." He glanced at the other visitors. "We're not alone. You'll have to come back another time."

"No, no," Elisabeth said, stepping forward. "We're here now. We've done everything you asked."

"We're not here alone. That was the agreement."

"The agreement," Elisabeth said, "was to talk with Margaret one-on-one. No guards, no me. That's what you said, and that's exactly what we're giving you. If there are other people here, I can't control that."

"Elisabeth—"

"No," she spat, "this is it." She had never felt so adamant about anything in her life. She had already gambled. She had already gone above and beyond. Time and time again, she had capitulated. She had given him everything he wanted. And now he was trying to wheedle out of their arrangement? No. She wouldn't let him. "You told me this was about trust," she said. "I'm here. Margaret's here. And now *you're* the one turning your back on us. *You're* the one betraying *my* trust. A deal's a deal, Alfred. If you don't—"

"All right. Okay." He hunched his shoulders and lowered his head, glancing again at the other prisoners and their families. He was embarrassed, Elisabeth realized. He was losing face like this, getting scolded by a woman. "You're right," he said quietly, "but you still have to wait outside."

"That was the arrangement." She looked at Margaret, and Margaret offered the slightest of nods. "Twenty minutes," Elisabeth said. She checked her wristwatch. "It's eleven twenty-five now. I'm coming back at a quarter till twelve."

"Fine," Alfred said. "Now go."

She had already planned this moment in her mind. She wouldn't say good-bye to Margaret. She wouldn't hug her. She wouldn't offer so much as an encouraging smile. For Margaret's sake and her own, she'd do nothing that would give more weight to the situation, nothing that might suggest there was anything to worry about. She would turn and knock on the door, and then she would walk through it. She would leave her daughter with a murderer, and she wouldn't look back.

And yet she couldn't help herself. As the door swung open, she turned her head and looked, just for a second. Margaret was watching her. Their eyes met, and the room seemed to pinch smaller, and in that brief moment Elisabeth almost went back for her.

But she didn't. She walked through the door and it closed behind her. As far as Elisabeth knew, Margaret was still watching her as she left.

"Wait a moment," Elisabeth told the guard, a young man she had never seen before. His coifed hair and gleaming patent leather shoes had all the signs of a new hire. His key was in the lock, but now he paused. "Can you leave that unlocked?"

"The door?"

"Yes."

"Why?"

She was ready for that. "My daughter's been sick with nausea all morning. She might need to run to the bathroom fast."

"We're at the desk right over there," the guard said, pointing down the hallway. "She only needs to knock. We'll hear her. We'll come in a flash."

"But it'd be easier to leave the door unlocked. Would you really mind?"

"We're not allowed to do that," he said, smiling sheepishly. He turned the key, and the lock clicked with all the tightness of a cocking gun. "It's a rule, you know?"

No matter. It was all right. Everything was fine. Margaret wasn't even alone; there were five other people in the visitation room. Five, and two of them were men. Maybe they weren't guards, but their presence was still a stroke of good fortune, and Elisabeth felt much more at ease. Yes, everything was fine. Better than expected.

She retrieved a chair from the lobby and set it beside the door. Her ear would have been pressed against it had she been any closer.

And she did hear their voices. Faintly, beneath the Athabaskans' halting words and the optimistic chatter of the two young women, she heard Alfred speaking to Margaret, and she heard Margaret speaking back in kind.

"Warmer," she heard Margaret say, and a few seconds later, as if reassuring Alfred, "It's fine."

Then Alfred spoke for a long bout, but his voice was so hushed that Elisabeth couldn't make anything out. She leaned closer to the door, but it made no difference. Silence for a time, and then came the rattling cacophony of the courtyard's door being opened, and Elisabeth jumped to her feet. She heard the door slam shut a moment later.

Sure enough, Alfred and Margaret had gone outside. Through the room's barred window, Elisabeth peered inside, but the Negro and the Athabaskan boy and their visitors were the only people seated at the table. Content and unalarmed, they were all still talking among themselves. The boy was smoking a cigarette now, staring into space as his mother idly talked.

But everything was fine. There was no reason to worry. Margaret could handle herself, and this was what they had all agreed to in the first place, wasn't it? The two of them alone. Her daughter and Alfred shut away by themselves.

But Elisabeth didn't feel like sitting down anymore. She paced in front of the door, peering inside every few seconds. Two minutes crawled by. Then five. She checked her watch as often as she checked the window. A guard walked past her, paid no attention, turned the corner down the hall.

Seven minutes. Ten. They were still outside. What in the hell were they doing outside? Maybe, Elisabeth thought, there were other inmates and their families out there, too. Despite the previous night's snow, it was warm today—a balmy fifteen degrees—and the sun was shining brilliantly. People would want to be outside, wouldn't they? Maybe Alfred and Margaret weren't alone. And even if they were, this was the arrangement. This was what she had gotten herself into. And she did trust Margaret. Alfred, too. Didn't she? Things would be fine.

Twelve minutes. Fifteen. With each second that passed, Elisabeth expected the courtyard door to come clattering up, two shadows casting across the floor like unfurling rugs. And there she would be—Margaret, her daughter, unharmed. *He asked me about school. I told him about Saturn's moons and the Battle of Barnet.*

But twenty minutes came, and the courtyard door never opened. The very second her watch read a quarter till twelve, Elisabeth tried to enter the visitation room, remembering the door was locked only after she had furiously rattled its handle. She knocked, staring at the others inside the room. Stupid. They couldn't unlock it either.

"Hey," she shouted in the direction that the young guard had walked. "Excuse me, can you open this?" She jiggled the handle noisily, as if that might catch his attention. "Hey, excuse me. Guard?"

Nothing. She loped down the hallway. And then she saw why the guard wasn't answering her: He wasn't at his desk.

"Hey," she said. Then louder, glancing around, "Hey! Hello?"

She walked farther down the hallway.

"Hello?"

No answer.

The lobby, then. The Walrus. She jogged down the hallway in the other direction, turned the corner, found him sitting at his desk. He was reading a magazine—a gossip rag, of all things. *The True Story of Joan Crawford*, its cover read, and Crawford stared straight at her with those piercing, sultry eyes.

"Can you unlock the visitation room, please?" Elisabeth said.

The Walrus looked up, raised one fat finger. "Ask the guard down there."

"He's not there."

"Not where?"

"At his desk," Elisabeth said. She stepped in the direction she had come from, hoping to usher him along. "Can you please just help me?"

"He should be there."

"He's not."

The Walrus leaned across his desk for a better view. "There he is." The fat finger again. Pointing. "Ask him."

The younger guard was at the far end of the hallway. Where had he gone? Where had he come back from? It didn't matter. Elisabeth was at the door in three strides, shouting and waving the guard forward.

"I need to get in," she said. "Come on. Open the door. Open the door."

And finally, she was back inside. The courtyard door was still closed, and she dashed to it, reaching for its handle by the floor. It was heavier than she expected, heavy and rusted, with wheels that screeched and fought against their tracks. She struggled with it, but then the door was up, and the light reflecting off the courtyard's snow blasted through the room like cold fire. She stood, and she stared.

The courtyard was empty. Margaret and Alfred were gone. Save for a few footprints, the yard was as peaceful and undisturbed as an old country cemetery. What Elisabeth didn't notice, not right away, was a space in one corner where the gathered bank of snow had been cleared. And carved into the crumbling wall was a hole, ankle high and eighteen inches wide, much too small for an adult, but just large enough for a child.

CHAPTER 36

The caustic cold against her forehead, cheeks, and chin. Her hands buried in the fresh snow. Weight around her chest and underarms, someone pulling her up from the spot where she had fallen. She never lost consciousness, so it wasn't that she fainted. But as soon as she saw the empty courtyard, all the power in Elisabeth's body left her instantly, and then she was lying on the ground. Not moving. Not crying. Not even blinking. It was like a switch had been flipped. She wasn't even human anymore. Just a pile of limbs and skin and bone, lifeless and without purpose.

But this initial paralysis was only temporary, and then the full reality of what had happened overtook her. From the courtyard, someone dragged her inside, and as she was lying in a heap on the floor of the visitation room, Elisabeth felt everything that had been suppressed in her immediate reaction.

She was sobbing. She was utterly destroyed. She still couldn't stand, but this wasn't for lack of strength in her limbs. Elisabeth wanted to lie there forever, curled up on the floor in ruin, and when she started clawing at her own face like her fever-stricken sister had done so many years before, the young guard and a team of other men restrained her. Sometime after that, two fingers were in her mouth, and a hand was shoving sedatives down her throat.

Wear and tear, the elements, and months of Alfred's own digging. Like a wolverine tunneling into a meat cache, Alfred had burrowed through the wall—a hoard of abraded forks and spoons were found behind the radiator in his cell—but he had needed Margaret to crawl through it. With her on the other side, Alfred had tossed Margaret an improvised rope: a line of knotted bedsheets, undershirts, and men's briefs that he had hidden within the embankment of snow, ready for use at a moment's notice. Margaret secured the line to a cast-iron gas pipe, and Alfred climbed up and over. The yard's withering barbed wire wasn't much of an obstacle, it seemed. After untying the rope from the pipe, Alfred and Margaret made their way to the pair of twelve-foot perimeter fences, which they scaled. Here, the barbs were sharper and new, fresh as springtime thistles, but Alfred unknotted his rope and draped the bedsheets and shirts over the wires for protection. They jogged to the road, and beyond there their footprints vanished. The whole thing took fifteen minutes. Twenty at the most.

The guards and the police took entire hours to figure out these details, and Elisabeth never heard this narrative directly. From a distance, she picked it up disjointedly, fading in and out, the hours slipping forward in fits and starts. They had her lying on a cot in the lobby, but she could hear voices and other sounds all around her. The chatter of police. Telephones ringing. A straight key's relentless tapping. The whirring drone of sirens as the prison locked down. A guard reporting the news over a radio. John's voice, distant and somber. Footsteps, thousands of footsteps, some hurried, others relaxed. She heard facts and times being reported and repeated ad nauseam, and frequently she heard voices talking about her.

"No, I think he's a friend of her family," one person said.

"Is she drunk?" another asked.

The drugs like fog in her veins, these voices came to her as rumbling echoes. She heard the world as if from underwater, and she thought of the drawing she had done for Alfred in September. Her self-portrait. *She's drowning,* Alfred had written, and as Elisabeth thought of that now, she started laughing, softly at first, but soon she was twisting and rolling with roaring convulsions. She laughed so hard that the muscles in her stomach felt as if they were tearing apart, her whole body rending itself to pieces.

"Else," came John's voice. But she just kept laughing. Then, louder, "Else!" and he slapped her across the face, waited a second, and then slapped her again. On a dime, she stopped laughing, and she stared up at him earnestly.

"I heard you the first time."

Sam York was not among them, but a group of police officers was gathered around the cot, and they wanted to speak with her. As best she could, Elisabeth answered their questions about Alfred, their meetings, their letters, the "exchange," Margaret, everything. She was past the point of feeling self-conscious. She remembered how she had once felt in York's office. Foolish. Like a child revealing some bit of mischief.

But today, she felt none of that. The sedatives' edge was already wearing off, and in its place was a new kind of numbness, one of her soul instead of her body. She felt dead inside, as if her core had rotted into wasted nothingness, and she answered the policemen's questions with unflinching sobriety.

"We've been having trouble at home. She tried to run away just this week."

"You could say that, yes."

"They had met only once before."

"That's what Margaret told me. I never heard him say it. But I believe her that he said it."

"Four times previously. This was the fifth, and the first time that Margaret had come with me."

"Talking mostly. Once, we drew pictures."

"No, I never noticed anything."

"No, he never mentioned it."

"No, I had no idea."

"No. If I had, I wouldn't have done it."

"About four foot six. Ninety pounds. Maybe less."

"Blond."

"Hazel."

"Joyce."

"Not that I'm aware of. She's never even broken a bone."

"You'd have to ask her teacher that. Catherine Curry. At the base."

In all the hours of questioning, Elisabeth never lost her composure. She had nothing more to lose. She was broken, and it wasn't just the sedatives. She listened to the questions, and she heard herself answer, but she knew there was no need for this. They wouldn't find Alfred, not if he didn't want them to. She had known that from the moment she lifted the courtyard door and saw that empty expanse of snow. If she had thought there was the slightest chance of catching up to them, she would have turned on her heels and sprinted out of the prison like a dog on the hunt. But she had known instantly that Alfred and Margaret were already out of reach.

Her daughter was gone. Carried off by a maniac. And to what end, she didn't yet understand. Stubbornly, the police were certain of themselves. "He needed her to bust out—that's all," they said. "She'll only slow him down, and if he really thinks of her like a daughter, he'll just let her go. He won't hurt her." Patrol cars were already combing the streets, and they expected to find Margaret at any moment.

Elisabeth had heard lines like that before: ignorance dressed as comfort, conceit disguised as conviction. *Everything is all right, ma'am. The situation is under control.* They didn't know what they were talking about. They had expected to find Jacqueline, too, and what good had that done? They had thought—

But Margaret wasn't Jacqueline. She needed to remember that. Margaret was smarter. Older. More resilient. The police were useless, but that didn't mean all hope was lost. What had happened, and why?

Concentrate on that. Alfred had needed Margaret's assistance, but he had needed her for something else, too. There was some other design here, something Elisabeth could only guess about. What she knew was this: There was no evidence of a struggle in the courtyard, nothing in the footprints that might suggest Margaret had been in any kind of duress. She had gone with him willingly, then. She had bought some story he had sold her, just as Elisabeth had done. He had lured her.

Elisabeth's mind flitted from the banal to the horrific. Perhaps Alfred wanted Margaret's company and nothing more. Perhaps he really did love her like a daughter and wouldn't harm her in the least. Or perhaps he was raping her this very minute. Perhaps he'd torture her. Perhaps he'd kill her. Or—and the sensibility of this was terrifying—perhaps Alfred would get in touch with the man who had taken Jacqueline. Perhaps he'd offer him a new bride.

This was what she had done to her own daughter, or what she might have done. It seemed insane to her now—the gamble she had made with Margaret's life. But she really had done it, and now this was it. Her new reality. *This is your life,* she kept thinking. *This is the life you've made.* A fate worse than death. A thousand times worse.

But in all her dry despair, Elisabeth tried to think about one thing above all else: the knife. Mack's hunting knife. Perhaps there was some hope left, and for that reason the knife was the only thing that Elisabeth didn't reveal to the police. In some strange way, she felt the need to protect that detail, as if revealing it to anyone else would somehow dilute what little hope it offered.

Yes, the knife. Think of the knife. She had to trust in Margaret. They wouldn't catch Alfred, but perhaps they wouldn't need to. Perhaps Margaret could solve this situation herself. She imagined Alfred by the side of the road, his throat yawning open like a wide, red grin. *Think of that,* she told herself. The possibilities. The potential. The knife.

"What else could have possibly happened?" John asked.

They were driving home. What else could they do? *We'll phone the second we learn anything,* one officer had promised, and then he had added, with unintended foreboding, *This will all be over soon.* Now it was almost ten o'clock at night, and this was the first time that John and Elisabeth had been alone all day.

"That's the only thing I'd like to know," he added. "What did you *think* would happen, Else? Give me the bottom line. How did you think this would end?"

Her seat was at an incline. She was staring out the window. Street-lights flickered across her face. Her voice was very soft. "I thought he'd take me to my sister."

John sighed. "Then you're even stupider than I thought."

He had to help her inside the house. Her mind was almost clear again, but her body still felt heavy and strange, as if her limbs belonged to another person. She hooked one arm around John's shoulders, and he limped with her to an armchair in the living room. After she sat, Elisabeth closed her eyes, but she could feel him still towering over her, watching. Then, he set something on the telephone stand beside the chair, and when she opened her eyes she saw that it was a dark brown bottle of pills.

"The doctor gave me those," John said. "They're sedatives, and I was told they're very strong." He hadn't bothered turning on the light, and his face was painted in shadow. He stared at her with eyes as black as the empty night sky. "The doctor said you shouldn't take more than one every six hours." He paused, and in that quiet he said everything else he needed to. "There are twenty-four of them in that bottle."

Then he left her, and she heard the bedroom door shut a while later. Elisabeth reached for the bottle, unscrewed the cap, shook out six pills. And she studied them for a time, six oblong capsules, yellowish white, like tiny sticks of butter. Her palm sweated against them, and their gelatin shells stuck to her.

She didn't resent John. She truly didn't. If anything, she sympathized with him. As much as he hated her right now, she hated herself even more. Their marriage was over, and if all the worst things came to bear on Margaret, Elisabeth's life would be over, too. She would see to that, and John knew this as well as she did. Could she really blame him, then? No. If he was guilty of anything, it was assuming that the worst had already happened to Margaret, and he had taken that assumption to its natural consequence.

But the knife. The knife, the knife, the knife. That was enough to keep Elisabeth going. Tonight was not the night. Not until she found out more about Margaret. She turned her hand over, and she watched as the capsules gradually snapped away from her skin, until at last only one stubborn pill remained. Then she clapped her hand against her mouth, swallowed the single pill, and tried to relax, closing her eyes once more, waiting for a sleep that she doubted would ever come.

B ut it did: a sweeping, thick sleep that enveloped her like rising water, and she was with her sister again.

It was winter but it wasn't. She and Jacqueline were standing on the ice of a frozen lake, but all around them the trees were blooming, rich with flowers and fruit. There were peach trees, pear trees, cherry trees, and apple trees, all of their branches fantastically long, reaching across the lake in a colorful embrace. She and Jacqueline stood near the center of the lake, but in the strange illogic of the dream, the branches hung only inches from their heads. Motionless, arms at her sides, Elisabeth watched her sister picking fruit.

"Margaret is so sad," Jacqueline said, her fingers working at a branch that dangled above her. "She's dreadfully sad."

Jacqueline was dressed in summer clothes—an off-white dress with a line of sunflowers stitched around the skirt—and she was barefoot. Elisabeth was, too. Against the soles of her feet she could feel the bite of the ice, a chill so cold that it felt like just the opposite, not the pinch of cold but the sting of heat.

"It's awful to see her like that," Jacqueline said, still balanced on her toes, picking through the branch. "Margaret's so sad, and do you even know why?"

Though the air felt warm and the trees were in bloom, clouds of frosty condensation trailed from Elisabeth's nose and lips as she breathed. She opened her mouth to speak, staring at her sister through a fog of icy vapor, but Jacqueline cut her off before she could begin.

"She's sad because she's waiting for you. She's frightened, and you're not coming to her." Reaching up a little higher, Jacqueline plucked a piece of fruit from the tree. Then she turned and, finally, faced Elisabeth. "I know how Margaret feels," Jacqueline said, "because you haven't come for me either. We're lost, Else, and you've abandoned us both," and with that she started walking closer.

Just tell me where you are, Elisabeth wanted to say. *I'll come to you. I'll find you, and I'll find Margaret, too. Tell her not to be scared. Tell her I'm coming. But first I have to know where she is, and where you are, too.*

That was what Elisabeth was going to say. Those were the words that gathered instantly on her tongue. But again Jacqueline spoke before she could.

"You'll never find us," she said, still walking. She stopped just a foot away from Elisabeth. Jacqueline's eyes were narrowed and sad. "You've already lost us, Else. We're already gone."

Just past the shores of the lake, something was rustling through the trees and underbrush. Elisabeth couldn't quite see it; the thing was only a shadow, a huge inky shadow, large enough to shake the fruit from the trees as it moved. Cherries and apples hailed to the ice. Watching the woods, seeing the shadow, Elisabeth gasped. But Jacqueline didn't look frightened at all.

"Here," she said, holding out her hand, offering Elisabeth the fruit she had just picked from the tree: a cherry, large and plump, as wide around as a tomato. "Take it," Jacqueline said. "They're delicious."

But Elisabeth was too terrified to react. The trees continued to shake and the shadow continued to move, plodding through the woods with steps so heavy that they shook the ice, each pace bringing it closer to the lake, closer to them.

"Jacqueline—" Elisabeth finally said, but as soon as she spoke the ice broke beneath her feet and she plunged into the water below.

The telephone was ringing. At first, still reeling from sleep, Elisabeth thought that she was back at the prison on the cot, surrounded by rushing bodies and the prison's droning alarm. But no. That sound—it was the phone. The phone beside her.

She was slumping in her chair, stuck in the midst of a slide to the floor, but now she straightened. Sunlight burned against the windows. It was daytime already? But the phone. It might be the police. It likely was. But only as she was lifting the receiver to her ear did Elisabeth realize the magnitude of that *might be*. Her daughter might be dead. Her daughter might be alive.

"First of all, Margaret is fine," she was told, but it wasn't the secretarial voice of a police officer. It was Alfred's. "She's fine, Elisabeth. All is well. There's nothing to worry about."

She couldn't breathe. Her body was a stone. "Where are you?"

"Delta Junction," Alfred said. "Do you know it? We're on our way to Tanacross. We'll be there within two hours, I'm told."

"Margaret—"

"—Is asleep in the back of the truck we've hitched. A supply truck. I had no idea piles of toilet paper could be so comfortable."

"Put her on."

"I'd like to let her rest," Alfred said, "and I intend to. We have a long hike ahead of us."

"Where—"

"Besides, I can only talk for a moment," Alfred said. "The truck's fueling up now, but we'll be off again soon. Have you seen the new military highway? It's quite an operation, and I've heard it's got young Tanacross growing up."

Elisabeth had heard that, too. The war had changed many things in Alaska, including Tanacross. It wasn't in the bush anymore. Impelled by the constant threat of a Japanese invasion, a highway was being built to span the length of the territory and facilitate the war effort. Thousands

274

of workers had been recruited for the project, and they worked on the highway day and night. As one of the largest settlements along the eastern half of the road, Tanacross was now the bustling home of construction crews and a frequent layover for army air traffic. The airfield was paved. Rows of one-room cabins had been built to house the highway workers. With the construction's breakneck pace, the road was nearly complete, and every day a parade of trucks traveled east: construction trucks, army trucks, rigs with open backs that seemed to haul nothing more than pillars of swirling snow. Tanacross was closer than ever—busier than ever. THE LITTLE TOWN THAT COULD, read a headline in the *Daily News-Miner* just weeks before, and beneath it had been a foggy picture of Henry Isaac and half a dozen others, all of them grinning ear to ear.

But she pushed Alfred's question away.

"Leave Margaret at the fuel station," she said. "I don't know what—"

"Again, I have no intention of waking her up. She needs her rest. She's coming with me."

"To Tanacross?"

"Not exactly. And in fact that's what I'm calling about: About a mile north of town is a small cabin. Mr. Sanford told me about it. It's a place your Indians keep for hunting. A shelter. Go to it. Margaret and I will be waiting for you there. And then"—he let that float in the air for a second, and she could almost feel his breath coming through the line, warm and moist and as acrid as burning oil—"then I'll keep my end of the bargain. I'll take you to your sister."

"What are you planning to—"

"They're waving me out, Elisabeth. They're all finished. I've got to go."

"Alfred, leave Margaret there. Listen to me. Please."

"A mile north. Walk straight north from the landing strip. You'll find it. It's there. We'll be waiting."

"Alfred—"

"Good-bye, Elisabeth. Don't worry. All is well. A mile north. Straight north."

She called out for him again, but he was gone. Then she was on her feet, and she was tearing through the house. Tanacross. Margaret was in Tanacross, and she'd be damned if she didn't join her. Her sister was wrong. *You'll never find us?* She would, and if necessary, she would bring Margaret back to Fairbanks over Alfred's dead body.

The closet in the master bedroom was where John kept it, and Elisabeth went there now. The room was empty. The whole house was quiet. The car was in the driveway—she had seen it from the corner of her eye as she sprinted through the living room—and Elisabeth could only guess where John might have gone. The police station? The base? A contemplative walk through the neighborhood? It didn't matter. She didn't need him, and she didn't want him. Not for this.

Like a broom, it was leaning against one corner of the closet. The Winchester rifle John had gotten at the potlatch. A minute later Elisabeth had the ammunition, too, which John kept with his tools in a utility chest beside the back door.

She wasn't an ace, but she was no fool around guns either. She had fired Winchesters before; at the start of each summer, as a kind of celebration, Tanacross would hold a shooting competition, and even the women were encouraged to participate. She had never actually loaded one, but she had watched John do it several times before, and she found now that it was just as easy as it looked.

She loaded five rounds into the feed, and then she pocketed the small box of bullets. The clock in the kitchen read eleven, and the time was so surprising that it made Elisabeth pause in midstep. She had slept for twelve hours. Twelve hours? Sedatives or not, she could hardly believe it. But it didn't matter. What mattered was that she was coming for her daughter, and again Elisabeth reminded herself of Margaret's capability. *The knife. Think of the knife.*

Until recently, the only way into Tanacross had been by plane. You'd had to find a bush pilot willing to take you, and most pilots had their own fixed routes. It could take hours, even days, just to find an available plane. But now Elisabeth had the highway. Now she didn't have to wait for anyone. Tanacross was four hours away, a stretch of time that seemed both brief and interminable. *Wait just four more hours, Margaret. Just four more hours.*

She was going to find her daughter. And then? Then she would have Alfred tell her where Jacqueline was. He could tell her, or he could die. She would leave that choice up to him.

CHAPTER 37

When Margaret was five years old, she was convinced that another little girl lived beneath her bed. It started simply enough. "What's under the bed?" Margaret would ask, and Elisabeth would crouch, peek, and tell her, "Nothing, sweetheart. Not even any dust bunnies." Then Margaret got more specific.

"Can you check under the bed?" she asked one night.

"For what?" Elisabeth said.

"For her."

"For whom?"

"The little girl," Margaret said. "She sleeps under my bed at night."

Elisabeth peeked beneath the bed and told her, "Nope. No little girl. Nothing at all."

"Oh," Margaret said. "Okay."

It went on like that for a month—every night, the same conversation. Elisabeth thought very little of the imaginary girl. John thought even less of her.

"As long as we don't have to feed her, I'm fine with it," he said.

And if Elisabeth had let it go, she would have been fine with it, too.

Then, on a whim, during lunch one day, Elisabeth asked if the little girl had a name.

"She does," Margaret said, "but she won't tell it to me."

Elisabeth nodded. It was just her and Margaret that afternoon. John worked weekends at a dairy farm, and he didn't return until dinner.

"Well, what *does* she tell you?" Elisabeth said. "What do you talk about?"

"She asks me to come under the bed with her."

"That's a silly thing to ask."

"Yeah." Margaret chewed her sandwich. "She wants to take me away."

Elisabeth frowned. "Take you where?"

"I don't know," Margaret said, sighing lightly.

"And what does she look like? Have you seen her?"

Margaret nodded. "When I don't get out of bed, she stands next to me and looks at me."

Elisabeth sat straighter. "But again," she said, though she wasn't even sure why she was pressing the matter, "what does she look like?"

And Margaret stared straight at her and said, flatly, "She has big black eyes, and she looks like Jacqueline."

That was the first time Margaret had ever mentioned Elisabeth's sister, and frankly, it was baffling. She and John had never told her about Jacqueline. They had never even mentioned Jacqueline in front of her.

"It's a name she heard someplace," John said. "Jacqueline Logan. Jacqueline of Holland."

"Jacqueline of Holland?"

"I don't know." He shrugged. "She could have heard it anywhere."

But Elisabeth couldn't let it go. That night, when Margaret asked her to check beneath the bed, Elisabeth leaned forward and said, "For Jacqueline?"

"No," Margaret told her. "Her name's not Jacqueline. She just looks like Jacqueline."

"Who's Jacqueline?"

Margaret yawned. "Aunt Jacqueline. The little girl looks just like her."

"How do you know what Jacqueline looked like?"

"Because she looks like you," Margaret said.

"But I thought she was a little girl. I'm your mom. I'm not a little girl anymore."

"No," Margaret said, and she yawned again.

They were quiet. Elisabeth tucked Margaret's sheets tighter beneath her body, glancing away for a moment, and then she turned back to her daughter. "How do you know who—" she started, but Margaret was already asleep. For a minute, she watched the rise and fall of her chest, the easy motion of her eyes behind their lids. Then Elisabeth turned for the door. *Tomorrow,* she thought. *Tomorrow,* and she left.

Five hours later, half past one in the morning, Margaret screamed. Their home at the time was very small—a two-bedroom apartment above a pharmacy on Cedar Street—and Elisabeth was up and on her feet almost instantly. The door, the hallway, the stairs to the pharmacy on her left, then bang, she was in Margaret's bedroom, but Margaret was nowhere in sight. Her bed was tousled but empty. The room was silent.

For a moment, Elisabeth just stood there and stared into the darkness. She couldn't even think to turn on the light. Margaret's babyhood was four years' distant, but Elisabeth still possessed so many of the tendencies that had come along with it: the lightness of sleep, the readiness for disaster, the expectation that the worst was right around the corner— that Margaret would choke, would suffer, would die if her mother wasn't ceaselessly vigilant.

And now, as Elisabeth stood in Margaret's doorway, staring at the vapid darkness, it seemed that her paranoia was justified. Her daughter was gone. Missing. Only a few seconds passed, but in that time Elisabeth felt a terror so absolute that all of the blood in her body seemed to freeze. Her heart didn't pulse but paused. Her fingers went rigid and cold. Then, before she really even knew it, she was on her hands and knees beside Margaret's bed, clawing blindly at the void beneath the mattress.

All the while, she expected a pair of eyes to come glinting back at her, not Margaret's but the other little girl's, the imposter's, the thief's.

Then she heard crying. Still on all fours, she turned and peered over her shoulder, and there was Margaret, sobbing in the corner behind the door.

"You didn't look," Margaret wailed. "You didn't look. You didn't look." Elisabeth had her in her arms. Margaret was shaking. "She climbed into bed with me," she said. "I woke up and she was lying beside me, and she was watching me."

Margaret slept in Elisabeth and John's room that night, and that was the last of the little girl beneath the bed. "She went away," Margaret explained a few days later, casual and calm, free of elaboration. And in spite of her own curiosity, Elisabeth let it go. She chalked it up to fantasy, to one of those things that kids do.

But now she saw it differently. It was an omen. Of course the little girl had stood beside Margaret's bed and watched her. Jacqueline wasn't just Elisabeth's twin sister. She was a specter that loomed over them all. She was a weight around their necks.

But she wouldn't be for much longer. The striving—the *running*—was nearly done. This was coming to an end. Either Alfred would finish this, or Elisabeth would. By the end of today, she would have the truth about her sister, or Alfred would be dead and the truth would be lost forever. Either way, it would all be finished, and in knowing this a concentrated calm overtook her. The road. The banks of snow. An overcast sky, thick and gray as porridge. Four hours passed in a haze. Elisabeth didn't cry. She didn't talk to herself out loud. She didn't pound her fists against the steering wheel, and she didn't think too much about what she was doing or where she was going.

Mostly, she watched the woods, mile after mile of trees weighed down with snow. They had been living in Fairbanks for only three months, but in that time something had been missing from her life that she didn't notice until now: the vast, suffocating bush. Fairbanks was wild in its own way—wilder than anywhere in Pennsylvania—but it wasn't anything like this, the Alaska that now unfolded in every direction like a boundless sea of green and white waves. This was the real Alaska, the Alaska that swallowed you whole, the Alaska where you could scream and it wouldn't even echo.

And yet it was beautiful. Perhaps being swallowed whole wasn't so terrible. There had been a time when the bush had intimidated her. Just months before they moved to Tanacross, a tragedy had struck the town, and Elisabeth had taken it to heart. Silas Denny, not seventeen years old, got caught in a snowstorm on his way back from a village north of Fish Lake. He was drunk, folks assumed. Why else would he have been so stupid as to set out at night, and in the dead of winter no less? He never made it to Tanacross, and a pair of hunters found him two days later— or they found what was left of him. He was torn to shreds, a mess of frozen gore and grinning, lipless teeth. Even his eyeballs were gone, Elisabeth had been told, the fast work of crows. The wolves had gotten the rest of him, and the hunters could tell from their tracks that the wolves had stalked drunk Silas for almost a mile.

That was what the Alaskan bush had once meant to Elisabeth: It was a place of unforgiving brutality, a place that would literally eat you alive. And for that reason she had been frightened of it, and that fear had made her see the bush as an ugly, monstrous blight.

But now she saw how wrong she had been. Now she saw the ragged elegance. The rolling trees. The cake-icing snow. The knuckled mountains in the distance, a thousand craggy peaks piled one after another. As she bumped through the icy tracks carved into the road, the minutes and the miles peeled away, and Elisabeth was so overcome by the beauty of the Tanana valley that all she did was watch, watch and drive.

Then she crossed the Tanana River twice in quick succession, and she snapped to attention. Tanacross was only a few miles away. It was almost three o'clock, and the sun was already dipping lower in the sky, bathing the world in a cool wash. She wasn't sure what to expect from Tanacross. She knew that the town had changed, but the article in the newspaper had included only one photograph, and the town itself had been shown very little. It would be bigger, she knew. It would be busier. That was no secret. In four hours of driving she had passed dozens of trucks—some of them army trucks, some of them work trucks, all of them moving fast, the gears of industry and urgency and deadlines to meet. Yes, Tanacross would be different.

It was the extent of that difference that shocked her. She turned off the highway at a sign that read TANACROSS, and then she rode for a quarter mile down an uneven road. The snow was so trampled in places that loose dirt actually showed through, spots of muddy brown poking out from the frost like sores. Then she came to a clearing and the wide expanse of the Tanana, belted now by a wooden bridge reinforced with steel bands.

The town on the other side of the river was barely recognizable. Dozens of new homes had been built alongside the river, and these were organized into three crescent streets. As the village had expanded, swaths of trees had been razed, and the whole of Tanacross now sat in soupy mud, even with the snow softly falling. Cars and trucks were everywhere, and the roads between the cabins were as pitted as minefields.

But it wasn't the construction or the mud or even the cars and trucks that surprised her. It was the sight of so many people. There were bodies hustling everywhere. The town was teeming, and yet Elisabeth recognized no one. Driving up the central avenue toward the landing strip, she felt as if she was driving through a bustling tourist town that she had never visited before. She stared through the windshield in shock, but no one seemed to think twice about her.

To hell with this. She could move faster on foot. She parked beside one of the new cabins, about a hundred yards from the landing strip. She tightened the scarves around her neck, and she tied an extra to the stock and barrel of the rifle, a makeshift strap. Then, with the rifle slung behind her, she cut between two rows of cabins, and she was back in the old Tanacross, the Tanacross she recognized.

But she recognized that something was missing, too. Her house was

283

gone, and the school with it. An empty slot now sat between Joseph Howard's on the north and Will Roy's on the south. There wasn't a single slat or board left behind. The space stood out like a missing tooth.

"Else?"

She turned. Teddy Granger was standing a few feet away, and he was staring at her in surprise.

"Else," he said again, smiling and rushing forward. He hugged her. He held a candy cane in one hand. "What in the world are you doing here?"

But Elisabeth ignored his question.

"The house," she said, glancing back at the empty space. "Where's the house?"

"It burned," he said, shaking his head in confusion. "Didn't you get my letters?"

No. Obviously not. Clearly not.

"What happened?" Elisabeth said, turning again to the space where the house had been.

"It burned in December. The curtains caught a lantern and the whole thing went up." Teddy frowned. "John's successor 'didn't know' about gas lanterns. That's what he said. 'Didn't know.' 'You didn't know fire catches things on fire?' That's what I said. He and his wife got out in one piece, but damn if that thing didn't burn." He raised one hand and pointed up the road. The frame of a new home already stood at the end of the row. "New school opens in April. Me and Buddy and Big Paul—"

But Elisabeth was walking away, and Teddy's voice trailed off. She felt his eyes still watching her, but she didn't feel much else. It seemed that she was floating down the road, and absurdly, out of nowhere, she thought of the National Bellas Hess catalogue from months before, the happy husband and the doting wife with their baby in the neat red stroller. *Look at these two. Now look at you. Now look again at them.*

"Else?" she heard Teddy say. "Else, where are you going? What's going on?" She could tell from the rising timbre of his voice that now he realized how strange this was—her with a rifle slung on her back, marching through the snow.

But it was all she could do just to tell him, "I have to go. I have something to do."

Forget it. Forget Tanacross. Forget the house. She was right—she had something to do, and now she was going to do it. She was going to get her daughter back, and she was going to put an end to this. Hell or high water, she was going to. Clutching her parka and her scarves, Elisabeth floated down the road in the direction of the landing strip.

A mile north. Straight north. Straight into the bush. She walked slowly but steadily, and she heard nothing more from Teddy. At the end of the road, Daniel Nilak was standing in the open door of Mack's old home. He was leaning on a pair of crutches, and after a moment, he lifted one hand and waved to her as she passed.

F or a quarter of a mile, the walk was easy enough. The snow was falling faster now, and what rested on the ground already reached halfway to her knees, but at first Elisabeth had the luxury of following a track. The path was no wider than her shoulders—on either side of it, the spruce trees and aspen trees leaned so far forward that their crests nearly touched—but the path was a track nonetheless, one that the Athabaskans used, well-worn and easygoing.

Then the track curved sharply west, and Elisabeth couldn't follow it anymore. *Walk straight north from the landing strip,* Alfred had told her, and he had even repeated those directions. *A mile north. Straight north.* She didn't have any choice. She left the track behind.

That was when the work began. If the first quarter mile qualified as the bush, the rest of the walk qualified as something else altogether. This was a different planet. This was swallowed whole. *This* was Alaska. Tarred with clumps of snow on every branch, the trees were so dense that Elisabeth couldn't see more than twenty feet in front of her. With no track to follow, she weaved through the forest with the stumbling gracelessness of a drunk staggering home. Here, the snow reached her knees, and yet everywhere the underbrush stretched through the frost like the slender tentacles of some hidden creature trying to pull her down.

And she did fall. Repeatedly. Once every few minutes, Elisabeth's foot would catch or slip on something beneath her, and then she would pitch forward and the snow would be up to her elbows and her nose would be brushing the frost. But each time, she pushed herself up, and she pushed herself forward. Each time, she reached into one pocket of her parka and glanced at the compass she had brought with her from the car. *Straight north. Straight north.* Often, it seemed to take her ten minutes to walk just as many feet, but she was undeterred. *Straight north. Go straight north.*

The temperature was in the single digits, and the air felt even colder than that. With each passing minute, the snow fell harder, and the sky grew darker. It wasn't even four o'clock, but dusk was already settling over Alaska, and the woods spread out in every direction like some blue-gray landscape in a dream. *Keep moving, and move fast. Go. It'll be dark soon. It'll be night.* Elisabeth neither heard nor saw any animals—not so much as a gray jay flitted through the trees above her—but she was thinking of Silas Denny. She saw the frozen heap of horror. The straggles of bloody clothing. Bones and masticated gristle. No matter the snow, no matter the temperature: *Keep moving.* She would get through this, and she would find Margaret. *Just keep going.*

And the walk did become easier. Not any faster, or less strenuous, but easier to manage. More tolerable. In time, Elisabeth concentrated just as she had done during the drive from Fairbanks. A foggy serenity overtook her, and she focused less and less on the soreness in her feet and the aching in her muscles and the snow that whipped against her face. Soon, she wasn't even cold. The rifle hung on her back and the bullets jangled in her pocket, and she moved.

She thought of John and the other men setting out on their hunting trip that afternoon when she had walked with them. She remembered how the woods had overtaken them, how it had enveloped them in an instant. That was her now, she knew. Today, she was on the other side of things—today, she was the one enveloped by the woods and the snow and the trees collapsing on top of her—and what she found was a world that existed in a kind of limbo. There were only the woods and the snow and the deepening dusk. *Straight north. Straight north.* She trudged. She pushed. She concentrated on the task at hand, so much so that she didn't even notice the cabin when she first came upon it, not until she was nearly at its doorstep.

The cabin blended in with the woods around it, a home more grown than built. Elisabeth stood outside of it for a long minute, studying the cabin, not entirely sure that it was even real. It was small, hardly any larger than her and John's bedroom had been in Tanacross. The cabin had no windows, just a door held on by a pair of wrought-iron hinges. It was made entirely out of tree trunks and, judging from the weathered darkness of the wood, it was clear that the cabin had been there for many years. It was buried under snow and ice. The roof sagged with age, and in its center, a small stone chimney jutted through the frost.

The chimney was smoking, pumping out a skein of gray that the driving snow bent instantly and blew away. But apart from the smoke, there were no signs of life around the cabin. No footprints. Not even a woodpile. The trees stood very close to it, just two or three feet from the cabin's walls, so close that it looked as though the whole structure might be absorbed back into the woods at any moment. Elisabeth pulled the rifle off her back, and she untied the scarf from its stock and barrel. Then she cocked the rifle's lever, and even with the wind and snow howling past her ears, she heard the bullet shift into place with a precise click. She stepped forward.

Nothing. No talking. No voices. No footsteps. She stood outside the door, listening, but she couldn't hear a single sound. The door was held shut by a simple iron latch, and she reached for it now.

He's going to be standing there with a gun against her head.

He's going to be there with a knife at her throat.

He's going to be on top of her. Crushing her. Destroying her.

But, when Elisabeth pushed the door open, a sallow light swept around her and she saw one thing and one thing only: herself.

Pictures, paintings, charcoal illustrations. Hundreds of them covered the walls, a lifetime of work, each illustration as eerily lifelike as Alfred's portrait of Lititz. There she was as a child. There she was on the front porch of her old home. There she was overlooking the field that lay past her back patio. There she was as an adolescent, a teenager, a young woman. There she was in the window of her and John's home above the pharmacy. There she was with her father, her aunt, her cousin Charlie.

She noticed photographs now, too, pictures taped between the larger illustrations like chinking between logs. Flanked by her girlfriends, she was walking out of Lititz Public School. She was strolling down the sidewalk. She was reading a book. There she was through the window of a diner. There she was through the window of her aunt and uncle's home. There she was sitting. Standing. At the post office. There she was sleeping. Pulsing orange light filled the cabin, and from the floor to the ceiling its walls were papered with her, her, her. She felt as if she was standing inside of a film projector, and the movie was her entire life.

"Do you understand now how much you mean to me?"

Alfred was walking toward her. Despite its small size, the cabin actually had two rooms. There was the space where Elisabeth stood now, but then—separated by a single wall and a wood-burning stove—a second, much smaller room comprised the cabin's eastern side. From where she stood beneath the frame of the front door, Elisabeth couldn't see the second room in its entirety, but she could see the tattered edges of a dozen piled blankets. A bedroom, it seemed, and Alfred was walking out of it. He had changed his clothes from the prison, and now he wore an ill-fitting, mismatched jumble that must have come from a shelter or a church or the trash. Threadbare denim overalls. Three layers of button-up shirts. Peeling black boots. A pair of dark mittens. Elisabeth lifted the rifle as he approached.

"Stop," she said.

And he did. He even raised his hands in surrender, turning his mittened palms out. But he raised them only slightly, and Elisabeth could feel his eyes taking her in. He was sizing her up, considering his options. Her feet were set firmly in place. Her heart was pounding. Her temples throbbed. Bent around the trigger, her finger already ached, and even through the supple stuffing of her parka, the stock of the rifle dug into her shoulder like the blade of a shovel cutting into earth.

"Where's Margaret?" she said, but the swift motion of her eyes asked a different question. The sight of the cabin's decoration was so strange, so utterly arresting, that Elisabeth couldn't stop herself from looking.

"Do you like it?" Alfred said. "It's my shrine. My shrine for you."

And when she stuttered for a moment, backing half a step away and sputtering some sound between a *what* and a *why*, Alfred went on.

"I've always been with you," he said. "Ever since that summer, I've watched you. I've waited for you. I never lost faith that you would come to me."

"What are you talking about?" she said, and she shook the rifle at him, feeling something rise in her chest, a knot of panic and unease and pure revulsion. "Margaret. Where's Margaret?"

"That summer," Alfred said. "We had a plan. We had it all worked out. Jacqueline was his, and you were mine."

"Stop talking like that. Who's *we*? Who's—"

"My brother and I," Alfred said. "Heinrich."

She was shaking her head, backing away from him. "Your brother," she said. "You told me—"

"I lied," Alfred said, "and I'm sorry." His eyes veered away from hers. He wilted. "I shouldn't have told you that, Elisabeth. I was worried you'd figure things out before the time was right, and I wanted to confuse you. I admit it. He's my brother, and he's my twin, but he's very much alive. I lied. I'm sorry." He clasped his hands together, pleading with her. "But everything else is true. All of it. Your sister is alive, and I know where she is."

"Then tell me," Elisabeth said, shouting now. Her arms were shaking—

her whole body was shaking—but the rifle never veered from its aim. "This stops now," she said. "Tell me where she is."

"Illinois," Alfred said, and he pumped his hands at her. "With Heinrich. They live on a farm. They go by different names. They have three children. They're happy, and we'll be happy, too. The plan—" His eyelids fluttered. "We were all going to run away together. Remember? You and your sister. Me and my brother. That was us. He and I had watched you two for months. We knew your father, and the moment we first saw you and Jacqueline we knew what had to happen. Your lives were so lonely, so tragic, and ours were, too. We had lost everything in the war, but with all of us together, the world could be good again." He lowered his hands, just an inch. Then, a single step forward. "We're meant for each other, Else. The four of us. Two pairs." Another step, slowly. "Two perfect pairs."

"Stop," Elisabeth said.

"You know it's true. You've felt me." Another step. "We're *Gleichgesinnte.*"

"Stop walking."

"I don't like you pointing that gun at me," Alfred said. "I'm no threat to you, Elisabeth. Look around." He flung up his arms, gesturing at the illustrations and photographs. "Do you realize how it could have been? There were hundreds of times—*thousands*—when I could have just taken you. Heinrich, that's what he did. Your sister put an end to things, and he took her. But me"—he touched his chest—"I'm the good one. I'm the one who's waited patiently for twenty years."

"This is all—"

"And do you know why?" He gaped at her, pausing for an answer. "Because I couldn't just *take* you. I couldn't force it. I didn't want to, not even when John came into the picture. I'm not like my brother. I'm patient. I'm a peaceful man, Elisabeth. I wanted *you* to come to *me.*" He shook his head. "For twenty years I waited for you to notice me. All that time, I was right behind you. I learned your routines. I followed you. I walked with you. I sat outside your bedroom window. But never once did you notice me. Never once did you reach out"—he held up one finger—"until that morning in Tanacross. And not only that . . ." He drew a long breath, clasping his hands over his heart. "You invited me inside your home."

"I didn't." She was reeling. The cabin rocked from side to side. "I didn't do that—"

"Twenty years," Alfred said. "Twenty years without you noticing me. And then the first time I came to Tanacross, the very *first*, you spoke to me. You smiled at the things I said. You brought me into your home. Understand, I had lost you, Elisabeth. Three years ago, and poof, you were gone. I knew you had moved to Alaska, but no one could tell me where. My job with the postal service, I got it to find you. Every route I could get, I would take. And I was starting to think I had lost you forever, but then I found you, and after twenty years it finally happened. You saw me. You *chose* me. That was when I knew it was time. That was when I knew that nothing could keep us apart." He sucked his teeth. "The Indian—I hated to do it."

"Mack—"

"I *hated* it, Elisabeth. And I wish it hadn't happened. But it did, and I make no apologies for it. He was going to keep you from me, and I couldn't let that happen."

"We're done talking like that," Elisabeth said. "What does that mean? Just tell me what you mean," and again she steadied the rifle, squaring its sights on his chest.

"Don't do that," Alfred said. "I don't like having a gun pointed at me."

"Mack. Tell me about Mack."

"Lower the rifle."

"Mack—"

"He found my illustrations." Alfred lifted his chin, defiant. "He was snooping around my plane. Helping me, he said, with the repairs. But he was snooping. Heinrich had sent me the dress, and I had brought that and a few of my illustrations from Anchorage. For you. As gifts. Proof of my dedication. But then, the Indian. The dress I had already taken inside, but he found my pictures, and I could see in his eyes what he was going to do. He would have told you to stay away from me. He would have stood between us and fate. *Our* fate."

"Our fate?"

"To run away together," Alfred said. "The four of us. We're a family, and the world is eating itself up all over again, and we need to protect ourselves. We need to be together. You want this, too. You said so yourself. You kissed me. You touched me." He moved forward again, hardly ten feet away now. "You *owe* this to me."

"Stop."

"I'll take you to her. Just like I promised. But first you have to lower that gun."

"If you come any closer, I'll kill you."

"You won't."

"Stop moving."

"Elisabeth—"

"Where's Margaret?"

But as she said that he lunged at her, one hand darting out. He reached for the rifle, but she had learned her lesson from the prison. She had learned how fast he could move, and she was ready for him. It happened in a flash, but as soon as he moved, she stepped to the side and swung her arms and caught the barrel of the gun against his head, just above his ear. She didn't fire, but he was on the floor a second later, and the barrel's steel sights must have cut him, because blood was suddenly trailing down his face, painting his left cheek in a dazzling crimson streak.

"Margaret!" Elisabeth shouted, and she turned and ran for the other room.

"She's not here."

"Margaret!"

But Alfred wasn't lying. The second room, no larger than a step-in closet, was empty. A burning Coleman lantern sat on a medical box beside the pile of blankets, and on the floor was a roll of masking tape, the adhesive Alfred had used to hang the illustrations. But there wasn't any sign of Margaret. No sign at all.

"Where is she?" Elisabeth shouted, darting back into the main room. Slowly, Alfred was rising to his feet. But he didn't make a move at her. His head hung. Blood streamed down his face.

"She's not here," he said. "But that's for the best."

"You said she was safe."

"And she was." He swayed on his feet, staggering sideways a few steps, but he did nothing to stanch the bleeding from his head. It seemed as though he wasn't even aware of it. "She was here with me," Alfred said. "All the way from Fairbanks we were together, but she's a child, Elisabeth. An incredible child, but still just a child. And she got scared. She left for the town just before you arrived."

Elisabeth's knees almost gave way. She couldn't breathe. Couldn't think. Margaret. The bush. The snow. The night. And as if Alfred could hear her very thoughts—as if the two of them really were *Gleichgesinnte*— he raised his hand in reassurance.

"But she'll be fine," he said. "She's no fool, and she'll find her way back to town."

That hand. That raised, reassuring hand, wrapped in its dark mitten. Fabric that seemed darker than before. Wetter. Soaked through.

"Take off your glove," Elisabeth said.

"I know it's hard to accept, but Margaret is not a part of this. Think of your sister. Lower the gun, and I'll tell you—"

"Take it off," Elisabeth shouted, steadying the rifle, aiming for his head now. "Take it off this second."

Silence. Panting. Watching. Then, very slowly, his left hand reached for its twin, and he pulled off his glove. His hand was wrapped in a hasty bandage, soaked through with blood. He had been cut. Slashed.

It was purely instinctive. A twitch reaction. And yet she knew exactly what she was doing, and she knew that she wanted to do it. She saw that bloody bandage, and she fired. The rifle exploded, and the whole cabin seemed to shake, and Alfred ducked and spun away from her.

But she missed. She knew that right away—a burst of detonated paper and splinters flew through the air—and of course Alfred knew it, too.

Instantly, he rushed at her. And then they were fighting for the rifle, stumbling back and forth and side to side around the cabin. Their shoulders slammed against the northern wall, tearing a group of illustrations to the floor, and a shower of dirt and dust rained down on them. His hands were wrapped around the stock and barrel of the rifle, but she wouldn't let it go. He was strong, and his eyes were wild with fury, but also with terror. Their feet tangled together, and she tried to trip him, pushing him back. But he didn't quite fall, and instead he stumbled backward—fast—wheeling toward the splintered wall and taking her with him. She shifted forward, nearly falling on top of him, and all of her weight landed awkwardly on one ankle. It rolled. Something snapped. Pain crashed through her whole body—she could feel it in her teeth—and she screamed. But she didn't let go.

They were on the floor now, Elisabeth on top of him, and neither of them would release the gun. She pulled him toward her, and when she felt him pulling back, she let her muscles relax for a fraction of a second and used Alfred's own momentum to slam his head against the wall. There was blood everywhere—on his face, in his eyes, on her hands, on dozens of illustrations taped to the walls—but Alfred still didn't let go.

But he was dazed. She could see that. She could feel it in the power already disappearing from his arms, and she pushed him back again, slamming him a second time—then a third, then a fourth—against the wall. She nearly had the rifle. She cranked its lever forward, felt a bullet shift into place. The barrel was pointed at the ceiling, and she was fighting to straighten it out. She pushed it one way, and he pushed it the other. But she was winning. Slowly, she was overpowering him. She cranked the rifle's lever back. She pushed. She ignored the screaming heat in her ankle, and she pushed. And now she summoned every trace of energy that her limbs still owned, and slowly the rifle moved. Alfred was watching it now, taking huge gulps of air, spattering blood on her face every time he exhaled. But at last the rifle pointed at him, lined up with his neck, and her finger found the trigger, and she fired.

They flew apart. Elisabeth went backward, and Alfred reeled to the side. The illustrations were what Elisabeth noticed first. They were doused in blood, so much dripping color against so much black and white. Then she saw its source. The bullet had eaten away at half of Alfred's neck, and a great gaping wound bloomed with gore.

Partly on his side and partly on his stomach, Alfred was crawling along the northern wall. Crying. Frantic with a fear too great for what feeble life he still possessed. He could barely move, but God, if he wasn't trying. One hand clutched at his throat while the other scrabbled at the floor. He was pulling himself forward—achingly, desperately trying to escape her. His legs were already dead. His breathing was a torrent of blood, and his eyes were closed tightly but streaming with tears. And then his voice.

"You shot me," he said. "Oh God. You shot me." He opened his eyes, turned his head, and stared at her in shock. "You shot me," he said. "Elisabeth, you shot me."

There wasn't much time for it now. She had to get her answers, and the urgency with which she had to do the asking drove her forward, and she was calm. She stood. Her ankle throbbed, but it didn't bother her. She cranked the rifle's lever again, and she stared down at Alfred.

"Where's my sister?" she said.

Alfred stopped crawling. He rolled onto his back, and his hand dropped away from his throat. He was bleeding fast—blood was everywhere now—but the pain had seemingly left his body. He looked up at her. Watched her.

"Jacqueline," Elisabeth said. "Tell me where she is. Give me an address. Give me their names. I kept my end of the bargain, and now you have to tell me where she is."

He was sputtering, drowning in himself. But his lips moved in earnest, working in vain to form a response.

"A farm in Illinois," Elisabeth said. "Tell me a street. A town. Tell me where my sister is. Give me an address."

His eyes were a vacant stare, but his lips kept moving, working again and again with the same single word. And then Elisabeth understood. "Up," he was saying. "Up," and with that she saw more than vacancy in his eyes. She saw direction. "Up."

She followed his gaze. And there, taped to the wall, was a picture that Elisabeth hadn't noticed before, not in detail. At a glance, she had mistaken it for a photograph of herself, but as she studied it now, she saw her mistake.

It was Jacqueline. A young woman, twenty or twenty-five, she stood in the center of a winding dirt drive. She wore a plain white blouse and a gray skirt checkered with stains. Her hair was simple and short, and a bobby pin lifted her bangs away from her eyes. She was thin, but not malnourished. Rough, but not unclean. She stood sideways to the camera, her arms crossed over her chest, and she seemed to be watching something. Waiting for something. Contemplative. Dignified. A young country woman, burdened but not without her pride.

Elisabeth reached up, plucked the photograph from the wall. It was her. It really was. Grown-up. Alive. She was floating. She was nothing. Elisabeth watched the picture turn over in her hands, and on the back was an inscription written in pencil: *Bond County, Ill.*

"Else," or a sound almost like it. Alfred was gagging, suffocating in blood, but his eyes watched her. He was crying. "Stay," he said. "Please."

She unbuttoned her parka and slipped the photograph inside. Then she was holding the gun at him, pointing its barrel at his face. *Don't close your eyes,* she told herself. *If you close your eyes, you'll miss again. You have to watch it. You have to look.*

"Please," Alfred said. "Stay." His lips popped and stammered, smeared with sticking blood. His eyes widened, and the man who stared back at her was the most wretched thing she had ever seen. "I'm scared, Else. I'm scared."

And she fired.

The blinding snow. The hurling, bitter wind. The crushing trees—everywhere, trees. Denser than ever. Darker than ever.

Night had fallen. The forest was black. The snow was past her knees. Her right ankle was broken. Her whole body ached. She could barely walk. But nothing would stop her from finding her daughter. It was all for nothing if she didn't have Margaret. Holding the rifle in one hand and Alfred's gas lantern in the other, Elisabeth trudged through the snow. She would find her. She would die out here if she had to, but she would find her daughter first.

And she did find tracks. The light thrown off from the lantern was little more than a dim custard halo, but in the darkness of the woods it was enough to see the snow. The tracks were faint, already blowing over, but they were footprints, clearly, deep pits narrowly spaced. A child's gait. Yet they didn't lead south. They weren't headed for the town. From the cabin, the tracks veered southwest—stumbling, it seemed, in confusion. Lost.

Why wouldn't she be? Never mind Margaret's trouble with direction and geography; the full strength of a blizzard was sweeping through the Tanana valley. Even in Alaska, it had been years since Elisabeth experienced a blizzard like this; tonight the snow fell and the wind blew with a strength so powerful that she could hardly stand or see or move. This wasn't a blizzard. This was a nightmare. A fantasy. Not a blizzard, but the legend of a blizzard.

"Margaret!" she shouted, but like the light from the lantern her voice seemed to travel only a few feet. The wind and the snow consumed everything. But that didn't deter her, and she called out again and again. *Margaret. Margaret. Margaret.*

She would lose the tracks for ten feet and then find them again, just barely able to string along Margaret's path. And as she trudged farther into the black woods, Margaret's footprints got more erratic, veering south, then west, then north. Soon, even Elisabeth lost track of which direction she was moving, and that was when she reached into her parka and felt for the compass. The bullets were still there, but the compass—the compass was gone.

The fight with Alfred. The staggering, rolling fight. Was that when it had slipped out? Or was it lying somewhere in the snow behind her, having slipped from her pocket after a misstep gave way to a stumble? No matter. She had the tracks. Her ankle was broken and she was buried in snow, but she still had the tracks. Through the darkness and the wind and the blistering snow, she followed her daughter.

"Margaret!" she cried, over and over, until her throat was raw.

But no answer ever came. The snow never abated, and the woods never brightened. And yet she moved and searched and screamed for her daughter. Time had no meaning. Twenty minutes passed. Thirty. An hour. A lifetime. But at last she lost Margaret's tracks. She could only guess how long she had walked—how long or how far—but finally she reached an area where the trees spaced out more widely, and there the wind whipped more fiercely and obliterated Margaret's footsteps. The lantern's light was dimmer now, nearly extinguished, so Elisabeth started crawling, searching the surface of the snow with the flailing desperation of a person drowning. She weaved left and right, forward and back, feeling at the snow, scrutinizing its every crest and ripple.

Yet she couldn't find anything. The tracks were gone. She was screaming, but the wind consumed her voice. She fell forward, and the lantern plunged into the snow and went dark. But her legs kept pushing, and her arms kept moving, and if the cold came to take her, she wouldn't be able to stop it. She would close her eyes, and she would die, but until then she would push herself, and she would stare into the darkness.

No, not darkness. Not complete. Like a mirage, she saw it: forty feet ahead, an odd splotch of color among the blackness of the woods and the whiteness of the storm. A boot. A leg. The domed hood of a parka. Margaret, facedown, collapsed in the snow. Elisabeth was moving for her. Screaming for her.

"Margaret! Margaret!"

But her daughter didn't move. Elisabeth had her a minute later, and for a moment she thought that she was dead. Layers of scarves snaked around Margaret's neck and face, but her eyebrows were caked in frost. Somehow, somewhere, her left mitten had slipped off, and her naked fingers were as white as alabaster. Shaking, not from the cold but from exhaustion and terror, Elisabeth pulled off one glove and touched Margaret's face.

She was alive. There was still warmth in her cheeks, and despite how little light filled the forest, Elisabeth could see how Margaret's cheeks still possessed the slightest shade of pink. And she could feel her breathing. She held one finger beneath Margaret's nose. Yes. Her breath was there, wet and warm. She had frostbite in her fingers—there was no doubt of that—but she was breathing. She guessed that Margaret had lain in the snow for only a few minutes. But why wasn't she awake? Exhaustion? An injury Elisabeth couldn't yet discern?

It didn't matter. She had her. Miraculously, impossibly, she had her. But they couldn't stay here, this unprotected clearing assaulted by the full power of the snow and the wind and the cold. Elisabeth unwrapped one of her scarves and tied it around Margaret's exposed hand. Then she scanned the area around them. Darkness, punishing darkness, and she couldn't see much more than that. Could they make their way back to the cabin? The compass was gone, but maybe she could follow her own footsteps, carrying Margaret in her arms.

No, they would never make it, not with her ankle broken and with the blizzard pounding them from every direction. They had to wait this out. The cold would persist—the temperature might even drop—but it couldn't snow forever. It would pass, and the forest would clear, and the going would eventually be easier, even without the lantern.

With both arms, Elisabeth lifted Margaret out of the snow and slung her over her shoulder. Then she lifted the rifle, and she started to walk. She was almost blind, but she moved, and she looked. For a dense crop of trees. For a grouping of rocks. For anything that might afford them some semblance of protection. She staggered forward, her ankle crushed beneath her own weight and Margaret's, and after fifty or sixty feet, she did find something: an uprooted tree, perhaps one that had fallen from this very storm. It had taken a swatch of the earth with it as it fell, exposing a gnarled pit of soil filling up already with snow. But the overturned tree and its severed roots sprawled open like a huge hand splaying its fingers, and even from a distance Elisabeth could tell that the wind and the snow would be lighter there. She moved for it.

It wasn't much, but it was something. She lay Margaret down, and then Elisabeth sat with her back against the tree and its gash of roots. She pulled Margaret onto her lap, cradling her like an infant. And the wind was less powerful here, the snow not as thick. This was the best she could have hoped for. The tree. At least they had the tree. This was their home for now—perhaps for an eternity.

No, don't think like that. They could wait this out. They could survive. They had their parkas and their scarves and their heaps of clothing underneath, and perhaps the snow would soon fade away. And the rifle— she still had the rifle, and she still had the box of bullets. She took them from her pocket now, and she pulled the rifle closer to her.

Teddy Granger. Daniel Nilak. They had both seen her go into the woods, and they must have sensed that something was badly amiss. Perhaps they would send a search party. Yes, that made sense. They would do that. They would almost certainly look for them. And maybe they would find them, too.

In fact, maybe Elisabeth could help them. She cocked the rifle and steadied it against her shoulder, and then she fired a shot into the air. She cranked the lever again, and she fired a second time. Then she cranked the lever once more, and one by one she loaded five bullets into the feed.

But she didn't fire again. She had to conserve her ammunition. She would fire two shots every twenty minutes, but she couldn't waste them all on the air. For now, she didn't see any animals around them, but if the snow cleared and the wind relaxed, she couldn't count it out. Bears. Wolves. They were here, or they would be soon, and she might not see them right away. She had to be ready to defend herself. To defend them both. And by God, she would.

She tried to breathe. She tried to stay calm. Listen, she told herself. Just listen, and she tried to concentrate. Listen: There's the sound of the wind. There's the creak of branches over your head. The swirling shuffle of snow. Listen: There's the sound of your daughter breathing. Don't you hear it? And isn't it the most wonderful thing you've ever heard? You might die in this very spot, this very minute, but for now, just listen. That's all you have to do.

"Mama."

Barely a whisper. The shadow of a sound. But it was Margaret. She was looking up at her with sleepy, blinking eyes.

"Mama," Margaret said, "we're lost."

But Elisabeth only smiled.

"No, honey," she said, pulling her tighter. "We're exactly where we need to be."

CHAPTER 38

You'll finish this yet.

At some point, you fall asleep. You're not sure how long it lasts. Perhaps an hour, perhaps a single second, nothing more than the time it takes for your head to slip and your chin to touch your chest. But in that time, you dream.

You see your father. You're back in Lititz. Your childhood home. You're sitting on the top step of the front stoop, and your father is standing by the door. He's looking back at you, and you know what he's going to say. You've lived this moment so many times. In your dreams. In your wretched waking memory. This is the moment that's haunted you. The pivot of your entire life.

"Else," your father says. "Go find your sister."

You stand. You turn and face him. And in place of what you really said, you stare at him and say, "I already have." Your dream self shrugs. "She's right upstairs."

That's when you feel a hand on your shoulder. You're being lifted, Margaret and all, and in the frigid blackness of the forest there's suddenly so much movement. You feel the strength of many hands. The heat of many bodies. A swirling, muted din. Your ears are ringing. Your eyes are foggy. But then you smell something—peppermint—and you know that they've come for you.

You drift in and out. You're made to drink tea, eat bread, chew what tastes like pure fat. You're in a cabin, and the voices around you are those of other women, and their words are quiet but calm and assured.

"Eat," they tell you. "Drink," they tell you.

When they strip your soaking clothes away, you cling to your parka and the secret it contains. But someone pats your hand and says, *"Êy t'o."* *It's okay.* *"Êy t'o,"* and you believe her.

They cover you in blankets, and already the world is coming together again. You're in Mack's cabin, or what used to be his cabin, and a fire is burning in the cast-iron stove nearby. Margaret is lying on a cot beside you. At first, you only sense her presence, but then you hear her speak—"Are we still in Alaska?" she says—and you begin to cry, overwhelmed with joy and relief and an almost holy sense of appreciation. Then you turn and vomit on the floor.

You're flown to Fairbanks. Checked in to the hospital. They set your leg and wrap it in a cast three inches thick. Your fibula is broken in two places, and your lateral ligament is so badly damaged that you'll walk with a limp for the rest of your life.

But that's nothing compared to Margaret. Overnight, they amputate three fingers on her left hand, and she loses the tip of one earlobe, too. This is what you've done to your child. Your limp will never be enough. You wish that they would take your own fingers as penance. You're a disgrace, and everyone knows it.

But you'll make it up to her. Just wait. You'll make it up to her.

When the police arrive, you know what to say.

"Ever since that summer," you tell them. "My whole life."

They're circled around your hospital bed, half a dozen of them. No one writes anything down, not even Sam York. They accept what you say as fact, because for once you tell them exactly what they want to hear.

"You were right," you say. "He took her, and he murdered her. He was disturbed. He was obsessed with me because I was her twin. He wanted to finish something he had started twenty years ago. All that while, he was toying with me, and as soon as he had the right moment to do it, he tried to kill me. He would have tried it sooner, but Mack intervened, and you know what happened after that."

Margaret listens from the bed beside you, and she doesn't contradict a single word you say. She sits quietly, her hands folded in her lap, and her face reveals nothing. They have no idea how incredible she is. How strong. How perceptive.

"Those are geese," she says the second night. With her right hand, the one not enveloped in bandages, she lays one finger on the photograph, pointing to a blur in the sky above your sister's head.

"Are you sure?"

She nods. "You can tell from the formation."

This is how you pass the time. When the two of you are alone, you hobble to Margaret's hospital bed and study the photograph. And already, you've learned so much. There's a parked car in the background, a black Chevrolet half-ton. Only a few years old, it looks like. You can almost make out its license plate number: 156-84, you think. Or maybe 758-84. In the distance, there's a distinctive silo in the center of a field: slightly flared at the top, with unmistakable freckles of rust near its middle. You'll recognize it instantly in person.

And now, the geese. That means there may be water nearby, and when an orderly brings you a map the next day—"For lessons," you tell him—you and Margaret find that there's only one large body of water in the county, Carlyle Lake, a reservoir on its southeastern border.

"You're brilliant," you tell Margaret, and she beams.

She's the only one who knows about the photograph, and you intend to keep it that way. Your biggest mistake was involving others. John. The police. Sam York. Everyone but her. And you won't make that mistake again. The truth, you've come to know, is a private thing. The right to know it must be earned, and no one has earned it but you and Margaret.

The truth about your sister is a secret for you and Margaret alone. For mother and daughter. For *countrymen*.

That's why she's coming with you. You'll finish this yet, and you'll finish it together.

The others make their own arrangements, and you play along. They think you're going to Pennsylvania. They think you're leaving Alaska alone. Ten days pass, and your aunt and uncle send you two tickets through the mail: one for a flight to Seattle, and the other for a train bound for Philadelphia. They want you to come live with them in Lititz. They want to help you "convalesce." To them, to all of them—John, the police, your own family—you're a mess that must be managed. You're a crazy woman, and an unhinged mother. John will remain in Alaska, and the idea is that Margaret will, too.

But that's not going to happen. The day before Margaret and you are to be discharged, you make your own arrangements. John has already delivered your luggage for the trip to Lititz, and that makes it all very easy. It takes one phone call. Nothing more. You call Elmer Whitlock and arrange for him to pick you up at the hospital. You've broken your ankle after slipping on some ice, and you need a ride home, just like you needed a ride to the penitentiary all those months ago. Not only that: To pay for your hospital bill, you'd like to sell him your Plymouth. Yes, the very same Plymouth that he sold you and John. Of course three hundred dollars will do. Never mind that you paid almost twice that hardly three months ago. You've simply got to pay this hospital bill.

From the house, you'll walk to the airfield. It isn't far, even on crutches. You'll exchange tomorrow's plane ticket for one that leaves to-day, and you'll purchase a ticket for Margaret, too. You'll have about two hundred dollars left over, at least. You'll stock up for the trip in Seattle, and from there you'll travel to Chicago.

And then? You'll finish what you started. You need to be patient, and you need to be careful—you'll arm yourself along the way—but sooner or later, you'll finish this, and you'll finish it together.

"You really think we'll find her?" Margaret asks.

Elmer Whitlock will arrive in ten minutes. You've already changed out of your hospital gown and into your street clothes. Margaret has, too. She's wearing your blouse, your slacks, your boots, and it's uncanny how much she looks like you. You've known this all her life, but now more than ever you can see the resemblance. Looking at her is like looking at a perfect image of your younger self. You smile, and you take your daughter's hand.

"That's the plan," you say.

ACKNOWLEDGMENTS

This novel has been in the works since at least 2012, and there are numerous people I'd like to thank for supporting its progress and inspiring my work as a writer.

First, my utmost thanks to Michelle Brower, my agent, whose professional and editorial guidance have been central to this book. I sincerely appreciate your expertise, Michelle, and your keeping faith in me all these years.

Likewise, my sincerest gratitude to Jen Monroe, my editor at Berkley. Jen: Your vision, feedback, and enthusiasm are deeply appreciated, and I feel truly honored to work with you. Thank you for taking me on, and for championing my work.

I'd like to thank the entire team at Berkley and Penguin Random House, particularly Lauren Burnstein, Jin Yu, and Craig Burke. This book simply wouldn't be what it is without your dedication and expertise, and I feel incredibly thankful and humbled to have such brilliant people promoting my novel. Thank you, too, to Laura K. Corless, Emily Osborne, and Anthony Ramondo for the gorgeous interior design and cover art, which I've proudly displayed above not one but two desks.

In addition to various family resources, several books and articles provided invaluable information for my research in writing this novel, particularly *Tanacross Learners' Dictionary* (editor: Gary Holton), Kenny Thomas Sr.'s *Crow Is My Boss: The Oral Life History of a Tanacross Athabaskan Elder*

ACKNOWLEDGMENTS

(editor: Craig Mishler), and William E. Simeone's article "The Northern Athabaskan Potlatch in East-Central Alaska, 1900–1930."

I'd like to thank my parents, Nicholas and Sandra, and I'd like to thank my sister, Lydia. Each of you has shaped the person who I am, and I'm profoundly thankful for your love and support. We may live many miles apart, but in my heart and my soul you're always close. So although I may go, I'll be coming home soon.

I'd like to thank my aunt and my grandparents, in loving memory. Like my parents and my sister, each one of you has been an inspiration, and you've made an indelible impact on my life. I miss you all, and I think of you every day.

I'd like to thank my professors at Ohio State University, in particular Michelle Herman, Lee Martin, Erin McGraw, and Lee K. Abbott. I'd also like to thank my entire MFA cohort, particularly Claire Vaye Watkins and Ali Salerno.

I'd also like to thank the Sewanee Writers' Conference and Richard Hugo House, in particular Peter Mountford and Ross McMeekin.

I'd like to thank *you*, the reader, for picking up this book, and for perusing the acknowledgments, no less. I've probably never met you, but I hope you enjoy(ed) the novel. Thank you for reading.

I'd like to thank my friends and colleagues at Indiana University, particularly Travis Paulin and the rest of the office on Park Street.

I'd like to thank my daughters: Lennon, Aurora, and Alice. Thank you for inspiring me, and for being the wonderful girls you are. You make my life complete, and you make this world make sense. It may be many years until you read this, but I am thinking of you, and if you're reading these words from a distant place and time, know that I am counting the very seconds until we're together again. My girls: I love you endlessly, and I always will.

And, finally, I'd like to thank my wife, Madeline. You are a dream come true. Thank you for your boundless support, and love, and inspiration. You've taught me so much, and it's my honor to be your partner and husband. Every day, I look forward to growing up with you. Every day, I want to live my life to the fullest because of you. I didn't know how good life could be before I met you, and I owe you everything. Past and present, future and forward, I cherish you. I love you, Madeline. You're my now and forever. My apple blossom.